About the Author

Bronwyn Scott is the author of over fifty books. Her 2018 novella, 'Dancing with the Duke's Heir' was a RITA® finalist. She loves history and is always looking forward to the next story. She also enjoys talking with other writers and readers about books they like and the writing process. Readers can visit her at her Facebook page at Bronwynwrites and at her blog at http://www.bronwynswriting.blogspot.com

Regency Rogues

Regency Rogues:

Exotic Affairs

BRONWYN SCOTT

MILLS & BOON

® and ™ are trademarks owned and used by the trademark owner and/or its licensee. Trademarks marked with ® are registered with the United Kingdom Patent Office and/or the Office for Harmonisation in the Internal Market and in other countries.

First Published in Great Britain 2020
By Mills & Boon, an imprint of HarperCollins*Publishers*
1 London Bridge Street, London, SE1 9GF

REGENCY ROGUES: EXOTIC AFFAIRS © 2020 Harlequin Books S.A.

Playing the Rake's Game © 2015 Nikki Poppen
Breaking the Rake's Rules © 2015 Nikki Poppen

ISBN: 978-0-263-27955-9

MIX
Paper from
responsible sources
FSC™ C007454

This book is produced from independently certified FSC™ paper to ensure responsible forest management.

For more information visit: www.harpercollins.co.uk/green

Printed and bound in Spain
by CPI, Barcelona

PLAYING THE RAKE'S GAME

For my awesome staff on the Disney Fantasy; Gabriella and Nicolas who kept us fed, and Puhl who had to clean my kid's stateroom *every day* and still greeted me happily every morning.

Chapter One

❧

Bridgetown, Barbados—early May, 1835

Ren Dryden believed two things about the nature of men: first, a wise man didn't run from his troubles and, second, only a foolish man ran from his opportunities. Ren considered himself in league with the former, which was why he'd spent two weeks aboard a mail packet aptly named the *Fury*, braving the Atlantic and sailing away from all he knew. In truth, a large part of himself had revelled in the danger of the adventure; revelled in pitting his strength against the sea. He even revelled in the unknown challenges that lay before him on land. At last, he could take action.

Ren levered himself out of the bumboat that had rowed him ashore, tossed the boatman a coin and stood on the Bridgetown dock, feeling a kindred spirit with the bustle of commerce about him. His blood hummed with the excitement of it. Ah, the Caribbean! Land of rum and risk.

Ren surveyed the activity with an appreciative eye,

taking in the vibrant colours of people, of fruits, sky and sea, the scents of citrus and sweat, the feel of heat against his face. It was a veritable feast for the senses and he engaged the feast wholeheartedly. Life began today, more specifically *his* life, a life of his choosing and his making, not a life predestined for him based on the caprices of earlier generations of Drydens.

There were plenty of people in London who would say he was avoiding his problems. The list was long and distinguished, ranging from his family, who'd found the 'perfect solution' to their little problem of 'dynastic debt' in the form of a weak-eyed, sallow-cheeked heiress from York, to the creditors who hounded him through the grey streets of London, even being so bold as to lie in wait for him outside his exclusive clubs.

There were also plenty of men of his acquaintance who would have bowed to the inevitable, married the heiress, paid the debt and spent their lives blindly acquiring new debt until *their* sons had to make the same sacrifices a generation later. He had promised himself years ago when he'd come of age he would not be a slave to the past.

Ren found it rather frightening that not only would those men have bowed to the inevitable, but they would have *preferred* to bow instead of breaking free. After all, there was a certain comfort to be found in the known. He understood the penchant for the familiar and he pitied the men who craved it. Ren had never counted himself among that number.

On the outside, perhaps he resembled his peers in clothing, clubs and mannerisms, but inside, he'd always been different, always railed against the things and people that kept him leashed, his hopes restrained by the narrow parameters that defined a gentleman's potential.

All that railing had paid off, all that hope was now fulfilled. He was here and he'd broken free, although it came with a price, as freedom always did. If he failed in this venture, his family failed with him; his mother, who had wilted after his father's death; his two sisters, one waiting for a debut, the other waiting to wed; and thirteen-year-old Teddy who would be the earl of debt-ridden lands should Ren not return.

Ren's hand curled tightly around the valise he'd brought with him from the boat. He'd not trusted it to remain with his trunks to be brought ashore separately. His future was in the valise: the letter of introduction and a copy of Cousin Merrimore's will bequeathing him fifty-one per cent interest in a sugar plantation—*majority interest* in a profitable business.

There would be shareholders to deal with, but technically the entire place was his to control. He would not fail. As unseemly as it was for a gentleman of his birth, he'd made it a point to know the dynamics of trade—he'd quietly made investments on the Exchange, invested in an occasional cargo. He'd listened to discussions in Parliament and taken an active interest in political circles when he was in London.

As a result, he did not come to Barbados without at least some knowledge of Britain's colonial gem. Nor did he come without his opinions. He would make an honest profit and he would pay an honest wage to see it done. He would not raise his family up by abusing the sweat of other men. Even a desperate man had ethics.

'Ahoy there, Dryden, is that you?' A tall, bronzed man with sun-bleached hair cut through the crowd, taking Ren by momentary surprise. Ren might not have recognised the man, but he'd know the voice of his one-time best friend anywhere in the world, case in point. London would have an apoplexy if it could see its one-time ballroom favourite now. The Caribbean had bleached his dark-blond hair and tanned his pale skin.

'Kitt Sherard!' Ren felt his face break into wide grin. 'I wasn't sure if you'd make it.' He'd sent a letter on the mail packet preceding him telling Kitt of his arrival, but there'd been no chance to receive a response.

'Of course I made it. I wouldn't leave you stranded at the docks.' Kitt pulled him into a strong embrace. 'What has it been, Ren? Five years?'

'Five *long* years. Look at you, Kitt. Barbados agrees with you,' Ren exclaimed. He couldn't get over the completeness of his friend's transformation. Kitt had always been wild at heart, but now the wildness had entirely taken over. His hair was not only bleached, but long, and his dress more closely resembled the loose clothing of those swarming the docks than the traditional breeches and coats Ren had on. They looked more comfortable too. But the eyes were the same: a sharp, shrewd sea-blue. It was Kitt all right and it felt good to see a friendly face.

'It does indeed.' Kitt laughed as a pretty, coffee-skinned fruit seller approached, swinging her hips.

'Fresh fruit, me loves, de best on de island. Is this

handsome fellow a friend of yours, Mr Kitt?' She wafted a firm round orange under Ren's nose, teasing him with its citrusy scent. The persuasion was effective. After two weeks without anything resembling 'fresh', the orange was a temptation nonpareil. She might as well have been Eve with the apple, and if Eve had been wearing a scoop-necked blouse like this island beauty, Ren completely understood why Adam had eaten it.

'He's come all the way from London, Liddie. You be good to him.' Kitt gave her two coins and took the fruit, tossing it to Ren.

'Are all your friends this handsome?' Liddie flirted with Ren, the loose neck of her blouse gaping open to offer a quick glimpse of firm, round fruit of a more erotic sort. She flashed him an inviting smile.

Kitt feigned wounded pride, a hand on his heart. 'More handsome than me, Liddie?'

Liddie laughed. 'You're too much for a poor girl like me, Mr Kitt. Are you going to introduce me?'

'Liddie, this is Ren Dryden, Albert Merrimore's cousin. He's going to be taking over Sugarland plantation.'

Ren thought he saw Liddie take the slightest step backwards. Her next words confirmed it wasn't his imagination. 'There's trouble out there.' She shot a warning glance at Kitt. 'You better tell him about the spirits and the witch woman, Mr Kitt.' She fumbled with a string about her neck and pulled a necklace over her head. A chunk of black coral hung from a strip of leather. She handed it to Ren. 'You're going to need protection. This will keep the bad spirits away.'

Ren took the charm, unsure of what to say. The idea there was trouble at his plantation was more than a little unsettling. That the trouble involved spirits and a witch woman seemed to portend the ominous. He looked a hasty question at Kitt, who merely shrugged at the mention.

'My friend and I are good Anglicans, Liddie. We don't believe in spirits.' Kitt dismissed Liddie's worries with an easy smile

Good Anglicans? Ren fought back a laugh at the notion. He didn't think Kitt had ever been a good anything except a good amount of trouble. Decent simply wasn't in Sherard's vocabulary.

Ren tucked the amulet inside his shirt and Kitt went back to flirting with Liddie. 'I am a bit jealous though, Liddie. What about me? Don't I get an amulet, too, just in case?'

Liddie's face broke into a pretty smile. 'Mr Kitt, I pity the poor spirits that mess with you, Anglican or not.' It was a good note to leave on. Liddie sauntered away, hips swaying.

'She likes you.' Kitt elbowed Ren. 'Do you want me to arrange something?'

'No. I think women will need to wait until I can get my bearings at the plantation.' Ren laughed. 'You're the same old Kitt Sherard, women falling all over you wherever you go.'

Kitt seemed to sober at that. 'Well, not quite the same, I hope. I didn't come here to be what I was in London and I'm guessing neither did you.'

Ren nodded in understanding. For them both, Barbados was a place for new lives. Kitt had left London five years ago rather suddenly and without warning. He'd shown up one night on Ren's doorstep needing sanctuary but unable to explain. He'd left the next day, slinking out of town towards the ports, leaving everything behind including his real name. Ren had been the last to see him. After that, Kitt had cut all ties with the exception of random letter to him and the third of their trio, Benedict DeBreed.

Ren had no idea what Kitt had been up to since then. A silence had sprung up between them, a reminder of the profundity of their choices. Ren steered the conversation back to the practical. 'Were you able to bring a wagon?' It was easier not to think about the larger scope of his decisions, but to take it all step by step. The next step was to get out to the plantation.

'It's right over here. I think they've just brought your trunks ashore.' Kitt gestured to the returning bumboat. Ren's questions had to wait while they loaded his trunks, but his nerves were rising. What had Cousin Merrimore done? What was wrong at Sugarland? He'd expected a bit of unease. There'd been four months between his cousin's passing and his arrival, but surely there was enough sense in the group of investors to manage things in the short term.

In fact, he'd assumed there would be very little to handle. Most plantation owners were absentee landlords who left the running of the estate to an overseer while they lived in England. But if that was the case, none of them had contacted him. It would have been simple enough to meet if they had been in England.

Since no one had come forward, Ren was starting to believe the landlords were in residence on the island. Even so, with or without his cousin's presence or the presence of any other shareholders, the overseer would keep the plantation going just as he always had. Ren ran a finger beneath his collar, the heat starting to make his garments uncomfortable. He shot an envied glance Kitt's direction.

'Take off the damn coats, Ren. We aren't in England any more.' Kitt laughed at his discomfort. 'Even the heat's different here, but you'll learn how to cope. You'll get used to it.' He winked. 'If you're anything like me, you'll even like it.'

Ren grinned and shrugged out of his jacket. 'I love the heat and I don't think London ever had a sky this blue. This is paradise.' Just minutes off the boat and he could see the allure of this place. Everything was different: the sky, the heat, the fruit, the people.

The talk of spirits and witches didn't bother him so much as did the fact that they were connected to his property. He'd risked everything to come here. Hell, he'd left the earldom unprotected, having turned the day-to-day affairs entirely over to his steward and solicitors. He could trust them, of course, and if he was wrong on that account he'd left his close friend, Benedict DeBreed, in charge to ensure he wasn't. He had protections in place, but still, if he'd been Trojan Horsed... well, the consequences didn't bear thinking about. He'd find a way to make it work.

Ren climbed up on to the wagon and squeezed in

next to Kitt. He decided to ease into the conversation. 'Thanks again for coming to get me.'

'I'm glad to do it, although I'm sure someone from the plantation would have been happy to come out.' Kitt chirped to the horse and caught his eye when Ren said nothing. 'They do know you're coming, don't they?' He paused, interpreting the silence correctly. 'Oh, hell, they don't know.'

'Not exactly,' Ren said slowly. 'I wasn't sure there would be a "they" out there. I assumed Cousin Merrimore was the only one in residence.' By the time he'd rethought that hypothesis it had been too late to send a letter.

Kitt shifted on the seat next to him and Ren's sense of foreboding grew. 'Well, out with it, Kitt. Tell me what's wrong at Sugarland. Are there really witches and spirits?' Ren absently fingered the chunk of coral beneath his shirt. Bridgetown was behind them now and there was an overwhelming sense of isolation knowing that they'd just left the only town on the island behind. For a city man used to having entertainments, food and anything else he needed at his fingertips or at least within a few streets, it was a daunting prospect indeed, a reminder of the enormity of what he'd chosen to do. He would be relying on himself and himself alone. It would be a true test of his strength and knowledge.

Kitt shook his head. 'It's a bad business out there—of course, I don't know the half of it. I'm gone most weeks.' Ren didn't believe that for a moment. Kitt was the sort who knew everyone and knew everything.

'You don't have to sugar-coat anything for me,' Ren

said sternly. 'I want to know what I'm up against.' Had he taken on more than he could manage? Assumptions were dangerous things and he'd made a few about Cousin Merrimore's property, but he'd had no choice. It was either marry the heiress or gamble on the inheritance.

Kitt gave another of his shrugs. 'It's the apprenticeship programme. It's a great source of controversy in the parish.'

Ren nodded. 'I am familiar with it.' Slavery in the British Caribbean had been abolished a couple of years ago. It had been replaced with the notion of apprenticeship. The idea was decent in theory: pay the former slaves who were willing to work the land they'd once worked for free. In practice, the situation was not far different than slavery.

Kitt went on. 'Finding enough labour has been difficult. The plantation owners feel they're losing too much money so they work the labourers to the bone, to death actually. As you can imagine, no one wants to work for those wages. Death doesn't really recommend itself.'

Great, his fields were rotting and there was no one to hire. But Kitt's next words riveted his attention. 'Except at Sugarland and that's what has all the neighbours angry.'

Ren let the thought settle. He tried to dissect the comment and couldn't make sense of it. 'You'll have to explain, I'm afraid.'

Kitt did. 'The plantation owners refuse to use the apprentice system fairly, except Sugarland. Anyone who wants field work, wants to work there where they are assured of a wage and safe conditions. As a result, Sugarland is the only place producing a significant profit right now.' That was good news. Ren breathed a little easier, but just for a moment. Kitt wasn't done.

'Someone put it about a few months ago, at the time of your cousin's death, that spirits were luring workers to Sugarland, that the woman running the place was in league with practitioners of black magic and that's why the plantation was successful. Since then, the rumours have multiplied: she's cursed the neighbouring crops, she's put a growing spell on her own.'

'Wait. Hold on.' Ren grasped the information one idea at a time. Spells? Witchcraft? A woman?

Kitt took pity on him, misunderstanding the source of his agitation. 'I know, the whole concept of black magic takes a bit of getting used to. The islands are full of it. The islands have their own names for it: voodoo, obeah. It's from Africa. It's full of superstitions and ghosts and spells.'

Ren thought of the chunk of coral beneath his shirt. Black magic was the least of his concerns. 'No, it's not that. Back up to the part about a woman. There's a *woman* at the plantation?' Cousin Merrimore's will hadn't said a thing about anyone, certainly not a woman.

Kitt nodded and said with the most seriousness Ren had ever heard him use. 'Her name is Emma Ward.'

A pit opened in his stomach and Ren knew with gut-clenching clarity there was no 'they'. There was no absentee landlord syndicate to write monthly updates to. There was only a 'she'. The other forty-nine per cent belonged to a crazy woman rumoured to be casting spells on her neighbours' crops.

Ren was starting to rethink the merits of surprise, especially when those merits were reversed. It was one thing to *be* the surprise as he'd planned to be. It was another to be the one who was surprised. Ren definitely preferred the former. A more cautious man would have waited in town until he could have notified the plantation. But he'd never been one to wait and he'd never been one to shy away from a challenge. He made a habit of meeting those head on, whether those challenges were notorious females or not.

Ren leaned back on the wagon seat, letting the sun bathe his face. Ah, the Caribbean. Land of rum, risk and apparently a little insanity, too.

Chapter Two

Waiting was driving her insane! Emma Ward took yet another long look at the clock on the corner of her desk. He should be here by now, Mr Fifty-One Per Cent. *If* he was coming. Emma idly shuffled the papers in front of her. They could have been written in Arabic for all she'd been able to focus on them today. Emma left the desk and began to pace, a far better use of her energies than staring at a paper.

Was she technically even waiting? Waiting assumed he was actually coming. What she really wanted to know was at what point could she *stop* waiting and be confident in the knowledge that he *wasn't* coming at all?

Her nerves were a wreck and they had been every mail day since Albert Merrimore's death. That meant she'd gone through this uncertainty for four months. Was this the day she got the letter saying Merrimore's cousin was coming? Or worse, would it be the day he actually showed up? Anything could happen. His ship could have been delayed, *he* could have been personally delayed and that was if he'd decided to come at all. It was just as likely he could have rethought the notion of coming halfway around the world simply to see his property when his profits didn't depend on whether he saw the place or not. Most gentlemen wouldn't bestir themselves if it wasn't required, especially since there was some risk involved. Who was she fooling? Not *some* risk. A *lot* of risk, starting with an ocean voyage. Ships went down even in the modern age of steam.

Emma scolded herself for such a morbid thought. It wasn't that she wished he was dead, merely marooned, her conscience clarified. It was possible his ship could founder and he could float to safety on an overturned table. For four months, she'd got her wish. How much longer before she could safely assume her wish had been granted on a more permanent basis? She didn't wish Mr Fifty-One Per Cent dead, she just wished he weren't here.

She had to stop calling him that. He had a name. It had been in the will and a terribly stuffy name at that. *Renford Dryden.* An old man's name. But of course, what sort of relations did dear old Merry have if not old ones? Merry had been in his late eighties. A cousin couldn't be expected to be much younger. Even twenty years younger would put him in his sixties. Which perplexed her further—why a man of advanced years would want to make such a dangerous trip that would only serve to disrupt both of their lives? Perhaps he wouldn't come at all. Perhaps she would be safe on that front at least.

Emma wanted nothing more than to grow her sugar

cane in peace and independence without the interference of men. After everything she'd been through, it
wasn't too much to ask. Men had never gone well for
her, starting with her father and ending with a debacle
of a marriage. The only man who'd done well by her
had been old Merry and now she had his relative to contend with. She couldn't stop him from coming, but she
didn't have to make it easy should that be his choice.

She'd already begun the campaign. She'd not written to him when she could have, explaining the situation when the solicitor had sent word to England. She'd
feared a letter would be viewed as a personal invitation,
as encouragement to come when that was the last thing
she wanted. She hadn't sent the wagon into town on
mail day these past months to see if anyone had arrived.

Guilt began to gnaw again. If he had arrived on this
packet, she'd left an ageing man to fend for himself in
the foreign heat. It was poorly done of her. She should
have sent someone into town just to check. That was
her conscience talking. She should tell Samuel to get the
wagon ready and go to enquire about the mail. Emma
glanced again at the clock, the knot in her stomach
starting to ease. It was getting late. The threat had almost passed for another two weeks. If he was coming,
he would be here by…

'Miss! Miss!' Hattie, one of the downstairs maids,
rushed into the office, hardly attempting any pretence
of decorum in her excitement. 'It's him, it's our Mr
Dryden! I'm sure of it. He is coming and that rascal
Mr Kitt is with him!'

'Kitt Sherard? Are you certain?' What would the

local scoundrel of a rum runner have to do with a man in his dotage? Sherard was the last person she'd want Renford Dryden to meet. Emma stopped before the mirror hung over the side table to check her appearance. Sherard was only one step above a pirate. 'I hope he hasn't got our guest drunk already.' Emma muttered, tucking up a few errant stands of hair.

She wanted to make a good impression on all accounts. She had plans for that good impression and Kitt Sherard did not qualify as part of it. Emma was counting on that impression to convince Mr Dryden to sell his interest to her or, at the very least, to sail back to England secure in the knowledge that his money was in good hands, which was mostly true, she was just a bit short on funds right now. The harvest would change that.

She would gladly trade some profits for independence. The autonomy of the last four months had given her a taste of what it would be like to be on her own, to be free. She was loath to relinquish even an iota of that liberty or responsibility.

'Do I look all right, Hattie?' Emma smoothed the skirts of her aquamarine gown, one of her favourites. 'Are they out front?'

'They're pulling up just now, miss. You look fine.' Hattie gave her a saucy wink. 'After two weeks on a ship, I think anything would look fine to a gent like him.'

Emma gave a dry chuckle. 'I'm not sure that's a compliment, Hattie.' Satisfied with her appearance, Emma set out to meet Dryden with a brisk step as if her presence could undo any damage that had already been done. The sooner Dryden was free of Sherard, the better.

She was a little breathless in her eagerness and anxiety by the time she reached the covered porch. This was the moment she both feared and welcomed. At last, the future could begin now that Dryden was here. Perhaps, she thought optimistically, that future would be better than the limbo she'd been living in. If she could manage an entire plantation, she could certainly manage one old man.

The wagon pulled to a halt in front of the steps and she saw the flaw in her hypothesis immediately. Renford Dryden wasn't an old man, not even a middle-aged one, but an astonishingly handsome young one. The man who jumped down from the wagon seat was certainly able bodied if those wide shoulders and long legs were anything to go on. So much for trying to caution him about the rigours of island life. He certainly looked as if he was up for it and much more.

Emma shot Hattie a sharp look that said: *Why didn't you tell me?* But she supposed Hattie had warned her in her own way. She should have known something was amiss the moment Kitt Sherard's name entered the conversation. Now she saw what it was. Up close, Renford Dryden was six feet plus of muscle topped with thick honey-blond hair and sharp blue eyes set above a strong, straight nose. He mounted the steps, oozing confidence and growing taller with each step he took. Still, he was a man and men could be managed, *must* be managed.

Emma took a deep breath. She needed to begin as she meant to go on. Men who weren't managed had run roughshod over her life to date and she was done with them. Emma held out her hand to greet him as if he was precisely what she'd expected. 'Welcome to Sugarland, Mr Dryden. We are so glad to see you.' She hoped he couldn't hear the lie.

His grip was firm as his hand curled around hers, sending a jolt of awareness through her. His eyes riveted on her, making her aware of the male presence of him. Never had a simple handclasp seemed so intimate. 'I am so very glad to be here, Miss Ward.' Was that a touch of irony she heard? Did he suspect she hadn't been entirely truthful?

There was no chance to verify the impression. In the next moment she was very nearly lost. Renford Dryden smiled, dimple and all. It was a most wicked smile that invited the mind to imagine all sorts of pleasantly sinful things without even meaning to. He was that type of man, all charisma. But there was more to him than a charming facade. There was self-assurance and intelligence, too. Those blue eyes were assessing eyes, eyes that took nothing at face value and when they looked at her, they were shrewd and wary. It occurred to her that in these initial moments they were both doing the same thing: measuring the opponent, selecting and discarding strategies.

It didn't take much guesswork to divine what his strategy would be. It was the strategy of all men when faced with a woman who had something they wanted. Emma stiffened her spine with a stern mental admonition to herself. She would not be wooed into giving up her independence. She had strategies of her own. It was time to teach Mr Dryden it wasn't easy to run a sugar-cane plantation, time to lead him to the conclusion that his best choice was to leave all this in her capable hands and go back to the life he knew.

She flicked her gaze down the length of him, taking in the cut of his clothes, the expense of the materials. Here was a man of quality, a man used to luxury. Perhaps she could use that against him. Luxuries here were hard won, something men of charisma and charm weren't used to. Those sorts usually didn't have to work too hard to get what they wanted, especially when they were endowed with a heavy dose of self-confidence like Mr Dryden. They just smiled. But smiles didn't harvest crops or pay the bills. Hard work was at the core of everything Sugarland had.

Emma gave him her hostess smile. 'I have lemonade waiting on the back veranda. We can sit and talk and become acquainted, Mr Dryden.' And he would learn how different they were and how he didn't have to be here to reap the benefits Sugarland had to offer.

'Call me Ren, please. No more of this Mr Dryden business,' he insisted, stepping aside as two servants came up the stairs with his trunks.

Emma looked past him to the wagon, using the disruption to ignore the request for informality. For now she would resist the temptation. First names were usually the first step in any seduction. 'Mr Sherard, would you care to join us?' Politeness required she ask. She hoped Sherard understood politeness also required he refused.

Sherard shook his head. 'No, thank you. I leave tonight on business and there's much to be done before I sail. Now that the wagon's unloaded, I'll return to town.' He gave her a strong look that reminded her Sherard was a man with a well-warranted reputation for fierceness. 'I expect you'll take good care of my friend, Miss Ward.' He nodded to Dryden. 'Ren, I'll look in on you when I'm back in port.'

Great. The notorious Sherard was on a first-name basis with her guest and now felt he could use that familiarity as a reason to call regularly at her house. Her conscience prodded at her again. The bloody nuisance had been busy today. It probably served her right for stranding Dryden at the docks. She'd left him to his own devices and this was what she got.

Having the new partner befriend Sherard was not what she needed, considering the other rumours swirling about her. Never mind most people didn't believe the rumours wholesale about her, the mere presence of those rumours was enough to still cast a certain cloud on her reputation. It called attention to her, something no decently bred woman deliberately sought. Nor did Sherard's presence help her disposition towards her new house guest. Sherard already acted as if Dryden were in charge with his damnable fifty-one per cent, no matter that he technically was. *She* was the one who'd been here. She'd seen to the planting and nurturing of the crop. If Dryden had been a few days later he would have missed the harvest too. How dare he swoop in here, *unannounced*, at the last and claim any sort of credit for *her* labour.

Emma tamped down her roiling emotions and led her guest through the house to the back veranda. She liked that word, 'guest'. It was precisely how she should think of Dryden. It was a far nicer term than 'Mr Fifty-One Per Cent' and, better yet, guests were temporary. She would make sure of it.

He could stay forever! Ren let the lemonade slide down his throat, cool and wet. He didn't think anything had ever tasted as welcome, or any breeze had felt as pleasant. Things were definitely looking up. When Kitt had pulled up to Sugarland, Ren had been more than pleasantly surprised with the white-stucco manor house, threats of witches and magic receding. He'd felt an immediate sense of affinity for the place. This was somewhere he could belong, somewhere he could thrive.

Such an intuition was an odd sensation for a man who prided himself on logic, yet Ren couldn't deny it was there. Possession, pure and primal, had hummed through his blood; *his, his, his*, it had sung. Then *she* had appeared at the top of the steps and his blood had hummed a more familiar tune of possession, a lustier tune. It was hard to mind being Trojan Horsed when it looked like Emma Ward. 'She doesn't *look* like a witch,' he'd murmured to Kitt.

'They never do.' Kitt had laughed as he leapt down from the wagon. 'Witches wouldn't be nearly as effective if they did.'

But Emma Ward did look like something else just as worrisome and perhaps more real, Ren thought as they sipped their lemonade. Trouble. She had a natural sensuality to her. It was there in the sway of her hips as she led him through the airy halls to the veranda, it was there in her dark hair, in the exotic, catlike tilt of her deep brown eyes. It emanated from her, raw and elemental; a sensuality that coaxed a man to overstep himself if he wasn't careful.

This woman was no virginal English rose. She was something much better and much worse. Maybe she was a witch, after all. He would have to reserve judgement. Ren raised his glass and stretched out an arm to clink his glass against hers. 'Here's to the future, Miss Ward.'

For someone who'd wanted to talk, she was awfully quiet, however. Perhaps he had misunderstood. He took the opportunity to learn a bit more about her. 'It is *Miss* Ward, isn't it?'

'Yes, Miss Ward is fine.' She supplied the bare basics of an answer and the briefest of smiles. Ren noted that smile didn't leave her mouth. Her eyes remained politely impassive. Perhaps her coolness was a result of his surprise arrival. She hadn't known he was coming and she was wary. A stranger had just arrived on her doorstep and announced his intention to live there.

'I am sure all of this comes as quite a shock…' Ren began congenially. He fully believed in the old adage that one caught more flies with sugar. It wouldn't do to put Miss Ward on the defensive without cause. 'It's a shock to me as well. Cousin Merrimore didn't mention anything about you in his papers and here we are, two strangers thrown together by circumstance.' He gave her a warm smile, the one he reserved for the *ton*'s stiff-necked matrons, the one that made them melt and relax their standards. It didn't work.

'In all fairness, Mr Dryden, I believe I have the upper

hand. I knew of you by name. Merry did mention you in the will quite specifically.'

Intriguing. Ren's critical mind couldn't overlook the self-incriminating evidence. She'd known of him. She could have contacted him, something his lack of details had prevented him from doing on his end. He could be forgiven for a surprise arrival having no information about who to contact in advance, but she'd known. She'd had the ability to send a letter with the copy of the will. She'd *chosen* not to.

Ren gave her a wry smile. What would she do if he confronted her? 'There is that, Miss Ward. You had my name. You were quite aware of my existence and yet you left me to find my own way here in my own time.' He would have to tread carefully here. It seemed Miss Ward was already on the defensive, a very interesting position for a woman. Given her circumstances, he would have thought she'd be quite glad to see him, to have him remove the burden of running the place alone. The past four months must have been daunting for a woman alone.

She flushed at having been called out. Good. She understood precisely what he was implying, a further sign Miss Ward was an astute opponent. 'It's nearly harvest season, Mr Dryden. There's hardly time for someone to sit for hours at the docks waiting for a ship to come in when it might possibly not and even if it did, it might not carry what you're waiting for.'

Touché. She had him there. 'Even for a relative?' Ren probed. It was a shot in the dark, but he was curious to know how Emma Ward clung to the family tree. Undoubtedly she was more familiar with 'Merry' than he was. Where did that familiarity come from? Was she a lover? A mistress? Or merely a distant cousin like himself? Ren had met Cousin Merrimore, as *his* family called the old man, perhaps three times in his entire life, the last time being eight years ago when he'd finished his studies at Oxford.

Emma Ward gave a short laugh at the reference, but it was not warm. Ren had the distinct impression things were not getting off on the right foot. 'You and I are *not* family, Mr Dryden. Merry was my guardian for several years until I attained my majority. After that, he was my friend.' There was no help for him there. In his experience, 'friends' came in multiple varieties, bedfellows included. But if Merrimore had been her guardian, he could assume nothing untoward had followed.

'Ren, please,' he suggested again, making the most of the opening the conversation provided. 'I should like for us to be friends as well.' If there was any naughty innuendo in his response, he would let her relationship with Merrimore be the measuring stick.

'*We* are business partners at present,' she replied firmly, moving the conversation away from the personal, although there were a host of questions he wanted to ask—how had a confirmed bachelor like his ancient cousin ended up as someone's guardian? Why hadn't she left the island? Surely Merrimore would have sent her to London when she came of age?

Those questions would have to wait until she liked him better. It was an unsettling, but not displeasing, discovery to make. In London he was accustomed to making a favourable first impression on women when he had to make one at all. Usually it was the other way around. Women sought to make a good impression on *him*. Not Emma Ward, however.

Then again, his title didn't precede him in Barbados. The York heiress had made it abundantly clear his antecedents were all she wanted. Her father would pay an outrageous sum for those antecedents to bed his daughter and give him a blue-blooded grandson. Ren had an aversion to being used as an aristocratic stud. A woman who didn't want him for his antecedents would be quite an adventure.

Ren grinned and set down his glass, ready to try out his theory. Emma Ward had been attempting to disconcert him from the first moment, now it was his turn. 'Miss Ward, I think you have not been entirely truthful with me.' He was gratified to see a flash of caution pass through her dark eyes.

'Whatever about, Mr Dryden?' she replied coolly.

'Contrary to your words earlier, you are *not* glad to see me. Since we've never met, I find that highly irregular.' It was not a gentleman's path he trod with that comment. But as she'd noted, *this* was business. More importantly, it was *his* business and quite a lot was at stake.

Miss Ward fixed him with the entirety of her dark gaze. 'I apologise if you find your reception lacking.'

'Really? I find that hard to believe when you don't sound the least bit penitent.' Ren pressed his advantage. If she meant to defy him, she would have to do it outright. Defiance he could deal with, it was open and honest. He would not tolerate passive aggression, not even from a pretty woman.

Her eyes flared with a dark flame, her mouth started to form a cutting rejoinder that never got past her lips. *Boom!* The air around them reverberated with sound that shook the windows and rattled the glasses on the table. Emma shrieked, bolting out of her chair, her eyes rapidly scanning the horizon for signs of the explosion.

Ren saw it first, his stomach clenching at the sight of uncontained flame. 'Over there!' He pointed in the distance to the telltale stream of smoke, clamping down on the wave of panic that threatened.

Emma had no such compunction for restraint. 'Oh goodness, no, not the home farm!' She pushed past him, racing down the steps, calling for her horse.

Ren bellowed behind her, 'Forget the saddles, there's no time!' But no one was listening. The stable was in chaos, people running everywhere trying to calm the horses after the explosion. Ren managed to pull a strong-looking horse out of a stall. 'Emma, give me your foot!' Emma leapt into his cupped hand and vaulted up on the horse's back. Ren swung up behind and grabbed the reins, kicking the horse into a canter as they sped out of the barnyard.

In other circumstances he might have taken a moment to appreciate the press of female flesh against him, the breasts that heaved against his arm where it crossed her and the excellent horseflesh beneath him. As it was, all he could focus on was the explosion. He'd been here a handful of hours and his fifty-one per cent was already on fire.

Chapter Three

The home farm was all disorder and confusion when they arrived. Ren leapt off the horse, hauling Emma down behind him, letting his senses take in the scene. Smoke was everywhere, creating the illusion or the reality that the fire was worse than it initially appeared, It was hard to say which it was in the haze. Panicked workers raced about without any true direction futilely attempting to fight the flames. A lesser man might have panicked along with them, but Ren's instincts for command took over.

Ren grabbed the first man who ran past him. 'You, get a bucket brigade going.' He shoved the man towards the rain barrel and started funnelling people that direction, calling orders. 'Take a bucket, get in line, a single-file line. We have to contain the fire, we can't let it spread to other buildings.' That would be disastrous.

Ren turned to Emma, but she was already gone, issuing orders of her own. He scanned the crowd, catching sight of her dark hair and light-coloured dress as she set people to the task of gathering the livestock away from the flames. Clearly, there was no need to worry about her. She had things well in hand on her end. He just needed to see to his. Ren shrugged out of his coat and positioned himself at the front of the bucket brigade, placing himself closest to the flames.

Reach and throw, reach and throw. Ren settled into the rhythm of firefighting.

After a solid half hour of dousing, his shoulders ached and his back hurt from the repeated effort of lifting heavy buckets, but they were gaining on the flames.

Confident the line could handle the remainder, Ren stepped aside and looked for Emma. He found her in the centre of the farmyard talking with a large, muscled African and another man dressed in tall boots and riding clothes, holding the reins of his horse. He was obviously a new arrival, having missed all the 'fun' of fighting the fire. His clothes were clean and lacked the soot Emma had acquired. Even from here, Ren could see Emma's gown wouldn't survive the afternoon. At a distance, too, he could tell this wasn't a friendly conversation on Emma's part. Emma waved her hand and shook her head almost vehemently at something the man said. Whoever he was, he was not welcome.

Ren strode towards the little group not so much for Emma's protection—she'd given every indication she could handle herself today and in fact preferred to work alone—as he did for his. Anyone who was a threat to Emma might very well be a threat to Sugarland. At the moment that was recommendation enough to intervene.

Ren didn't hesitate to insert himself into the conversation. 'Do we know what happened?' he asked, his question directed towards Emma. Up close, she was a worried mess. Her hem had torn in places and a seam at the side had ripped, the white of her chemise playing peekaboo. Her hair fell loose over one shoulder. She looked both dirty and delicious at once, a concept his body seemed to find very arousing in the aftermath. All of his unspent adrenaline needed to find an alternate outlet.

The big African spoke. 'Dunno. One minute we were working and the next, there was a bang.' He snapped his fingers. 'The shed just went up. There was no warning, no time.' He shook his head.

'The building was a chicken coop.' Emma explained to Ren, filling him in. 'Some of the chickens were outside, but we likely lost at least twelve.'

Ren nodded. It could have been worse. As fires and damages went, this was minor; Just chickens and a shed. The loss would be an inconvenience, but they would recover from it. It could have been the hay, the cows, the food staples, human lives even. Fires were dangerous to a farm's prosperity.

The business of the fire satisfied for the moment, Ren turned his attention to the newcomer. Ren stuck out his hand when it became apparent Emma wasn't going to make introductions. 'I'm Ren Dryden, Merrimore's cousin.'

The stranger shook his hand, smiling. He was a strong man, tall, probably in his early forties. 'I'm Sir Arthur Gridley, your neighbour to the south. It looks like you've come just in time.' He gave Emma a side-ways glance of friendly condescension that perhaps explained her reluctance to make introductions.

'Our Emma's had a struggle of it since Merrimore passed away. It has been one thing after the other for the poor girl. She's had quite the run of bad luck: a sick horse the other day, the broken wagon wheel last week, trouble with the equipment at the mill. We've all tried to pitch in, but Emma's stubborn and won't take a bit of help.'

Emma's mouth hardened into a grim line. Ren wondered what she disliked most, being talked about as if she weren't here or having her weaknesses exposed to an outsider. Or maybe, on second consideration, it was Gridley she was most opposed to.

The man seemed nice enough, certainly eager to be neighbourly but Ren noticed Emma had stepped closer to him during the exchange. Closer to himself or away from Gridley? Perhaps there was more there than met the eye. He'd have to follow that up later. Right now he had an explosion to solve. 'I'm going to walk through the ruins and see if I can't unearth any signs of what might have started the fire. I'd welcome any assistance.' He'd let Gridley prove himself. After all, Emma didn't much like him at the moment either. She might have an aversion to men in general or just to men who posed a threat to her authority.

Ren moved towards the remains of the chicken coop, Gridley on one side, Emma on the other. 'Look for anything that might have triggered an explosion: a wire, a fuse, a match. I don't think the fire had time to get too hot, clues have likely survived.'

He'd meant the instructions for Gridley, but Emma moved forward, ready to brave the ashes. Ren stuck out an arm, barring the way. 'Not you, Miss Ward. What's left of your slippers won't last. Hot or not, any residual ash could burn right through those flimsy soles. I need you to talk to people, they know you. Perhaps someone might remember some strange activity around the coop before the explosion.'

She shot him an angry glare. He wasn't scoring any points in his favour with this latest directive, but she went. Did she go out of acquiescence to his request or as a chance to be away from Gridley? His curiosity would liked to have seen what she'd have done if Gridley hadn't been there.

Digging through the rubble was more difficult than expected. Ren had thought it would be fairly easy to determine the cause of the fire—after all, the coop hadn't been that big to begin with once the smoke had cleared and there wasn't that much debris.

Ren pushed back his hair with a dirty, sweaty hand and looked around him. They were nearly done and nothing had shown up. Gridley waved at him a few feet away and strode over.

'I think I've found something,' he called out loudly enough to draw attention. He held up a small bundle of grey cloth. The people working near him gasped and moved out of the away with anxious steps. Out of the corner of his eye, Ren saw Emma hurry towards him.

Ren took the item from Arthur Gridley and turned it

over in study. 'What is it? It looks like a child's doll.' A poorly made one. It was nothing more than cloth sewn into a crude resemblance of a human form.

Gridley and Emma exchanged glances laced with challenge. Emma's voice conveyed a quiet anger when she spoke. 'It's obeah magic. This is a bad-luck charm.' She shot an accusing glare at Gridley.

Gridley blew out a breath, sounding genuinely aggrieved. 'I'm sorry, Emma. It's the last thing you need.' He stepped forward to put a consoling hand on Emma's arm. This time Ren didn't imagine her response. She moved out of reach, stepping on the toes of his boots as she backed up. Gridley's eyes narrowed, but he said nothing, opting instead to pretend he didn't notice the slight.

'This doll didn't start the fire,' Ren put in, drawing them away from whatever private war waged between them. He fingered the doll. Something wasn't right, but his mind couldn't grasp it.

Gridley gave a harsh laugh. 'I'm not sure it matters what started the fire. I'm not even sure it matters only a chicken coop burnt down. It's not the fire that's damaging.' He nodded to the huddle of people forming behind the big African. 'Emma's likely not to have any workers in the morning. Obeah magic is powerful and they believe in it.'

The tension between Emma and Gridley ratcheted up a notch. Gridley shifted on his feet and Ren flicked a covert glance over his person, noting the telltale beginnings of tightening trousers. Gridley tugged at his coat front in the age-old effort to disguise a growing arousal. For all of Gridley's bonhomie, Ren would wager his last guinea

Emma didn't care for her neighbour as much as the neighbour cared for her, if caring was the right word. He wasn't convinced yet that it was. There were other less flattering, less worthy words that recommended themselves.

The big African approached tentatively. 'Miss Emma, no one wants to go back to work today. The healers need time to purify the farmyard, to make it safe again.'

Gridley spat on the ground and prepared to respond. 'Now you listen here, you're making a working wage—'

Emma interrupted firmly, her anger directed openly at Gridley. 'This is my place. *I* will handle any business that needs handling.' Ren had to give Emma Ward credit. Even in a tattered gown, she commanded authority. She'd acquitted herself well today in the face of a crisis.

Emma stepped forward towards the foreman, distancing herself from him and Gridley. 'Peter, tell everyone they can have the rest of the day off. They may do whatever they need to do. But make it clear, they are to be back at work tomorrow. If the harvest fails, we all fail and failure doesn't pay the bills.'

'You are too generous with them,' Gridley warned in low tones. The man was treading on dangerous ground. Couldn't he see Emma was spoiling for a fight? Maybe a fight was what he wanted. Perhaps it was the presence of conflict that fuelled his desire. Some men were like that.

Emma's chin went up in defiance and Ren didn't think much of Gridley's chances. 'It is my mistake to make then. The last time I checked, it was my name on the deed, not yours. If you'll excuse me, I'd like to go home and clean up.'

Ren laughed to himself as he gave Emma a leg up

on the horse. She'd neatly dismissed Sir Arthur Gridley and Gridley had been furious over it. Perhaps he'd been expecting an invitation to tea? Or perhaps not, given Emma's overt dislike of him. There probably hadn't been invitations to tea for quite a while. Such dislike didn't grow up overnight or without cause.

Ren wasn't laughing when she did the same thing to him back at the house, the sun starting to set in the sky. She wanted a bath and would it be all right, given the excitement of the day, if she took dinner in her rooms? She didn't think she was up for company.

He'd granted her request. He had little choice otherwise. She'd prettily made her excuses, playing the delicate maiden to the hilt, which had been entertaining to watch but hardly believable. He'd seen her in action today. Anyone who handled herself the way Emma had wasn't going to be put off by company for dinner. Still, he played the gentleman and gave her the reprieve. He allowed himself to be handed over to her house servants and hustled off to his quarters.

Ren stepped inside his rooms and immediately understood what she'd done. The minx had not only dismissed him, she'd relegated him to the care of servants *and* tucked him into the far reaches of the house. Even worse, Ren could find little to complain about. It wasn't as if she'd put him in the attics or that the house was so large it needed a map to navigate. It was the principle of the matter and what it signified.

The *garçonnière* was a novel idea borrowed from the French, a large spacious set of rooms put aside for a family's bachelor sons. On the surface, the rooms were the practical answer for housing a male guest. It was what lay beneath that surface Ren took issue with. He could indeed come and go as he pleased through a separate entrance without tramping through the main house. In fact, he need not even interact with anyone in the main house if he chose or vice versa; the main house need not interact with him, which he suspected was more the case.

The footman, Michael, offered to stay and unpack, but Ren excused him. He wanted time to think and sort through what had happened that day. Ren pulled off his cravat and undid his waistcoat. There was no sense in standing on ceremony for oneself. He was alone.

The impact of it hit him hard as he stacked his linen and filled the drawers. For the first time in his life, he was entirely alone without his family, his friends and without his title; it meant nothing here at the moment. Even the institutions that had filled the backdrop of his life to date were absent. What he wouldn't give for a quiet evening at his club, laughing over brandy with Benedict. Ren set out the personal effects he'd brought; his game board, his writing kit. He would need to pen a letter to his family and let them know he had arrived safely. He even rearranged a few pieces of furniture to better suit himself. He'd put his stamp on this place yet whether Emma Ward liked it or not, starting with these rooms.

The welcome he had received today was not what he'd expected. The element of surprise had served him well. Emma had not been able to hide behind the pomp and ceremony of a planned reception. She'd been forced into an impromptu situation which had left her exposed. Surprise worked both ways, though, and there'd been surprise for him as well. He'd not expected a single shareholder. He'd been prepared for a consortium of businessmen. He'd expected people would be glad, even relieved to see him. The burden of running a plantation would be lifted from their shoulders. The reality had proven a bit different. Emma Ward was clearly not eager to be relieved of her duties or to share them.

It did make him wonder what Emma Ward had to hide. Ren set out his shaving gear, a plan of attack starting to form. With another woman, he would have chosen a strategy of overwhelming kindness and politeness. He knew already that gambit would have disastrous outcomes with Emma Ward.

Emma would need to be handled directly and firmly. He'd seen how she'd treated Arthur Gridley, with unabridged disdain. She'd eat a 'nice' man alive, the sort of man who made the mistake of thinking she was a delicate flower. Ren chuckled at the thought, another image taking shape in his mind. If she was a flower, she would be the sort that lured their prey with their beauty and then shut their petals tight until there was no escape for the poor unsuspecting soul.

She would learn soon enough he was no fool to be played with. It would take more than bad manners to deter him. If Emma Ward thought a cold welcome would send him packing, she was in for another surprise. Of course, she had no idea of what he had faced in England—not even Kitt knew. Emma's bad-mannered welcome couldn't begin to compete against the consequences of genteel poverty awaiting him if he failed here; of watching his sisters become spinsters for lack of attractive dowries, or watching them settle for questionable matches simply because only men of dubious character would take them; of watching the estates dwindle into disrepair for lack of funds to fix roofs and replace failing furniture; of watching the tenants move off the land one by one looking for more lucrative fields.

Genteel poverty was a slow social death sentence. He would not go easily down that road. He would fight it with every resource he had for the sake of his family. Even if he could afford to leave Sugarland, which he couldn't, even if his family wasn't depending on his success here, which they were, this was his fifty-one per cent and more—this was his future. He was here to stay. Both practice and principle demanded it.

Ren Dryden couldn't stay! Emma slid deep into the soapy bubbles of her bath. Watching him manage the fire today had been proof enough of that. He'd done a good job, stepping in at a moment's notice. Too good of a job. He'd been a natural leader the way he'd formed the bucket brigade and then joined in, working alongside the others. Perhaps he'd been afraid it was his fifty-one per cent on fire, Emma thought uncharitably, soaping her arms. The men had respected him, too. She'd seen it in their faces when he'd given orders. He was *not* what she needed—a man with enough charisma to usurp her years of hard work.

That was exactly what would happen if he knew the truth of things. She'd desperately wanted to paint a pic-

ture of idyllic prosperity, that all was well in the hopes
of convincing Ren Dryden there nothing to do here. He
might as well go home. Then the chicken coop had ex-
ploded, the obeah doll had shown up and Gridley had
nearly let the rest of the cat out of the bag with his 'poor
Emma' remark. If Dryden thought his investment was
in danger, she'd never dislodge him. He'd shown today
that he was a protector by nature and protectors were
warriors by necessity. They would fight for the things
they cared about.

Heat that had nothing to do with the bath water began
to simmer low at her core. Such a man was intoxicating,
his strength a potent attractant and how she'd been attracted! She'd been poignantly aware of him today even
amid the crisis. Her eye had followed him throughout
the afternoon, her gaze drawn to the rolled-up sleeves
and the flex of his arms hauling the buckets, to the ash
smearing his jaw, the blaze of his eyes as he barked
orders. There'd been the feel of him behind her on the
horse, all muscle as his power surrounded her.

There was an intimacy about riding astride with a
man, about being captured between the power of his
thighs, nestled against his groin, home to more intimate
items. It was a position Dryden had been comfortable
with. He'd not thought twice about the potential indeli-
cacy of drawing her close against him. It suggested he
was a man comfortable and confident with his body,
a man who would be good at a great many things, bed
included.

Oh, it was poorly done of her to harbour such
thoughts about her guest, especially when she wanted

that guest to leave. She suspected she wasn't the only woman who'd entertained the idea of bed with Ren Dryden. He was the sort who could conjure up all sorts of hot thoughts with a single look, a single touch.

That makes him dangerous! her more logical side asserted. He was particularly dangerous to a woman like herself, who valued her independence, who didn't want to be protected. Protection meant sheltering, shielding. She wanted neither. If she wasn't careful, Ren Dryden would undermine all she was simply because it was in his nature to do so. Her best interests required she stay the course— ignore him when possible and when it wasn't, resist.

In the meanwhile, she needed to continue life as usual. That meant praying her workers showed up and firing the fields tomorrow as planned in preparation for the harvest.

Firing the fields! Emma shot up in her bath, sending water and suds splashing on the tile floor. She should have told Ren. It was too late. She'd already effectively said goodnight with her dismissal and going to him now would require getting dressed. She wasn't about to traipse through the house in her dressing robe. Ren might believe she'd rethought her welcome and that certainly wasn't what she wanted. Ren Dryden was a spark she couldn't risk igniting.

Chapter Four

Fire! Ren came awake in a rush of awareness, his senses bombarded on all fronts: the heat, the overpowering stench of smoke and the blinding darkness. His brain raced. Teddy! The girls! He had to get to them. Panic engulfed him, adrenaline propelled him.

He lurched out of bed, stumbling in the darkness. His foot tripped on the corner of the bed and he swore. Outside the slats of his blinds orange flames flickered. His senses registered the scent of smoke more thoroughly now. It smelled of burning leaves. The panic receded infinitesimally. This was not England. Teddy and the girls were safe. But his fields…

Ren pulled up the blinds and stared in horrified amazement. This was not even the fire from yesterday. It wasn't a chicken coop this morning, it was the cane fields. *His cane fields!* Talk about money going up in literal smoke. The panic returned momentarily before his brain caught up with his senses. He remembered his research. The fire was deliberate, a prelude to the harvest, burning off the leaves and the cane's waxy outer layer to make reaping and milling more efficient.

Ren braced his arms against the window sill, breathing deeply, letting the shock pass. His family was safe half a world away. His fields were secure. All was well. But his panic was understandable. Knowing didn't make the fire appear any less harmless or smell any better. The dawn sky was black with smoke and the orange flames looked menacing. It would have been easy to misinterpret the fire for something more sinister, especially when one was groggy with the fog of a sudden awakening.

Perhaps that had been the intent? In his more alert state, it occurred to Ren that Emma could have warned him, just like she could have written, informing him of the business situation. Again, she'd elected not to, choosing instead to let him find his own level.

Ren looked down at himself. He was stark naked and in his standard, early morning, state of arousal. He usually slept nude and he'd seen no reason not to continue the practice last night. If he had misunderstood the fire, and if he had let his initial panic drive him out the door, Miss Ward might have been in for quite the surprise. As it was, she might still be in for one, although this one would be clothed. If she thought she could burn his fields without his presence or permission, or if she thought she could force him into the role of the silly, uninformed newcomer, she would be wrong on all accounts.

Ren dressed in trousers and a clean shirt. He pulled on his boots and took time to put on a jacket. He didn't want to give any ounce of credence to the idea that he'd rolled straight out of bed and raced to the fields. He wanted Emma convinced he'd not panicked.

Once outside, he spied a group of men gathered at the edge of the field and strode towards them. They were standing a safe distance from the flames, monitoring the fire's progress with a nonchalance that affirmed his conclusion: the firing was deliberate. All three heads turned towards him as he approached, but not all were male. Of course she'd be there.

Emma Ward stood between two men, dressed in trousers, tall boots and a man's cut-down shirt, her hair tucked into a tight, dark braid that fell over one shoulder; a look that emphasised long legs, high firm breasts and did absolutely nothing for taming his morning arousal.

Emma met his gaze with a cool stare of her own. 'We are firing the fields today.' Firing the fields, firing his blood, his temper. There was fire aplenty today.

Ren chose to ignore the obvious quality of the statement and went straight to the pronoun. 'We? That seems an odd choice of words considering you left me in bed.'

Emma coloured, his innuendo not lost. 'I did *not* leave you in bed the way you suggest. You'd had a long journey. I let you sleep.' She turned towards the other two men with her. 'Mr Paulson and Peter, allow me to introduce Albert Merrimore's relative, Mr Renford Dryden. He arrived yesterday afternoon. Mr Dryden, this is my overseer, Mr Paulsen, and my field foreman, Peter, whom you met yesterday.'

Paulsen was a tall, slender man with leathery skin, a man who'd seen years under a hot sun. Peter was the thick-muscled African from the home farm. Ren offered his hand to the two men and took the opportunity to establish his ground. 'I'm pleased to meet you. I will want to discuss the plantation with each of you over the next few days.'

That brought a shuffling of feet from Peter, who hastily looked away, and a hesitant nod from Mr Paulsen. Ren was pleased to see they were loyal and not wanting to betray their allegiance to Emma, but resistance was resistance. As such, it was only a step away from outward defiance. Ren decided to address it head on with a smile. 'I am the primary shareholder now. I will, of course, be ably assisted by Miss Ward, but you should accustom yourselves to a new line of authority.' Ren shot a stern look at Emma. 'This is a partnership now.'

Partnership, her foot! This was a slippery slope to dictatorship if it was anything at all. Emma glared out over the smoky fields, arms crossed. If he was going to begin as he meant to go on, she should, too. His 'partnership' would have to be nipped in the bud, but that nipping would have to wait until they could return to the house. She was not petty enough to argue in front of Mr Paulsen and Peter.

Nor was she naive enough to think she was going to get away with nothing more than the veiled scolding of Ren's last remark. That remark had been a warning and now he was making her wait for the other proverbial shoe to fall. She was not a patient person by nature and he'd already tried what little patience she possessed over the past four months *waiting* for him to arrive or not. Apparently, she was not done waiting.

She waited until the burning was nearly complete and could be left in Mr Paulsen's capable hands. She waited through the walk back to the house. She waited while they filled their plates with a late breakfast and sat down at the table. She waited as he took a few bites of his eggs and buttered his toast.

Ren took a bite of that well-buttered toast and looked a question at her with an arch of his brows. 'Yes? Do you have something you want to say?'

'No, do you?' Emma sipped at her coffee in hopes of disguising her agitation. She wanted him to engage first.

'I have nothing to say that you do not already know.' His eyes held hers, blue fire simmering in them. 'You tried to play me for a fool this morning.' His tone was even, neutral. 'We both know it. You deliberately didn't tell me about firing the fields.'

Emma gathered her practised defence. 'By the time I remembered, I had already undressed for the evening.' It had sounded better in her head. Out loud, it only proved to be provocative and Ren had indicated already he wasn't above innuendo. He would not let such a reference pass.

'Were you now?' His gaze was steady but the faintest ribbon of a smile played across his mouth, bringing to mind images that were entirely too intimate for the breakfast table, images that left her stripped bare beneath his gaze and not the least bit protected from the direction of his thoughts and hers.

Emma looked down at her eggs. 'I couldn't very

well traipse around the house in my nightgown.' That was even worse. She was making a mess of this. Usually, she was considered quite the wit. Not today. Not with this man.

'I, too, had retired for the evening,' Ren said drily. 'In fact, I was wearing far less than a nightshirt. Had you come, you would have been overdressed.' The last comment brought her eyes up, her cheeks starting to heat. 'I sleep in the nude, Emma. In case you were wondering.'

'I wasn't,' Emma snapped in mortification. It was absolutely a lie, however. She *had* been wondering, her mind filling rather quickly with images of a naked Ren Dryden.

'More to the point, I awoke naked and nearly ran out to the fields in my altogether. I wonder who would have looked foolish then—me, for running out naked in concern for my crops, or you for having overlooked the simple courtesy of notifying me?'

Emma's cheeks were twin ovens now, her mind a riot of inappropriate images of her guest. She tried to sound oblivious to the implications of his words. 'I think we're being a little dramatic about a harmless episode.' Hot cheeks or not, she positively *refused* to let him turn this into an inquisition. Nor would she let him turn this into a favour he'd done her in which *he'd* saved *her* from embarrassment.

Ren's eyes were shrewd when they met hers. 'A harmless episode, but not an isolated one. In the past…' he stopped here and flipped open a pocket watch, doing a quick calculation '…eighteen hours since my arrival, you've made it clear you don't want me here. But I *am* here and this *will* be a partnership. There will be no more of these attempts to dissuade me.'

'My apologies if you feel that way,' Emma replied, but her tone was unrepentant. He'd proven to be a worthy opponent at present, catching on far too quickly to her strategy. That didn't mean she had to admit to it. It did mean, however, she would need another. Simply ignoring Ren Dryden wasn't going to work.

Her brain began to recalibrate. The new gambit would have to be something more subtle, something that would bind him to her without arousing his suspicions. After all, if he was going to stay, how could she best use him? Could she make him an ally against Gridley? He'd been quick enough to support her yesterday.

Emma studied Ren, well aware that he was watching her, waiting for her to cede the terms of their partnerships. *Watch me all you like.* He was not entirely immune to her. He knew very well what he was doing with his innuendo and his eyes. A man didn't play such games with a woman he wasn't attracted to. She was used to men watching her, men like Arthur Gridley and Thompson Hunt. Men who were always wondering about her, thinking they knew how best to manipulate her for their own gains.

Like them, perhaps Dryden's own confidence could be played against him. But how to do it? Perhaps a temporary show of agreement was in order until she sorted things out.

Emma stuck her hand out across the table, evincing appropriate reluctance. Her about-turn would have to be convincing. Ren Dryden would not find complete, immediate capitulation compelling. 'Very well, since it seems I have no choice, I agree. A partnership it is.' She would honour that partnership until it was no longer judicious for her to pursue a course of assumed equality. Her next gambit, whatever it was, needed to be something *more*. Her first gambit had not worked, based as it was on faulty assumptions about who Ren would be. She needed time to think the next one through. Agreement bought her time and this time she had to succeed. She wouldn't get another second chance.

Ren relinquished her hand, but his eyes didn't stray from hers. 'Perhaps we should seal our partnership with a tour of the property. I would like to start learning about the plantation immediately.'

A little spark of excitement travelled down her spine, a most unwanted reaction. She had the distinct impression he wasn't necessarily referencing the plantation. Her pulse raced, oblivious to what her mind already knew: it was only a game. Ren could flirt all he liked, but in the end, she needed to be the one in charge. If this was to be a game, she preferred it to be one played neutrally, at least on her part.

'I can arrange to have Peter or Mr Paulsen show you around.' After a morning of sharpening wits with him, a little distance was in order. She needed time to plan. Emma rose to make her departure, but Ren was ready for her. He rose with her, blocking her access to the door.

'I'm sure they're capable, but I'd prefer you. We can go right now.' He held his arms wide, showing off his riding attire with a laugh. 'Fortunately, I am dressed for it and so are you.' He gave her a conspiratorial grin at the inside joke. 'You're not in your nightgown and I'm not in my altogether, so there's no excuse.'

Emma recognised defeat. She'd been flanked. She would not be able to dismiss him as easily as she had yesterday by pawning him off on her servants. She smiled tightly. She *had* to capitulate, there was no way out of it and he knew it, he'd orchestrated it that way. 'Very well, I'll call for the horses.'

His grin widened. 'No need, I've already done that. I told the groom to have them ready at half past.' Not *your* groom, but *the* groom. Beneath his casual manner there was a sharp reminder that while Sugarland was her place, it was also his. *Theirs. Together.*

Emma let the comment pass and led the way out to the drive. Sharing would take some getting used to. It would demand she reshape the way she viewed him entirely. At least temporarily, she had to move away from seeing him as the interloper, someone who was here only on Merry's posthumous good grace. Still, she had to be strong. Otherwise, Ren would think she was soft. Men exploited softness.

Horses were indeed waiting outside and Ren gave her a leg up, tossing her into the saddle with ease as he had done yesterday. He adjusted her stirrup and checked her girth one last time. It was either quite gallant of him, or quite patronising. Emma shot him a wry look, assuming the latter. 'You should know, Ren Dryden, I don't like high-handed men.'

Ren gave her stirrup a final tug and looked up, blue eyes sparking with amusement. '*You* should know I don't like scheming females. I think that makes us even.'

He swung up into his saddle with athletic grace, the heels of his boots automatically going down in the irons, his thighs naturally gripping the stallion, a bay Merry had bought from an officer who was returning to England. She felt a sharp stab of heat at the memory from yesterday of those thighs gripping her.

'You're a horseman,' Emma said as they turned their mounts out behind the house to begin the tour.

'I love to ride. My family prides themselves on their stable. We all grew up in the saddle.' Ren drew his horse alongside hers, his tone easy, inviting conversation as the path widened to easily accommodate two riders abreast.

'Do you have a large family?' The way he'd said 'all' implied that he did. She'd not imagined him having siblings. She'd spent her time planning for the arrival of an old man with few ties.

'Big enough. Not as large as some,' Ren answered. 'I have two younger sisters and a younger brother. How about yourself, do you have siblings?'

She shook her head. 'I barely had parents, let alone brothers and sisters. It was mostly my father and me. He was in the military and we travelled.'

'That must have been exciting.' Ren was studying her, giving her the full attention of his gaze. It was warming and unnerving all at once. This was supposed to have been a safe conversation but it was proving contrary to her intentions. Was it real or was it merely his brand of superficial politeness? Worse, was it the beginning of a seduction? Was he being nice to capitalise on the truce they'd established over breakfast? She'd seen such niceness often enough from those who had something to gain. If he thought to kiss the plantation out of her, he wouldn't be the first to try and he wouldn't be the last to fail.

This was where seduction, if that was what he was up to, became tricky. One had to be careful not to forget the game, no matter how appealing the fantasy. She wouldn't make it easy for him or for herself. Neither could she appear to be entirely resistant. Resistance would not convince him she'd rethought her position on his presence. Still, things didn't have to go too far.

Emma decided to put a halt to the moment before she had herself imagining he cared about something other than his fifty-one per cent. 'It was lonely. My father's career was all consuming. He lived for it and the adventure of always moving can be something of a burden when one is craving the stability of a normal home and friends. There was no one to fall back on when my father died.' They reached a fork in the rough trail. She gestured they should go right.

'There was my cousin,' Ren answered, swiftly coming to Merry's defence.

'Yes, there was Merry and I will always be grateful. He was all that was generous and kind to a lonely sixteen-year-old girl.' The trail narrowed and Emma pushed ahead of him. They were climbing now. Emma was glad for a reason to proceed single file. Even after four months, her grief over Merry remained raw. Too much sincerity, feigned or not from Ren Dryden, and she'd be a gusher.

They reached the top of the incline and dismounted. Emma went to stand at the edge, using the time to gather her emotions. But Ren did not give her long. He came up behind her, his boots giving fair warning as they rustled the grass. He was close, close enough for her to smell the scent of honest sweat mixed with the scents of horse and morning soap. The combination was decidedly male and not at all unpleasing. There was power to it and strength.

'This is the highest point on Sugarland, from here you can see everything.' It was one of her favourite places to visit. She and Merry had come up often when he was well. The last time had been two days before he died. The trip had taken all of his strength. She remembered worrying that he *would* die on the hilltop, that it had been his reason for coming; he'd wanted to depart the earth where he could see his legacy spread before him. It was the day he'd warned her of his suspicions about Gridley. She wished he'd warned her about Ren Dryden, too.

Ren let out a low whistle of appreciation. 'That's an amazing view. I can see why you'd want to come. A man could be a king here, surveying his domain.'

'Or a queen surveying hers,' Emma amended. This was her kingdom, a reminder of all she fought for, of all she defended. A reminder, too, of what she stood to lose if she was not a vigilant guardian. Gridley would wrest this place from her if she gave him half a chance. Perhaps Ren Dryden would, too.

'Tell me about it, tell me everything we see.' Ren's voice was quiet, intimate at her ear. It sent an unlooked-for trill of awareness down her spine, so unlike the prickles of hatred, even fear, that Gridley's presence roused.

Ren pointed in the distance. 'What's that building over there?'

'That's our sugar mill. Once we harvest the cane, it will be refined there. We're big enough to support our own mill. We're lucky. We mill the cane for some of the smaller plantations, too, who don't have their own,' Emma explained.

She moved their gaze to the east. 'That's the main house. Then there's the cane fields.' They were black beneath the sky, the recent firing causing them to stand out stark and naked against the lush background. 'There are the vegetable fields and the home farm.' She paused to glance over her shoulder, taking in Ren's expression. 'You're surprised. We're self-sufficient here. The trick is to balance the land between what we need to feed ourselves and what we can afford to grow for cane. Sugar cane is our money crop, but it won't do us any good if we starve or if we have to spend our profits on food. Already, so much of what we need has to be imported from England. It would be a shame to have to import food, too.'

Ren nodded slowly. She could almost see the wheels of his mind turning behind those eyes of his. He was interested in the plantation. Well, she'd see how interested he was in the middle of a sweltering summer when there was work to be done, although he'd done well yesterday with the fire. He hadn't hesitated.

'Is cane difficult to grow?' he asked, his gaze going

back to the charred fields. 'From my reading, it doesn't seem to be.'

'Not too difficult. The cane regenerates itself.' She started to explain the process, acutely aware of the potent male presence behind her. Ren was making it difficult to talk about ratoon crops and he wasn't even touching her. He was just standing there. Only he wasn't. He was flirting silently with his body.

No, flirting was too superficial of a word. Flirting required witty banter and gay repartee, not an agricultural discussion. This wasn't flirting, this was *sampling*. He was letting her sample his physicality—the smell of him, the heat, the sensuality of him as he turned even the most mundane comment erotic by murmuring it near her ear.

There was no doubt he was a man who understood precisely how to use the nuances of space and touch to create a certain appeal. The bigger question was why? She had yet to meet a man who didn't have ulterior motives when it came to women or when it came to her. She didn't need to be a genius to figure out what Dryden was after. She'd been alert to that potential ever since he'd climbed down from Sherard's wagon in all his broad-shouldered, blue-eyed glory.

His subtle flirtation here on the bluff confirmed what she'd suspected. Even being alert for such a move from him, it was disappointing. Perhaps a small part of her had hoped the man she'd seen at the fire would be different. Not that knowledge of his likely game was enough apparently to stop her pulse from racing, or a little *frisson* of excitement from running down her spine as he abstrusely put his body on invitation. But it needed to be.

She was a smart woman and experience had made her smarter than most when it came to the nature of men. Those experiences would need to be her armour now. Emma stepped forward, away from the heat of his body. 'We should be getting back. I have work to do.' Anything would be better than being near Ren and his intoxicating presence without a plan of her own. Too much of him and she'd forget her resolve and his agenda.

Emma filled the ride back with business. She talked about the native flora and fauna, the seasonal changes on the island, even the hurricane of 1831 which had left much of the island devastated and claimed fifteen hundred lives. All of it done in an attempt to create distance and a reminder they were business partners and would be nothing more. She couldn't afford to be *more* with him.

The house came into view and Emma felt a surge of relief. Sanctuary! She would not have to deal with Ren again until dinner. She could bury herself away in the office behind closed doors. That relief was short-lived. As they approached the drive, it was evident she had company. A rider was dismounting from a tall sorrel stallion. Damn and double damn. Hadn't yesterday been enough for him?

Ren drew his horse alongside. 'Expecting guests?'

Emma grimaced. 'Sir Arthur Gridley isn't exactly a guest.' He'd probably seen the smoke from the crops and wanted to poke his nose into Sugarland's business, something he'd made a habit of doing since Merry's death.

'A nuisance then?' Ren joked wryly.

'Something like that,' Emma responded tersely. Gridley was more than a nuisance. He was insidious. He liked to portray himself as the nosy neighbour who had her best interests at heart. Only she knew better.

'If he's not a nuisance or a guest, what is he, then?' The protectiveness she sensed in him yesterday gave an edge to Ren's voice.

'Nothing for you to worry about. I've got him under control.' She hoped she did anyway. She wasn't about to admit otherwise to Ren and alert him to the possibility that not all was perfect at Sugarland. Neither did she want to give Ren a possible weapon to use against her.

Arthur Gridley strode down the steps towards them, smiling pleasantly, playing the good neighbour to the hilt, definitely a bad sign. It seemed she was about to trade Ren Dryden for something worse, a classic case of out of the frying pan and into the fire.

Chapter Five

'Emma, my dear, you've been busy!' Arthur Gridley effused his usual charm and was dressed in the height of luxury. The packet was always bringing him expensive clothes. If the island had a dandy, he was it.

Emma smiled tightly, aware of how dirty she was again compared to Gridley's pristine neatness. He most certainly hadn't spent the morning firing fields and touring his land. Gridley wasn't exactly a hands-on manager when it came to his plantation. 'Sir Arthur, it's good to see you. Did we have an appointment?' She would not give him an inch. She would show no fear in his presence. It would only give him one more weapon.

Sir Arthur grinned, showing even, white teeth. Many women on the island found that smile attractive, including the governor's wife. Emma did not count herself among their number. Gridley's appeal had worn out ages ago for her. 'Since when do old friends need appointments to call on one another?' He gave her a friendly wink. 'I came to talk to Dryden. We didn't have a chance to become acquainted yesterday with all the chaos.' He said 'chaos' as if she'd planned the fire deliberately. 'It was not the most ideal of circumstances for introductions.'

Emma saw Gridley's intentions immediately. He'd come to be the serpent in the garden, to woo Ren with a false show of friendship. She should have warned Ren when she'd had the chance. Gridley had the devil's own tongue and she could easily imagine the tales he would spin now that Merry's heir was here, a new uninformed target for Gridley's ambitions to acquire interest in Sugarland. Gridley was not a man to face without forewarning.

'Albert and I were close. He was a good friend,' Sir Arthur supplied with a sad smile when she offered nothing to qualify the nature of his relationship. What she said or didn't say hardly mattered. He was never above a little self-promotion.

Gridley's smile softened and fixed on her just long enough to create an impression of caring before turning back to Ren. 'I'm not just a friend to Merrimore, but to his dear Emma too, I hope?'

'You must forgive my manners, it's been a long morning,' Emma ground out with the barest of civility. It was the only demur he was going to get from her. Proper etiquette required she say something like 'I did not mean to imply otherwise' when she really did. She would not play the politeness game with him and avow him publicly in any form.

'Yes, I see you fired the fields.' Gridley raised a scolding eyebrow at Emma but he directed his next comment to Ren. 'Not all of us fire the fields, Dryden. It's too risky for some of us veteran planters, but Emma has a penchant for all the latest novelties.'

'You make it sound as if I fired the fields on a whim,' Emma cut in crisply. She would not let him reduce her farming methods to a female foible in front of the man she was desperately trying to impress with her capability. It was a sound decision to burn the fields and when she had her crop in first, she'd prove it to the others.

'I am confident Emma knows what she is doing.' She felt Ren move up behind her, the heat of his body echoing against her back. He was proprietarily close. Something dark flitted through Gridley's eyes, but his ever-present grin was benevolent when he spoke.

'Nonetheless, I'm glad you're here, Dryden. You can take things in hand now and let Emma focus on running the house.' Goodness, he was in full form today! He'd all but chucked her under the chin like a doting uncle, an identity which was a complete misnomer when it came to their dubious relationship. Gridley had no intentions of being a father figure to her. He had far lustier aspirations.

'I'd invite you in, but I'm busy today,' Emma said sharply, making apology for her breach in social manners.

'Never mind about me, you go on with your business. As I said, I'm not really here for you.' He gave another of his winks to indicate a friendly joke. 'I'm here to see Dryden and give him the lay of the land. We'll stay out of your way, just send a pitcher of falernum to the back porch where we can have a nice long visit.' He slapped

Ren on the back. 'I'll give him a proper welcome to the neighbourhood.'

'A *proper* welcome?' Ren shot her a discreet glance and she could almost hear the private laughter in Ren's voice, laughter that was there just for her, some inside humour only the two of them shared. 'I think I'd like that very much.' The inside joke made Arthur Gridley a momentary outsider and in a subtle way let her know she had an ally.

Emma could feel the beginnings of a smile play on her lips. It could just be part of a larger strategy Ren was playing, but for now it felt good to know he had her back. It was certainly a new way to view Ren's presence and it just might provide the new gambit she was looking for. *The enemy of my enemy is my friend. For now.*

Enemy? Friend? Concerned neighbour or ambitious interloper? It was hard to know how to classify Sir Arthur Gridley. Ren took a seat in one of the twin rockers on the veranda, gathering his thoughts. Emma certainly didn't care for the man. But was that dislike or fear she felt? What was she hiding that Gridley might expose? All in all, Ren thought it would make a rather insightful afternoon.

'What do you think of our little piece of the world so far?' Gridley stretched out his legs, settling into his chair and looking quite comfortable at a home not his own. He'd said he was Merrimore's close friend. In all fairness, he was probably used to being here, but the action struck Ren as overtly territorial, the tactic of a man who wants to remind everyone of his superior claim to ownership.

'It's hot,' Ren replied affably. It couldn't hurt to be nice. Knowledge was power and Gridley would want to demonstrate his. If Ren played this right, Gridley would talk all afternoon, thinking he was establishing his ground, when in reality Ren would get precisely what he wanted—information.

Ren had learned years ago it was the listener who held the upper hand when navigating the social waters of the *ton*. He had to start making friends in this new place. He wanted those friends to be the right ones. He had a hunch there might be wrong ones and he still had to figure out where Emma fit into the balance. Who to trust? The supposedly crazy woman running Sugarland or the well-dressed, seemingly well-intentioned neighbour?

'It *is* hot, in an entirely different way than London,' Gridley agreed. 'You'll get used to it. We have our rainy seasons and our fever seasons, but it's not a bad way to live. There's no cold, no ice, no grey skies that go on for months.' Gridley was all friendly assurance.

A servant brought a tray carrying a pitcher full of an amber liquid and two glasses. She set it down on the little table between them and poured. 'You'll like falernum,' Gridley said. 'It's sweet, full of spices and a hint of vanilla.'

Ren sipped tentatively, relieved Gridley was right. He could pick out the hints of ginger and almond, even a bit of lime. 'It *is* good.'

Gridley chuckled. 'You sound surprised. Don't be.

Emma has the best falernum on the island, there's something about how her cook mixes it.' Gridley sighed and dropped his voice. 'Emma has the best of everything. The best cook, the best field manager, the best overseer, the best household staff. It's made her some enemies and I'm worried for her. I'm glad you're here. Perhaps you can talk sense into her.'

Gridley slid him a sideways glance, no doubt looking for compliance. But Ren was more astute than that. He needed information before he made any decisions about his support. Ren decided to play the 'fresh off the boat' card. 'I'm afraid I don't quite understand what you mean?'

'Of course not, no one expects you to. We'll show you the ropes around here. You'll get the hang of how we do things in no time at all.' Gridley gave him another friendly smile, but Ren was cautious.

'I'd appreciate that,' he said neutrally. Ren was starting to wonder if Gridley had come of his own accord or if the neighbours had elected him to be the one to call and sound out the newcomer. He was used to this discreet vetting process. It wasn't all that different from the way the gentlemen's clubs tested a member's viability in London.

'It's not Emma's fault.' Gridley was quick to establish. 'It's the damn apprentice system. It looks good on paper, but it's costing the planters a small fortune in profits and there's hardly enough labour to go around.'

Ren raised an eyebrow in query, hoping Gridley would take it as a sign to elaborate on the process. Gridley took the hint and continued. 'Under the new system, former slaves can choose if they wish to work on the plantations and they can choose *which* plantations. We can't compel them to do it. Naturally, they want to work for the places that pay more and demand they do less.' The complaint against Emma was implied in the comment. 'She might as well tuck them all in with quilts and feed them meat three times a day.' Gridley chuckled, but Ren heard the contempt beneath the humour. 'You saw such a display yesterday with the afternoon off over the obeah doll.'

'You disapprove of such equity?' Ren asked, eyeing Gridley carefully. Something more was at work here in his social call. Was his ulterior agenda political? Economic? Social?

'I disapprove when those choices jeopardise one's neighbours' ability to make a decent living,' Gridley answered squarely. Ren shot a quick glance at Gridley's expensive boots. He didn't think Emma's choices were hurting Gridley too much.

Gridley dismissed the harshness of his comment with a wave of his hand. 'Emma doesn't know better. She's too kind-hearted and impulsive as well, not the best combination for business. She doesn't see the big picture—the consequences her actions have for all of us.' There was anger and heat in the man's words.

Ren felt himself bristle at the cut to Emma's character. It was a strangely protective reaction to have towards a woman who had made it clear she was intent on disliking him. Still, what sort of neighbour maligned another in her own home? 'Perhaps you judge her too harshly,' Ren offered in Emma's defence. 'She believes she's doing the best she can to sustain the property.'

Gridley's demeanour became intensely serious. 'She doesn't quite grasp the larger implications. It is *us* against *them* and *they* have us vastly outnumbered. If we don't stick together, they'll be asking for seats in the assembly next or taking them outright.' The voracity of his comment was almost disturbing.

Ren understood the reference. The white plantocracy was outflanked by the ex-slave population by nearly ten to one. The sheer numbers created a certain unrelieved tension between the two groups. The plantocracy minority held all the legitimate power, but the ex-slave faction held the overwhelming majority of force should they attempt to exercise it.

Rebellion, *successful* rebellion, was possible, even likely. He knew from talk in London that other islands in the West Indies had experienced such rebellions. There were people like Gridley who believed such rebellion against the legitimate power was inevitable, their only weapon being the ability to legislate punitive codes to keep rebellion at bay.

Even though Ren understood the motivation for the plantocracy's logic, he could not condone it. His position was something he apparently had in common with Emma. It was also something that would not endear him to Arthur Gridley and his other neighbours if his position were known. Caution suggested he wait to reveal his feelings on the subject.

'Perhaps if people work together they might find a middle ground.' Ren put the unformed idea forward.

He didn't want to lie to Gridley or profess to hold an opinion he heartily disagreed with. However, he had navigated the shoals of London society long enough to know there were bridges one couldn't afford to burn. If Emma had already burned hers, he needed to maintain his for Sugarland's sake. He was staunchly in favour of the decision to abolish slavery and even of reallocating seats in the assembly to more accurately reflect the population.

Gridley's response was curt and immediate. 'I don't know that there's any middle ground to be had, or any ground at all. I mean that quite literally. Once you've seen the island in its fullness, you'll understand. We don't have any unowned land. It's all claimed. The freemen want to work their own land, but where would that be? There's no land for them to buy, no land to give them, without breaking up the existing plantations.' There was a defensive gleam in his eye that belied the intensity of his convictions.

Ah, illumination. Land was the real threat, the real fear, that somehow Britain would legislate land be taken from the planters. Ren nodded thoughtfully, allowing Gridley to pour him another glass of falernum. Ren had no doubt if that came to pass, Arthur Gridley would meet people at the door with a gun.

'But enough of politics, you'll learn all that,' Gridley said, his earlier bonhomie returning in a sudden wave of good humour. The man definitely possessed a mercurial range of emotions. One moment he was serious, almost fanatical in his commitment to his positions, the next he was easygoing. 'As for Emma doing the best she can, that's another issue. We all understand she has a huge responsibility. It doesn't have to be that way. She needn't shoulder the burden of Sugarland alone, but she refuses to listen to reason.'

By 'we' Ren supposed Gridley referred to the neighbours, all of them male. 'What sort of reason?' Ren asked, although he could already guess how their brand of reason had gone over with Emma. Even on short acquaintance he knew she would see the solutions as infringements on her independence.

'The usual,' Gridley said sobering. 'I was close with Albert Merrimore, especially during his last year. He was worried for Emma and what would become of her. He knew his time was limited. I promised him I would be there for her. If she wanted to go to London, I'd see it done. If she wanted to stay here, I promised him I'd make it possible. We were neighbours, our plantations abut one another, of course I'd watch over his charge.'

'And the options you put to Emma?' Ren steered the conversation back towards his original question. 'What did she want?'

'She wanted to stay.' Gridley gave a sad smile. 'A woman cannot be out here alone trying to run a plantation without all nature of hardship, so I offered her marriage and she refused.' His eyes met Ren's, convincingly full of a man's regret that something he valued had slipped through his fingers. 'I shall ask again once she has found her centre. In my eagerness to fulfil my promise to Albert, I rushed my fences. I see that now. She was grieving, she was sorting through the estate and the will.' He shot Ren a wry look. 'She was adjusting to the news that a relative was coming who'd been given the majority of the shares. She was in no state to appreciate what a proposal would mean to her.'

This was what Gridley had really come to discuss. He was staking his claim to Emma. Ren assessed Arthur Gridley with new eyes. This was a man who was more than a neighbour, even more than a random suitor who fancied Emma. He'd been a family intimate with Cousin Merry. He had attempted to wed Merry's ward and meant to try his luck again, regardless of Emma's rather obvious feelings on the subject.

Even if Emma professed undying love for Gridley, allowing such a thing to happen was not in Ren's best interests as long as Emma held the other portion of ownership. It provoked the question of what drove Gridley's persistence. It was an academic question only. Ren could not allow Gridley's persistence to win out.

His protective streak rose, coupled this time with a competitive urge. This wasn't only about protecting Emma, but about protecting himself and his family. If Emma married Gridley, Ren would have to share the estate with *him*. It was not an idea he liked. It was one thing to drink a casual glass of falernum with the man, but it was another to make him a business partner and tie his family's interests to Gridley's. The prospect sat ill with Ren. His sixth sense told him that was not what his cousin had intended. He supposed he could buy out her share. He wondered if Gridley would still want her if she was without property…

'That's where you come in, Dryden,' Gridley was

saying as Ren dragged his thoughts back to the conversation. He must have missed the beginning.

'How is that, exactly?' Ren asked obliquely.

Gridley have a short chuckle. '*You're* to help her see reason, show her the best options for Sugarland. She can't go it alone forever without risking the plantation's viability.' There was a dark glint in Gridley's eye and Ren wondered if he referred to a risk that had less to do with Emma's ability to make agricultural decisions and more to do with what might be termed her 'personal welfare'.

'I will do my best to live up to my cousin's faith in me,' Ren said honestly, although his best might not lead to the decisions Gridley was hoping for. Ren took the opportunity to rise, signalling their conversation had come to a close. He had quite enough to digest. Gridley had discharged his duty to the so-far-anonymous neighbours quite well. All that needed to be shared had been shared and any necessary warnings had been given. Perhaps even more than was necessary. Were the neighbours astute enough to know that Gridley would advocate for himself as well as them? Gridley's measure was clear. He was a man who did what benefited him.

Gridley shook his hand. 'It's good to meet you, Dryden. I want to have a dinner for you, give you a chance to meet everyone. I'll set it up and let Emma know.'

'I will look forward to it.' Ren showed Gridley out, understanding that the next move was up to him. Gridley had initiated, had laid out the rules of the game. Gridley and the neighbours would wait to see what his response would be. They could be in for a surprise. He might not know much about sugar cane, but he knew a little something about navigating society, especially when a game was afoot. If Emma Ward thought she had everything under control, she needed to think again.

Chapter Six

She had everything under control. Emma took a deep breath and moved her pip on the backgammon board, embracing the silent mantra that had sustained her throughout the evening. *Everything was going to be fine.* Not just the game but *everything*: the harvest, Arthur Gridley's unwanted attention, the plantation. She was balancing a rather precarious load just now, not counting the arrival of Ren Dryden.

One false step and it would all come tumbling down. But it wouldn't. It simply couldn't. To lose Sugarland was unthinkable. To allow Gridley to triumph, even more so. She told herself it was a good sign Ren hadn't run to her immediately after Gridley had left. It meant there was no need to worry. Right? Ren had said nothing during dinner. They'd talked about the plantation and adjourned here to the library for backgammon.

Across from her, Ren critically surveyed the board, jiggling the dice in his dice cup. 'Double would be useful about now. I won't get off the bar without at least one five.' It was the only open point he could move to. She'd completely blocked out her field.

'You'll never get it.' Emma laughed, feeling confident she would have the advantage for another turn. She was starting to relax and enjoy the novelty of having someone to share the evening with. Surely, if something had alarmed Ren he would have brought it up by now.

'You're a very cocky minx, Emma Ward.' Ren grinned, looking devastating in the lamplight. He'd dressed for dinner, but he'd shed his coat when they'd begun to play. She'd thought he'd been handsome in his evening attire. He was far more attractive in his shirt and waistcoat, his cufflinks set aside, his sleeves rolled up.

The gesture had created a sense of domestic intimacy and a domestic fantasy, too; a glimpse of what life might be like for a husband and wife spending a quiet evening at home after a busy day with the plantation. He was a master indeed if he could conjure such images for her with the simple gesture of removing a coat.

If there wasn't so much on the line, the plantation, her own future; if she didn't have to be vigilant regarding any covert game Ren might be playing with her, she would have allowed herself to fall for him. It had been a long time since she'd let herself fall. Surely, she'd learned enough in the interim to fall safely, to enjoy the fantasy.

Without the trappings of her present circumstances, an affair with Ren Dryden would be a delightful diversion. As it was, at this point it could only be a dangerous diversion, a delusion. 'Are you going to roll?' Emma prompted with a sly smile. 'Staring at the board won't change anything.'

Ren sat back in his chair, his eyes on her. 'You are so sure I won't roll double fives. Why don't we wager on it? If I get double fives, I claim a forfeit. If I don't, you claim the forfeit.' He shook the cup and then halted, his eyes dancing with mischief. 'The forfeit should be something little, Emma. No property, no crazy requests that either of us abdicate our percentage of the plantation. I don't imagine you'd be terribly good at cards, my dear. Your thoughts are written all your pretty face.'

Emma feigned indignation over the teasing. 'Very well, I'll take your bet. I'm already thinking of all the "little" things you can do for me. It's just so hard to choose one.' The banter was almost enough to take her mind off her real worries: what had Gridley told him this afternoon? What was Ren thinking about her now? What sort of poison had Gridley added to the proverbial well?

Ren rolled his dice and let out a whoop. Emma stared in disbelief as double fives tumbled out. Emma shook her head. 'You have the devil's own luck. I'd thought to have you trapped on the bar a little longer.'

Ren gave a confident grin and moved his marker off the bar. 'Now I have a chance to catch up, I might make a match of this yet.' There was a warm twinkle in his eye and Emma realised he was having a good time. Whatever Gridley had imparted, it hadn't dampened his spirits.

'And your forfeit?' Emma asked, bearing off her first pips.

'I think I'll hold on to it a while.' Ren's voice was low and mysterious, conjuring up images of a decadent

forfeit. 'It will give you something to worry about besides Gridley's visit.'

Emma gave him a sharp look. 'I'm not worried about
Gridley's visit.'

Ren took his turn. 'Yes, you are. You've been worried all night.'

'As I told you, I have Arthur Gridley under control.'
Emma rolled a disappointing two-three combination
that slowed her march towards victory. She reached out
to move her pieces.

Ren grabbed her wrist over the board, his eyes boring into hers, the sudden ferocity of his move startling
her. 'No, you don't have him under control. You have
a rejected suitor who isn't taking your refusal as final.
It makes me wonder what motivates his perseverance.'

Emma swallowed, her heart sinking. Gridley had
told him! Goodness knew how Gridley had cased *that*
particular story. 'That's private business. He should not
have told you.' She pulled her wrist from Ren's grasp.

'Probably not. Nonetheless, I was glad for the information. It adds a certain layer of understanding to
the local dynamic.' There was an accusatory edge to
his response. He'd asked what Gridley was to her and
she'd prevaricated. But Gridley had not. Gridley had
seized the advantage and told the story first, no doubt
to his advantage.

Ren played, rolling another set of doubles and neatly
evening out the game. 'The way I see it, a man would
only share such personal information with a stranger
because he was still wounded over the rejection and not
thinking clearly, or because he has another agenda to

advance. What do *you* think Gridley's reason is?' He was more serious now, the fun-loving Ren from a few moments ago had disappeared.

She tossed the dice. Another disappointment. 'I think Gridley has overreached his ambitions.' It was a non-answer, but she wasn't about to voice her suspicions of what Gridley really wanted or what he'd done to get it. She hadn't any proof of it. Even so, she didn't know if she could trust Ren Dryden to side with her. He had done so briefly today because it had suited him. Gridley's revelations might have changed that.

Ren made his last play, claiming victory with another miraculous roll. Emma shook her head. She'd had that game right up until the end. 'You play like Merry. He was always coming from behind for spectacular finishes. Whenever I thought I had him, he'd surprise me. The dice never failed him. If he needed doubles, he got them.'

Ren laughed. 'I'm glad to hear it. I have to confess I didn't know my cousin all that well. He was here, I was in London. There was an ocean between us in distance and in age. I enjoyed his company the few times he visited, though. The last time was when I'd completed my studies at Oxford, about ten years ago.'

Emma gave a soft smile. 'Merry was a good man, one of the best people I've ever met. He was always thinking of others.' Ten years seemed a lifetime. She'd have been fifteen, her father still alive, their own arrival to the island new.

She hesitated and then took the plunge while the moment was poignant and they were both feeling charitable. There was unfinished business between them. She didn't want to put it off any longer. 'I hope Arthur Gridley said nothing today that would undermine Merry's memory.'

Ren began stacking his pips. 'It seems Gridley and Cousin Merrimore were close friends, especially at the end. I must confess to finding it an odd friendship. Gridley is younger by several decades. I would not think they'd be natural companions, but perhaps one cannot be choosy about who one's friends are out here?' It was a question, not a commentary. He was the one probing now, daring her to confirm or deny Gridley's assertion.

Her probe had not resulted in a direct answer. Emma opted for a different tack. She wanted to know where Gridley stood in Ren's estimation before she committed. 'And you? How did you find our neighbour? Will he be your friend?' They were both dancing around the conversation gingerly.

'I suppose he could be,' Ren answered vaguely, closing the case. 'I can't say I know him well enough after one visit. I think in large part that decision depends on you.' Ren paused 'Do you want me to be his friend? Is there something useful we might cultivate there for Sugarland?'

She noted the reference to *we*. *Something useful we might cultivate?* It was a reminder he meant to be an active participant in the plantation. Still the question remained: did he mean to partner her or usurp her? In that regard, what made him different from Gridley? She'd had indications of both today.

'I fear I have upset Gridley,' Emma ventured cautiously. 'My choices are not his choices and it has become a contention between us, one that has created irreconcilable differences.' She was sure Ren would press her for more. Her answer was both descriptive and oblique.

Ren seemed to ponder her words. He moved towards the open French doors, his back to her. Without his coat, he presented a nice view of his backside, evening trousers pulled tight over firm buttocks, the tailoring of his waistcoat delineating the outline of broad shoulders before tapering to a trim waist. Not only did he possess a handsome presence but a commanding one, one that inspired confidence, even trust if she dared. She had to admit, it was easier to dare such a thing in the intimacy of the evening.

'I suspect Gridley is not a complacent loser,' he said at last.

She stood and went to join him at the doors, hoping the pleasant evening breeze would dispel the hot images in her mind. She needed to focus on the conversation, not on undressing her guest. He was fishing for something with his questions and she might inadvertently give it up. 'Yes,' Emma said carefully, 'Gridley likes to win.'

'Do *you* like to win, Emma?' His voice was quiet in the darkness.

'I like to protect what is mine. I think that's a fundamental difference between men and women.'

'You're very direct. Such directness has wounded Gridley's ego a bit.'

Emma let out a sigh. They were back to that dratted proposal. 'How much did Gridley tell you?'

'He explained he'd felt moved to act swiftly out of loyalty to Cousin Merrimore, but that you were in no state to properly assess the benefits of that proposal.' He turned his blue gaze on her in full force, his voice low and private, moving a business conversation into something more intimate, just as the removal of his jacket had turned a simple backgammon game into a domestic fantasy. 'Gridley indicated he meant to ask you again. Would his suit be welcome now that you've had time to settle and reconsider your situation?'

'That is a bold question,' Emma prevaricated. Her answer would be no. Gridley's suit would never be welcome, but telling Ren Dryden that on the acquaintance of a day would be giving away too much. It might even be encouraging him to pursue his flirtation. She did not know if she could trust Ren any more than she'd been able to trust Gridley. But who to play off against whom? If she said yes, would the gentleman in Ren feel compelled to back off? If she said no, would the seducer in him pursue and could she could use his interest as a buffer against Gridley?

'It's meant as a business question,' Ren answered. 'Who you marry affects me greatly. I'll have to work with them, trust them with forty-nine per cent of my livelihood.'

'Perhaps I'll never marry for exactly that reason. I, too, have to trust them with my forty-nine per cent.' At some point in the conversation, Ren had picked up her hand and was tracing circles on the back of it with his finger. It was idly done, but the gesture was doing warm, tingling things to her arm.

'Then Gridley will be refused?' Ren brought the conversation full circle. 'I sensed there was some tension between you this afternoon and yesterday.' It was all she needed to be reminded of the favour he'd done her, taking her part without being asked. For literally stepping up. Now, she owed him and he wanted payment in the form of an answer.

'Yes. Gridley will always be refused.' She did not offer the reasons why. She'd paid her debt. Ren would have to judge the rest on his own.

Ren nodded. 'The neighbourhood might not take kindly to that.'

'I know,' she said simply. There were advantages for everyone if she married Gridley, not the least being the cessation of her version of the apprenticeship programme. 'Your presence should appease them for now. They want a man in charge and now they have one—at least nominally.'

'More than nominally,' Ren corrected with a wry grin. 'Perhaps this means you've revised your opinion of me. Under *these* circumstances which have newly come to light, I'd think you would be glad to see me. Although yesterday, you led me to believe otherwise.' There was a teasing quality to his words, but the topic was serious: where did they stand with each other? And why?

Emma felt as if she were fighting a battle on two fronts. On one side, she had Gridley to contend with, an enemy she knew in full measure. On the other, there was Ren, a man who could be either enemy or friend. That decision was up to her.

She did need him. She needed him to stand between her and Gridley's proposals. She needed him to stand between her and the neighbours who felt a man, even a man who didn't know a thing about sugar cane, would be a better manager of the plantation than a woman who knew everything. He'd aptly summed up the battles that had consumed her since Merry had died. She so desperately wanted to do this on her own, to show everyone who doubted that Sugarland could be run by woman, that a woman could do anything a man could do. Maybe then she could be left alone.

Emma clenched her fists covertly in her skirts, her nails digging into her palms, frustration mounting. She'd been managing decently until Ren Dryden had come along, now she had Gridley on her doorstep persistent as ever, obeah magic threatening her workforce and exploding chicken coops. How would she ever convince Ren she had it all under control when that control seemed bent on slipping away? The noose around her independence was tightening.

'The truth is, Emma, you need me.' He made the pronouncement sound like an invitation to sin, the way he'd made their discussion of cane crops on the bluff sound like foreplay. They were standing close, no longer side by side staring out over the dark lawns, but face-to-face, having turned during the course of the conversation. Ren's knuckles skimmed the curve of her jaw, his touch warm against her skin.

Emma felt the door frame hard at her back. He had her effectively trapped. There was no escaping his hot blue eyes or the thrum of her pulse as it raced in anticipation. 'What are you doing, Ren?' she murmured, although she knew very well. He'd been staking his claim all day in little ways, pushing all other claims out of the way by her own denial of them.

Ren's mouth bent to the column of her neck. 'I'm claiming my forfeit.'

Chapter Seven

'Give over, Emma.' His mouth was close to her ear, whispering his decadent suggestion, the feel of his body intoxicating as she arched into him, giving him full access to her neck, letting him trail kisses up its length to her earlobe. She let his teeth nip the tender flesh, his breath feathering against her ear. She couldn't give over any more without giving over entirely and that would be foolish. She knew what this was. The game of seduction he'd begun on the bluff was adding another delicious layer.

Tonight she seemed helpless to resist, even knowing better. Maybe that wasn't such a bad thing. Maybe it was best to get this first initial contact out of the way, remove all the anticipation and curiosity that often motivates first kisses. And perhaps she should play a little after all? She wouldn't know what Ren intended if she didn't let him advance. At least that's what she told herself as his mouth closed over hers, his tongue running over the seam of her lips. She gave him entrance, her own tongue eager to duel, eager to taste.

Surely, there could be no harm in letting her guard down just for a moment. She had been fighting for so long, been on constant alert to the hidden agendas of others. Ren was no threat to her forty-nine per cent, he already held the majority and she knew what he was playing for. His agenda was not nearly as secretive as those who'd come for the funeral. They'd come to assess the spoils, to assess how they could best use her for their own advancement. But Ren's agenda was clear even if she didn't agree with it.

Ren's hands were at her waist, strong and firm. It would be a very little thing indeed, only a matter of inches, to raise her hands to those broad shoulders. It didn't have to mean anything, just a few moments of freedom, a few moments for herself. That decided it.

Emma slid into his arms, revelling in the feel of his mouth, the caress of his tongue as it claimed hers with the confidence of an expert lover, a man sure of his reception, her mouth drinking him in as much as he drank her. He tasted faintly of dinner's wine, smelled of vanilla and clean, healthy male.

Her body moved against him of its own accord. This was a kiss that demanded full participation, not just mouths but bodies. She could feel the heat of him, the masculine strength of him where their bodies met, the power of his thighs where they pressed against her skirts, his body fulfilling the promises it had alluded to on the bluff. It was a potent signal that here was a man who understood pleasure was best when shared. Here was a man who would not seek pleasure only for

himself. It was also a signal that this had gone too far.
This was only to have been the experiment of a moment.

Emma broke the kiss with a little shake of her head.
'We have to stop.' Her voice sounded breathless to her
own ears.

'Why?' Ren rested his forehead against hers, his eyes
dark and dancing.

It was hard to think of a reason with him so close.
'We hardly know each other,' she said softly. Even that
was a lie. She knew enough about him to know this was
the road to no good.

'I think you underestimate how much kissing can
tell you about a person, even strangers.' Ren gave her
a wicked grin in the gathering darkness. He had one
arm braced against the wall over her head, his body
still indecently close to hers, giving her no quarter. 'For
instance, you're an extraordinarily passionate woman.
You do not kiss only with your mouth, but with your
hips, your arms, with all you have.' His free hand had
dropped to her waist, his thumb drawing lazy circles
low on her hip, pressing firmly, erotically, through the
fabric of her gown. 'You deserve a lover who is worthy
of your passion.' His mouth was at her neck again, his
implication blatant.

'You think you are that lover?' Emma fought to
sound aloof when her body was surging with desire.
Never had she'd been so overtly pursued and she found
the honesty of that pursuit heady in the extreme. She
was passionate, yes. An easy conquest? No.

'I could be, Emma. You've been alone too long.' His
eyes lingered on her lips. 'I've issued a bold invita-

tion, nothing more. The rest is up to you.' Then he was gone, levering his weight off the door frame and slipping out into the night, the Caribbean darkness swallowing him entirely the moment he stepped beyond the reach of the lamplight.

Emma stared after him, thoughts forming, disintegrating and reforming in the wake of his departure. Gridley's aggressive visit today had reshaped her perception of what Ren could mean to her. Instead of seeing him as a second antagonist to fight, he could be an ally given the right incentive.

Ren could stand between her and Gridley by virtue of being the majority shareholder. And he would. He'd demonstrated as much already. But for how long? What if Ren decided to sell in the future, or what if Ren returned to London? How could she entice him to stay?

What a difference a day made. Initially, selling or leaving were things she'd favoured in order to maintain her independence. But she'd underestimated Gridley. If Gridley had told Ren he meant to push his suit, more trouble than she'd realised was brewing. Being married to Gridley not only put Sugarland under his control, but it put her under his control as well.

This was her greater fear. Having been under a man's control before, the experience did not recommend itself as worth repeating. Emma closed her eyes, pushing memories of Thompson Hunt and his cruelties to the back of her mind. Whatever Thompson Hunt had done, she had no doubts Arthur Gridley would be worse.

Thompson Hunt had been a selfish con artist with a malicious streak, nothing more. Arthur Gridley was a sadist and, in her opinion, a murderer. Those were two claims no one would believe if she made them as his wife, assuming she lived long enough to make them at all. She was certain their marriage would be a short one, just long enough for him to ensure Sugarland was his at last.

Emma opened her eyes and blew out a breath, refocusing her thoughts on the present. She needed Ren to stay, perhaps in a more permanent capacity than majority shareholder. How to ensure that, especially if he ever learned Sugarland wasn't as solvent as perhaps he'd been led to believe? Did she dare to risk with him what she would not risk with Gridley? Marriage was the most permanent bond she could think of.

But even then, marriage wouldn't prevent Ren from leaving her and sailing back to London, especially if it was an empty marriage done for convenience. It didn't have to be empty. If she could give him a passion to stay for, a warm bed he'd be reluctant to leave… He was a man unafraid of passion, of his own sexuality. Tonight had proven she could rouse those passions, ignite them. Her past proved sex could be a powerful weapon. It certainly had been when wielded against her. She would never stoop to Thompson Hunt's level, but she would fight with all she had.

Emma twisted a strand of hair that had come loose, an idea coming hard and fast. What had she thought earlier? *A woman could do anything a man could do…* Men seduced women out of inheritances all the time. Ren might even be trying to do that very thing. He had made it clear he couldn't be pushed away. Maybe he could be pulled in. Emma tapped a thoughtful finger against her chin. It would take time, she'd have to go slowly. Ren would never believe she'd done a complete about-turn so immediately. Nor would he trust a woman too loose with her favours. But it would be perfect. She'd use his own seduction of her as a smokescreen; while he was seducing her, she'd be seducing him. Into bed, and with luck, beyond.

'I believe he can be seduced to our side,' Arthur Gridley announced confidently to the men seated at the round table in his library: Miles Calvert, Elias Blakely, Hugh Devore and Amherst Cunningham. All Englishmen, all upstanding citizens of St Michael's parish, all of them bound together under the common standard of having suffered financial setbacks over the last five years and, most importantly, all of them having concluded that wresting Sugarland out of Emma Ward's control lay at the heart of any successful solution to their cash-flow problems. Outside of those commonalities, there were other private agendas that drew them together, politics making very strange bedfellows indeed, in some cases literally, and Gridley knew them all.

Cunningham nodded slowly, his dark eyebrows knitted together in thought. 'We'll have to act quickly before that hellcat gets her claws into him.'

'I am working on that,' Gridley said. 'Dryden and I had a long visit today.' He hoped a few salient seeds had taken root, particularly the one that warned Dryden off pursuing anything with Emma Ward. Emma was *his*. If anyone was going to wed her, or bed her, it was going to be him. He'd paid his dues. It had been unsettling to discover Dryden was a younger man. He'd been counting on someone older, less physically appealing.

'Does Dryden have money?' Miles Calvert asked. The light of the candles in the centre of the table cast his face in shadow, the whole of his expression inscrutable.

The darkness didn't bother Gridley. He knew without seeing Miles's nervous pale green eyes that Miles would be wondering if he could entice the newcomer to buy his moderate-sized plantation and add it to Sugarland's holdings. Miles had been privately contemplating a buyer so he could take the profits and return to England.

Fortunately, Miles had done that contemplating over absinthe in the evenings with him. So far, Gridley had dissuaded Miles from such a course of action in general. It hadn't been hard, there'd been no buyer until now. Miles was wondering if the arrival of Ren Dryden changed that. Gridley would have to make sure it didn't.

'I'm not sure,' Gridley answered truthfully. 'He dresses well and presents himself as an educated man. I would think he's not entirely without funds, but how much?' Gridley shrugged to indicate he thought it unlikely Dryden possessed enough to buy a plantation.

Hugh Devore broke in with a shake of his head, dismissing Calvert's financial concerns. He was a beefy, heavier-set man with greying hair and he spoke with a commanding voice. 'It's not money that matters, it's relationships. What I want to know is who Dryden's connections are. How well did he know Merrimore? We know he's a cousin, but were they close? Was Merrimore likely to have told him about us? If so, what might that have been? Are we friends or enemies?'

The last was said with the faintest hint of accusation. Gridley bristled at the implication that somehow he was to blame if they were exposed. 'I assured you months ago and I assure you now that the risks we so covertly refer to are secure. Merrimore suspected nothing, he told no one because in his mind there was nothing to tell.'

Hugh Devore was not satisfied. 'We took an *enormous* risk at your urging, Gridley, and we lost. You were wrong in your assumptions. Nothing turned out as you purported and now we have a cousin on the scene, one more person that stands between us and our goals.'

Elias Blakely nodded his head in concurrence. Amherst Cunningham said nothing, but looked distractedly at his hands. So that was how things stood these days. A little faction was growing within his group, Gridley noted. He would have to calm them with a reminder of what he held against them. He wasn't above a bit of blackmail to ensure compliance. But first, perhaps some soothing was in order.

'I don't recall seeing you in Merrimore's sickroom taking those risks,' he reminded Devore and Blakely. 'That was all me. In that respect, gentlemen, your hands are clean.' Never mind that they'd given permission for what he'd done in there. He'd remind them about that another time. Accomplices were just as guilty as those who executed the act.

Devore sat back in his chair, hands laced across a healthy show of stomach. 'Be that as it may, Emma Ward has refused you, making our risky efforts for naught. Sugarland, either through legal deed or marriage, is beyond our grasp at present.'

That statement had everyone's attention. The men at the table leaned forward in earnest. Six months ago when Merrimore's demise was imminent, they'd decided the best, least intrusive way to take Sugarland from Emma would be to marry into it. The most likely candidate had been himself. Devore and Cunningham were already married, Miles was a 'confirmed bachelor' and Elias Blakely wasn't much to look at and prone to ill health besides.

'I will renew my courtship now that she's had a chance to see what reality looks like,' Gridley replied. 'I will remind her of my promises to Merrimore and play to her sentimentality.'

'And Dryden?' Devore asked astutely. 'Does he have matrimony on his mind?'

'I'm not sure what Dryden has on his mind. I only spoke with him the once and he's only just arrived,' Gridley reminded the group with a note of censure. 'I'm not a mind reader, although at times many of you think I am. I think the best course forward is to hold a dinner party for him so each of you can take his measure. We can plan how to deal with him from there.'

Elias Blakely spoke for the first time. 'In the meanwhile, there must be something we can do to urge Emma Ward towards our conclusion. I don't need to tell anyone here that time is critical. We are poised at the beginning of the harvest. Once the harvest is in, decisions will be made about next year. All of us will be making those decisions, too, and money is tight. If we cannot secure Sugarland, some of us might make different decisions about the following year.' He swallowed and said quietly, 'Plantation prices are dropping. Some of us may decide to sell before prices drop further.'

Gridley fixed him with a hard stare. 'If anyone were to do that, it would ruin the cartel we've worked so hard to put together. All of us standing united can drive the prices of sugar back up. Then, we'll be in the money.'

'Only if Sugarland is with us,' Miles put in, his eye always on the bottom line. 'If Sugarland continues to stand alone, we'll never achieve the ability to control the prices.'

Gridley gave a tight smile. He was growing weary of the effort of dragging the group along behind him, but he needed them. It would pacify them if he resumed an active courtship of Emma, so he would do it. He would give her two weeks' respite from exploding chicken coops and obeah dolls before he launched his new campaign. His dinner party for Dryden would be the perfect venue for resuming his courtship.

Privately, he didn't think such measures would be enough. But there were other ways to urge Emma to the altar that had nothing to do with the delicacies of romance and everything to do with the hard choices a person makes to save the things they love.

Chapter Eight

Ren stood impatiently while Michael put the finishing touches to his cravat. Arthur Gridley's dinner party was tonight and Ren felt as if he were donning armour instead of evening dress.

The metaphor of battle was not amiss. The peaceful hiatus of the last two weeks while planters focused on their own crops had been a detente of sorts between Gridley and Sugarland. In the quiet of the interim, Ren had not forgotten Gridley and his self-serving intentions lurking just beyond the harvest. The dinner party marked the end of any reprieve. Gridley would be waiting to see how Ren would align himself—with the parish or with Emma.

'Be patient, Mr Ren. Mr Merrimore was a stickler for perfection and you should be, too.' Michael stepped back with the reminder that he was as capable as any London valet. 'I dressed Mr Merrimore for many of Sir Arthur's dinner parties. He liked to wear his stick pin just so. Perhaps I should adjust yours?'

Ren lifted his chin and tolerated the effort, a thought coming to him. 'Were Merrimore and Gridley good friends?' Who would know better than Merrimore's footman-cum-valet? Currently, he only had Gridley's word on the subject. Frankly, Gridley would be biased on that account.

Michael's brow knitted as he reset the stick pin. 'They were always friendly, but it wasn't until the last year that they were what you'd call close. Sir Arthur was here every day, playing backgammon or chess. When Mr Merrimore wasn't well enough to do that, Sir Arthur read to him. Sir Arthur would have me carry Mr Merrimore downstairs and they'd sit and read for hours. He was here when Mr Merrimore passed away and he was here every day after until Miss Emma couldn't stand it any more.' Michael stood back. 'That looks much better.'

Ren gathered up his watch and chain from the dresser. 'She kicked him out, did she?' He was starting to piece together where Emma's loathing for Gridley came from. He'd rather have had Emma tell him herself, but since she'd been reticent on the subject of Gridley except to say she would not consider his suit, Ren had to look elsewhere for information.

'She was grieving, Mr Ren, and Sir Arthur wanted decisions made. It was just too much for her,' Michael offered. 'They fought one day. We could hear them yelling at each other all the way down in the kitchen. We couldn't hear what they said exactly, just the rise and fall of voices. Then we heard something shatter. Later we found pieces of a vase when we were cleaning up. Miss Emma must have thrown it at him.'

Ren stifled a laugh. He could imagine Emma doing just that. She was a woman of passions and that included her temper. These weeks had seen progress on that front, too. The forfeit he'd claimed had accomplished its purpose. She was starting to reshape how she viewed him. That was exactly what he wanted. He wanted her to stop seeing him as an enemy and begin to see him as a man with potential, someone who could help Sugarland, help her if she'd let him. If that potential started with a kiss, so be it. If she would not welcome him as a business partner, perhaps she'd welcome him as a friend or something more. He'd left that invitation open. She was an exciting woman, a woman aware of her own desires and she was not immune to him.

'Thank you, Michael. I can handle things from here.' Ren dismissed the eager footman-cum-valet with a smile and strict orders not to wait up. He could get himself to bed and he knew Michael would have an early day of it no matter when he got in. He'd learned that during the harvest everyone had early mornings. Regardless of one's usual status the rest of the year, everyone was in the fields these crucial weeks, including himself and Emma.

He'd been astonished by the amount of people needed to run the place. In part due to inherent labour shortage and in part due to the lingering effects of the obeah charm, Emma had ended up with only about two-thirds of the hands she needed. Everyone had been pulled to the fields. Jobs in other areas of the plantation went undone. The two of them had even joined in, stripping stalks of cane and tossing them on the wagons. It was back-breaking work. His friends at home would have laughed to see him sweating in the fields.

Thankfully, Sugarland was nearly done, but other plantations might continue to harvest or even start their harvests at staggered intervals for the rest of the month depending on the readiness of their fields.

Ren stretched to relieve the soreness of his muscles, a testament to the long hours and hard work. He didn't mind. It felt good to be actively doing something on his family's behalf, to feel that he was making progress in achieving financial security for them. Soon the harvest would be in and there would be money to send home, a good chunk of it, too.

He was already imagining the relief on Sarah's face when the notice came, already hearing Annaliese's happy laughter as she danced through the hall dreaming of all the ribbons she could buy in the village. Sarah would buy those ribbons and licorice drops for Teddy but she would know what it really meant. They were saved. She could go back to London and carry on as if nothing had happened. She could have her pick of husbands and in a few years Annaliese could too.

This would be the first of many infusions. He would not be there to celebrate with them, of course. His efforts would be required here, but his absence was a small sacrifice for their security. He'd known quite well when he'd left England there would be no going back. Maybe for a short visit in a few years, but never to live. This new life would require all of him. And in truth, he didn't mind that either. London had paled for him long ago. If it hadn't been for his sense of duty, he might have left with Kitt. But he'd been the heir and Kitt a mere second son. Kitt's choices couldn't be his.

Ren took a final look in the mirror. The image made him smile. It had been five weeks since he'd left England and already he was changing. His hair was a little lighter—more the colour of paler winter wheat, less the colour of deep wild honey. His face was tan, his arms would be too beneath the sleeves of his shirt. Even his chest was tan after weeks of working shirtless in the equatorial sun. He doubted Arthur Gridley would sport such evidence of hard work tonight. Emma had said Gridley did not take an active hand in his harvest.

Satisfied with his appearance, Ren picked up his evening cape from the bed. It seemed silly to take the garment with the weather being warm, but Michael had assured him Sir Arthur's parties were formal affairs and one did not go to war without the proper weapons, after all.

Emma was waiting for him in the drawing room. She turned from the window and his breath hitched. She was stunning, exotic. Gone was any trace of the trouser-clad, boot-wearing woman who'd sweated and laboured beside him, although that woman had been appealing, too. In her place was a lady London would find no fault with.

Emma's dark hair was piled high on her head and threaded with pearls. The *coiffure* was both demure and seductive, showing off the elegant length of her neck. At the base lay a thin gold necklace, simple but expensive. No jewel could have looked finer. The gold was the perfect foil for the deep coral of her gown. In

London, the colour would have been scandalous, too bold among the whites and pinks of debutantes, but here among the lush colours of the island with its rich green grasses and deep azure skies, the vibrant red-orange seemed entirely appropriate.

It certainly suited her colouring: dark hair, dark eyes and skin tinged a healthy shade of light toast from days in the sun. It suited her figure, too. The cut of the gown made the most of her natural assets; a bare neckline exposed slender shoulders, a tight bodice lifted her breasts high, the fullness of her skirt fell sensuously over the curve of her hips, accentuating the provocative sway of her hips.

'I thought the man was supposed to wait for the woman.' She gave a throaty laugh and crossed the room, her eyes running over the length of him in silent approval.

Ren picked up her cloak from the chair and held it out for her, letting his hands skim bare skin as he settled it about her shoulders. 'I assure you, I'm worth waiting for.' He felt her telltale pulse leap beneath his fingers where they lingered.

'You're certainly the most arrogant man I've ever had to wait for.' She slanted him a coy look.

'I don't think you mind.' Ren smiled, enjoying the flirty sparring and gave her his arm. Perhaps tonight would be a chance to launch an offensive on this particular front. Goodness knew his body had been on edge since the night of their kiss, the proximity and long hours together since then working all sorts of magic in honing his physical desire to sharpness. Five weeks of enforced celibacy didn't help.

The carriage, an open-air landau, was already outside. He handed her in and took the rear-facing seat, determined to be the gentleman. Women responded to manners and, oh, how he wanted her to respond. *Give over, Emma*, he thought. *You know you want to, stop torturing us both.*

She wasn't the only one affected, not by a long shot. He was attracted to her, had been from the moment he'd stepped off the wagon and seen her standing on the porch. In all fairness, the kiss had not been all strategy. There was a certain thrill to seducing her, to feeling the infinitesimal tensing of her body as he'd come up behind her on the bluff, to seeing her pulse beat in anticipation at the base of her neck when he came near, to see those eyes darken in response to his innuendos.

The kiss had tested all sorts of waters and now he was waiting, rather impatiently, to see what she would do. The intervening weeks had been her test as well as his. He'd provoked her and, in turn, she was teasing him with a toss of her hair over breakfast, a lingering glance at dinner, flirtation and witty banter over backgammon, even a light brush of her fingers on his sleeve when she said goodnight.

All of which had conspired to leave him in a perpetual state of slow burn. He was starting to wonder who was playing whom. It was time, Ren decided, for her to take the invitation. Perhaps he could help that decision along tonight.

The drive to Gridley's took half an hour and Emma had filled it with talk about who he would meet. It was a briefing more than a conversation. Ren's head was swimming with names and details by the time the carriage pulled up to the impressive front of Gridley's neoclassical home with its pillars and fountain.

'The house makes quite a statement.' Ren helped Emma down from the carriage, letting his hand linger at her back in silent persuasion.

'It's a pretentious monstrosity if you ask me.' Emma shook out her skirts. 'No other great house on the island is built this way.'

Ren offered her his arm. 'Then that's probably why he did it.' He was starting to understand this neighbour a little better. Arthur Gridley was a man who coveted the best and the rarest of things. No wonder he had proposed to Emma. She was a rare beauty. Gridley would have coveted her even without the plantation.

The others were already assembled in the drawing room, drinks in hand. Gridley noticed their arrival immediately and strode forward. 'Everyone, our guest of honour is here!' The announcement was met with a small round of applause. Gridley shook his hand. 'It is good to see you, Dryden. You're looking well. Emma hasn't worked you to death yet.' He turned to Emma and bent over her hand, bestowing a kiss on her knuckles. Ren could feel Emma freeze beside him, unable to avoid the physical contact. 'You look lovely. I'm so glad you didn't wear black. Albert wouldn't have wanted you to mourn.'

'I'm very clear on what Merry wanted for me,' Emma answered sharply, pulling back her hand. 'Shall I introduce Mr Dryden around?' It was a ploy to escape Gridley.

'Let me do the work, Emma. You relax and enjoy yourself. The ladies will want a good coze with you. I know it's been ages since you've seen them.' He gave Ren a knowing, manly look. 'The ladies have little suitable company on the island, one of the drawbacks of living in the colonies.'

Gridley spirited him away to meet the gentlemen, leaving Emma to join the women gathered on one side of the drawing room. He met the neighbouring planters, shook their hands, listened to them discuss their harvests which were just getting under way while Sugarland's was nearly done. But Emma remained relegated to the other side of the room, a bright, brilliant burst of colour against muted blues and grays. It occurred to Ren that Gridley might be attempting to divide and conquer.

Dinner was much the same. Ren sat at Gridley's right hand with Gloria Devore on his other side, *her* hand resting occasionally on his thigh in blatant invitation. Alexandra Cunningham was across from him affecting the same sort of invitation with her eyes. Emma was at the other end of the table, holding court with Elias Blakely and Miles Calvert. By the time cheese and fruit were served, Ren did not doubt the meal, the whole event even, had been orchestrated and not solely for his benefit, but for Arthur Gridley's.

Gridley had trotted out the best china and crystal, he'd shouldered the expense of preparing excellent food and opening the finest imported wines in the hopes of getting something in return. *From him.* He was the guest of honour for a reason. Ren finished the last of the wine in his glass and shot a quick glance at Gridley. The man was watching Emma again. Ren had caught Gridley watching her all night. Perhaps he shouldn't be so egotistical and think it was only himself Gridley wanted something from. This was a display for Emma, too, a reminder of all he could provide for her, the lifestyle she'd have if she said yes.

Something possessive flared to life in Ren's core at the thought of Emma in Arthur's arms, of Emma kissing another the way she'd kissed him. Emma had made it clear she didn't want Arthur Gridley, but he still didn't know why.

Ren fingered the stem of his wine glass. Why *did* a woman turn down a man like Arthur Gridley? Gridley was wealthy, good-looking, well mannered, had a house that would impress a certain type of person, he even had a title. It wasn't one that could be inherited, but he'd demonstrated his upstanding citizenry by providing a valuable service to the Crown. What wouldn't appeal about that package? That it *didn't* appeal was far stranger than if she'd accepted his proposal, especially when it was made at what Ren considered a very opportune time.

Devore's wife rose from the table, her hand finally admitting defeat. 'Ladies, let us adjourn to the drawing room. Conversation at this end is quickly turning to dull business.' She flashed him a last look, invitation openly written in her hazel eyes as she led the ladies, Emma included, from the room. Gloria Devore was handsome, but Ren didn't make a habit of dallying with married women. Unlike Kitt, who actively sought a new woman every night, married or not, Ren preferred the mixture of adventure and stability that came with long-term mistresses. Kitt was easy and he was hard, damn hard these days when it came to Emma.

Chapter Nine

Ren's senses went on alert the moment the double doors were drawn behind them. Whatever purpose Gridley had in putting on this lavish dinner, it would be exposed shortly. It was just the men now and business would be discussed, talk would be freer.

Gridley began buttonholing the port around the table. There was general, unfocused conversation as everyone poured a glass. 'As you can see, Dryden, we are not without our comforts. We live well out here in the colonies.' Gridley raised his glass once everyone had served themselves. 'A toast, gentlemen, to our success, hard won as it is.'

Ren drank to the toast although he couldn't help but think Gridley's success was due to force more than the winning of anything, much less loyalty. The atmosphere at Gridley's was different from Sugarland. At Sugarland, the staff was much like a house staff in wealthy English homes. There was a sense of being in service, working for a wage, as opposed to being in slavery.

Gridley might profess to follow the apprenticeship programme, but the climate of his home didn't suggest a
sense of freedom or personal pride in one's work. It did,
however, suggest a sense of fear driving the excellence
that surrounded Gridley.

'I won't beat around the bush, Dryden. We want to
discuss business with you.' Gridley put down his glass
and refilled it. 'Sugar prices have fallen in the last few
years. We are of a mind to form a sugar cartel in order to
drive up the prices. We'd like you to join, to bring Sugarland in line with the other plantations in the parish.'

Ren sipped slowly, letting the rich port travel down
his throat. So this was what Gridley wanted. What they
all wanted. The others nodded their heads sagely. 'I will
need to discuss that with Emma.'

Gridley gave a friendly laugh and leaned forward,
his hand on Ren's arm in a gesture of familiarity. 'You
control the majority of the estate. You don't need to
ask Emma anything. Take charge, Dryden. Don't let
her lead you around by the short hairs.' He winked
and added conspiratorially, 'Although you wouldn't be
the first man she had thinking with the wrong head, if
you know what I mean.' There was general masculine
laughter around the table.

Ren bristled at the remark. It was insulting on so
many different levels he didn't know where to aim his
anger: at slander against his masculinity and the idea
that his head could be so easily turned or the crude reference to Emma. 'As the will stands, Emma and I are
partners. The division of the estate is all but equal.' He

made the protest even while his own sense of caution silently challenged him not to act rashly.

Was it slander or did Gridley speak the truth? Emma was no blushing virgin. He'd not thought it when he arrived and he certainly didn't think so now after the flirting and kissing that had passed between them. Emma definitely had a sense of her own feminine power. Did that mean she lacked virtue as Gridley suggested? Up until now, he hadn't realised how heavily he'd been relying on Merrimore's judgement to serve as Emma's character reference.

'But it's *not* equal when it comes right down to it. Don't you let her convince you otherwise. Merrimore left *you* the majority for a reason,' Hugh Devore put in briskly. 'Emma's impulsive, she's emotional and we know she misses Merrimore. She's not equipped to make a good decision and we can't wait. We need the cartel in place before we sell this year's crop.'

Elias Blakely backed him up in softer tones. 'It's not as if we haven't waited. We've given her time. I think Merrimore would have joined us, but she's backed off. Sugarland is the largest producer in our parish. Without you, the cartel will have no teeth.'

Ren nodded noncommittally. The game wasn't a complicated one. They were trying the age-old back-door strategy. They couldn't get to Emma so they were trying to go through him. 'I will look into it.' He put enough steel into his voice to end the conversation.

Gridley understood the message and intervened before Devore could argue. 'Check the books at Sugarland if you haven't already, Dryden. You need the cartel as much as the cartel needs you.' He beamed at the group. 'Now that's settled, let's go join the ladies.'

Emma looked up with relief as the door between the drawing room and the dining room slid open. She wanted nothing more than for the evening to end. Being *inside* Arthur Gridley's home was nothing short of being in prison. There'd been a cold pit in her stomach all night, put there by the irrational fear she'd disappear inside these walls and never be seen again. It was what she feared if Gridley succeeded in marrying her.

Nothing all night had been able to distract her fear, not the fine food which she barely tasted, and certainly not conversation with the women. The women had bored her with their agenda of barely veiled concern over her being alone at Sugarland with a man. Emma had no doubt their husbands had put them up to it. They wanted her to move. Gloria Devore had offered her rooms with them. 'Let Mr Dryden run the plantation, you needn't be alone there any more,' she'd said with false sweetness. Emma had politely declined. Gloria probably would have preferred to offer those rooms to Ren based on the amount of time her hand had spent under the table tonight.

At least the men hadn't taken very long, only a half hour. She wondered if that was good or bad. Ren looked a little grimmer than he had at dinner. But whatever had happened had not got the best of him. With that grimness came an air of command. His presence dominated the room. She'd felt that presence before when they were alone. It was one thing to think he was powerful when there was no one to compare him to. It was another to think it when she saw him against the backdrop of the parish's leading men. He stood out even in the company of large men like Devore and supposedly attractive men like Arthur Gridley.

Ren's eye caught hers and the nerves in her stomach began to relax. She'd missed Ren tonight. After having had him to herself for dinners and days on end, she'd not had him at all this evening. He'd been whisked from her side the moment they'd walked in. She was sure it had not been accidental. She'd not realised how used to him she'd become. They'd worked together, they'd taken their evening meal together, they'd played backgammon games together before retiring. One might say they lived in each other's pockets.

And yet, she worried. What she would have given to hear what had been said behind those doors! How had Ren responded? She might know his backgammon strategy, but she had no idea how he'd answer the leading members of the plantocracy. Would he undo all of her hard work? Would he use his fifty-one per cent to force her into accepting decisions she would not have made? Would he have betrayed her? Men had betrayed her before. Would Ren prove to be the same?

Betrayal was a strong word with only a kiss between them, yet betrayal was the emotion she felt when she looked at him; this strong, masterful stranger who'd entered her life. Would he betray her? Ren was speaking with Gridley. She smiled at him, hoping to signal that he should join her but it was Gridley who approached the sofa where she sat.

'My dear Emma, come take a turn about the room with me. I don't think you've seen my new painting.' She couldn't refuse, nor could she ignore the warm glances the women cast her way as Gridley led her apart from the group. It was no secret everyone's lives would be easier if she accepted Gridley or if she disappeared, leaving them free to pursue their cartel at the expense of the backs they built their empire on.

The knot in her stomach returned. She felt vulnerable in his home with him, even surrounded by others. Who would come to her aid if Gridley decided to act less than gentlemanly? Would Ren? Had Ren decided over port that life would be smoother if her stubbornness was removed? Emma thought of the knife strapped to her thigh beneath her skirts and drew a deep breath. She would use it if she had to. She had no doubt she could plunge it into Gridley's black heart if the need arose.

'Is this the beginning of another courtship?' Emma asked sharply. 'If it is, you may also consider it the end. You already have my answer.' She pretended to study the painting.

Gridley stood close, too close. She fought the urge to move away, so unlike her response to Ren. 'You should re-examine your options, Emma. Look at all I have to offer you. My wealth is on display for you tonight. I can provide for you the way Merrimore wanted you to be cared for.' He lowered his voice. 'I am a patient man and I do not think you'd find my presence in your bed intolerable, my dear. I'm asking for so little in exchange for so much.'

Her temper began to override her fear. 'Do not play

the lovesick suitor with me,' Emma answered in low, angry tones. 'How dare you stand there, acting as if nothing else were at stake but your heart when we both know it's Sugarland you want.'

Gridley gave a dry laugh. 'You underestimate your charms, Emma. I assure you, I want you. I lie awake at night, dreaming of how it will be when you are mine.' He lowered his voice, his eyes glinting with evil desire. 'Shall I describe it for you?'

'No!' Emma almost shrieked. Only the steel grip she kept on her self-control prevented her from causing a scene. In her mind, she willed Ren to approach. Surely this didn't *look* like a normal conversation to anyone, further proof that no one in the room particularly cared how Gridley achieved his ends, only that he achieved them.

Emma opted to play her one ace in an attempt to regain some control. 'You are a slave-master and a murderer. If you continue to pursue this issue between us, I will be forced to go to the magistrate.' She sought to walk away, but Gridley held her arm tight, his grip a vice.

'Is that what you think you saw in Merrimore's bedchamber?' he hissed, his breath warm and sour on her face.

'You killed him.' Emma held her ground. Let him be scared. 'I saw you with the pillow.'

A leer spread across his lips. 'I saw something a little different. I saw *you* put the pillow over the old man's face.'

'Liar!' Emma all but spat in his face for the accusation.

'Who is to say who the liar is, Emma?' He shrugged. 'You say I killed Merrimore and I say you did. Who will the magistrate believe? A knight of the realm who has shown you every courtesy, including the protection of marriage, or you a woman who has a dubious past and who doesn't exactly reek of good judgement? I think we both know to what I refer. I would think this line of attack over more thoroughly if I were you.'

She tugged but he wouldn't let go of her arm. Instead he smiled as if the conversation were friendly. 'You haven't shown Dryden the accounts yet. How long do you think he'll stay after that or even want to consult your opinion? I imagine he'll lose interest unless you've offered him some other incentive?' The type of incentive he referred to was obvious. 'That's what you offered Thompson Hunt, wasn't it?'

'How dare you imply—'

'How dare *you*!' Gridley interrupted, his fingers digging painfully into her arm. She would have bruises. 'I am tired of hearing what I dare when it is *you* who insults me at every turn. You need me more than you think. Some day you will beg me on your knees for help.' He licked his lips, his eyes dropping to the low swell of her neckline. 'I will wait for that day. After all, I am a patient man with a vivid imagination.'

The fear her temper had held at bay clawed at her stomach. She'd seen Gridley angry before. There had been that one quarrel when she'd thrown the vase. But this anger was different. There was an unholy light in his eyes, a fierceness in his grip. He'd never laid hands on her like this. Gridley was a strong man, a tall man.

In the past she'd always thought her word was enough to stop him. No meant no. Now, she wasn't sure.

What if Gridley decided not to wait for her capitulation? What if he could physically force her to his will? No one would stop him. Everyone supported Gridley's quest to see their lands united, to see *them* united. The others either didn't see the evil in Gridley or they didn't care. Who would stand up for her if Gridley came for her? She felt a presence behind her as if in answer to the question. Ren.

'I think Emma has recovered her balance sufficiently to stand on her own.' Her knees nearly buckled from relief. 'You did lose your balance, my dear, didn't you? Are you feeling faint? I can't think of any other reason for a gentleman to grip your arm so tightly.' The last was said strictly for Gridley's benefit, a threat neatly wrapped in polite enquiry.

'I'm fine now.' Emma edged closer to Ren and took his arm, her courage returning. 'The painting was most, ah, enlightening.'

Gridley looked from her to Ren, trying to gauge their level of involvement. She felt her pulse catch. She was playing a dangerous game, pitting them against one another. Ren would not appreciate being used. 'Just so, I think I'd like you to take me home,' she appealed to Ren, eager to be away from this nest of smiling vipers.

Ren saw to the carriage and they were off within ten minutes, their lanterns lighting the way in the darkness. She was grateful for his efficiency when it came to arrangements. She was a little less grateful when it came to conversations. The driveway was hardly behind them when Ren started the questions. 'What were you and Gridley discussing so intently?'

Emma shook her head. 'Nothing. He's jealous, that's all.' She fought the urge to spill everything to Ren, but that would give him power he might not deserve. *Not yet*, she cautioned herself. She had to be sure of him first. Not yet.

Ren's eyebrows arched in the shadows. 'Why would he be jealous?' There was a hint of teasing beneath the question, their conversation taking on a lighter, flirtier edge now that Gridley's house was behind them.

Emma smiled and moved to sit beside him. 'Because he thinks I prefer you to him.'

'And do you?'

Emma slid a hand up his thigh. 'Yes, as a matter of fact, I do.' This was a dangerous gambit too, but she had to be sure of Ren. There was so much at risk, she would do whatever it took to secure her future—which was a far better justification for her actions than simply admitting to herself that she wanted him, but far less true. She would have wanted him without the planta-tion between them. In the back of her mind, she knew she had planned to make her intentions known tonight regardless of the evening's outcome at Gridley's.

Ren's hand covered hers in caution. 'Emma, do you think this is a good idea?' Good idea or not, it didn't matter. It was the only idea she had, if sex would be something irrevocable to bind him to her. Besides, it seemed an natural evolution of their relationship at this point. Everything since their kiss had been leading to this. He had started it with his wicked forfeit over backgammon, but by heaven, she would finish it. Her safety and Sugarland's security demanded it.

'It's the best idea I've had in a long time.' She leaned forward and kissed him hard on the mouth, as if everything depended on it, because it did.

Chapter Ten

This was a bad idea on multiple levels, starting with the most obvious: there'd been *a lot* of wine served at dinner. They'd both imbibed thoroughly. There were more complicated reasons, too, Ren knew: whether she admitted it or not, Emma's encounter with Gridley had left her feeling vulnerable, feeling in need of a hero. He was aware he'd been that hero for her in the drawing room, coming to her side when he'd noted the conversation had taken a less friendly turn. Perhaps the hand running up his thigh was being grateful for his assistance. Perhaps she felt she needed to offer recompense.

Mentally, Ren knew he should put a stop to that hand before it reached a more critical juncture. His mind didn't want 'grateful' sex, but his body didn't seem capable of making those distinctions. His body was responding to her with the wholehearted enthusiasm of a healthy man who'd been celibate for over a month.

Emma had managed to get a leg over his lap, straddling him, with her coral skirts riding high, her hand between them cupping the hardened ridge through his trousers, her mouth on his in a full-bodied kiss, her tongue in his mouth, his own tongue giving as good as it got. As much as his mind willed, his body would not be mounting any resistance to her intimate assault.

Emma ran a thumb over the outlined tip of him and he moaned. It had been so long since anything had felt this good, this physically inviting. His hands ran up her legs past the curve of her calves to her thighs and came to an abrupt halt as one hand made contact with a leather sheath. 'Good lord, Emma, what is this?'

'An old habit,' she murmured between kisses. Why did a woman take a concealed weapon to a dinner party? He should have pushed the issue right then, but his mind had finally registered the sensual reality of bare flesh. His hands had moved on, clenching around the soft swell of her buttocks, 'You minx!' Ren nipped at her bottom lip with his teeth. 'You've been naked beneath this dress all night.'

She gave a throaty laugh and squeezed him, her eyes dark with desire. 'I'm hungry for you, Ren Dryden. Are you hungry for me?'

'Oh, yes.' Ren groaned. She was bold, beautiful, sure of herself, all the things he liked in a woman. The nakedness beneath her skirts confirmed it. She'd planned to have him, a most titillating and flattering realisation. Confident lovers were hard to come by. Apparently so was privacy.

They both recognised they'd reached the limits of what could decently be accomplished. There was no question of taking this any further in the open-air car-

riage with the driver's back so near. Emma flashed him
a frustrated glance. They had another mile to go before
they were home.

Inspiration struck. There was one thing he could do.
'Can you be very quiet?' Ren whispered at her ear, his
hand sliding again beneath the bunched fabric of her
gown to the damp, hot core of her. Whatever reservations his mind had about taking her, there was no arguing she wanted this, wanted *him*. His fingers were wet
with her honey as he found her secret place, the centre
of her pleasure. He ran his thumb over the hidden little
nub, watching her eyes widen, feeling her body shudder with delight.

She arched against his hand, her body instinctively
wanting to be closer to the source of pleasure. He revelled in her response, intoxicated by the knowledge he
could render this beautiful woman boneless. *She wanted
him,* without any inkling of who he was, or what his
title meant.

He stroked her again, and the tiniest of mewls escaped her lips. 'Shh,' Ren warned with a wicked grin.
He silenced her with a kiss, long and deep, while he
stroked, while he rubbed. It became an intense, intimate game to see who would break first. Emma writhed
against him, the kisses coming hard and fierce as her
climax neared.

'Do *not* scream,' Ren instructed hoarsely, feeling
her body tighten. Her hands dug into his shoulders in
an effort to keep her silence. She gave a gasp and Ren
smothered it with a kiss as she collapsed against him,
her relief palpable. Ren was almost jealous. She was mo-

mentarily sated while he was still very much aroused and painfully so, craving her touch, craving the release that would come. His mind urged his body patience. This was good, but there was better waiting. This was just the beginning.

They pulled into the drive, the carriage coming to a stop in front of the house. He helped Emma down, the sight of her, ravished and dishevelled, fuelling his desire to the brink of breaking. Her hair had come down in dark glorious waves, her lips were swollen from ardent kisses, marks of his possession, signs that she was his. And she burned for him still, her eyes hot with wanting as they mounted the front steps. The momentary release he'd given her now becoming only a prelude, a sample of something greater to come.

She might have sparked what had happened in the carriage, but Ren had become the master of it, driving her to the edge of pleasure and over it, but even that hadn't been enough for his wild Emma. She was burning, her body on fire for more, for him. Knowledge of it stoked his passion to the breaking point. He was a well-primed powder keg of male desire by the time they gained the hall. She tugged at the lapels of his evening coat, dragging him to her for a hard kiss. Any thought he'd entertained about making it upstairs to bed vanished in the wake of his wanting.

Ren answered her with a devouring kiss of his own, his mouth claiming primal possession. Her arms were about his neck. Her body pressed into his, her hips undulating in an unspoken request. 'Take me, Ren. Here.' Her voice was a feverish murmur against his mouth.

It was all the invitation he needed. Desire rode him hard. He bore her back to the wall, lifting, balancing, as her legs wrapped about him and her skirts fell back to reveal bare skin, the grip of her thighs urging him closer. He released the fall of his trousers and, by all that was holy, he couldn't recall wanting a woman with such uncontrolled abandon. He felt rough and wild as he thrust into her, not in the least a gentleman.

Her head went back, her neck arched, a feral cry escaping her. He was a king in that moment, watching her thrash in passion, knowing that the wildness was not his alone. He thrust again and again, pushing both of them to the completion that waited just beyond the wildness. He gave a last, rough thrust, his body pulsing into hers as she screamed his name one last time.

They could not stay here, locked in an intimate embrace in the hall. It was Ren's first thought once sanity returned, a thought mobilised by necessity. His muscles were starting to ache from the strain of balancing her against the wall.

'Emma love, let me help you upstairs.' He disengaged as gracefully as possible and gently lowered her until her feet touched the ground, but she was boneless in the aftermath of their exertions. While he might take manly pride in that accomplishment, it had its own consequences. She gave only the slightest of protests, his muscles giving rather more, when he swept her up in his arms and mounted the staircase.

By the time he'd tucked a sleeping Emma into bed still fully dressed and reached the *garçonnière*, Ren's brain had started to register the fullness of what he'd done, what they'd done. It was perhaps more sobering than any amount of coffee. From the wicked game they'd played in the carriage to the unrestrained love-making in the hall, the interlude had been savage and uncivilised in the extreme.

Ren supposed he could chalk it up as the natural repercussion of a healthy man and woman living and working in close proximity. There was bound to be curiosity. They certainly had been aware of each other from the start and heavy flirting had followed. Under those conditions, what happened tonight had been inevitable. But now that the curiosity was satisfied, what next? How did they go on from here?

Was this to be a one-night experiment or was it the beginning of an affair, or even the beginning of something more, a relationship? Ren undressed for bed, carefully laying aside his evening clothes for Michael to brush in the morning. He wished his thoughts could be set aside just as easily.

Had this evening been only about the physical? His thoughts might have strayed in such lusty directions, but in the end Emma had started it. *She'd* been the one to straddle him, to intimately cup him. One could not mistake an overture like that. Even exhausted as he was, his body roused to the memory. What had she been looking for? Satisfaction? Appeasement? A safe harbour?

She might have started it, but don't forget you finished it. You were the one to play a decadent game of 'don't scream'. You were the one to push her up against the wall, to thrust into her until she cried your name, his conscience scolded. It wasn't done. *Whatever to-*

night was, you enjoyed it far too much for it not to matter. His pleasure was not inconsequential. Tonight had been as much about his pleasure as it had been hers. At the end, his own climax had ripped from him like a river breaking its banks and for a while it had obliterated everything in its path— common sense and reality.

The truth was, tonight had been a moment out of context. He knew deuce little about Emma Ward beyond the present. Ren lay down on his bed, his hands behind his head, his eyes fixed on the stuccoed ceiling. He knew of her only what their short time together had taught him. What he'd learned were attributes. She was strong, determined, independent. But attributes were not history. How did those traits translate into events? Had those traits worked for or against her? Sir Arthur Gridley suggested those characteristics led Emma to be impulsive, to make rash decisions in business and in sex. Gridley believed she needed to be protected against that rashness. Was Gridley to be believed?

Gridley would be livid if he knew what had transpired here tonight. Ren drew a deep breath and exhaled, making the argument with himself. He hadn't poached on another man's territory. Emma had made it plain she did not welcome Gridley's attentions, but Gridley wouldn't see it that way. Ren wondered if that had been some of Emma's impetus. Had she merely been caught up in the moment and looked for a quick way to strike out at Gridley?

He didn't relish thinking of himself as a pawn in her neighbourly war. Yet, that was the one thing he didn't doubt. Tonight, Emma had been frightened. The war between her and Gridley was real, suggesting the stakes for Emma were high. Ren had seen her fight fire and marshal her troops without hesitation. She was not a woman who scared easily.

That Gridley unnerved her spoke volumes, some of it rather difficult for his ego to contemplate. Had fear forced her into his arms tonight? The idea that her seduction had been planned was starting to pale from its original flattery. Had she been scared long before this and decided to seduce him as security?

'Oh, Merrimore, what have you sent me into?' Ren mused, feeling a bit guilty. No matter how pleasurable it had been, he'd acted rashly this evening. Would he have dared such a thing if Merrimore had been alive? What would Merrimore think if he knew Ren had tupped his ward in the hall, nonetheless? That was something Kitt Sherard would do. It wasn't that he wasn't an imaginative lover. He was. He just wasn't normally an exhibitionist, given to performance in potentially public places. Good heavens, what had he been thinking? Any late-night servant could have run across them.

But that was just it. He hadn't been thinking. Every ounce of his being had been focused on succouring his desire, sating his want. Tonight, the pursuit of pleasure had stripped him of all logical thought. He hadn't even possessed the decency to do it in a bed in a private room with the door shut. Not that those details made it better in the end. In the final analysis, he'd bedded—he did use that term loosely since there had been no real furniture involved—a woman he knew very little about and knew even less what he meant to do about it.

To make matters worse, Ren had to be honest. Despite the afterthoughts, he *would* do it again, even though it might be best if he didn't. If sex with Emma Ward was so consuming he forgot all decency, celibacy might be in his better interests. He had a plantation to learn to run. He had a family back home relying on this money-making venture. *He* was relying on this venture. If he wanted to escape the clutches of the York heiress, he had to think with his brain, not his—

A memory from earlier in the evening stirred; something Gridley had said. *Don't let her lead you around by the short hairs.* Initially, Ren had thought Gridley was merely referring to the division of the estate and the comment about who was really charge. Given Gridley's longer-standing relationship with Emma, Ren had to wonder if that was all he'd referred to.

An uncomfortable feeling began to take up residence in his gut. Gridley had implied Emma was not above using seduction and had done so on at least one occasion. He had to exercise caution. He knew logically the interlude was a mistake, yet he also recognised he'd willingly make that mistake again if the opportunity arose.

She started it. Another discomforting truth presented itself. Emma had planned this. She'd gone to dinner stark naked under her gown. It was fair to say there'd been some premeditation there. A woman didn't forgo undergarments on a random whim. Had she anticipated that when the act came it would be fast and furious, no time for undressing or for dealing with inconvenient underclothes? If she had, what did it mean?

The truth crashed about him in the darkness of his chambers. The longer he thought about it, the clearer it became. All roads led to the same conclusion. He, Ren Dryden, one of London's most sought-after lovers, had been seduced by a master.

Chapter Eleven

Emma gave a languorous stretch, letting the morning sun caress her body. She'd slept better last night than she had since Merry passed away. She felt rested, in both body and mind. It was the first morning she could recall where she hadn't awakened with her mind an immediate riot of lists full of things that had to be done. She gave another long stretch and stopped mid-action. Something didn't feel right. She felt confined as if she was wearing a tight garment instead of her loose nightgown.

That was funny; she couldn't remember putting her nightgown on last night. Emma ran hands down her body, her fingers halting when they met with satin instead of cotton. She looked down and confirmed her suspicions. She was still in her dress. Ren! The latter part of the evening came back to her in hot, vivid flashes; Ren's naughty game in the carriage, Ren taking her hard and swift up against the hall wall. All the pent-up passion that had lurked beneath the surface of their interactions since his arrival had been given its head last night to the delight of them both.

There was no ignoring that what had happened last night had been rough and spectacular. There was also no ignoring that she'd started it. She'd been the one who had slid her hand up his leg, who had boldly straddled his lap. But he'd not been resistant. He'd been more than ready for her when her hand had found him through his trousers.

Emma sighed and sat up, ringing for Hattie. She couldn't get out of the dress on her own. She'd have to tell Hattie something to explain it. She'd have to tell Ren something, too. She doubted she could let the interlude go unremarked. One didn't have sex against the wall with a guest living under one's roof and *not* address it.

Hattie came and exclaimed, as expected, over the crumpled gown. Emma murmured a vague excuse about being late and tired and not wanting to wake her. 'I just laid down for a moment…' Emma offered an apologetic smile 'the next thing I knew, it was morning.'

'Well, I can press most of the wrinkles out.' Hattie undid the fastenings in the back and helped her slide the gown off but the scowl of disapproval on her face suggested she suspected far more had happened.

Emma offered no further discussion of the evening. Her mind was already examining and discarding possible explanations she could give Ren for her behaviour as Hattie combed out her hair. She could blame it on Arthur Gridley. No, she would sound weak, desperate for a man to solve her problems. Ren would take that opening to further increase his involvement at the plantation.

She could blame it on the wine. That would sound irresponsible, but plausible. It would be better than blaming it on her curiosity, her physical attraction to him, or on the idea she'd been alone too long. All of which implied she wanted him to stay, even needed him in ways that superseded the practical tasks of running the estate. She had started this with the intent of using it to bind him to her, but she had to admit her plans were only a part of what had compelled her boldness last night. There'd been other, selfish, personal reasons, too. Those reasons also implied she might want to continue what they'd started in the hall.

A little shudder went through her at the thought: Another night with Ren? Is that what she'd wanted? He'd been a lover nonpareil, giving her exactly what she'd been after, a rough, impetuous joining, and doing it most thoroughly. She'd been completely lost. She might have started it, but he'd taken control almost immediately. Instead of satisfying her curiosity, the encounter had merely made her hungry for more. What would it be like to lie with him, skin to skin, to linger in the act of lovemaking instead of sharing a brief, heated encounter?

'Miss Emma, are you all right?' Hattie was staring at her in the mirror. Emma focused, embarrassed to see twin pockets of colour rising on her cheeks.

'I'm fine.' Emma stood up from her dressing table. 'I'm just hungry.'

Hattie nodded, giving her a considering look. 'There's breakfast downstairs. Mr Dryden already ate. He had a big appetite this morning, too.' Ah, she wouldn't have to face Ren right away.

'Where is he now?' Ren was up early for such a late night.

'He said he wanted to look through some of his cousin's personal belongings. Michael showed him where Mr Merrimore's room was.' Hattie paused. 'I hope that was all right?' Merry's chamber had been shut up since his death. At first, Emma hadn't been able to bring herself to enter the room. Later, she simply hadn't had time, at least that's what she told herself. Perhaps she still wasn't able to face it. It seemed she'd have to, though, if Ren was in there.

She smiled at Hattie to relieve the other woman's concern and maybe her own. She'd not planned on bearding that particular lion today. 'It's fine. I'll go see how Mr Dryden is doing.'

She had only the length of the hallway to decide how she wanted to handle facing Ren after last night. Did she want to excuse the encounter as a one-time slip of moral judgement or did she want to go ahead with her initial thought of seducing Ren as a means of binding her to him?

When she'd had that idea it had been before she actually knew what she was getting into—it had been before he'd carried her up the staircase and put her to bed, before he'd claimed her so thoroughly against that hall wall. She might have meant to seduce him last night, but in the end, it had been difficult to tell who was seducing whom. She needed to remember he had his own gambits in motion as well. If she continued on the path of seducing of him, she'd be allowing him to do the same with her.

Merry's door stood ajar, making no secret of the room being open and occupied. The coward in her had hoped Ren would have finished before she arrived. She pushed the door all the way open, drew a deep breath and stepped just inside. She could not will her feet to go further than the threshold.

The room was unchanged except for the basics. The big bed was made up. The bureau and the table tops were straightened, the medicines that had marked Merry's last months were gone, but his personal brushes and other sundry items still decorated the room. Sunlight streamed through the large window, toying with fluttering dust motes. If she threw open the wardrobe and bureau drawers she would find Merry's clothes pressed and ready. It was as if the room itself was waiting for Merry to walk through the door. But she knew better. This had not only been a place of death, it had been a place of murder.

She spotted Ren seated at Merry's small escritoire near the window, reading through a book. To reach him, she'd have to cross the room. Emma opted to call out, 'Good morning, I hear you were up early.' She tried to sound cheery and nonchalant.

Ren looked up from his reading. Seeing her, his face broke into a smile, his dimple deepening. He didn't seem nervous at all. Perhaps he had more experience than she with morning-after encounters. And, of course, the room wouldn't mean the same to him.

Ren held up his reading material, a brown leather

journal. Not a book, but a personal diary. 'I've been looking for answers and I think I may have found some.' Emma knew a different kind of anxiety. She'd never looked through Merry's personal journals, deeming it too great of a privacy violation when he was alive and not having the heart to do so when he was dead. Had he written about her in there? If so, what? She had her secrets and she preferred to keep them that way.

Emma forced a smile. 'What kind of answers? Perhaps you'd care to show me over breakfast. I'm starving.' She wasn't nearly as hungry as she had been earlier, the room had sucked most of her appetite out of her, but it was a clever ploy to get Ren out of the room and herself, too. Her breath was coming fast. She put a hand on the door frame to steady herself.

Ren rose from the desk, journal in hand, and moved towards her, concern etched on his face. 'Breakfast is a good idea. You look a bit peaked. Are you sure you're all right?'

He took her by the elbow and ushered her downstairs. In the breakfast room, he insisted she sit while he fixed her a plate.

'What would you like this morning? There's sausage, eggs, fresh toast.' He rattled off a list of offerings. Her stomach rumbled, her hunger returning.

'Sausage, please, and some eggs. Breakfast was always Merry's great weakness.' The good aromas of morning cooking were triumphing over the evil of Merry's bedroom. 'We serve many local dishes for dinner, as you've probably noticed, but Merry could never give up his English breakfast.'

She took the plate from Ren. 'Thank you.' It was filled perfectly if not excessively with a balance of the things she liked: eggs, two slices of toast, two sausages and a slice of melon on the side. She was impressed. This wasn't their first breakfast together. Apparently, he'd been paying attention.

Ren smiled at the mention of Merry and resumed his seat with a plate containing his second breakfast of the day. 'I'm sorry if I was out of line by going into my cousin's room. It clearly upset you and I must apologise.'

'No, you have every right,' Emma stammered. 'This is your home, too.' Although it was still hard to imagine it as such, it was a necessary part of her plan that he did see Sugarland that way. He'd be far less likely to want to leave a place he felt a connection with. She needed to foster that connection on any level she could. Emma summoned her courage. 'What were you looking for?'

'Cousin Merrimore's thoughts.' Ren paused to take a drink of coffee. 'It was suggested to me last night that my cousin would have supported the sugar cartel Gridley has in mind. But you don't. I am hard pressed to reconcile the idea that Merrimore would have sided with Gridley over you, but I have no real evidence for that.' He held up the journal. 'I was hoping this might provide some objective illumination.'

He studied her, his face sombre. 'It is difficult to be the newcomer. Everyone is eager to share their versions of the truth. In most cases, that truth is no more than a pretext. I have no context for assessing its value or validity except my own intuition.'

Emma swallowed, moved by his admission. He was

vulnerable in that moment. He was letting her see how exposed he really was. She'd not thought of him that way. He'd been in command since the moment he'd arrived, never showing an ounce of self-doubt, never backing down from her or from Gridley, or hard work, never once showing weakness as he adjusted to a new life. As a result, it had been easy for her to overlook what he'd given up to come here: the family he must have left in England, his home, his friends, all of his comforts. She'd been so focused on herself, on what his arrival meant to her, she'd not thought about what it meant to him.

Careful, Emma, her conscience warned. *This might all be part of his game. If he shows you vulnerability, perhaps he hopes you will show him your vulnerable side, too.* She'd almost made it easy on him. Emma set aside her napkin. 'Did the journal provide you with any answers?' She kept her tone businesslike.

Ren gave a polite, tight smile, disappointed in her response. 'Yes. Cousin Merrimore makes it clear he had concerns over the cartel. He saw it as temporary success with no likely long-term viability.' Ren opened the journal to an early entry about a third of the way through the book and passed it to her. A footman came in to begin clearing away the sideboard.

'Is that as far as you read?' Emma scanned the date— February of last year.

'Yes.' Ren hesitated, his voice dropping in deference to the lingering servant. 'Is there more I should know?'

'I don't know what Merrimore wrote about,' Emma answered vaguely. She could guess though. 'I have never made a habit of reading someone else's private journal.'

Ren shook his head. 'That's not what I meant. What else do you know that I don't? What is really going on with Gridley?'

Emma shot Ren a warning glance. Her servants were loyal, but she didn't like them worrying over bits and pieces they might overhear. In the last year of his life, Merry had made it a practice to discuss business with her away from Sugarland. She supposed that ritual had rubbed off on her.

In a louder voice, she changed the conversational direction entirely. 'There's nothing like a good breakfast to set things right. Thank you for suggesting I eat something.' She gave Ren a broad smile.

He took his cue admirably. 'I must say that I agree. After Oxford, I did a grand tour through Europe. Nowhere else did breakfast rival the English version in my mind. Elsewhere it was a small meal: some bread, some cheese, maybe a piece of fruit.'

'You've travelled then?' He'd not mentioned it when they'd talked of her travels with her father.

'Just the usual venues.' Ren wiped his mouth with his napkin. 'Paris, Vienna, Rome, Greece, Ephesus.' Usual venues? Hardly. They sounded far more glamorous than the destinations her father had been posted to. Ren leaned across the table, a handsome smile on his face, a little spark leaping in his blue eyes. 'I've been a lot of places, but I've not seen much of the island since my arrival. Why don't we take the day and you can show me around? We'll pack a lunch and explore.'

The suggestion caught her off guard. Nothing this morning had happened the way she'd envisioned it. Her first thought had been to confront the issue of the prior evening, but they had yet to do that. They had instead addressed other concerning issues of business: the cartel and Gridley. It was just a matter of time before Ren asked her about the unpleasant conversation with Gridley last night. 'I don't know, there's work to be done—' Emma stalled.

'There's always work to be done,' Ren interrupted before she could begin to list all the things that needed doing. 'I've checked with Peter. There's nothing that can't wait, nor is there anything that needs your especial attention. Peter can handle it, it's his job after all.' Ren leaned back in his chair. 'When's the last time you had a day off?'

She hesitated too long and Ren laughed. 'That's what I thought. You can't remember. I'll give you twenty minutes to get ready and then I expect you in the front hall.'

Chapter Twelve

Expectations fulfilled. Precisely twenty-one minutes later they set out, a covered basket and towels in the small bed of the gig. Emma hadn't even considered protesting. Ren might ask politely, but she was certain he'd have come looking for her if she'd not shown up. In truth, she hadn't wanted to protest. After the surprises of the morning, she wanted to get out of the house, away from the dark memories.

'I want to see the island,' he'd said and he turned over their direction to her care. She decided their first destination would be the limestone caves between Sugarland and the beaches. Along the way, she pointed out the natural flora, saying things like, 'That tree with the pink flowers is frangipani. Those long red-orange leaves belong to the croton plant.' They passed a cluster of yellow-and-purple flowers. 'That's allamanda. It has no smell.' It was an easy conversation to make. There was no risk to it. Flowers were harmless and the small talk helped her relax.

'You're amazing. You know everything,' Ren complimented. He steered the gig beneath a tree and got down to picket the horse in the shade. 'I'm duly impressed with your botanical knowledge.' He bent down and plucked a flower from a nearby bush. 'Allamanda, right?'

'Yes, but be careful!' Emma jumped down from the gig. 'It's a milk flower. Its nectar can blister you if you're not cautious.' She grabbed the flower from him.

Ren laughed and held up his hands. 'I am at your mercy, my dear.' He glanced around, taking in the lush green surroundings. 'Where is this cave of yours?'

'We'll have to hike the rest of the way. It's not far.' She led the way, the path winding through tall grasses and over stones. The hike was only about a quarter of a mile. She found the entrance and stepped inside. The cave was cool and it was far larger than it appeared. Emma reached for the old lantern that was left on a hook near the entrance and struck a match, illuminating the area.

She moved to the side, wanting to catch a glimpse of Ren's reaction. She had been here several times since coming to live on the island, but it never ceased to dazzle her.

'Oh my.' Ren's words came out in a gasp of delight. 'It's beautiful.' Long stalactites hung from the ceiling, stalagmites rose up from the ground in ponds of milky-turquoise water.

Emma led the way, holding the lantern out. 'There's more to see.' She led him past pools and along a trickling river, their voices echoing off the cavern walls. The underground river gathered and grew until they came to a ledge. 'Look down there.' The water cascaded in a fall, dropping into a pool twenty feet below.

Ren put his hand in the water. 'It's warm.' He sounded

surprised. He looked at her and back at the water. 'Can we get down there?'

'I don't know,' Emma said honestly. 'I've never gone any further than this.' She'd always been with Merry or with her father. They'd always stopped here.

Ren took the lantern from her and swung its arc of light around. 'Look, over there. It's some sort of natural staircase.'

Crude but wide stone steps were cut into the wall. 'I've never noticed them.' Emma advanced towards them, eager to see them, but Ren put out an arm to stop her.

'Let me go first. Take my hand.' It was Ren who led them to the bottom of the stairs, her hand in his firm grip, warm and reassuring on the ancient steps whenever she stumbled. The trip down the stairs was worth it. The waterfall pool steamed in the lamplight, looking magical.

'It's like a fairy grove,' Emma exclaimed in quiet, awed tones.

'An underground hot spring.' Ren slanted her a naughty look. 'It would be a shame to have come this far and not try it out.' He was already tugging at his boots. 'Are you game, Emma? How about a swim?'

It was all the invitation Emma needed. She hadn't swum for some time. She'd used to love it. 'You'll have to help me with my dress.' She was envious of the speed which with Ren was able to undress. His shirt was gone, his boots off before he came to work the fastenings at the back of her gown. She shivered a little at the warmth of his hands, competent and sure as they worked the buttons. How many women had he undressed? His prowess last night suggested he was more than gifted at bed sport.

She shrugged out of her dress and set it aside with her shoes. Ren stood at the water's edge, pushing down his trousers, revealing taut, muscled buttocks and long legs. It wasn't polite to stare, but she couldn't stop herself. There'd been nothing to see last night, only feel. She couldn't help but wonder what the source of all that pleasure looked like. She wished the lantern light was stronger. If he would just turn around... Darn it, Ren stepped into the water, not turning towards her until he was up to his waist in water.

'It's warm!' he called back to the shore. 'Let me swim out and see how deep it is.' In a few powerful strokes, he reached the waterfall and waved. The water reached mid-chest. 'I'm standing just fine. It's maybe five feet.'

But Emma hadn't waited. She'd stripped out of her chemise and undergarments and was feeling self-conscious standing on the shore naked, never mind the light didn't show much. It would be better to be naked in the water. She executed a shallow dive and swam out to him, revelling in the warm water. 'This is heaven. We have a giant bathtub all to ourselves.'

They swam, they raced, they dived beneath the surface. They floated lazily on their backs when they tired of their games. They were having fun, Emma realised. There was nothing in their way today: no politics, no Gridley, no plantation. She hadn't had this much fun with a man, *ever*. Men were creatures to be guarded against, to be used perhaps, but never enjoyed. One al-

ways had to be wary of the strings attached to any pleasure they offered. She'd learned that lesson first with
Thompson Hunt and her dealings with Arthur Gridley had reinforced it. In the end, she didn't expect Ren
Dryden to be any different, but for today he was. Today
there was a truce.

Ren swam up under her and grabbed her leg. She let
out a scream before she realised it wasn't a sea monster.
He popped out of the water, hair streaming while he
laughed. 'I got you!'

'You scared me!'

He hauled her to him, wrapping her in his arms. 'I
didn't think anything scared the great Emma Ward.'
He kissed her then, more slowly, more intently than last
night or the night he'd claimed his forfeit. Oh, this, too,
was a kind of heaven, to be held in his arms, to have
her mouth ravished with his kisses, the water lapping
against her body.

He lifted her in those arms and carried her to the
shore, finding a soft, sandy patch. He laid her down, his
hair dripping on her skin as he rose over her. 'They're
like stalactites.' She laughed, reaching a hand up to
squeeze the water out of the strands. His eyes burned
into hers, hot coals of desire as skin met skin, wet and
slick. Her tone turned husky. 'But I don't mind.'

Ren's mouth sealed itself over hers. He raised her
arms above her head, shackling her wrists in one hand.
Their bodies had no choice now but to meet and to meld.
Her breasts thrust upwards against his chest, her legs
parted to cradle him. He felt right, as if he belonged
with her. Maybe it was the magic of the falls, the sense

of being part of an ancient world here in the cave. She wanted, she *hungered*. Her body throbbed for him.

He was nuzzled against her entrance, but he wasn't done playing, wasn't done stoking her fires. His mouth sought her breast, his tongue working her rosy peak, sucking and tugging ever so lightly until her hips arched up into his in protest. *No more waiting, only claiming.* Her body was eager to see if the magic would happen again. She'd shattered for him not once, but twice last night. Would it always be like that?

Ren chuckled at her impatience, his lips pressing kisses to the column of her neck, but she sensed his own desire was pushing him. She spread her legs wider, an invitation he could not refuse. He slid into her and she sighed, luxuriating in the feel of him filling her, of her body shaping itself around him. She wrapped her legs around his waist, urging him, securing him. He thrust once, twice, and she picked up the rhythm, raising her hips to meet him, to join him. This—lying naked in a primeval cave, joined with a man in the oldest pleasure on earth—was decadence defined, sin at its very best.

Their rhythm increased, moving them towards the edge of ecstasy. She bucked hard beneath him, wanting her hands, wanting to bury her nails into his shoulders as an anchor against what was to come, something to hold on to while she broke. But he held her fast, forcing her to free-fall into the pleasure. And she did, one cogent thought in her mind—it was indeed possible.

Chapter Thirteen

Emerging into the sunlight and heat was akin to being born into another world and almost as difficult. Ren would like to have remained by the waterfall, savouring the magic of their cavern glade, but the horse would be getting restless and reality called. They kept silent as they climbed back into the gig and resumed their drive towards the beach.

Ren was reluctant to the break the spell, perhaps Emma was too. He cast a sideways glance at her profile beneath her straw hat, the slim nose, the sweep of her jaw, all conspiring to create the sharp beauty of her face. But there was tenseness, too. Whatever the reason for her silence, she was absorbed in her thoughts, breaking her contemplations only to gesture toward the cut-offs leading down to the water. He wondered if her thoughts followed the same pattern as his. Was she thinking about them, too? What did the events of the last two days mean to her? Or was she thinking of something else? She'd been frightened last night with Gridley and she'd been frightened again this morning, although a less perceptive man would not have noticed. Emma was a master at using boldness, her bravado, as her shield against that fear.

They rounded a final curve and the ocean opened up before them, sparkling in deep blues and greens beneath the sun, the sand nearly white.

Ren couldn't help but smile at the incredible view. 'I thought the cave was breathtaking, but this easily rivals it. The average person in England can't begin to imagine the beauty here, it's so vibrant. Even the colours are different. Our ocean is dark and cold, hardly inviting.'

He jumped down and unharnessed the horse. In this secluded cove, the horse couldn't go far. He went around to Emma's side and helped her down, his hands lingering at her waist, looking for some sign of what was going on behind her dark eyes. She was by far the loveliest, most mysterious woman he'd yet to meet, but that also made her the most complicated and the most intriguing. 'Will you walk with me, Emma?' Ren asked quietly.

They made short work of their shoes. Ren rolled up his trousers and Emma tied her skirt in a knot to keep it out of the waves. Everything *was* different, not just the colours of the ocean, Ren reflected as they made their way to the water, the sand warm between his toes. Emma was different, too. She'd not hesitated to take off her shoes, to knot up her skirt. No English girl would have dared such immodesty, certainly not the heiress in York. But modesty was often impractical here. He couldn't picture Emma *not* enjoying the beauty of the ocean for the sake of keeping her toes covered. Propriety was not worth the sacrifice.

'A penny for your thoughts…' Ren began as the waves gently lapped at their feet. The warmth of the water was a marvel to him. His brother Teddy would be in awe.

'A pound for yours. You smiled just now. What were you thinking?' Emma bent down and picked up a white shell.

'I was thinking of my brother and how much he would love this place. We'd never get him off the beach.'

Emma threw the shell out into the water. 'Do you miss them? Your family?'

Ren gave a short laugh. 'Not yet. I am sure I will, though. Back home, I saw them every day. It can be overwhelming to have a house full of females, especially when one is used to living alone.'

Emma knit her brow, not quite understanding. He elaborated. 'When my father was alive, I kept my own apartments in London. It was the right balance of distance for a young man. I like my family, but I like my freedom, too. A young man's pursuits aren't always appropriate when surrounded by nosy sisters. When my father passed away, I moved into the town house so I could take care of the family.'

When he'd become the earl, everything had changed right down to his way of life. 'Overnight I went from being a carefree buck to a man of responsibility.' Great responsibility. He not only had a family to look after, he had estates, investments, debts to manage, decisions to make, his sister Sarah to launch into Society. That had been four years ago, four years of trying to make ends meet and realising that traditional methods of aristocratic money management weren't going to work.

Emma looked up at him from beneath the brim of her hat, her eyes thoughtful and sincere. 'I'm sorry. You never mentioned your father had died. Were you close?'

'We were.' Ren couldn't help but smile. He could see his father in his mind, tall, striding about vigorously, laughing, wrestling with Teddy, teasing the girls, full of life. 'He loved us. None of us doubted it. My father saw that I was ready to take his place some day, that I was educated and prepared for life, socially, academically. He did the same for his daughters. But it was all so sudden.'

His voice dropped, the memory of those first moments flooding him. 'I'd met him for a drink at our club the previous afternoon. We'd talked about a horse he wanted to buy. I was supposed to meet him and my family at a ball that night, but he didn't feel well after dinner and went to lie down. The next morning he was gone.'

He felt Emma squeeze his hand, her words quiet. 'We're never prepared, sudden or not.' She looked away, her eyes going out over the ocean. 'It *is* beautiful here, but it's dangerous, too. Sometimes I'm not sure we were meant to be here. There are hurricanes, deadly insects, fevers and there's nothing to be done when they strike. We can't hold back the storms, we can't stop the fevers. We are so very vulnerable.

'My father was a strong man. He'd weathered the rigours of military life for years and yet the fever took him within a week. People told me I was lucky. We'd had a chance to say goodbye, he'd had a chance to make last plans. Merry sat with him, writing furiously when my father wasn't delirious and reassuring him when he was. But in the end, it didn't matter. I still missed him, still grieved. I suppose that gives us something in common.'

They moved a little further along the surf line, hands interlocked. He felt connected to Emma in those moments in a way that defied any other connection he'd felt. Perhaps it was the lingering intimacy of the caves that had provoked his disclosure. Perhaps it was something else. He only knew he'd not planned to tell her such a thing when they'd come down to the water. In truth, he'd meant to draw *her* out. He knew, too, that he'd never shared those feelings with another, *ever*. Kitt had left before his father died, and he'd not wanted to burden his sisters in their own grief with his.

They turned back towards the wagon and the picnic basket. His stomach was rumbling. Breakfast seemed ages ago, part of a different world. Ren spread the blanket and helped Emma set out the food. She wanted to hear more about England. 'I haven't been there since I was a little girl,' she confessed, biting into a cold ham sandwich. 'I don't remember much except that it was gloomy and it rained a lot.'

Ren laughed. 'Then you remember it pretty well. It hasn't changed. But summer in the English countryside is not to be missed.' He regaled her with stories of his family, their country home where they picked strawberries and rode horses and swam in the river.

His tales took them through the sandwiches, the

mangoes and the sponge cake the cook had packed. Ren finished his cake and set aside his napkin. Emma had already stretched out on her side of the blanket, propped up on an elbow, her hair falling over one shoulder. She looked utterly provocative on that blanket. His body stirred with a thousand possibilities. Actually, he wasn't sure it had stopped stirring since the caves. Her every move, her every glance, touch, word seemed to keep him on the edge of arousal.

Ren stretched out beside her and she welcomed him with a smile. Ren fought the urge to give in to that welcome. What she wanted would have to wait. 'I think we have to talk before things go any further.'

She did not protest. Part of him had hoped she would. 'I thought we had been talking,' she said coyly, dropping her eyes to the blanket.

'We have, and it's been good. We haven't talked, not like that, since I arrived. Sometimes I'm struck about how little I know about you and you about me, considering how much time we spend together and our circumstances.'

Her eyes came back to his, her gaze direct. 'By circumstances you mean having made love?'

'Among other things.' Ren met her directness with a bluntness of his own. 'We have a plantation between us, we are partners whether we choose it or not...' he made a back-and-forth gesture with his hand between them, 'and now, we have *this*. It's profound and heady and I don't have a word for it, just "this" and "it". What are we doing, Emma?' He paused, watching her pleat the blanket between her thumb and forefinger. 'Is this an affair, something to entertain ourselves with? Is it guided by real feeling or is it part of some political agenda against Gridley? Maybe it's just a personal agenda. Which is it, Emma?'

'You think too much, Ren.' Emma gave a slow smile to take the edge off her response and perhaps to distract. 'Can't it just be sex? Very, very good sex?'

'I wish it could be, but I don't believe it can be, not for a minute. There are too many strings pulling at us.'

Emma scooted closer to him, the heat of his body rising with her nearness. Her arm went about his neck. He could smell the scent of water and salt on her, the scents of the Caribbean in her hair. 'Were there strings pulling at us in the cave?' Her voice was husky as she dropped slow kisses along his jaw.

Ren swallowed hard. This conversation was going nowhere—well, not *nowhere*, it was going somewhere quite nicely, just not the place he'd hoped. He was starting to think resistance was pointless. 'Emma, you know what I mean.' It was a half-hearted attempt to call upon her own sense of reason.

She gave a throaty laugh against his neck, her hand reaching for him. 'I shattered for you twice last night, and you brought me to it again this morning. Is that something secret agendas can control?' Her words were an aphrodisiac as she thumbed him, the friction of cloth and her hand driving him to the edge of insanity. Her next words, whispered at his ear, sent him over that cliff. 'I've never experienced anything like it before. Does that mean nothing?'

She bit his earlobe with a gentle nip. 'Only you, Ren

Dryden. I've shattered only for you. Forgive me if I don't want to look for reasons for it.' She worked the fall of his trousers. 'Let me return the favour. Shatter for me, Ren, no strings attached.'

It was the fantasy every man must dream about: a beautiful woman in a setting that rivalled Paradise, taking him in hand. Before now there'd only been moulding, cupping. There was no material between them this time, just her warm, firm hand on him, easing itself up and down his length. He would shatter for her. There was no doubt in his mind she would bring him to climax.

That didn't mean everything was settled between them. He should probably stop her; force her to keep the contract that nothing could happen until they'd decided what this was going to be between them. She thumbed the tender tip of him, spreading moisture over the head, a shudder of absolute delight taking him. He knew there was no chance of stopping her just as surely as he knew he would shatter under her touch. Their discussion had been postponed. Which was just as well. A moment later he was beyond any coherent thought, his hips bucking upwards against her hand, a groan ripping from his throat as she brought him to completion.

Emma's eyes were dark with excitement, a little smile hovering on her lips as she watched him. He was not the only one who had received pleasure from the act. The look she gave him was almost as moving as what had just occurred. It was an honest look, a look of having been swept up in the moment. In his experience, there was much about pleasure that could be contrived or feigned, but not *that*. It went a long way in alleviating his worries over there being a larger, more sinister agenda at work. After this, Ren didn't want there to be. He didn't want to face a reality where this pleasure had an ulterior purpose. He'd already faced one in the York heiress and found such a situation cold, lacking.

For once, he wanted something to be pure and unadulterated. He'd been pursued by women since he'd come into the title—not because they wanted him necessarily, but because they wanted what he represented. He, too, had been forced to pursue certain women because of what *they* represented as well—fortunes that could redeem the earldom.

Here, in the Caribbean, he could have the best of both worlds; he could escape that fate as Kitt had escaped it and he could save his family from social ostracism. But he wanted Emma to want him, no strings attached. He certainly wanted her. He'd have wanted her with or without the plantation. He wanted her still, even with Sugarland acting as a barrier between them. She was used to independently running the place, she did not easily welcome his interference and yet, wanting her overrode those concerns. He wanted to believe the passion they shared overrode those concerns for her, too, that passion could lay the groundwork for trust. But even if it did, he was right back to where he'd started. What did this mean for them? An affair, or something more?

In his world, a gentleman's world, 'something more' implied marriage without exception. A man didn't behave with a woman as he had with Emma without offering her the protection of marriage unless that woman was of a certain sort and class, a class Merrimore's ward didn't fall into by any means. Had Merrimore been expecting her to now fall under Ren's protection as his proxy? Or had Merrimore thought something more?

Emma moved into the crook of his arm, her head on his shoulder. 'You're thinking again, Ren.'

Ren kissed the top of her head, breathing in the light floral scent of her hair. 'Only about you, surely that's fair enough.'

She nestled closer, running a hand up inside his shirt. 'As long as the thoughts are good ones.'

It was on the tip of his tongue to ask why they wouldn't be, but his mind wasn't entirely finished with the previous ones. What if Cousin Merrimore had brought him here for more than just the plantation? What if Merrimore had brought him here for *her*?

Chapter Fourteen

The more Ren thought about it, the more the idea had merit. It was still on his mind as he paced in the drawing room, waiting to take Emma into their usual dinner for two. The question was—what shape did that inheritance take? Had Merrimore wanted him to be a proxy protector? If so, Ren had done a poor job of it. He'd been here a handful of weeks and he'd already bedded Merrimore's ward, hardly a sterling recommendation for a protector, which raised another question. Had Merrimore wanted him to be something more permanent? A husband, perhaps?

Ren wasn't sure how such a possibility sat with him. In part, he'd left England to avoid an arranged marriage. It seemed the height of irony to have come all this way only to have another arrangement waiting for him. It was a much prettier arrangement, a more passionate arrangement to be sure, but it was still an arrangement, *someone else's arrangement*, that would guide the rest of *his* life. Ren very selfishly wanted to make those sorts of arrangements on his own.

Had that been what Cousin Merrimore had wanted? Ren trailed his hand over the curves of a porcelain figure of a dog sitting on a small side table. He'd been so sure Merrimore had been looking for a plantation manager. Had Merrimore instead been looking for husband material for his rather wayward ward? It had not escaped Ren last night or this afternoon that he'd not been her first lover. She'd been sure of her skills and he'd thought from the first that such sensuality didn't come with virginity, but from confidence and experience. He had no complaints. Virgins had never held much charm for him, but society adored them. His cousin might have been anxious about Emma's future based on that social preference.

Ren did, however, chastise himself for not seeing the possibility sooner although he knew the reasons for it. He'd been self-absorbed in the adventure; overly focused on the plantation and what it could do for the salvation of his family in England, overly focused, too, on his own freedom, his narrow escape from the clutches of the York heiress. The busyness surrounding his arrival hadn't helped things. There'd been the exploding chicken coop, the burning fields, the neighbours to meet, new and unexpected circumstances to adjust to. He'd been swept up immediately into the daily processes of plantation life. There'd been no time, as one of his professors at Oxford was fond of saying, 'to see the forest through the trees'. The larger scope of why he'd been called here had escaped his notice, lost in the technicalities and events of the daily routine.

It was only now when things had slowed that he could see the patterns and the subtle intentions.

A swish of skirts alerted him to Emma's arrival. He looked up, a slow smile taking his face. She always managed to look stunning in gowns, or the breeches she wore about the estate. He couldn't imagine Emma *not* looking stunning. Tonight she'd done it in a gown of pale blue that turned her hair impossibly dark and her skin beautifully tanned. A single, slim strand of pearls rested at the base of her neck, calling attention to the fact that there was quite a lot of skin artfully revealed in the sleeveless vee cut of the bodice. There were no trimmings or flounces to disguise what was on display. As a result, the gown was far less girlish than the silly London confections designed to be demure.

Dinner was waiting for them. Tonight, it was a spicy rice dish liberally filled with shrimp, accompanied by fresh baked bread, fried okra, which had been new to Ren, and a light white wine.

Ren took a bite of the rice and shrimp, savouring it as if it were a great luxury. 'I think I like the food in Barbados, especially the seafood dishes.'

Emma laughed, her eyes twinkling as she leaned forward. 'You haven't tasted pudding and souse yet. Do you know what that is?'

Ren grinned and leaned back in his chair, waiting to be regaled. 'You know I couldn't possibly.'

'It's a special Barbadian dish made of pig parts for the pudding and pig's head with trotters boiled down for the souse.' Emma smiled and took another sip of wine, waiting for his reaction. He almost gave it. The dish sounded positively disgusting but that was what the little minx wanted. Ren fought the urge and opted to tease her a bit.

He merely fingered the stem of his glass and said, 'Ah, a Barbadian version of haggis, is it? Why do you suppose so many cultures seem bent on stuffing things into intestines?'

The comment caught her entirely off guard as he intended. She'd not anticipated a humorous response from him. If she had, she might not have taken that sip. Wine spewed out of her mouth, just missing her plate of rice and shrimp. She choked, gasping for breath, until Ren had to come to her side, patting her on the back as if she were a small child. 'I'm sorry. I should have timed my remark better.' Ren offered her his napkin, but he couldn't help laughing.

Emma was laughing, too, unable to stay angry. 'You timed it just when you wanted it. You knew what you were doing,' Emma scolded in friendly tones, wiping her eyes.

Ren took his seat. 'Well, maybe I did,' he confessed. 'Do you need a new plate? I could call Faulks.'

'No, I missed the plate.'

'This is one of the reasons I prefer eating this way, everything is on the table at once. Can you imagine resetting Gridley's table if you'd spat your wine out last night?' Ren shook his head in mock despair. 'One plate we could have managed, but all of his? And the glasses and the silverware?'

Emma laughed with him. 'I assure you I don't make a habit of spitting out my wine. But it's true, Gridley does prefer excess. He wants everyone to remember he is English and a knight of the realm.'

Ren laughed. 'So his house is too big, his art too ostentatious, his table too full.' Ren paused. 'He's jealous, you know. He wants everyone to remember he's equal to Sugarland. He told me during our afternoon visit that you had the best of everything. The best food, the best cook. No matter what he does, he still finds himself lacking when measured against you.' Ren gestured to the room about him. 'Sugarland is a stunning home. The dining room rivals anything one would find in London, as does the service.'

Emma smiled. 'Sugarland does sport the best dining room on the island. It was one of Merry's pride and joys. He had the Wedgwood specially commissioned and the crystal hand blown in Ireland.'

'My cousin had good taste or did he have you to thank for it?' Ren gave her a warm smile. He liked this easy conversation with her. They'd made progress today relaxing with one another.

'More like the merchants on Swan Street, but I certainly helped.'

They'd finished their meal and it was the perfect opening to move the conversation towards the questions in his mind. Ren rose and offered Emma his arm. They'd developed the habit of taking a walk about the lawns after dinner before settling into a game of chess or backgammon. Tonight, it seemed the perfect venue for a more intimate discussion. 'My cousin must have valued you a great deal. Tell me about Merry. I suspect you were closer to him those last years than anyone, even Gridley. I have difficulty understanding that friendship. It's rather odd to be friends with a man one is jealous of.'

It was still warm outside, but not uncomfortably so. The stars were starting to come out. It was somewhat of a magical novelty to Ren that darkness actually fell in a land so warm, but it did, a constant reminder of how close they were to the equator. There were no long or short days here, all the days were the same.

'Gridley always has a reason for his friendships,' Emma said, looking up into the night sky where the stars were beginning to come out. 'There's usually something he wants.' She was trying to sound blasé. Ren wasn't fooled. The nonchalance was just another aspect of her brave facade.

'You?' Ren offered bluntly. 'His eyes made no secret of the fact last night. Even without his gaze following you around the room, he made that abundantly clear the afternoon we talked. In retrospect I see his confession more as a warning than anything else.'

Emma gave a nervous laugh. 'I thought we were talking about Merry.' He had her off-centre—interesting. What was he getting close to? He had meant to talk about Merry, but perhaps this was the opportunity to talk about Gridley the way he'd meant to earlier in the day.

'I think the two are inseparable,' Ren said, his voice low in the darkness. He wanted to build an aura of intimacy, wanted her to feel comfortable with a confession if there was one to make. 'What did Merry want for you? Did he want Gridley for you? Did he want you to go to London?' His mouth was next to her ear, his nostrils breathing in the clean scent of her. 'Did he want you to have me?' *I want to have you, to hell with what Merry thought or anyone else.* It was probably unfair to ask such a question standing here in the warm evening, their bodies close, primed with reminders of the day, but he asked anyway.

'I don't know what Merry intended. I was anticipating an older man.' She gave a short self-deprecating laugh. 'I wasn't sure if anyone would even come.'

'I'm sorry to disappoint you.' Ren chuckled.

She gave him a coy smile. 'You don't exactly disappoint, Ren Dryden. But if you're asking me what Merry intended for you or for me, or for us, I don't know.' Even in the darkness, intuition told him she was holding something back. She might not know in truth, but there were things she suspected. Ren tried to pry her thoughts loose with a little disclosure of his own.

'There were plenty of people who advised me not to come. My mother, my friends. Such a journey was too risky and unnecessary, they said. I should stay home and collect my portion of the profits and do nothing. But I sensed Cousin Merry hadn't willed me the interest in Sugarland for me to stay home. I don't know that to be the case factually speaking, but I *felt* it. It seemed to suggest itself based on circumstances.' He stopped, taking a moment to watch her profile. She was thinking, hard. 'Surely you must have some intuition about what Cousin Merrimore wanted for you? There must have been conversations in the past, even at the end that would at least suggest some answers?'

Ren was pushing hard tonight and it made her wary. He was using all the tools at his disposal: a day of exquisite sexual practice, the deepening intimacy of the night, the proximity of his body, the easy humour over dinner. It all combined to create a heightened sense of comfort between them. And it was working. She did feel comfortable with him despite what she knew he was doing. He'd seduced her and now he thought to use that intimacy to get his answers. Well, Thompson Hunt had already beaten him to that strategy and she would not be fooled twice.

She had her own strategies, too, for what their intimate encounters might be used for. Then there were her hopes that maybe here was a man who would be different from the rest. She'd never know unless she tested that hypothesis, too. Tonight, she'd risk a little more, perhaps risk a lot. She sensed the time for truth, at least about Gridley, had come. Emma drew a breath. 'Towards the end, Gridley was with him and the solicitor constantly. Those last days were fearful to me. I was afraid of Gridley's influence, afraid Gridley might convince Merry to do something foolish at the end.'

'Like what?'

'Something medieval like Merry compelling me to marry Gridley in order to keep the plantation or forcing me to join Sugarland to his. Gridley talked of it nonstop.' She said it casually, with a laugh to make it sound even more ludicrous. She might be ready for Ren to know what had transpired, but she wasn't ready for him to know how real that fear had been.

'Merry suspected Gridley had more than friendship

on his mind, however. One day shortly before he died, we went up to the bluff and he told me about his concerns,' Emma added quietly. 'Whatever Merry wanted for me, it was not Gridley. I wonder, too, if Merry wrote those suspicions down in his journal along with his thoughts about the cartel.' Or if he'd had a chance. He'd seldom been alone. 'Every time the solicitor came, I worried. It sounds selfish, but I breathed easier once the will was read and nothing of the sort was mandated.'

'It's good to know that Merry knew,' Ren said after a while. 'I wouldn't have liked knowing that he died duped into a false friendship.'

Emma stopped walking and faced him. Ren meant the comment to be consoling, but it was far from that and she could not let it pass unaddressed. This was no ordinary land struggle or arranged marriage drama. It was time to disabuse Ren of any notion he harboured in that direction. It was time for the truth about Gridley. She took a deep breath, her grip on Ren's hand tightening. 'In the end, Merry knew Gridley's measure precisely. He lay there helpless, unable to do anything but watch while Gridley put a pillow over his face and snuffed out the last of his life.'

'Dear God!' Even in the dark, she could tell Ren was stunned. 'How do you know?'

'I saw the last of it. I saw him lift the pillow from Merry's face.' Her voice was starting to shake. Tears burned in her eyes. Even a few simple, unemotional words were too much for her. She could see it in her mind as if it had just happened.

There was a stone bench nearby and Ren led her

there, forcing her to sit, his arm about her drawing her close for comfort and strength. 'You don't have to tell me,' he whispered into her hair.

'Yes, I do. You have to know what you're up against. Gridley is a monster.' She forced her thoughts into coherent sentences. 'The solicitor had come downstairs and stopped to talk with me. We spoke for maybe five minutes before he left. Then I went up to see Merry. It was time for his medicine,' she explained, although the detail didn't matter. 'I entered the room without knocking and that's when I saw him. It was plain what he'd done and Gridley made no attempt to excuse it.' Her voice caught and she swallowed hard. 'He looked at me and said, "The old man was bound to go tomorrow or the next anyway. It might as well be today." Then he winked at me and said, "This will be our little secret. We can't have anyone thinking you might have done this", as if he were taking the blame for me.'

She felt Ren's arm tighten about her in protection and anger. She'd been right to tell him. 'Oh, my dear girl, you must have been frightened beyond words. No wonder you were so pale in that room this morning.'

'I was too numb to be frightened,' Emma admitted. 'Gridley simply walked out of the room and went home as if nothing unusual had happened.'

She could feel Ren's breathing change as he began to think. She could almost predict his next question. 'Did you tell anyone?'

Emma shook her head against his shoulder. 'No. It's the one and only time I've ever done anything Gridley's asked. How could I have done otherwise? I was alone with no one to protect me and Gridley's threat had teeth. When I thought about it, who would believe me over Gridley? So I let it go.'

'And in doing so, you've given Gridley a tidy piece of blackmail to hang over your head,' Ren summed up. 'Why hasn't he used it to force your hand already? Marriage and Sugarland in exchange for not taking you to trial.'

'That's easy, Ren,' she murmured. 'Timing and you. He had to wait for the will to be read. He honestly thought it was going to be changed, that something had been agreed upon that last day. He was eager to see Merry removed before Merry could change it again. But he'd guessed wrong. The solicitor and Merry had outwitted him at the last.

'Then there were his promises to Merry. He'd been very public about having been charged with "watching over" me. There had to be an interval of decency. I think there's some fear for him, too, in making his claim public. I'd at least smear his reputation by telling everyone the murderer was him. I'd be the one who loses in court. I would hang, but he'd be ruined in other ways.

'Then just when that was ending, you showed up to complicate things further. Blackmailing me into compliance isn't enough any more. You have the other fifty-one per cent.'

Emma felt Ren's hand still where it had been running up and down her arm in a comforting motion. His body stiffened. His voice was terse when he spoke. 'Is that why you slept with me?'

A blow to the stomach could not have been more effective. This was the pivotal moment, the moment where she could lose him. She could not lose him now! Not now when she'd invested so much in the hope Ren embodied for her future and when she'd invested so much of herself not just physically, but emotionally. She'd trusted him tonight. Emma disengaged herself and rose, combining truth and lie into the only answer she could defend. 'I slept with you because I wanted to.' The terse set of Ren's jaw started to relax. She played her ace. Regardless of his misgivings, Ren could not resist her. Emma held out a hand, putting his acceptance of her answer to the immediate test. 'And I would like to do it again, only tonight I might suggest something different.'

Ren stood, his eyes hot with rising desire. The crisis was past. A rill of elation surged through her at the little victory as he took her hand. 'What would that be, Emma?'

She smiled coyly and tugged him towards the house. 'A bed.'

Chapter Fifteen

Bed changed everything. Ren's blood ran hot with the thrill of deliberately taking a woman to bed, of watching her undress and undressing for her in turn. The mere prospect honed a man's arousal to a sharp edge of anticipation. There was a titillating intimacy to the formal art of sex in a bedroom that was absent from hotter, more spontaneous encounters—the sort of which had populated their couplings to date.

He liked those encounters as well. They didn't require thinking, only doing, only living in the moment of passion. One could be swept away, let oneself go and then use that very spontaneity as a carefully constructed excuse later to explain 'the mistake'. One did not have such leniency in the bedroom where it was all clearly premeditated. One had to be honest with oneself afterwards.

A single lamp illuminated Emma's bedchamber, casting a rosy-gold light on the walls. Like the other walls in the house, they were white stucco. Wallpaper didn't last in the humidity. But the other items in the room leant the chamber its colour. A braided rug in oranges, pinks and reds lay on the polished hardwood planking of the floor. A quilt of matching colours lay folded at the foot of the bed.

Ah, the bed! It was a four-postered wonder done in teak, covered in an immaculate white quilt turned back to expose the thick mattress and tight fitted sheets. Pillows were plumped sumptuously against the headboard. But what stood out most to Ren was how high it was set up from the ground in what he was coming to know as the Caribbean style. His own bed in the *garçonnière* was set unusually high, too. Michael had explained it was for protection against anything that crawled or slithered: scorpions, snakes, stinging beetles. Necessity it might be, but it also precluded any romantic gesture of carrying one's lover to bed since getting into bed required a mounting block. A laugh escaped him at the humour.

'What's so funny?' Emma had sobered, too—perhaps she'd also realised what a bedding in the bedroom entailed.

Ren nodded towards the steps set beside the bed. 'I was just thinking how appropriate it was to need a mounting block for mounting of another sort.'

She tossed him a hot look. 'You have a wicked mind, Ren Dryden.'

'It makes me more interesting.' Ren tugged at the end of his cravat, pulling it loose and letting the yards of cloth slide around his neck, giving Emma ample warning of what was coming next. He tossed the strip of cloth on to the end of the bed. One never knew when a cravat could be put to other uses.

Emma took her cue and sat down in an upholstered

lady's chair by the window. She spread her skirts about her, managing to look both demure and worldly as she prepared to watch him disrobe.

Ren started with his waistcoat, making her wait as he took off his watch chain and cufflinks, setting them in a trifle dish on the table next to the bed. He undid the buttons of his paisley waistcoat and started on the studs of his shirt, pulling his tails out of the waistband of his trousers as he went. His shirt came off. He heard Emma's breath catch at the sight of him.

He was magnificent! Emma's hands fisted in the folds of her skirts, her breath catching at the sight of him. There was something poignantly erotic about seeing a lover revealed for the first time, a gorgeous package being unwrapped just for her. Ren Dryden in clothes was a sight to behold. Ren Dryden without them was beyond words.

The dark shadows of the cave had not done him justice, nor had their lusty half-clothed couplings. Here was a man who knew how to take care of himself. His chest was a sculpted atlas of muscles, his shoulders blatantly displaying their breadth. *This* was what she'd lain her head against at the beach, *these* were the arms that had held her against the wall and carried her up the stairs to bed.

Ren's hands went to the waistband of his trousers, his eyes on her making it known that part of this seduction was this decadent voyeurism—him studying her studying him. A slow smile crept across his face. 'Watch me, Em.'

As if she could do otherwise. Her throat was dry with anticipation, her eyes riveted on his hands, taking in every minute motion of those long fingers as he undid the fall of his trousers and pushed them down past narrow hips, muscled thighs and well-shaped calves. She couldn't recall when his boots had come off, but they must have at some point. It was hardly important when there was so much more to look at, to wonder over. Her eye was drawn to the manly core of him, to that nest of dark hair and what was jutting up sharply from it. She needn't be shy, he meant for her to look, to drink her fill. A trill of feminine possessiveness took her. *Her* lover was extraordinary.

Ren climbed the steps to the bed and stretched out, posing on his side and letting the lamplight fall over the length of his body; every plane, every angle, every muscle of him on display as he propped himself up on an elbow, resting his head on his hand, one leg bent. There wasn't an ounce of modesty to him. He was all brazen male. He gave her a nearly imperceptible nod. Now it was her turn.

Emma rose from her chair, thankful she'd inadvertently chosen a dress she could get off by herself. She'd not planned this when she'd dressed for dinner. The idea of taking Ren to bed had been spontaneous, a product of the warm night and their quiet disclosures and, to be honest, a product of distraction. His questions were getting too close to disturbing subjects she'd rather not discuss until she must. Already, she'd told him so much. And yet, a secret or two remained.

Emma reached behind her, freeing the three hooks that fastened the gown. She let the dress slide over her body and down, leaving her in the soft, thin cotton of her undergarments. 'Move into the light,' Ren instructed in low, hoarse tones from the bed. 'I want it to play behind you, my very own erotic chiaroscuro.'

'Ah, an artist's distribution of light and shadow.' Emma replied, complying. She knew full well what the light would do, what it would expose: the deep rosy brown of her nipples pressing against the thin linen of her chemise, showcasing the dark juncture between her legs.

Emma lifted a leg to the middle step of the mounting block and began to peel off her stocking. She felt Ren's eyes following the roll of silk down past her knee, down slim calves. She did the second one, hearing the sheets rustle as Ren shifted his weight. She was careful not to look at him, inviting him to participate in a different sort of voyeurism than the kind he'd invoked. She undressed as if she was alone in her room, unaware of a man watching her private ablutions.

Emma raised the chemise over her head, letting the lamplight catch her breasts in profile. She discarded the undergarment and cupped her breasts, lifting them, palming them as if studying their suitability, something she'd done a hundred times in front of a mirror, testing her own attractiveness. But in front of a man, the act took on something bolder, wilder.

'Goodness, Emma. You'd drive a saint to sin,' Ren growled appreciatively from the bed, lust lacing his words. She pretended not to hear, her hands moving to the delicate string of her pantalettes. She turned her back to him and moved her hips, drawing the loosened pantalettes downward over the slim curve of her buttocks until they pooled in a white puddle at her feet.

'Come to bed, Minx.'

'Not yet,' Emma said softly, knowing he was enjoying the view from behind as much as he'd enjoyed the other views she'd presented. She reached up to her hair and pulled out the pins, letting the heavy tresses fall down her back, a dark curtain. She heard Ren moan. After a moment more, she turned to face him for the first time, fully naked, enjoying the desire that flared in his eyes, knowing she'd been the one to put it there. 'I shall take pity on my poor subject and grant him a boon. What do you want? Name anything.'

'I want to be your steed, my lady. Will you ride me?'

Emma climbed the steps to the bed and straddled him, her knees sinking into the soft mattress. 'Gladly. I will ride you and more,' she promised. His hands were warm where they framed her hips. She lifted herself over him, rising over his rigid shaft and lowered, slowly slipping on to him, letting herself savour the slide of him as she took him inside. Oh, this was exquisite! This was power! One look at Ren's face and she knew he shared the sensation, too. There was awe and amazement written there, as if nothing had ever felt this good, this right.

Emma began to ride, up and down the length of him, his hands holding her hips so she didn't stray too far. She clenched about him, delighting in the gasp of surprise that claimed him. Ren had not anticipated such a show of feminine strength. She did it again and felt him respond inside her. His grip tightened on her hips and she gave a little scream as he rolled her beneath him, a swift move that kept them joined. 'I thought you wanted *me* to ride you. You lied!' Emma protested, looking up into his blue eyes.

'I didn't lie. I changed my mind,' Ren clarified with a wolfish grin.

She adjusted her legs about him, shifting ever so slightly to accommodate this new position. 'You're a most demanding subject.'

Ren bit at her neck. 'You're a most tempting queen who needs to be taught a lesson about provoking said subject.'

Emma raised her hands above her head in surrender, her voice a husky whisper. 'Then teach me.'

Ren didn't have to be asked twice. He stretched out his arms, reaching up to capture her wrists in his grip. Using her body as leverage, he began the rhythm she craved; thrust and withdraw, each cycle building the delicious tension. She felt herself die a little each time he pulled back and live again when he surged into her, her body flowing about him until the tension he'd wrought was unbearable, pushing her to the breaking point. Ren's voice was harsh at her ear, a victim of his own efforts. 'Let go, Em.'

That was when she broke, taking him with her over pleasure's cliff. A strangled cry escaped her. She was falling, falling with only Ren to hold on to, her anchor in the free fall into pleasure's oblivion. Her one cogent thought, brief and fleeting: how was it that a game of seduction, a game she'd designed to counteract his own efforts to render her vulnerable, a game designed to *pro-*

tect her, had failed her completely, leaving her exposed to the very things she sought to avoid?

How, in heaven's name, had this happened? But she knew the answer in part already. This was what happened when one dared to use sex as a weapon, forgetting that quite often weapons are turned on those who wield them.

'How the hell has this happened?' Arthur Gridley brought the palm of his hand down hard on the polished mahogany surface of his desk. The inkstand jumped, the heavy paperweight gave a shudder.

The man standing before him played with the brim of his straw hat, too nervous to meet his gaze, as well he might be. The man had nothing good to report. Ren Dryden had turned out to have a voracious sexual appetite if the man's information was to be believed. But then, Dryden couldn't take all the credit. Arthur imagined Emma Ward could bring out the best in any man's more intimate appetites.

'They went out into the gardens and when they came back in, they went upstairs.'

'Which room?' Arthur interrupted.

'Second room on the right in the front.'

'Her room.' Arthur nodded his confirmation, his groin tightening at the image of Emma taking a man into her private chambers.

The man coughed discreetly. 'There was a lamp, sir, there were shadows visible from the front lawn. There's no doubt what they got up to.'

'And what was that?' Arthur Gridley pressed. He was making his messenger uncomfortable, but he wanted the details, wanted to know exactly what Emma and Dryden had been doing. He listened intently, his mind providing the erotic images of Emma undressing against the light, her hair coming down, her hands on her breasts, teasing Dryden in ways she ought to be teasing *him* instead; Dryden stripping out of his trousers, his naked, muscled body covering Emma. Dryden was a well-made man. Arthur was flexible enough to appreciate Dryden's physical features, although he'd appreciate them more if they weren't being used to seduce Emma out from under him.

In fact, once his lurid fascination was appeased, there was only anger left; anger at Emma, who had betrayed him by throwing herself after an Englishman she barely knew, yet again; anger at Ren Dryden who fashioned himself a gentleman and ought to have known better than to accept the offer. Arthur pulled a quill from the inkstand, playing with it. A gentleman didn't take advantage of a woman on her own, especially when the gentleman in question had been told she was taken. The quill in his hand snapped. Well, the gloves were off now. If Ren Dryden didn't feel the need to act like gentleman, neither did he.

It was difficult to strike against Emma as he would like. To destroy her cane crop, for instance, would bring her to her knees financially and quite possibly in other ways. She'd be begging him to help her through the season. But the move seemed illogical. To hurt Sugarland would be to strike against himself. He would ultimately pay for any destruction he did to the plantation and that defeated his purposes. He wanted Emma Ward in his bed, but he wanted Sugarland in his bank account. He would have to pull the financial rug out from under her in other ways.

He doubted Ren Dryden would be as eager to take her to bed if she wasn't a plantation heiress. The reported activities of the last two days suggested Dryden had not yet taken his advice and looked at the books. Arthur tapped the broken end of the quill against the desk. It was time to make sure Dryden did. A glimpse of financial reality might also encourage Dryden to join the cartel regardless of the pleasures Emma provided in bed. When money talked, men usually listened. He would be there first thing in the morning to make sure Dryden didn't prove to be the exception.

Arthur undid his trousers and put a hand on himself. He leaned back in his chair, eyes closed, his mind conjuring up a vision of Emma on her knees before him, her hair unpinned, begging him, pleading with him. His hand slipped up and down as a dialogue formed in his head. She was sorry she'd given herself to the wrong man. He'd been right; Dryden had only wanted her for her money. Dryden had made a whore of her with his demands. She'd forgotten how powerful Arthur was, how she should have come to him from the start, how he'd always been there for her. If he would only forgive her, she would spend her life showing her gratitude.

Arthur began to jerk in his excitement. In his fantasy, he saw himself place a priestlike hand on her head, offering absolution. 'Take me in your mouth, Emma, and all will be forgiven.'

Chapter Sixteen

Ren could almost forgive the sun for rising when he recalled the night that had preceded it. Shortly before dawn, he'd found enough willpower to drag himself to his rooms in order to maintain a facade of decency and to rest. What he couldn't forgive was being awakened by Michael after what had seemed like only a few minutes of deep sleep.

'Sir Arthur Gridley is here.' The rush of Michael's words mirrored his actions. Michael was hurrying through the room, laying out clothes. 'He wants to see you.'

Ren pushed himself up, his eyes squinting against the bright light from the opened blinds. 'If he wants to see me, he can wait,' he said, sounding grouchy.

'But it's Sir Arthur.' Michael's comment vacillated between a protest and a warning. Apparently, Sir Arthur sat at the top of island society.

'And he's waking *me* up. Maybe he should think about that before he comes calling.' Ren stretched, starting to feel more awake as Emma's revelations flooded to the fore of his mind. That murdering bastard was not going to jangle the keys to *this* kingdom any longer. 'I'll see Arthur Gridley when I'm ready to see him and not a moment sooner.' Protectiveness of his realm and his woman surged and he dressed quickly. Gridley didn't call the tune at Sugarland, but neither did Ren want that snake wandering the halls unaccompanied.

Something was afoot. Even in his groggy state, he knew that much. What he knew about Gridley's personal habits did not recommend the man as a morning person. If Gridley was here so early, it meant something. Ren swung his feet out of bed. 'Did Gridley say what he wanted? There hasn't been an emergency, has there?' He would feel terrible if there was truly a crisis and he'd decided to play a little game of social one-upmanship just to prove a point.

Michael shook his head. 'He didn't say. Faulks told him to help himself to breakfast and you'd be there presently.'

'And Miss Ward? Did Gridley ask to see her, too?' Ren held out his arms and let Michael help him into a shirt.

'It was only you he asked for.'

If he hadn't asked for Emma to join them, he'd likely come for his answer about the cartel. 'We'll let him wait, but not for too long.' Ren sniffed at the air. 'Is that coffee you brought? I think I'll have a cup.' He wanted to meet Gridley with his mind fully functioning. After Emma's disclosures about Gridley, Ren was starting to feel as if he were caught in the middle of something that ran deep and sinister. The depths to which Gridley had sunk suggested he was desperate for Ren to choose a side. Gridley could not make his next move until Ren did.

Ren sat down, waiting for his customary shave. He closed his eyes as Michael bathed his face in warm water, the ritual giving his thoughts a chance to regroup. Gridley wasn't the only desperate party. Emma was desperate, too—desperate for protection against Gridley, desperate to save her home. She was certainly the more innocent party here. She hadn't committed murder or forced another into a completely untenable position, but what *had* she been willing to do in her desperation? When he'd asked her point blank in the garden last night, she hadn't really answered.

After a night of unbound lovemaking, thoughts of having been used or having been manipulated through that lovemaking were unsavoury ones to wake up with. Yet, Ren could not dismiss the potential. Emma had motive. *But she'd wanted you*, his male ego was quick to argue. *That sort of response could not be feigned over and over again, not once, not twice, but multiple times.*

But why? He hoped he didn't know the answer. He didn't want Emma in his bed because she was desperate. That brought him up short. He paused in the hall, reluctantly contemplating his train of thought. He wanted her in his bed because it meant something to him to have her there and he wanted it to mean something to her, too. As Ren approached the breakfast room he couldn't help but feel that something was not all it seemed and that he and Emma were poised on the edge of something that transcended the problem of Gridley and his sugar cartel.

'Ah, Dryden, there you are. I'm green with envy. Your cook has the English breakfast down to perfection.' Sir Arthur's booming tones met him as he entered the room. Usually, Ren had taken Gridley's easy bonhomie at face value. Today, with his new knowledge, Ren fought the urge to plant the man a facer and throw him out of the house. He'd not counted on such a visceral response.

'I am glad you have availed yourself of the hospitality.' Ren schooled his features, deciding to play the gracious host. How had Emma managed to tolerate the man for so long? No wonder she carried a knife beneath her skirts. If he'd had a knife on him, it would now be embedded in Gridley's black heart. Being in the same room with his cousin's murderer curdled his stomach.

The fist at his side clenched and unclenched at the sight of Gridley tucking into his food. But Ren couldn't give in to those baser emotions. He couldn't give any hint Emma had shared that information. Intuitively, he felt to do so would place Emma in grave danger. He fixed himself a plate since it would appear odd not to and sat at the table, even though sitting down with his cousin's murderer caused the bile to rise in his throat. Ren hoped he could give a decent facsimile of eating.

'What brings you over so early in the day?' It couldn't hurt to point out the hour, a subtle reminder that Gridley had called without an appointment.

'Early?' Gridley's sandy eyebrows went up. 'Eleven is hardly early.' He leaned forward with a chuckle. 'But maybe your nights are more exciting than the rest of ours. Is that it, eh?'

Ren met the implication with a stiff reply. 'I sense there is an inappropriate innuendo underlying your comment. If so, I take offence at it.' Not only did Gridley make a habit of arriving without invitation, he also seemed to be in the practice of slandering Emma in her own home. All minor sins, of course, compared to the one that lurked beneath the surface of those questionable behaviours.

The other man was not put off. He waved his hand in one of his dismissive gestures. 'Come now, Dryden, we are both men and we can be honest with each other. Emma Ward is past the first blush of innocence and a beauty besides. You wouldn't be a full-blooded male if you didn't notice the way she walks through a room, the sway of her hips, those lips, those eyes. You don't need to pretend with me.' He nodded at Ren's plate. 'Are you finished? If breakfast doesn't appeal, perhaps we might adjourn to the library? I have some things to discuss with you that require more privacy than a dining room affords.'

The movement offered a chance to drop Gridley's latest slur of Emma's character. Ren was beginning to think he'd have to call the man out. Such comments would not have gone unchallenged in London, to say nothing of murder. As hot as his blood was running right now, a duel was starting to look like quite the appealing option.

'Ahhhh,' Gridley exhaled as they stepped inside the library with its smells of leather and books. 'Albert and I spent hours in this room. His collection is excellent. He took a regular shipment of books that came every three months.' He smiled fondly at Ren. 'But these aren't the books I came to discuss. I came to discuss the accounts. Have you looked at them?' He ran a hand over the spines in a casual gesture. But Ren had Gridley's measure. Everything about the man was a facade designed to conceal the evil within.

'No, not yet. I imagine Emma and I will sit down and do a thorough rendering of them once the harvest is settled,' Ren said honestly. 'I don't have reason to think I'll find anything amiss, however.'

'I think that depends on your definition of "amiss", old chap.' Gridley faced him, his eyes friendly, tinged with the slightest hint of pity. Really, the man was a master at dissembling. 'We've all been losing money, the whole plantocracy. The hurricane four years ago was a costly disaster, which we might have survived if the Crown hadn't gone and abolished slavery and instituted this mixed-up apprentice system which is bleeding us dry with wages. All of it taken together has created something of an economic depression for us. Sugarland is no exception no matter what Emma tells you.'

Gridley was eyeing him, watching for a reaction. He was expecting shock, outrage. Ren was careful to show him neither, although inside he was starting to reel. Phrases like 'losing money' 'bleeding us dry' and 'economic depression' were digging a pit in his stomach. There was no need to panic yet, he told himself. 'It can't be that bad. You seem prosperous enough.' Ren smiled affably. 'I've seen the boots you wear, the opulence of your fine home. Those are not the signs of a man suffering hardship.'

Gridley met his smile with a patient one of his own.

'I suppose the quarterly cheque sent to your bank account didn't look desperate either.'

Ren tensed. He'd only received one quarterly cheque, the one issued after Cousin Merrimore's passing. It had looked fairly healthy. It had arrived after news of the will reached him. That cheque had been the deciding factor in his decision to come, to use the plantation as the bulwark that would stabilise his family's failing finances. He did *not* want to be told the cheque was a fraud.

He wasn't concerned about the money. It had been real enough when he'd spent it. However, Ren feared what that cheque represented wasn't. He'd been lured here under false pretences of prosperity. The feeling he'd experienced upon arrival of having been Trojan Horsed, resurfaced. His sisters, Teddy, his mother, were all counting on him, on this.

Consider the source. What does Gridley gain if you panic? The realisation carried a calming quality with it. Anything out of Gridley's mouth was highly suspect.

'Albert wouldn't tell you, although I insisted he should,' Gridley went on. 'Albert wanted to make sure you received the full share. I told him it would give you the wrong impression.'

Ren found Gridley's knowledge of his cousin's finances almost as disturbing as the news. 'I appreciate the insight.' Ren studied a shelf of books, gathering his thoughts.

'Of course, the cartel is an opportunity to turn things around,' Gridley offered in consoling tones. 'We're all in the depression together, we all might as well be in the success, too. This time next year, things could change if we all come together. It's true plantation prices are plummeting. There was a fellow in another parish who sold last year, a mere pittance really. It doesn't help that we're not the only ones growing cane any more. Now the Americans have crops and the other islands in the West Indies have turned to cane. But a cartel that can corner the market and control the supply can balance those scales.'

Ren nodded absently. In theory, Gridley spoke the truth. The venture was economically sound. It was the ethics of it that bothered him. He'd be throwing his lot in with people who treated their workers like slaves, people who for all intents and purposes, behaved as if slavery had not been abolished. There would be blood on any of the money he made through them. Yet, if he didn't take this opportunity, who would save his family? Who would help his sisters make matches worthy of them? Who would give his mother the comfort of her own home in her widowhood, or send Teddy to school? 'As I said, I haven't looked over the books.'

Gridley had taken up residence in a chair. 'I'm not sure at this point that looking over the books even matters. You need the money and even if you didn't, the rest of us do. Joining the cartel is the neighbourly thing to do. It would be selfish to hold the rest of us back.' Ren heard the threat. If he wasn't *for* them, he was *against* them.

Gridley studied his nails in another pose of feigned casualness. 'Miles is thinking of selling as it is. I'd hate to lose him. We've all been through a lot together, we're like family out here.'

A weird sort of family full of covetousness and lust, Ren thought. Family didn't make comments about one another that bordered on lecherous. He and Gridley must disagree about what family denoted.

'I know Emma doesn't want any part of it and I know that's why *you're* hesitating.' Gridley adopted a tone somewhere between a well-meaning older brother and a wise uncle. Ren thought it sounded condescending. 'She's got her delicious claws into you, there's no shame in admitting it. You're not the first man who has succumbed to her charms. You should ask her about Thompson Hunt some time.' Ren didn't want to hear about Thompson Hunt. Gridley's words were uncomfortably close to his own ruminations this morning.

'Don't play the offended gentleman with me, Dryden. Your defence of her honour does you credit, but she gave away her virtue long before you. She knows how to bring a man around to her point of view.' He held up a hand to stall Ren's burgeoning protest. 'You seem like an ambitious, smart man, Dryden. Think about it. Seeing the books would naturally be one of the first things a man like yourself would do in a venture like this. Don't make any more excuses. Yes, there was harvesting, but now it's over. She knows it's just a matter of time before you ask to see the accounts unless she can distract you, make you forget.'

Gridley paused. 'Face the truth, Dryden, regardless of what she's indicated, she doesn't want you here. Why would she? You threaten her autonomy. Where else on this earth can she be the mistress of her destiny, own property, have a man's life? She has two choices. She can send you packing or she can find some way to emasculate you and render your fifty-one per cent impotent.' Ren wondered if Gridley's crass references were deliberately sexual. The man seemed to have a one-track mind where sex and Emma were intertwined.

Gridley looked at him thoughtfully. 'Is she that good? Is she worth social castration? Because I assure you, that is exactly what will happen if you throw your lot in with her.'

'And yet you seem quite eager to marry her,' Ren ground out, fighting the urge to plant Gridley a facer for the umpteenth time that morning. If he'd had his way, Gridley's face would be black and blue and his mouth short a few teeth.

'I'd marry her to tame her, to control her,' Gridley answered. 'She's impulsive, wild and she will ruin the district if she's not brought to heel.' Something hot and lurid leapt in his eyes.

'I think you should leave.' Ren stood up.

Gridley rose and held out his hands, palms up. 'Remember, Dryden, I'm merely the messenger. Sex is her weapon. *You* look at the books, *you* talk to Emma. When you've seen the facts, you will come to the right decision.' He tapped his skull with his forefinger. 'Just make sure you're thinking with the right head when you do.'

Gridley was as audacious as they came. He probably should have taken a swing at the bastard anyway for marching in here, thinking he could dictate terms, thinking he could insult Emma, thinking he could insult Ren's own masculinity. There were so many reasons. But hitting Gridley for any of them accomplished nothing. The niggling worry that had taken up residence in his brain had become full bloom. *What if Gridley was right?*

One did not hit a man because he was right. An opinion wasn't necessarily wrong just because he didn't like the man who held it. Ren's mind reeled with *what ifs*. What if Emma had been using the attraction between them for her benefit? It wasn't as if he hadn't wondered that himself. What if she was miraculously able to fake such pleasure time and again? What if she was distracting him from seeing the truth of the accounts? What if Sugarland was indeed foundering in economic seas as Gridley suggested? He would be betrayed on all fronts. The few bites of breakfast sat like a rock in his stomach.

Ren drew a deep breath. He'd never know if he sat in the library sulking. He needed to see those books. Ren made his way to the office, half expecting to see Emma materialise on the stairs, but there was no sign of her. He was glad she had not been present for the interview with Gridley. The beginnings of a self-satisfied smile played on his lips. She was sleeping late because of him, because he'd kept her up half the night and then some; further proof that she felt *something* for him at least, further proof that Gridley wasn't entirely correct about the nature of their relationship.

In the office, Ren found the books behind a glass cabinet, each one neatly labelled by year. There was something reassuring, solid, about seeing decades of ledgers. Ren ran his hand over the spines. A place that lasted this long, that had passed from owner to owner through centuries even, couldn't be in dire straits. He found the ledgers from 1831 to present and pulled them out, deciding he would test Gridley's supposition that things had started to fail after the hurricane.

Ren seated himself behind the desk, opened the first ledger and began to read. He recognised his mistake right away. He needed to go back a few more years and see what the norm was before the hurricane. He went to the cabinet and pulled out the three years preceding 1831.

Those were good years. There was hope in the stories told by the columns and balances. But there was another story, too. The plantation did not diversify. It relied almost exclusively on cane for its export profits.

Ren sat back in his chair, absently rubbing at his temples. He'd file that bit of information away for another time. When it came to business, putting all of one's eggs in a single basket was not solid practice. It worried him that Sugarland had done so, especially if Gridley was right. It worried him, too, that the cartel was seeking to do the same thing. A monopoly might provide short-term financial solutions, but it wouldn't solve long-term problems. There would be other hurricanes, there would be other places establishing their own sugar-cane trade.

Ren reluctantly reached for the post-1831 ledgers. He suspected he'd read the good news. Now it was time for the bad, if Gridley was to be believed. He opened the first book.

An hour later he pushed the ledgers aside, fighting panic along with the facts. The money he'd thought Sugarland had was a myth. What would happen to his family now? Sarah and Annalise, Teddy and his mother, were all counting on him, on something that had never been.

The great adventure had failed before it had really begun. The ledgers told the whole story. By 1834, the downward pattern was clear. Gridley had been right. The pit in Ren's stomach clenched in sickening realisation. Ren reached for the bell pull. He had to confront Emma. If Gridley was right about the economics, what else was he right about?

A footman came right away. 'Tell Miss Ward I'd like to speak with her in the office immediately.' His voice sounded hollow even to himself. He'd been Trojan Horsed after all. The next question was how deep did the deception go? Had everything been a lie?

Chapter Seventeen

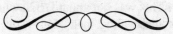

Emma answered the summons with no small amount of trepidation. She wanted to be angry. She wanted to rail: how dare he act with such presumption! How dare he think a night in her bed meant she was at his beck and call. It would be easier to be angry over the summons, but it would also be a lie.

She wasn't angry, she was nervous. What did Ren want? Hattie had told her Gridley had been here early. She'd opted for the coward's way out and let Ren handle him. Had Ren called for her as a result of Gridley's visit? What kind of vile rumour had Gridley let loose this time? Or had Ren called her for another reason? The thought of that reason set butterflies fluttering in her stomach in girlish anticipation. Perhaps that reason had to do with last night? The night had been erotic and beautiful and, heaven help her, it had meant something to her despite her vow to the contrary. Had it meant something to him, too?

Emma pressed a hand to her stomach, trying to still her nerves as she made her way down the hall toward the office. It wasn't supposed to be this way. She wasn't supposed to have fallen for her own ploy. She was to have been neutral and calculating, treating the sexual attraction between her and Ren with cool detachment. He was supposed to have been the one who was seduced.

Emma pushed open the office door and all thoughts of seduction fled at the sight of the ledgers spread open before him. This was not about Gridley or last night, but something else altogether.

Ren looked up at her entrance, his jaw tight, his skin ashen beneath his tan. 'Sugarland is losing money.' It was part accusation, part questioning disbelief.

He knew! Her stomach tightened. Yet another of her secrets was up. Would he blame her for it? Would he opt to use this as proof of her inability to run the place? Or use it as proof to force her into the cartel? Emma fought the urge to give any outward show of dismay.

'Sugar prices have dropped.' Emma decided to play it coolly. She would let him come to her with whatever had provoked this sudden desire to look in the books. She took a seat in a chair and arranged her skirts. *Show no fear!* It was the number-one rule of engagement with any man looking to get the upper hand.

'I can see that. Based on these numbers Gridley's cartel seems a good idea.' Ren's tone was cool as well, his blue eyes shrewd as they studied her, his demeanour distant. It was hard to believe this was the same man who'd been so passionately alive in her bed last night, who'd cried her name at climax, who had teased her so sinfully with his body.

The man behind the desk was detached and businesslike as he went on. 'But, of course, there are ethical, personal reasons why we can no longer pursue a cartel arrangement with Gridley no matter how much profit it offers. We will not do business with a murderer.'

Emma met his gaze calmly. Inside, she was a roiling mess of emotions. She hadn't lost him yet. He was still saying 'we', and he was aligning himself with her on the position of Gridley. Whatever Gridley had come to say, it had not swayed Ren into betraying her. She held Ren's gaze and went on the offensive.

'What prompted this sudden look at the accounts? I have to say it isn't the usual response after a night of rabid lovemaking.' She let her eyes flirt a bit, her gaze lingering on his mouth. Perhaps it wouldn't hurt to mix a little business with pleasure and strengthen the lure that currently bound him to her.

'Arthur Gridley paid me a call this morning before I was even out of bed.' Gridley had put Ren up to this? It was the worst prompt Emma could think of. She'd far rather have had the peek into the accounts prompted by his own curiosity. If Gridley had made the suggestion, it no doubt came with a personal commentary as well. She could imagine how Gridley would have shaped his case. But Gridley's arguments were for naught. Ren had already indicated as much, which meant Gridley hadn't provoked the ashen pallor beneath his tan.

'You should have sent for me. I would have met with him as well. If we are to be partners, we need to show a united front. Clearly, Gridley called for *you*, thinking we are not united.' Blame and misdirection were usually standard tools for launching an offensive. But Ren was quick to respond, not in the least stymied by her shift.

'Partners?' The anger rose in Ren's carefully controlled voice. 'You hid this from me. You led me to believe Sugarland was doing well.' He made a sweeping gesture towards the open ledgers in front of him. Emma's heart sank. This was about money. Well, now at least she knew.

'Omissions seem to be a habit for you. These ledgers are not all you haven't mentioned. You didn't tell me about the cartel and your efforts to resist it. I had to learn that from Gridley. You didn't tell me there isn't really a choice when it comes to that cartel. Despite our ethical reservations about doing business with a murderer, lack of participation in the cartel will make life unbearable for us, if not downright dangerous.'

Ren had risen, ticking off on his long fingers the list of her omissions.

'You're upset...' Emma began, hoping to placate him. His face was positively thunderous and she was reminded of the power of his presence. Ren's hand slammed the page of an open ledger in a forceful movement. She jumped, startled by the sound.

'Damn right I'm upset. I've travelled halfway around the world to discover I've not inherited a plantation, I've inherited a viper's nest!' He moved around the desk, halting in front of her, his height accentuated from where she sat, forcing her to look up. 'Everywhere I look, you're at the heart of it, Emma—you and Arthur Gridley with your schemes and secret histories.'

Oh, no, she was losing him. He might as well have

stabbed her with a knife if he was going to compare her to the likes of Gridley. Emma felt herself pale with real, desperate fear.

He narrowed his eyes, twin cobalt flames burning into her. 'Tell me, did you seduce me? I asked you last night, but you didn't give me a straight answer. Is this the reason why? Did you hope once I had a taste of your charms I'd not care what I found in the ledgers or anywhere else?'

'That is the outside of enough!' Emma rose swiftly, her hand making hard contact against his cheek with a resounding slap. 'I will *not* allow you to stand in this room and call me a whore when you know what I've been through, what I've had to fight. A woman has far fewer weapons at her disposal than a man.'

They were standing toe to toe, chests heaving with emotion. She could see a tic jump in his cheek. He was keeping himself barely leashed, the imprint of her palm red on his cheek.

'Answer the question, Emma,' Ren growled. 'Did you seduce me?'

Oh, mercy. She had hurt him, and in doing so she hurt herself, too, something she hadn't thought possible when he'd arrived. He'd been an object then, a stranger. The realisation that he had become more made her uncomfortable. She was a good person, she wasn't in the habit of scheming, of perpetrating evil, that was Gridley's market. Even more than that, she didn't want to hurt Ren, not even to protect Sugarland.

'It wasn't like that, not last night...' Emma began, resuming her seat. The heat of the fight had left her.

How to do this? Did she dare the truth? It would expose her entirely in ways that left her vulnerable. She drew a breath to steady her voice, her decision made. She would risk the truth if it meant keeping Ren. 'All right, maybe in the beginning I thought I might be able to use our attraction to my advantage.'

'Aha!' Ren accused.

'Let me explain,' Emma protested the interruption. 'If you want answers, you can't twist the facts.'

Ren nodded, backing off, giving her space while he opted to pace by the window and listen. 'That night when you claimed your forfeit, you wanted me, it was there in your eyes. I thought I could do it, I thought I could use that desire to keep control of Sugarland. But when it came right down to it, I couldn't.'

'And yet, we've had quite the last three days.' Ren's tone was cynical. 'I'm having trouble believing you had difficulty doing it. You seemed to be "doing it" quite well.'

Emma crossed the room, coming up behind him, her hands on his arms, her lips pressed to his back. 'Then believe this. I couldn't do it for the reasons I'd set out to do. I'd meant to use you, to bind you to me. But when the moment came, I only went forward because I wanted you for myself too much. I couldn't be neutral, detached. Everything that has happened, happened because I wanted it, not because it furthered some hidden agenda.'

He had to believe her! She'd given him the truth—what more was there to give him? If he refused to accept it, something valuable would be lost, broken beyond repair even if Sugarland was saved.

He turned, his body as stiff as his tone as he disengaged her hands and stepped away from her. 'All right. I will take that into consideration.'

It wasn't what she was hoping for. Desperation galvanised her. 'Ren, this is Gridley's divisiveness at work, I feel it.'

Ren merely nodded. 'I will take that into consideration, too. If you will excuse me, I have to go into Bridgetown.'

'Why?' Panic gripped her. He couldn't leave, not now when everything was a mess. She hated feeling this way. She was not one given to panic. It was testament to how deeply he'd affected her, how quickly his opinion had come to matter.

He fixed her with a steely stare. 'The way I see things, there're two problems at work. We have a plantation and a burgeoning relationship, both in jeopardy. I think I can save the former. I'm not sure about the latter. The plantation is worth my effort, I don't know if the relationship is.'

His words made her feel small and petty. She'd misplayed her hand with him from the start and now she had to pay. 'I'll come with you. We can talk over your ideas for the plantation on the way. I can help.' Emma stood up and smoothed her skirts, eager to mend fences, eager to earn back his trust and respect, assuming she'd had it in the first place.

Ren shook his head. 'No. I want to go alone. I think you've helped enough.'

Emma stood in silent shock, watching Ren walk away. It was the most complete dismissal she'd ever received. Goodness, it hurt. Never mind that she might have deserved it. In all fairness, he *had* walked into a viper's pit. There was much she had deliberately held back and even when the revelations had come out one by one, he'd borne each one reasonably. Except today. The money had bothered him greatly, the proverbial straw that had broken the camel's back. Why had the money mattered so much? At the moment, it seemed to matter more than her, more than her soul-exposing disclosure.

To her credit, she had meant what she'd said today. She had not given herself to him in the hopes of playing his desire against him. She welcomed his passion, welcomed the fire he raised in her. She'd taken him to her bed because she'd wanted him, because her body cried out for him. He made her feel alive, free.

A tear slipped down her cheek. Now he was gone. What had she done? 'Is that why you did it, Merry? Is that why you wanted him to come? To protect me?' she said aloud to the empty room. From the start, she'd seen Ren Dryden as a nuisance while Merry had seen him as something more. Not just for Sugarland, but for her, too. Emma had the sinking sensation that in her desire to protect the plantation, to protect herself, she'd inadvertently chased away the one man who could save them both.

Chapter Eighteen

'I need a secondary export to save Sugarland,' Ren said over ale in one of Bridgetown's less glamorous public houses where he'd found Kitt Sherard. When he'd left the plantation he'd known only that he needed to talk, needed to be listened to and needed to listen in return. In short, he needed a friend and Kitt was it. He'd hoped the entire five miles into town that Kitt would be in port.

'Is it as bad as all that?' Kitt eyed him over the foaming tankard.

'It will be. Sugar prices have continued to drop, the cost of labour will rise. The books are already showing the effects.' Ren pushed a hand through his hair. 'I think diversifying is an obvious answer. A second export would give us something substantial to fall back on in hard times.'

'May I suggest rum?' Kitt offered. 'Sugarland has its own still, if I recall.' He leaned forward and lowered his voice. 'Around here, most planters produce rum for themselves and for local businesses. But I'm talking about mass-producing the rum. Sugarland is large enough to have the molasses to do it. A lot of places don't have the resources to go big.'

'Where do I sell all this rum? It wouldn't be enough to just sell it here on the island.'

Kitt laughed and dropped his voice to a whisper. 'To the British navy, you numbskull. They're the world's largest consumer of rum. I also think you work on a special line. Sell the regular stuff to the navy. Their rum doesn't have to be fancy. Then start to make another rum designed for a finer palate, something that might appeal to all your snob friends back home. Run up the price on that. Snobs like to pay for their pleasures.'

Ren nodded slowly, processing the idea. They could start right away. With the harvest finished and the cane just now going to the mill, there would be fresh sugar-cane juice, a fresh supply of molasses. 'I don't suppose you could arrange for me to meet with the naval quartermaster?' Ren asked drily. He didn't think for a moment Kitt had offered this out of sheer humanitarianism.

Kitt's grin widened. 'Stay over in town with me tonight and you can see him tomorrow. I have an appointment to discuss other business with him.'

Ren leaned back against the wall, studying his friend. 'Is this what you've been doing for five years, Kitt? Running rum?'

Kitt nodded, unashamed. 'Pretty much. It's not illegal any more. But everyone in the islands needs it, wants it. Not everyone can produce it. The best rum in the islands comes out of Barbados. What I've discovered in these parts is that transportation is the key. It takes time to get from one point to another. The first thing I did when I arrived was buy myself a boat. I just started hauling whatever people needed delivered to wherever it needed to go.'

Ren didn't want to ask what some of that might have been. Kitt's code of ethics was a little different from his. But at least Kitt had one. Ren was starting to think that was a rare commodity on the island. He reached across the table and gripped Kitt's forearm. 'Thank you for this, my friend. I won't forget it.' One problem was potentially resolved if he could deliver the rum.

'What else is on your mind?' Kitt asked quietly. 'Is there more to this than finding a secondary source of income?'

Ren stared into his emptying tankard. Why not tell Kitt everything? It was surprisingly hard to talk about this latest intimacy, even with Kitt. They'd shared talk about women before plenty of times back in London, but those had been casual liaisons, society games. He and Emma were…different. What they had shared was sacred somehow, more personal, something he had just begun to realise before the doubts had set in.

Ren braved the disclosure with a carefully couched sentence. 'Things with Emma Ward have become complicated.' An understatement if ever there was one.

Kitt gave an embarrassingly loud hoot of laughter that drew stares towards their table. 'You bedded her! After all your protests about how you didn't think you had time for a woman.' He winked at Ren. 'There's always time for a woman when she's the right woman, isn't there? Emma's as pretty as they come and as prickly, too.'

Ren rubbed the back of his neck. 'I think she seduced me to minimise my power. I think she hoped if I bedded her, I wouldn't contest her authority.' He didn't want that to be true. Hearing the words out loud made them sound so cold, the complete antithesis to what he and Emma had shared.

'That you'd be too caught up in her charms?' Kitt nodded knowingly. 'That's no good, my friend.' He thought for a moment before leaning back in, his voice thankfully lower again. 'Why do you think that? Did you come up with that idea on your own or did someone suggest it?'

'In part, both. You know me, I'm an analyst. I'm always thinking of things from different angles. She wasn't pleased to see me the day I showed up and then a couple weeks later we're in bed. One might say that's quite an about-turn.' Only he hadn't seen it that way. He had been caught up in her flirtation and he'd been so sure of himself he hadn't thought to question things.

Kitt shrugged. 'You know how to turn a lady's head, Ren. I've seen you do it countless times in a ballroom. Even the stiffest old matron melts for you. I wouldn't underestimate your charm. Perhaps she saw your, ah, "potential" and changed her mind. But you said in part. What else influenced your conclusion? It wouldn't be Arthur Gridley, would it?'

'I had a rather unpleasant interview with him this morning,' Ren said. 'The subject came up, not for the first time.'

'Gridley's hot for her, has been for ages. He won't like her choosing you over him. I wouldn't let his opinion colour mine too much since he's got an agenda.' Kitt had made his point. 'As for me, I don't think it seems like something Emma Ward would do. If anyone in these parts has a social conscience, it's her. She supports an honest application of the apprenticeship programme, she pays a fair wage. She doesn't use people, but Arthur Gridley does.'

Ren thought about the day the chicken coop burnt down, how Emma had understood the request for time off and a chance to practice local customs. He thought, too, about his earlier argument with himself. She could not have feigned such passion.

He thought, too, about what she'd told him regarding Gridley. She didn't merely loathe the man, she feared him. She stood to lose more than a home if Gridley succeeded. She stood to lose her freedom, maybe even her life. Under those circumstances, even if she had used him, he could hardly blame her. In her situation, he might have done the same, although she'd suggested this morning that she'd not gone through with it for those reasons.

He might have lied to Kitt when he'd told him Emma had thought to prevent his usurping of her authority. He saw now that she hadn't set out to emasculate him, far from it. She wanted him to be her buffer. She didn't want him to run, she wanted him to stay. And he'd done just the opposite. He'd left her to fend for herself against Gridley. But perhaps he could remedy that situation ,too.

'Kitt, what do you know about Arthur Gridley…?' he began hesitantly—he'd already asked Kitt for so much.

Kitt shook his head. 'Nothing good. His background is a little murky, but that's true for a lot of folks out here looking for new beginnings. Beyond the obvious, why do you ask?'

'I have reason to believe he killed my cousin. I'd like to investigate, but…' Ren let the implication hang in the air.

Kitt nodded knowingly. 'I'll look into it and see if Gridley has the magistrate or the police force in his pocket.' Before they could bring charges, they had to determine if it would be safe to do so. If the officials were bribed, it would be dangerous and futile.

He'd done what he could for now to help Emma, a mere peace offering after their quarrel. Guilt swamped Ren. He'd been too hard on her. He'd been in financial shock, upset over the reality of Sugarland because it wasn't what he needed and he'd channelled some of that disappointment in her direction. He groaned when he thought of the hot words they'd spoken, the things he'd accused her of. They were not things a gentleman accused a lady of *ever*. 'I may have some apologising to do,' Ren murmured into the last of his ale.

'I know someone else who might have some to do, too…' Kitt began slowly. 'I know you have lady problems of your own. I hate to add one more, but there's something you need to see. Just don't kill the messenger.' Kitt slid an opened letter across the table. 'This came in my post. I happened to intercept the mail packet a little sooner than the rest of you.'

The letter was from London. Ren swallowed, his heart starting to race. There would only be a few reasons why Kitt would show him a personal letter. 'It's from Benedict,' Kitt supplied as Ren scanned the contents. Ren felt his nerves ease. Benedict DeBreed was wild, always up to something crazy.

'What has Ben got himself into this time?' Ren gave a chuckle.

'Matrimony.' Kitt answered. 'To your sister. It's all in there. He even included the announcement from *The Times.*'

Ren looked at the newspaper clipping in disbelief.

Mr Benedict DeBreed announces his engagement to Lady Sarah Dryden, sister to the Earl of Dartmoor.

'Apparently, Benedict has come into some money, a tin mine or something.' Kitt said tentatively.

Sarah was going to marry one of London's most notorious bounders? How had this happened? But Ren knew. Rumour of their finances must have got out. 'I asked Benedict to watch over the family, not to marry into it,' Ren muttered. Benedict was a good friend, a loyal one, but that didn't mean he wanted a rake marrying his sister. Sarah must have felt forced to it, must have felt there was no other choice. Ren looked at the postmark. They might be married already if Benedict had proposed in haste. Even so, there was nothing he could do at a distance.

'This is my fault.' Ren groaned. He should have been

there. He was feeling selfish. He'd come for a lot of reasons, but especially to escape his own matrimonial entanglement. Now, his sister had gone and done the unthinkable. 'I should have come up with a better solution.'

'Short of marrying that horse-faced heiress out of York, I don't know what that solution would have been.' Kitt reminded him.

'Perhaps I should have. Then Sarah wouldn't have had to marry DeBreed.'

'Maybe she wanted to. DeBreed's handsome, now he's rich. He's a legend in bed.' Kitt shrugged, not taking the issue with half as much seriousness. Then again, Kitt didn't have sisters.

'Shut up, Kitt,' Ren growled.

'What? You don't want your sister to enjoy marriage?' Kitt was brimming with laughter. 'If I had a sister, I'd want her to enjoy certain aspects of marriage.'

'Well, you don't, so you hardly know what you're talking about.' Ren tried to keep a straight face. The conversation was so ridiculous it was hard to scold Kitt for his crassness. Ren lost the battle, his face breaking into a grin. 'I had forgotten just how pathetic you are, Kitt. Thanks for reminding me.'

Kitt reached over and clapped him on the shoulder. 'Don't worry. DeBreed might be wild, but deep down inside, and when I say deep, I mean pretty deep, it is DeBreed we're talking about after all, he's a decent fellow. Besides, Sarah's a big girl. She can take care of herself and you have your new rum enterprise. I think you're missing the silver lining here. Sarah's married money and you're making money. The great Dartmoor line will be in the black in no time at all.' Kitt raised his hand and called for another round. 'Tonight, *you* should be celebrating.' He grinned. 'And I'll help.'

It didn't help matters that Ren hadn't come home the previous night from Bridgetown. How could she apologise? How could she win him back if he wasn't here? Emma looked out the front-room window for the millionth time since the sun had started to sink. There was no sign of life in the long drive. To hell with peeking out the windows. She was going to sit on the porch and stare down the road until he showed up. And she did, until it was too dark to see. So much for that idea.

The sun was completely gone and even with the assistance of a lantern, there was only so much visibility. That was when she decided it: she would wait for him in his bed. That way, even if she fell asleep, she wouldn't miss his return and he wouldn't be able to overlook her. For the first time since his arrival, she was regretting putting him in the *garçonnière*. It would be far more convenient to have him in one of the bedchambers in the main house near her.

Emma smiled when she entered his rooms. At least this would be private. Privacy would be welcomed if everything went well. She changed into her nightgown, a filmy white confection of lace and chiffon. She took down her hair and brushed it out. Then she settled into his bed to wait, knowing full well it would be hard for him to resist. She'd seen herself in the long mirror in the corner, her hair loose, her gown doing little to conceal her feminine assets.

She breathed in the scent of the linens. They smelled like him, all vanilla and sandalwood. She looked around the room, noting the little changes he'd made with the furniture, seeing the personal effects he'd set out. It was tempting to get out of bed and look at those items up close. Emma talked herself out of it. If she was going to earn back his trust, the last thing she needed to be caught doing was going through his belongings.

Waiting was boring. Snooping was starting to look more appealing. She had to do *something*. Emma opted for the book on his bedside table. She hoped for poetry, or a novel. What she got was an agricultural treatise on the Caribbean, interesting as far as research went. In other circumstances she might have enjoyed it. But in terms of keeping a girl awake, Emma had her doubts about its effectiveness. She made it through two pages before she began to yawn...

The sound of booted feet woke her with a jolt. She experienced a moment of panic, a sense of being invaded before she realised where she was and who was coming through the door. Ren! He was home. A surge of elation replaced the panic. She rose up on her elbows. 'Hello, stranger,' she said in her best sultry tones.

Ren grinned. 'You make coming home worthwhile. I could get used to a sight like that. I was starting to think I'd never make it back.' He came over to the bed and sat down. He did look exhausted. She couldn't recall ever having seen him look so entirely unkempt even after a day of riding the estate. His clothes were wrinkled, his shirt cuffs looked dingy where they peeped out from his jacket sleeve.

He leaned forward to pull his boots off. 'Those were the longest five miles ever. I misjudged how much time I'd need and I left it too late to get home before the sun set. I misjudged the darkness, too, that's pitch black out there. No lamplights, no nothing.'

Emma smiled and scooted over to him. 'I'm just glad you're home. You are right, though, the darkness can be dangerous. People get lost, wander into the interior, stumble on to a snake, and it's too late by the time we find them.' She meant to put her arms about his neck, to hold him close, let him feel the press of her breasts and remind him of what they could share but she recoiled at the last moment. 'Eww, you stink! Ren Dryden, you're drunk!'

Not even on the good stuff either. His clothes reeked of cheap ale and brandy—well, maybe the brandy was higher quality, it was hard to tell. No wonder he'd misjudged the time, no wonder he looked so dishevelled. Emma threw back the covers and slid out of bed. 'I'm disgusted with you! You left here and went straight to Bridgetown for a drinking binge without even telling me how long you would be gone. I've been here, worrying while you've been out doing who knows what with who knows whom.'

But she did know with whom—with the disreputable Kitt Sherard. And she probably did know what, too. Had he really left her bed and found another so quickly? Her heart sank, her visions of a happy reunion fading.

Could she blame him? He'd left Sugarland believing she'd used him, believing there was nothing between them that required any loyalty.

She started towards the door, only to feel Ren's hand close over her arm. For a drunk man, he moved fast and in a straight line. 'Em, wait. It's not like that. Yes, I've been with Kitt. He spilled an ale, it got all over me, and, yes, things got a little wild, but I wasn't on a binge. I was at a meeting Kitt set up.' He forced her to turn and look at him and those beautiful blue eyes, which were clear. It would be easier to stay angry if he had been drunk.

'Em, listen to me. I found a way to increase our revenue. I have a contract with the British Navy to sell them rum, casks and casks of it.'

She stared, her brow knitting as she tried to process what he had said. Then the implications hit her and she felt her mouth drop. 'We won't have to rely solely on sugar any more. Ren, do you know what this means?' She hardly noticed his smelly clothes as her mind raced with the possibilities. 'We could branch out, make a special label for a finer-quality rum.'

Ren laughed. 'You might not like Sherard, but you sound an awful lot like him. That was his suggestion, too.'

There was hope after all. She wasn't fighting a losing battle. Ren had come back and he'd brought an answer with him. She threw her arms about his neck and kissed him full on the mouth. But Ren did not respond. Instead, he put his hands on her hips and set her away from him.

'Emma, this is an answer to *one* of our problems, not

all of our problems. Even if we're successful with the rum, the cartel will not be happy. Gridley has suggested quite openly they will retaliate if we don't comply.'

Emma shook her head. 'Tonight I don't care. Tonight I'm just glad you're home. Ren, I'm so sorry.' She reached for him again and again he sidestepped her advances.

Ren looked at her, his eyes serious. 'Are you? Are you excited about the rum, or about me? I need you to be sure. No man wants to be appreciated solely for his fifty-one per cent.'

Emma answered his stare with an even gaze of her own. 'I came to this room to wait for *you*. You know it's true because I had no knowledge of your deal with Kitt, or if you would be back tonight. I don't know what we can be to each other, or even what we want to be to each other. You're right. That remains to be sorted out. But I do know what I want from you has nothing to do with your fifty-one per cent and a hundred per cent to do with the man.' Emma took his hand. 'I want you naked in bed, Ren Dryden. But before your ego gets too inflated, it's because you'd stink up the sheets otherwise.'

Ren swept her a bow. 'Your wish is granted. Naked I will be. It's no trouble since I sleep naked anyway.' He winked.

'Yes,' Emma said drily, climbing up on the bed to watch. 'I seem to recall it was one of the first things I learned about you. You were so eager to impart that piece of information at the time.'

Ren pulled off his coat and tossed it to a corner. 'I

will bathe if you want me to,' he offered, his fingers working the buttons of his shirt.

Emma shook her head. 'Here's a little something you should know about me. I'm impatient and I've waited too long for you already.' To prove it, she pulled her nightgown up over her head and tossed it into the corner with his coat.

Chapter Nineteen

Dryden was back. Gridley's little spy had reported first thing in the morning. He wasn't surprised, but he'd hoped to get a lucky break. The mail packet was due in soon and it would be perfect timing for Dryden to make his exit.

Gridley drummed his fingers on his desktop. The fact that Dryden had returned worried him. It meant there'd been a reason to come back even after the nudge he'd given the man. What more could he do to convince Dryden? He'd shown Emma to be a woman of loose morals, a manipulator of men. He'd all but opened the books and put them under Dryden's nose to round out the impression Emma had deluded him. All the things Dryden had come to believe in had been exposed and found wanting. Yet he'd come back. Did it mean he was going to join the cartel? Or did it mean he'd found a way to revive Sugarland's flagging profits outside of the cartel? Or worse, there was always an outside chance Dryden had come back for Emma. If he had, it was only a matter of time before Dryden knew Gridley's dirty little secret. He couldn't rely on Emma keeping that quiet forever.

He looked up as a servant announced the arrival of Hugh Devore. Normally, Arthur liked to plan alone and announce his intentions after the fact. Today, he'd felt the need for reinforcements.

'Dryden has certainly thrown a wrench in our plans.' Devore settled into a chair and crossed a leg over one knee, cutting straight to the heart of the matter. 'It was one thing when we thought he'd be gone, or that we could rely on Emma helping us along with her own desire to be rid of him. But it seems that has changed. He means to stay and Emma has figured out he can be an ally.'

'Exactly,' Arthur agreed with Devore's assessment. 'The problem is what to do next? Anything we do, short of ignoring Sugarland's choices, will commit us irrevocably to a path of division. It will openly be us against them.' He preferred more covert tactics that relied on assumed friendships, the building of trust and then the ultimate betrayal with him riding to the rescue, no one the wiser as to his part in bringing the crisis about in the first place.

Devore thought for a moment. 'We need to reshape the way we've looked at our options. We have always built our assumptions around the premise that Sugarland had to be factored into our plans. We've tried to buy it, tried to marry into it, tried to partner with it. None of those options have worked. What if it was just gone, no longer a variable to contend with?'

Interesting and risky. Arthur leaned forward. 'How would we do it? Eliminate the players or the thing we're playing for?' He was a little nervous, too. He'd always engineered the plots, making sure he was in a position to use Sugarland as leverage to force Emma. 'With Sugarland gone, I would lose a powerful piece of persuasion.'

'Would you?' Devore queried. 'She'd be completely exposed without the plantation, her source of income gone, her source of stability gone. She'd be homeless, nothing more than a rabbit flushed from the brush running without cover. Perhaps she'd see what you have to offer differently. Right now, a home doesn't mean much to her because she has one. Neither does an income, or a lover,' Devore said pointedly.

'We could have done without the last,' Arthur growled. It galled him to know Dryden had superseded him in all ways.

Devore steepled his hands over his stomach. 'It's a simple case of supply and demand. Everything is in the end.'

Arthur gave Devore's advice a considering nod. 'We get rid of Dryden, we burn Sugarland. But Emma remains unharmed. I must have that last condition. I promised Albert Merrimore…'

Devore gave a harsh laugh. 'Right before you put a pillow over the old man's face. Don't get sanctimonious on me, Arthur. You'd make promises to the devil if it advanced your cause. Not that I have a problem with that. I understand you and you understand me. We're businessmen, cut from the same cloth. We're both ruthless when it comes to something we want. Still, I want the cartel, you want the girl. I think that can be arranged.'

'When do we do it?' Arthur was warming to the idea now that he could see the benefits. Really, the plan was almost too good to be true. They would get their cartel, sugar prices would go up, Dryden would conveniently go away, Emma would be his either by coercion or by persuasion.

'I think soon. Crop Over happens at the end of the week. All the workers will head to Bridgetown for the celebrations.'

'It should be a fire,' Gridley said. He didn't want Devore calling all the shots, it would give the man an exalted sense of his own power and make him forgetful of who led their exclusive coterie. 'They've already had one fire with that chicken coop. There's precedence.'

'Precedence for arson.' Devore gave an evil grin. 'I don't believe for a moment that coop burned on its own.'

Gridley returned the grin. 'It had help.' Never mind that the ploy hadn't worked as effectively as he'd hoped. The plan had been to have a minor catastrophe that would scare off enough of Emma's work force to subvert her ability to harvest. But Dryden had chosen that day to show up unannounced. Dryden had taken charge. There'd been little Arthur could do to work up panic among the workers by the time he'd arrived, short of making sure everyone saw the obeah doll he'd planted among the ashes. It had cost Emma a half day's labour, but nothing more. Until now. That fire was going to be useful after all.

'How do we take care of Dryden?' Devore enquired.

Burn him along with the house, lose him in the interior, set him aboard a ship sailing for parts unknown. Arthur could devise any number of unfortunate accidents. This would be one area, however, where he wouldn't mind Devore taking the lead. He'd handled Merrimore, clearing the way to leaving Emma open to the next layer of their attempts. Now it was someone else's turn. Devore could handle Dryden. Then, if it became convenient to expose Devore to Emma in the future to win her affections, he'd be able to turn on Devore. Ah, yes, things were starting to come together nicely.

The morning was starting well: Emma tucked against him, his body replete with sexual satisfaction. Two out of three wasn't bad. Any gambling man would take those odds. Unfortunately, Ren wasn't so much a gambler as he was a perfectionist. He'd prefer three out of three, but he couldn't get his mind to conform, to accept the here and now without looking forward to the future. How would the here and now affect the later? He was an analyst, too, along with being a perfectionist and both of those qualities were wreaking havoc with his mind at the moment.

Emma stirred against his shoulder, her dark hair grazing his chest. Ren looked down at his sleeping beauty. What was he going to do with her? She'd stirred his passions from the moment he'd laid eyes on her. But it had all happened so fast. In many ways she was a stranger still. Every revelation proved it. The very idea that Gridley's insinuations had the power to at least sow doubt reinforced that proof as did her own reticence to be forthcoming with him. And yet, he was drawn to her. He didn't want to let her go, but to what end?

His options were few. There was only one choice really. If he meant to keep her, to make her his, he should marry her. If he didn't marry her, he'd have to walk away. The island wasn't big enough for both of them. Walking away would mean returning to England. It was the more logical choice. He could open up an office in England to oversee the rum imports. He could build the business from that end and still be able to run the earldom as he should instead of at a distance through solicitors. He could be on hand to take care of his family, to make sure there were no more disasters, like Sarah marrying Benedict.

Perhaps he'd always known it would come to this. He'd wanted to believe coming here would be a new start, a new life for him. But deep down, perhaps he'd known it couldn't be permanent. He was the earl, he had responsibilities. If it came to choosing between Emma and his family, there wasn't really a choice. There couldn't be.

No matter that he honestly liked it here. Kitt was right, one got used to the heat. He loved the beaches, the ocean, the lush colours of sky and grass, the informality of life, the ability to work for that life. Did staying here preclude going home ever? That was the one issue he'd refused to address when he'd left home— would he ever return? It wasn't that he minded *not* seeing England again, but he did very much mind the idea that he would never see his family again, that his only contact with them would be through letters. He should have been there to negotiate Sarah's marriage settlement. He should have been there to head DeBreed off in the first place.

You could take Emma with you, came the niggling thought. *Why not become an absentee landlord like so many in the other parishes? Peter is a trustworthy overseer. With him in charge, you could keep an eye on the business from England.* Emma could be his countess in the truest sense. If he married her, she'd be a countess wherever they were, but in London it would count. London would require a certain lifestyle. He tried to imagine Emma there, navigating a ball, turning away the envious gentlemen that would flock to her side. He tried to imagine what his family would make of her. And he failed. Not because it was impossible to see her succeed, but because he couldn't see her being happy.

Gone would be the Emma who strode about the plantation in breeches. What would she wake up and do each day? He couldn't see her happily assimilating into a lady's routine of shopping, teas and charity work. The Emma he knew would be bored within a month. He knew in his gut, London would be nothing more than a cage for her.

In the light of morning, his choices seemed crystal clear. Keeping Emma meant staying here, making Sugarland his home and protecting Emma from Gridley. Marriage would be the best protection Ren could provide her. It would put her beyond Gridley's reach. Ren could see himself happily piecing together that life. Although there were trade-offs. Certainly, he might return to England occasionally as Merrimore had done, but he'd become an absentee earl in truth. It was possible to pull it off. He had good solicitors, a regular mail service and DeBreed would be there now with some legal power as a brother-in-law to oversee things until Teddy was old enough.

If he *didn't* marry Emma, it meant leaving and soon. It wasn't fair to her or to him to carry on this affair indefinitely if nothing was to come of it. He selected a deadline in his mind. The end of August. There would be time to deal with Gridley. He couldn't begin to think of leaving Emma alone with Gridley on the loose. Their rum business would be up and running by then, too; everything under control to a point where Emma could manage it and he would be waiting on the other side to receive the shipments. He might even make it home in time for Sarah's wedding if he wrote and told them to wait, that he was coming.

Emma lifted her head, her hair was tousled, her voice sleepy. 'You're awake. You should have woken me. We could have got our day started.'

'There's no hurry.' The logic of his earlier analysis started to slip. What man left *this* behind? What sort of man gave up a woman like Emma? He could almost hear Kitt laughing in his head—*only a fool, Ren.* 'Where did you want to start your day?'

She laughed, a low throaty sound, as she swung a leg over his hip. 'In bed, the same place I finished it. Then, we should ride out and see the still.'

It occurred to Ren as she straddled him that Emma was a woman who knew what she wanted and he hadn't worked that into the equation of his thoughts. He'd been concerned about what he wanted. Did *she* want to marry him? Maybe she'd be happy enough to see him leave in August? This wasn't going to be a decision he could make on his own. He would have to discuss it with her and her answers would affect the outcome. But in order to discuss it, he would have to tell her who he was in his other life and why he was really here. Rather belatedly, he realised the shoe was on the other foot now—his foot—and it pinched. Once she knew, she would be justified in pinning on him the same secrecy he'd accused her of.

His thoughts had come full circle. No matter how much he thought about it, they were still just two strangers in bed together and it was as much his fault as hers. Fortunately, Emma reached between his legs and stroked him into readiness, saving him from having to think too much with his brain. He was much preferring a different kind of logic at the moment.

Emma was almost giddy with excitement at the still. The prospect of starting up a new business was a heady one. She might have been entirely given to giddiness if she hadn't sensed Ren's distraction so strongly. He'd been distracted during lovemaking. She'd climaxed without him, their morning coupling lacking the intense connection that had marked their other joinings.

He was distracted now, too, although he was making a valiant effort to hide it. They'd talked about rum on the ride out to the distillery. He told her the details about his meeting with the quartermaster, how he'd already placed an order with a cooper in town for the casks they'd need. But his mind was only partly on the conversation. She wondered what else he might have done or discovered in town to bring on such distraction or if the distraction stemmed from something internal, perhaps remnants of their quarrel. She wasn't naive enough to think those more interpersonal issues had been fixed just because business had been resolved.

'There won't be an immediate profit, but you should see one by next year,' Ren was saying as they stepped outside the distillery and into the sunlight.

Ah, that was it. Emma halted, her heart sinking. She caught the discrepancy right away. 'Don't you mean "we"? *We* will see the profit?'

'Of course, I meant "we".' Ren smiled and tried for some humour. 'We'll be bound together forever through this place. You'll never really get rid of me.'

She knew instantly where this was leading. The man who'd declared he was here to stay had decided he was leaving. Maybe he wasn't leaving tomorrow or on the next packet, but he was moving in that direction. How much time did they have? Two months? Three? Everything had suddenly become short-term. 'You've decided the Caribbean doesn't agree with you,' Emma said matter-of-factly. Maybe it was the Caribbean that didn't agree or maybe it was her. Perhaps he'd decided they didn't suit. 'When did this happen?'

They stopped under the shade of a tall palm. Ren took off his straw hat and ran a hand through his hair. 'I didn't say anything about leaving.'

'Do not play semantic games with me,' Emma cautioned sharply. 'Something has happened. Is it Gridley again with his fallacious claims?'

Ren put his hat back on and shook his head. 'It's personal and it's more complicated than that. Emma, I can't stay and continue to compromise you. Already Gridley is spreading talk. I don't think I can just be your business partner. I can't be here and simply stop the affair. I want you too badly. It would be torture to live under that roof, to see you, to work with you every day and not have you. The sacrifice wouldn't be enough anyway. Even if I were to play the monk, no one would believe it.'

Emma turned away from him, her emotions stirring to the surface. Part of her was flattered. No man had ever shown her such a fine consideration. Part of her knew it was too fine. 'Your concern for my reputation is quite chivalrous, not that I have much of a reputation left to protect. But I'm not foolish enough to believe that is enough to send you back to England. There's more.'

She heard his hesitation in the silence that followed. 'My sister is getting married. Kitt had a letter arrive with the news while I was in Bridgetown.' He paused, perhaps realising as she did how incomplete that explanation was. People could travel. Weddings were not occasions that required him to stay in England permanently. A wedding did not explain his earlier chivalry. He started again slowly. 'Did Cousin Merrimore tell you anything about me? About my family?'

'No.' What she did know about Merry's family was very general. They were thousands of miles away and he had no immediate family. Knowing cousins and relatives Merry hardly knew himself hadn't seemed a priority. They'd had each other and that had been family enough. Until now. 'I think he said once that he was a relative of your mother.'

'He was a cousin of my mother's father,' Ren supplied. 'My mother's family is landed gentry out of the south-east of England, Sussex area. They're comfortable landowners with a nice income for their station. But my mother wasn't satisfied with that lifestyle. She went to London for a Season and aimed a little higher. She came home betrothed to the heir to the Earl of Dartmoor, one of the finest catches of that Season.'

Pieces slid together in a terrifying puzzle in her mind. Ren's father was an earl. Emma recalled bits of other conversations. His father was deceased; Ren had told her as much that day on the beach. His brother, the one called Teddy, was younger than Ren. She felt the truth overwhelm her. She'd always known he was a gentleman, it had been there in his clothes, his bearing, his manners, the way he'd taken charge the day of the fire. That wasn't surprising. She'd known Merry was from a comfortably situated family. It had stood to reason his distant cousin would share some of that comfortable life, but she'd not dreamed of the extent. Emma braced an arm against the palm-tree trunk, oblivious to the prickly bark cutting into her hand as she tried to take it all in. 'You're the earl!'

She felt him move towards her. 'I'm still Ren Dryden, I'm still just a man. This doesn't change anything.'

Emma whirled on him, not sure what emotion to feel first: anger, betrayal, hypocrisy. He'd been so worried about what she'd held back, so upset about the viper's pit she'd led him into and the whole time he'd withheld the truth of himself. 'Yes, it does. You've already admitted it. You wouldn't be leaving otherwise. *This* changes everything.'

Chapter Twenty

'It doesn't change the important things.' Ren was trying to placate her with comforting reassurances. It was a sweet gesture, a protective gesture and she was absolutely *not* in the mood for either.

'Stop right there. Do not give me platitudes about how it doesn't change your feelings for me. You have no idea what those feelings are.' Those feelings hardly mattered now. She should have refused the temptation of taking those feelings out and looking too closely at them before reality struck. Earls didn't marry daughters of colonels. They didn't marry women who hadn't set foot inside English society since they were eight and earls certainly didn't wed women who carried scandal for a calling card. If she showed up in England with Ren, there would be curiosity and curiosity would lead to enquiries. Eventually, her sordid past would come out. Earls needed pure innocent girls to be their countesses. Nothing could come of Ren's feelings even if they ran deep. It was best if he realised that before he decided chivalry could take forms other than leaving. Who was she fooling? It would be best for her, too.

'Perhaps we should talk about this back at the house,' Ren suggested. 'I've picked a poor place for this discussion.'

'No, we'll talk about it now.' Emma drew a deep breath to steady her mind. 'There's too great of an opportunity for interruption. We'll have privacy here.' Her thoughts were starting to move past the initial shock. 'What else don't I know, Ren? What are you really doing here?' Not for the first time, she wondered why he'd bothered to come at all, especially now when it was clear he had demanding responsibilities in England. Adventurers and businessmen could move around. But Ren was neither. Earls did not have the luxury of that freedom.

By silent, mutual consent, they started to walk. Ren was reluctant to talk. His words came haltingly. 'I'm here because the earldom is nearly broke and Cousin Merrimore's inheritance looked like manna from heaven at the time, a chance to restore our fortunes. I had to come and see if that was true.'

Guilt consumed her. She could have stopped that journey if she'd written, if she'd done more than wait around to see if he'd come or not. She could have written about the truth of that last payment to his account, that it reflected an illusion. She'd gone without her usual allowance to make that payment. He would have known from the start there was no real money. That would have changed everything.

Perhaps not for the best for her at least. What if he'd

sold his share? What if he hadn't come? She would have had to face Gridley alone and possibly a second villain in the form of the new owner. She never would have stumbled on the rum contract. How long would she have lasted without Ren? She felt less guilty now, but a lot more selfish.

'I could have managed the inheritance from England, but I wanted to come. I was selfish.'

The words so closely mirrored her sentiments, Emma thought for a moment she'd spoken out loud. 'I beg your pardon?'

'I was selfish,' Ren repeated. 'This was an escape from an arranged but unwanted marriage.'

There was another woman! Her head swam. She'd desperately wanted to believe Ren was different from the men she'd known. She'd been terribly wrong. Did all men have women stashed in every corner of their lives? This was shaping up to be a rather unpleasant morning all around. 'How do you mean unwanted? Unwanted as in you didn't want to go through with it, or unwanted as in you *did* go through with it under duress?' She stopped walking and fixed him with a stare. 'I will not be a party to adultery or bigamy or anything of the sort.' The thought of encountering such circumstances a second time after Thompson Hunt made her stomach churn. She was supposed to have been smarter now.

Ren shook his head. 'I'm not married. I couldn't go through with it. There was an heiress in York who was willing to trade her fortune for my title, but we did not suit.'

Emma breathed easier. Not quite Thompson Hunt,

then. She was still free to believe Ren was different; upstanding and noble. 'It's not selfish to avoid unhappiness.' She knew a thing or two about that.

Ren gave her a sharp look. 'It is when your sister sacrifices herself on the matrimonial altar in your place.'

'*She* married the York heiress?' Emma wasn't following the twist and turns of the story.

'No, she's marrying, or has already married, a man for his wealth in order to save the family from scandal. She did what I should have done.'

His remorse was palpable and it moved her. Above all, Ren Dryden was a responsible man. If the weeks of knowing him had shown her anything of the man it was that. 'Is the money that important?' She felt impotent. She would give him the world if it was hers to offer. But she didn't have the kind of money he was looking for. No wonder the ledgers had upset him. He'd come looking for the pot of gold.

'The money is everything, or was.' Ren paused. 'I suppose everything has worked out for now.'

But not the way he'd planned. Clearly, these new developments pained him. He'd been the one who had thought to provide for the family and given time, he would be, if he could just see that. Meanwhile, she hurt for him. When had she started to care so much about this man? It had been easier to fathom him when he was nothing more than an adventurer looking for fast money. She might be wary of such men, but at least she understood them. The islands were full of such men, every last one of them looking for an opportunity to make riches, men like Kitt Sherard. Ren Dryden was entirely out of her league. She didn't know what to do with a man of principle. Her experience there was admittedly limited.

'Is he a good man?' Emma could think of nothing else to say that would assuage Ren's guilt or feelings of failure.

Ren nodded. 'He's a good friend of mine.'

'Then he's a good man. I can't imagine you having bad friends.'

'What about Kitt Sherard? We went to school together.' Ren stopped himself from saying any more. Kitt had his secrets.

'You're trying to pick a fight now and we're not discussing Kitt Sherard. We're discussing you,' she gently reminded him. If they wanted to quarrel there was plenty of more immediate material to fight over than Sherard. 'Do you really see leaving as your only choice?' She brought the focus of the conversation into sharp relief with her words.

Ren faced her, his face serious, his eyes sombre. 'If I stayed, we'd be talking about marriage. We cannot live under the same roof without its protection. I could not do that to you.'

'That's definitely not the most romantic of proposals.' Duty and obligation were written all over his suggestion and not an ounce of feeling, or love. However, she'd reached for the fairy tale once before and found it to be just that. Fairy tales weren't real. Neither were Prince Charmings. The fairy tale had been overrated. 'It would be no different from what you left England to escape, a marriage of convenience,' Emma posited.

Ren shrugged. 'Perhaps we can't really run from our fates.'

Emma shook her head and stepped away. If he touched her, she would lose control and she did not want to cry. It would be too easy to fall in love with him. She suspected she was already a good portion of the way there. To completely fall and to know he only saw her as an expeditious arrangement that suited him in bed and out would break what was left of her heart. 'I'm sorry, Ren. I couldn't do that to me. I am selfish, too. I need to be more than a man's convenience. In truth, I couldn't do it to you either.'

'I haven't even asked.' Ren tried to smile, but she could see that her outright refusal had surprised him. She realised he'd already tried the idea on in his mind and found the offer probable. He thought he could be comfortable with it. She ought to be flattered. An earl didn't come asking for her hand every day. But he was only asking because he didn't know better.

He studied her for a moment. 'I understand your reticence. I can only tell you I don't think it would be like that.'

They started walking again as if they could put distance between themselves and the awkward subject if they moved the space that had witnessed it. 'Have you ever thought Cousin Merrimore wanted us to marry?' Ren said after a while. 'Maybe that was why he divided the estate as he did?'

'No. It's a fairy tale of a thought, Ren, the perfect happy-ever-after is an impossibility under the best of circumstances. Merrimore knew better.' She paused, holding on to the last of her damning secrets for a moment. 'He watched my first marriage fall apart.'

It was her turn to stun him and that did it. If anything could trump the disclosure that Sugarland's majority shareholder was an earl in his other life, this was it. But all Ren said was, 'Perhaps you should tell me about it.'

She was glad they were walking. Talking was easier when the rest of her body had something to do. She didn't have to look at Ren and watch his reaction to just how ruined she was. What had happened had happened almost nine years ago and she'd thought she'd put her past behind her. More importantly, she'd thought she'd come to terms with it. Ren's arrival had shown her she had not. He tempted her to make the same mistakes again. More than that, he'd shown her what an imperfect shambles her life was without even meaning to do it. She was a treasure trove of scandal.

'I married at eighteen, perhaps too young, although lots of girls marry before they're twenty. I was dazzled by him and I rushed in. In retrospect, I think it was because I was lonely after my father's death. I had no family, no sense of place, except for what Merry had given me. But I was acutely aware of how temporary that might be. I wanted something solid of my own. I wanted to build a family that was mine, something to replace all that I'd missed in my nomadic childhood.'

The parallels to what was happening right now were overwhelming in their symmetry; the death of a close protector spurring her to subconsciously cast about for a replacement. Her father's death had encouraged her towards an early marriage, and now Merry's death was encouraging her towards Ren. She'd always thought of herself as strong and independent, but this pattern indicated otherwise.

She slipped a sideways glance at Ren. He nodded, focused on the outer story itself. 'You felt this man could give you those things?' He was taking it all in with a great deal of calm, she thought. But he didn't see the parallels yet. He didn't understand this story was a form of rejection, full of reasons why she couldn't marry him if for no other reason than to prove to herself she'd learned something from her past and would not repeat those errors.

'All that and more,' she admitted honestly. 'He was comfortably situated. He was older, in his late thirties. He'd been married before. He seemed to know everything about the world. He could make me laugh, he showered me with little gifts. He always had a little treat in his pocket, a ribbon or a bonbon. I worshipped him. He was Prince Charming, so handsome and gallant. Merry encouraged me to wait, to give it more time, but I didn't want to. I was afraid he'd leave and never come back. After two months of courtship, I married him. Merry gave us a lovely wedding in the gardens. Then it all fell apart.'

Very slowly, to be sure. Her new husband had been too smart to show his hand right away. He'd helped Merry with the plantation, gradually usurping the role she'd held. He'd befriended Sir Arthur Gridley and the other planters in an attempt to be seen as the new face of Sugarland. After all, even nine years ago, Merry had been old. Then he'd tried to formalise that arrangement, pressuring her to get Merry to acknowledge him in the will.

'When that failed, the laughter stopped, the gifts stopped. He became an entirely different creature from the man I thought I knew,' Emma confessed. 'It was clear he'd married me to get to the plantation. It was a far easier route to landownership than starting up one of his own.'

'There'd likely been nothing to start from,' Ren put in. 'Gridley once mentioned there's no land for sale on the island.'

Emma nodded. 'It's true. The only way to acquire a plantation of any size is to buy it from someone else. But my husband wasn't interested in buying, only in taking. He thought he could woo Sugarland out of me. Fortunately, Merry was onto him. Unfortunately, too. Once he realised Merry wouldn't acknowledge him, he took his frustrations out on me.'

Those had been dark days. She'd tried to hide the bruises from Merry, but her husband had not been careful, or perhaps he had. He'd wanted his mark to be visible, wanted Merry to be coerced into reconsideration. She could feel Ren bristle beside her, his chivalry on full display. Ren's gentleman's code would not tolerate such treatment. 'Tell me how this story ends, Emma.' His voice was tight.

'Merry ordered him from the house at gunpoint one day. He was a coward at heart. He left. Shortly afterwards, we learned he'd gone to Jamaica and was living openly with a wealthy widow. Some even said he'd married her, but we have no real proof. I didn't care at the time. I was glad he was gone. Forever only lasted three years, and happy-ever-after lasted even less than that.'

'Where is he now?'

'Mouldering in a grave, shot dead by a jealous husband. It seemed the wealthy Jamaican widow wasn't enough for him. He had quite an enterprising career here in the Caribbean.' This was the more embarrassing part to admit. 'It's likely he was married to someone else while he was married to me. I can add bigamy to my list of accomplishments. Not everyone can claim they were a bigamist at eighteen or a widow by twenty-four.'

'You were an unknowing participant. It's hardly your fault—' Ren began.

She cut him off. 'Are you trying to absolve me or yourself? I don't need absolution, Ren. I made a mistake and married a bad man against the advice of those who cared for me. I can't pretend it didn't happen or excuse it. Society certainly won't. They feast on it.'

'He's lucky he's dead,' Ren said. 'If he wasn't, I'd have to shoot him myself. Even though he was gone, he kept you trapped in that marriage for two years after he left.'

'In name only was far better than having him here. But now you see the whole of me. You understand now why it's best I remain alone. I'm ruined and I'll never be anything but trouble to any man.'

Ren ignored the dismissal. 'What was the bastard's name?'

'Thompson Hunt.'

Chapter Twenty-One

⁂

He'd known the name before she spoke it. Gridley's last cryptic comment had been solved. Their walk led them in a loop back home. Ren felt as if their talk had led them in a circle, too. He knew so much more, but none of it brought him closer to resolution. He was still back where he started in all senses of the concept.

Emma gave a rueful laugh. 'You're a contrary creature, Ren Dryden. This morning you were talking of leaving, now you're talking of staying and marriage.' Her eyes were sad as she reached up to push an errant strand of hair back behind his ear. 'You only want me because you can't have me.' It was a comfortable, intimate gesture that fired his blood as surely as any erotic touch and it spoke volumes of what this relationship had become, something far more than bed sport, something he did not want to let go of, something he was willing to fight for.

In that singular moment, in that gesture, was the clarity he sought. She wanted him, she wanted what he offered, but she couldn't risk it, not just for herself and the fear of making the same mistake twice, but for him, too. She wouldn't allow him to be dragged down by her past. What woman turned down a countess's coronet? What woman gave up her own happiness in order to protect a man? That was when he knew. She was pushing him away because she loved him.

Emma loved him! Ren captured her hand where it lay against his ear, bringing it to his lips and pressing a kiss against her palm. Elation poured through him. She loved *him*, not his title, just Ren Dryden the man. His decision was made—go or stay, he wasn't letting her get away. When a man had a woman like Emma Ward, he had something worth fighting for.

The hall was unnaturally quiet. There was no one around, no maids polishing the bannister, no one moving in and out of rooms cleaning. 'Where is everyone?'

'They have the day off. It's Crop Over. Everyone has gone into Bridgetown for the celebration.'

A thought struck him. 'Did you want to go? I didn't mean to ruin any plans.' He'd been so excited about the rum still he hadn't stopped to think. 'We could get rooms at the hotel, you could shop.' Bridgetown was only five miles away, but life out here was so entirely consuming it might as well be fifty. If he could get her away, where it was just the two of them without constant reminders of the past, maybe he had a chance. Now that he'd made his mind up, he wanted that chance more than he wanted anything else except Emma herself.

He took her hands and danced her around the hall. 'What do you say?' He gave her a boyish grin. 'You deserve some fun, Emma and maybe we can think of something to celebrate.'

She was laughing, a sign she was starting to crack as he swung her about in a fast country-dance step. 'All right!' she conceded with a breathless gasp. 'I can be ready in half an hour.'

Bridgetown was a city besieged by revels and the atmosphere was contagious. Emma hugged Ren's arm spontaneously as he carefully navigated the gig to the livery off the crowded main street. 'I haven't been to the festival in years!' She twisted around on the seat, trying to take it all in at once. Street vendors filled every available space, calling out their wares, delicious smells peppered the air, there were handmade toys to buy, and street entertainers on stilts dressed in bright colours.

Ren laughed. 'You're going to fall off the seat if you aren't careful! There's plenty of time to see everything.'

They parked the gig and the horse at the livery and went to the hotel to claim rooms for the evening. Most people would be staying with friends or sleeping out in the open. There were plenty of rooms available and Ren insisted on getting two for propriety's sake, but they both knew one bed would be cold. No matter how things ended, Emma wanted whatever she could have. Oh, she knew what Ren *thought* he wanted and she knew what she had to do to protect him from his own chivalry. She hoped she had the courage to do it when the time came. Until then, however, there was no room for sad thoughts. Bridgetown at Crop Over was to be enjoyed, it was a time to be carefree.

Out in the streets, music was everywhere, on every corner; guitars and shak-shaks played as they wandered the bright market. They stopped to buy fishcakes wrapped in plantain leaves and fried dumplings, washing them down with tumblers of falernum. 'These are delicious.' Emma peered into her leaf wrapper, disappointed. 'I've eaten them all.'

'You've devoured them!' Ren laughed and bought her some more. 'This is quite the festival. Have you folks been doing it long?' His hand was at her back, ushering her towards a slightly less populated portion of the market.

'It's Crop Over, or Harvest Home, and we've been doing it since the sixteen hundreds,' Emma explained between bites of fishcakes. 'It's the celebration of the sugar-cane crop being in.'

'I love it, it makes our English fairs looked positively staid.' Ren took the last dumpling out of its wrapper and popped it in her mouth with a smile. 'I saved it for you since you like them so much.'

He spoiled her the rest of the day, dancing with her in the streets, buying her an endless supply of sweets, winning her a pretty green hair ribbon at a knife-tossing game and stealing a kiss when he did, much to the cheers of the crowd gathered around them. By the time they headed back to the hotel several hours later, her stomach was bursting from the food, her feet had started to hurt from all the dancing. She was tired and she was happy.

Best of all, they hadn't run into any of her neighbours. There hadn't been a sign of Devore, or Gridley, or any of the others. Ren was having fun, too, she realised. These efforts were not designed to entertain only her. *This was what it must feel like to be courted*, she thought. *What it must be like to be honestly in love with someone.* Did she dare trust that feeling? Did she dare reach for the happiness Ren offered? She believed she'd felt this way for Thompson Hunt once, too. But that had been blind infatuation. She hadn't known him, hadn't spent time with him the way she had with Ren.

They stepped into the hotel with its wide lobby and made their way up the curve of the staircase, both of them too tired for any more adventures in the streets. The hotel was full of whites, planters who'd come to town for the celebration. But still there was no sign of her neighbours. 'Does Gridley come to town for this?' Ren read her mind as he fitted the key into the door.

'Sometimes. He feels it's a bit beneath him.' Emma slipped through the door in front of him. Ren followed her in and shut the door behind them, shutting out the noise of the hotel. It was just the two of them. The room was cool and dark, quietly intimate after the exuberance of the streets.

'Ren, this has been the most amazing day…' Emma began, unsure of what she meant to share. The silence was unnerving after a day of noise and sound.

'An amazing day, with an amazing woman.' Ren moved towards her, a finger on her lips. 'Shh, Emma. Just enjoy. We could have many more days like this. Did you think about that today? What it could be like next year with our rum venture underway and no worries? I did, I thought of nothing else.' He kissed her neck and she shivered. His touch could undo her in short order.

'Ren...' She wanted to protest, but could find no arguments. Of course she'd thought about it. It had been there in the back of her mind. This man could be hers if she would give up the fight. That fight had started out as a struggle to resist him, but it had since become a battle to protect him from her, from the scandal she'd bring and the danger. 'It's not a good idea.'

He had her in his arms now, peeling away her clothes with his hands, his mouth at her neck, at her ear, his voice thick with persuasion. 'I'm not him, Emma. I am not Thompson Hunt or Arthur Gridley or any other man who has wronged you. I promise. I will cherish you forever, starting tonight if you'll give me a chance.'

He pushed her dress from her shoulders, stripped away her chemise and undergarments until she stood naked before him, his gaze hot on her, devouring. He'd seen her naked before and in better light than this. But this time was different, this time *he'd* done the undressing. She felt claimed, the act marking her as his. Would he look at her the same way once the scandal started? If only she could be his without destroying him.

Ren's voice was hoarse when he spoke. 'Get on the bed, Emma.'

There was a hint of wickedness to his suggestion and a tremor of anticipation took her as she complied. Ren tugged at her legs, drawing her forward until her legs dangled over the bed, her *derrière* resting on the edge. He knelt between her legs, his hands resting on her thighs. 'When one finds something worth cherishing, one wants to start right away.'

He caught her eye, his intentions becoming clear. Oh, mercy, he meant to… Emma's mouth went dry. Never had she been approached so intimately, cherished so erotically. His breath was warm against her damp curls. Her head fell back on the bed, her legs utterly open to him. There was no point in resisting. She wanted this, wanted him. Neither of which were new revelations, but the intensity of them was.

His tongue flicked over her secret nub and she cried out, again and again as he repeated the delicious caress, each cry louder than the one before as pleasure rose, hope rising with it. Ren would stay for her—was she brave enough to let him? Could she believe in the fairy tale one more time? Her last cries were sobs, her control wouldn't last much longer. Then Ren was whispering to her, calling to her from somewhere within her pleasure, 'Emma, let go.'

She did. It didn't occur until later that if she let go, she might fall forever.

The morning came too soon, although it was more like late morning before Emma managed to rouse. She might have slept longer if her body hadn't subconsciously registered the absence of Ren's beside her. How quickly she'd become used to him, to his presence. She raised up on an elbow and searched the room, finding him by the open doors of the chamber that looked out into a quiet courtyard.

He seemed lost in thought as he gazed into the yard. From below, the sounds of a fountain burbled up. The quiet, the pose of her man, elbows resting on the railing of the small balcony, struck her as a moment out of time, a piece of serenity in this little paradise of theirs. Emma held still, closing her eyes tight to capture the image in her mind. No matter what happened, she'd always see him like this.

'Good morning,' she called from the bed. 'What has you up and about?'

He turned from the railing, a sheet of paper in his hand. 'I went out to get breakfast. There's coffee and rolls.' He gestured to the little table where he'd laid everything out. 'I brought the post, too. The mail packet came in yesterday in time for the celebration.'

'A letter from home?' Emma asked, trying to sound casual.

'From my sister. She wrote to tell me about Benedict DeBreed and their hasty engagement.' A little smile played at the corners of his mouth. 'It seems all's well that ends well. You and Sherard were right.' He folded the letter into squares and tucked it into his pocket. 'She has found happiness in a most unlooked-for place and with an unlooked-for person. I would not have imagined her with Benedict. It appears I was wrong.'

'I'm sure that doesn't happen often,' Emma teased, relieved there wasn't bad news, nothing to take Ren away from her before decisions were made. She wanted those decisions to be made between them and not because external circumstances dictated them. There'd been too much of that already.

'Of course not.' Ren smiled, picking up on her joke. 'After we eat, there's one place I want to stop before we head home.'

* * *

That place turned out to be St. Michael's Cathedral with its tall bell tower. If it wasn't the most perfect cathedral, it was understandable. 'It's survived quite a bit.' Emma stepped ahead of Ren into the dim interior. 'There was the hurricane of 1780. It took nine years to rebuild and then there was the hurricane of—'

'1831,' Ren finished for her. 'I wasn't even here for it and I feel like I know that storm personally.'

'It's how we define time in these parts,' Emma said seriously. 'If I understand my history correctly, London marks time around the Great Fire, is that not true?'

'Touché.' Ren laughed, putting a hand to his heart. 'Your arrow has hit its target, my dear.'

'Why did you want to come here? I'm guessing it wasn't to assess the storm damage.' Emma led him over to a stand of candles. Only a few were lit. The church was quiet the day after the festival.

'I don't want to go back.'

The words seared her. She'd not been expecting that. He was leaving now. Of course, the mail packet was in port. It was just so much sooner than she'd thought. It wasn't going to be her decision after all, even after everything he'd said.

'Not go back to Sugarland?' she stuttered through the words, stepping away. What had she misunderstood about yesterday, about last night? Just yesterday, he'd been talking about forever and she'd been the one hoping she'd have the courage to let him go, but it seemed that courage wouldn't be required. He'd seen reason. He understood her limitations whatever his fantasies dictated to the contrary. It shouldn't be a surprise. Earls didn't marry possible bigamists.

Ren gripped her hands, pulling her back towards him. 'I don't want to return to Sugarland and go back to how things were between us before we left. I want to go forward. I want to return knowing how things stand between us.'

In the candlelight, she could see for the first time the signs of strain on his face, how much this was costing him to ask. He wasn't sure of her, of how'd she answer. He might be the bravest man in the world, taking such a risk, sailing his soul into unknown waters. His next words confirmed it. 'I would like to go back to Sugarland knowing that you will be my wife and that we'll build a life together here in Barbados.'

She stared at him, stunned. He wasn't leaving. He was staying *for* her, *with* her, because of her. 'Why?' She barely breathed the word, her eyes never leaving his face.

'Because I love you and I want to stand up with you in this church, in front of God and everyone, and say, "You are my choice. This life is my choice." Will you marry me, Emma? Not because it's good for Sugarland, not because it will subdue Gridley's advances, not because I have money, because I don't, not right now at least. And not because I'm an earl, but because *you* want to, because you love me and I love you and that means something.'

It was to be her decision after all. Her knees threatened to give out. Could she throw caution to the wind? Could she grab a bit of happiness for herself with this man? He'd been brave moments ago, asking for what he wanted, knowing that his future hinged on her answer. He would go or stay on her choice. Now it was her turn to be brave in a far different way than the one she'd imagined yesterday. It required one sort of bravery to send him a way. It would require an entirely different type to let him stay, to let herself be happy. Emma seized her future with two hands and one simple word. 'Yes.'

Ren kissed her then, softly, reverently, on her hands, on her lips. 'You will always be safe with me, I promise.'

Chapter Twenty-Two

The day was promising to be one for the memory books, one of the best of his life. Ren was certain he'd look back in his old age and this day would be among the days that shone. He'd come to Barbados looking for a new life, a fresh start, and he'd found it. It wasn't the way he'd imagined it. His imaginings hadn't predicted a beautiful, headstrong woman waiting for him. Nor had his imaginings figured in the financial and social trials he'd faced. But he had triumphed. The woman dozing against his shoulder was proof enough, prize enough.

Ren mentally ticked off the blessings of the morning. His sister was happy, his friendships with Kitt and Benedict had proven true. His family was safe, although not through the means he'd expected. He was going to marry, not for convenience, but for love and for passion and for partnership, things he'd not thought to have or find when he left England. He was a satisfied man and the day was good indeed.

Two miles from home, Ren saw it; a grey funnel of smoke spiralling up into the sky, odd but not alarming.

There were any number of reasons there'd be smoke this time of year. Someone could be burning leftover cane debris or clearing a field for a new crop. At this distance, it wasn't entirely clear the smoke even came from Sugarland, which of course it wouldn't. There was no one there. Workers would be trickling in later today, home from their holiday in Bridgetown. There'd be no real work until tomorrow, no real reason to wake Emma, who dozed against his shoulder.

One mile from home, the grey funnel became blacker, more intense, its location closer to Sugarland, although it was hard to tell with the twists and turns in the road exactly where the smoke was located. But Ren's anxiety grew. He was running out of counter-explanations. The plume was bigger, darker than it had been earlier. He thought he could even see the orange prongs of flames at the base of the funnel.

Beside him, Emma stirred, lifting her head and crinkling her nose. 'What is that smell? It smells like… smoke!' She caught sight the black cloud.

'Something's on fire. It's hard to tell where it's coming from.' Ren hedged, not wanting to panic her without cause.

Emma had no such reservations. She scanned the horizon and her judgement was instant. 'It's *Sugarland*. The estate is on fire! Ren, hurry!'

Ren whipped the horse up to top speed with the gig. He turned into the long drive, urging the sturdy chestnut to greater speeds. Beside him, Emma looked desperately for the source of the fire. 'It's out in the fields somewhere, I can't tell where.' Her voice edged with desperation. 'Gracious, Ren, how did this happen?'

The house came into view, untouched, but smoke was thick in the air, a precursor to impending disaster. Ren slowed the horse and they jumped down, racing through the house to the back veranda where any relief Ren felt at seeing the house safe evaporated into fear. Fire crossed the fields, racing towards them, eating up everything in its path. The flames ran horizontal, stretching the width of the fields, a great orange wall of fire.

Ren's mind was a whirlwind of thought. There was still time, but to do what? They couldn't fight the centre of the fire, just the two of them. If the fire kept on, it would reach the house, it would surround them given time. But perhaps they could flank it from a different location? He did not think they could save the home farm, it would be in the thick of the conflagration. But maybe they could save the still?

'We'll lose everything,' Emma breathed, her face white with panic as her mind registered the consequences of such a fire.

'Not everything.' Ren cast his gaze eastward. What to save? Should they try for the house, which seemed a futile battle, or the still, their source of income? The flames eastward seemed weakest. They could make a stand there, salvage something. There was no time to second-guess his instant analysis. He was running, already on his way to the office, calling instructions over his shoulder, 'Emma, you have two minutes, grab anything from the house you value: blankets, clothes, medicine. Meet me at the gig. We'll make our fight at the still.'

In the office, Ren grabbed a throw from a chair and

spread it open on the floor. He opened the glass-fronted cabinet holding the ledgers and important papers and tossed items on to the throw. He flung open desk drawers, grabbing anything that looked official. He heard Emma's feet pounding down the stairs, her voice calling his name. Ren gathered the ends of the throw up into a makeshift pack and hefted his bundle onto his shoulder. He cast one more look around the room. Had he got everything? There was no more time.

Emma was outside, tossing her bundle into the shallow bed of the gig. She scrambled up and he leapt up beside her. They were off, paralleling the line of flames as they raced for the east edge of the property.

His gamble was well founded. The flames weren't as strong, weren't as greedy at this end, the smoke not as thick. The still was thick-walled. It would prove to be flame resistant to some degree, providing safety for them as well if they needed it. There were tools there, too: shovels and buckets, a rainwater barrel and the water for running the mill wheel.

'Do we have a chance?' Emma shielded her yes with a hand, watching the smoke.

'More than a chance. We can do this,' Ren said confidently, hoping to reassure her. It seemed a horrible irony that just two hours ago he'd promised her he'd keep her safe and now there were no guarantees he could keep even a portion of that promise. The best day had become a nightmare.

'We need help. The fire is too big,' Emma argued, but she took a shovel and started helping him dig an impromptu firebreak.

'We can fight for a while on our own and help will come. The workers will see the smoke plume and race to our side.' He hoped. She'd been a fair employer, they would come to her aid. He was counting on it. A ruined Sugarland meant no jobs for them. They had nothing to gain by not helping.

'They're five miles away,' Emma countered, flinging dirt into a pile. They'd passed people on the road, making the slow walk back to their jobs, no one in a hurry to see the holiday end.

'The neighbours are home,' Ren offered, remembering that Gridley and Devore and the others had not gone into town. 'They'll see the smoke.'

'And rejoice,' Emma said sharply, grunting between shovelfuls as a ditch started to take shape five hundred yards in front of the still. 'This is exactly the kind of catastrophe they've been waiting for. Without us to independently sell our sugar outside of their cartel, the cartel can control prices.

Ren leaned on his shovel, her words driving home with sickening reality. 'You think they set the fire? They would go that far?'

Emma met his eyes. 'Gridley would do it. He warned you, warned *us*, didn't he? And this is nothing compared to murder.'

Ren put his back into the shovelling. Emma was right. Aid was unlikely. They were on their own. This firebreak would be all that stood between the still and utter defeat. If the fire jumped the ditch... He didn't want to think about it. He would not fail Emma. But his mind hadn't given up trying to fathom the motives for such destruction. If Gridley had laid the fire, his decision was hard to grasp. It was drastic and counter-intuitive.

'Why would Gridley destroy something he covets?'

'To bring me to my knees,' Emma said simply, but Ren heard the unspoken logic. There was something, *someone*, Gridley coveted more than the estate: Emma. Without income, without an estate, the two things Merry had left to protect her, Emma was exposed. Ren could see Gridley's perverted reasoning. Emma would need him, be reliant on him for everything. But Gridley had forgotten one variable and that was Ren himself. *He* would stand between Emma and Gridley when the estate and the crops failed. He and the rum. He would fight for her just as he was fighting for her right now.

'He would go to such lengths, but I can't believe the others would allow it.' The depravity of the neighbour-hood was hard to grasp. It bordered on madness.

'The Caribbean doesn't draw the finest of men. These are self-fashioned gentlemen who checked their morals at the dock and have given themselves airs.' Emma panted her words between shovelfuls.

He'd very much like Emma to be wrong. Ren stepped back from their digging and surveyed the work. It might be enough. 'Clear away any vegetation on our side. We don't want the fire to have anything to cling to if it crosses the ditch. Fires need fuel. If it's starved, it can't burn.'

Ren strode toward the gig and reached under the seat. He drew out the travelling pistol and tossed it to Emma. 'Here, take this. I hope you won't need it. I'll be back.'

'Where are you going? You're leaving me?' Emma cried in angry disbelief.

'I'm going to go scout the fire. I want to see how close it is and what else can be done.' The wind was picking up and it would either help them or hurt them. He hoped for the former, hoped the wind would blow the fire away from the still. If so, they might be able to leave it and make a second stand somewhere else, a chance to save one more thing.

Emma's hand was on his arm. 'I don't like it. Ren, fire is dangerous, wind is dangerous, it can change everything in an instant. Please, don't go. You could be surrounded and there'd be nothing you could do.'

He kissed her then, long and sweet. There was nothing else he could say or do. He couldn't make her any more promises. 'I won't be long. Don't worry, your defences will hold. You'll be safe here.'

'It's not me I'm worried about, you silly man.' She gave him a wry smile and released him. 'Go, then, but hurry and don't be a hero. Sticks and stones aren't worth it.'

The fire was magnificent, a work of art, Arthur Gridley thought as he and Hugh Devore sat on their horses watching Albert Merrimore's estate burn, the fields and the home farm, consumed in flame. From their vantage point, they could see the fire marching towards the main house. It would be a shame to lose that building, but if it stood Emma would never relent. The house couldn't generate income, but Emma was a sentimental fool. She wouldn't see the house as useless, she'd see it as a remainder of her inheritance. 'Dryden's gone for the still,' he told Devore. 'The gig headed in that direction.'

'Inspired, that. Dryden's a smart man. Too bad he didn't side with us,' Devore said, fingering the club he carried at his side. 'It will cost him.'

Gridley had to give Dryden credit there. The man had astutely decided to go for the still instead of the house. Gridley hadn't counted on that. He'd thought Emma would sway him to save the house. That was insightful. Perhaps Dryden carried more influence with her than Gridley had factored. Good to know. Ultimately, that would only help his cause. This was all going very well.

He and Devore had their men lay the charges under the cover of night. That hadn't been the risk. There'd been no one around to see. Everyone had been gone to town. It had been igniting them, the timing, that had contained the risk. That had to be done in the light of day. He wanted Dryden and Emma to see it, to know he'd made good on his warnings. He wanted them to rush towards it. The fire would play to their emotions. Both Dryden and Emma would try to fight it. Everything was going according to plan. They were down there even now, making a stand.

A breeze kicked up, drawing their eyes skyward. Clouds were moving in from the ocean, grey ones, heavy with rain. Well, let the weather come if it must. 'It's time.' He nodded to Devore.

Devore gave a devilish grin. 'I'll track down Dryden, you get the girl.' They kicked their horses into motion. Rain or not, the damage had already been done. Rain couldn't save much of Sugarland, and it wouldn't save Ren Dryden. It was time for phase two.

Emma checked the rain barrel and watched the sky, watched it darken with rain clouds. There was hope in those clouds. But the fire crept closer and the minutes dragged by. Where was Ren? Would he bring good news? Was the fire dying out? Was the house safe? If the house was safe, they might salvage something yet. How had this happened? But she knew how.

She had done this. In her arrogance and in her selfishness, she'd brought down the wrath of Arthur Gridley. She'd not been careful. He'd come for Sugarland and it was only a matter of time before he came for her, his prize. She would have nothing left to resist him with, nothing left to fight with, all her barriers stripped away. Except Ren.

Would he be enough? Would she *allow* him to be enough? There would be yet more danger for him, danger he didn't deserve. He'd come here looking to be a businessman, looking to save his beloved family, and he'd found peril after peril in knowing her. Her brashness this morning seemed ill founded based on the ruin around her. She should set Ren free, send him back to England where he'd be safe whether he willed it or not, whether her heart willed it or not.

Emma turned at the sound of noise behind her, the sound of someone coming. Ren! Her heart leapt even as her hand closed reflexively around the butt of the pistol and the first raindrops fell, flat and wet on her face.

'Emma, come away, this is foolishness! You can't

save it.' It wasn't Ren, but Gridley who crashed into the courtyard of the still on his horse, concern pasted on his face. He slid off his horse, one hand on the reins, the other stretched out for her.

Another woman, a frightened woman, would have been fooled. Not Emma. He was here for her as she'd known he would be one way or another, one time or another. The last thing she wanted was to give up her ground and go anywhere with him. She knew in her heart this was to be the final battle. Better to face him on Sugarland ground even if it was burning. She raised her pistol, levelling at his chest. 'Drop the facade, Gridley, I am going nowhere with you.'

'You're not thinking clearly.' Gridley persisted in playing her friend, a role he'd played for months even when they both knew better. He dropped the reins of his horse and stepped forward. 'Put the gun down. Where's Dryden? We need to find him and get all of ourselves to safety. The fire will be here any minute. For the love of Albert Merrimore, come away with me. He would not want you to risk yourself needlessly.'

'You were never his friend! You murdered him in his bed.' Would she have to fire? Would Gridley call her bluff? The rain was coming down harder now, making it difficult to see, to hold the gun steady with slippery fingers. She would have to make her choice soon or it would be too late. Emma gathered her courage.

'I am done with you, Arthur Gridley. No one would think twice finding your body amid the ashes. I will make it clear to everyone you risked yourself to come to our aid. You will be a hero.'

Gridley laughed coldly. 'You won't shoot me. It's not in you, Emma. But gracious, the defiance! You *are* glorious. I've never wanted you as much as I do now with those dark eyes of yours staring at me from behind the barrel of a pistol.'

'I don't think she'll shoot, Gridley,' Hugh Devore called out, edging his horse around the corner, drawing both their attention. 'Not when she sees what I've got.' He shook his head in mock regret, revealing the body slung across the horse's hindquarters. 'Poor Dryden never saw it coming.'

Chapter Twenty-Three

'Ren!' Emma's scream tore the air. She dropped the gun and ran to him, hauling his limp form off the back of the horse with both hands. The weight of him nearly staggered her once she had him down. She got her hands under his arm pits and dragged him away from Devore and Gridley, panting from her efforts. 'What have you done?' The fire, the rain, the mounting wind, all of it ceased to matter. Only Ren mattered.

'What have we done? I think that's easy enough to see. We've disarmed you, for starters.' Gridley smiled evilly, stooping down to pick up her discarded pistol. He tossed it to Devore. 'Looks like we've also exposed her weakness, Hugh. Appears she has a *tendre* for our Englishman, after all.' He smirked. 'We did wonder, my dear, if it was just a romp in the sheets or something more. Apparently, it's something more.'

She barely registered the crass commentary. Emma ran her fingers through Ren's thick hair, searching for evidence of Devore's club. She found a bump on the side of his head. Ren groaned as she touched it. Sound was good, it meant he was alive, but in pain. Those bastards! Her anger surged. How dared they hurt him like this? But she knew how they dared and why. *All* of her defences were gone.

Gridley was stalking her like a big cat. He circled her, all pretence of niceness gone. There was nothing to stand between her and Gridley now. There was only her to stand between Gridley and Ren. Devore stood to the side under the eaves out of the rain, an interested spectator. How did she take on both of them? If it had just been Gridley, maybe she would have thought of something. She'd been managing Gridley for years.

The rain was coming down hard now. The fear of the fire reaching them receded, replaced by worry over taking a chill. Ren was soaked. She shivered, cold. She needed to act fast. 'What do you want, Gridley? Name your price.' She might as well cut straight to it. She had to get Ren to a warm bed.

'You know what I want. I want you.' His eyes glinted dangerously as he circled.

'What do I get in return?' Emma held his gaze, matching her footwork to his so that she began to circle with him, both of them moving around Ren's still form.

Gridley cast a disparaging glance at Ren. 'You can have Dryden's life. See him nursed back to health and put him on a boat. That's what you want, isn't it? What else is there to bargain for?'

'There's Sugarland.' Emma dared to push her luck. 'You've destroyed it. You should rebuild it for me.'

'As a wedding gift.' Gridley gave her a mocking bow. 'The place will be ours, after all.'

'It will be Dryden's,' Emma corrected. 'He owns fifty-one per cent and you've already promised me his life.'

'You ask for too much, Emma.' Gridley reached out a boot and kicked Ren in the stomach, laughing when Ren groaned. 'I have let you bargain for your lover. I didn't need to allow that. I could simply have taken you. You can't stop me.' As if to prove it, he lunged for her across their circle.

His sudden movement took her by surprise. She was no match for the weight of him in motion. Emma went down, crying out as Gridley landed on top of her. She struggled, kicking with her feet, jabbing with her knees, her hands. But Gridley was stronger. He got her hands, imprisoning them in his grip. 'Come hold her, Devore.'

'Not man enough for me?' She spat at Gridley, earning her cheek the back of his hand.

'Hellcat!' Gridley's eyes were dark with lust and anger as he straddled her in the mud.

Devore was there, laughing as he took her hands and stretched them over her head. 'You've got a live one, Arthur. Are you sure this is the one you want?'

She kicked out against at Gridley, not giving him a chance to answer. 'What do you get out of this, Devore?'

'I've already got it. Sugar prices will go high and that's all I wanted.'

She'd liked to have spat on him, too. But he was above her head, out of range. 'You disgust me. What sort of man thinks sugar prices are worth watching a woman being raped, a home burned, a man nearly killed?'

'It's hardly rape. He's going to marry you. Consider this your engagement. Besides,' he chuckled malevolently, 'you promised him. I think it's time you started holding up your end of the agreement.'

Gridley reared back, his hand working the flap of his trousers. 'You did promise, my dear. I've let the Englishman live, but perhaps I should reconsider. A shot to the knee would hurt and it might convince you to keep your word. Do you have her, Hugh?' He rose up slightly, reaching around for his pistol. 'I don't think Dryden will thank you much for a permanent limp.'

'No!' Emma screamed. Gridley was absolutely over the edge of sanity. A leg wound could finish Ren. 'Don't do it, don't.' She sobbed.

Gridley laid the gun down, his attention back on her. 'Don't what, my dear?'

'Don't, *please*.' Emma gritted her teeth. She hated to beg, hated to be helpless. But only helplessness would save Ren.

'And?' Gridley ran a finger down her jaw. Her skin crawled.

'I'll be good,' she said meekly.

'That's more like it, isn't it, Hugh? Now where were we? Ah, yes, I was just about to share intimacies with you and you were going to let me and Devore was going to be my best man and watch.'

Ren pushed up to his hands and knees, his vision a blur, his head pounding. But he could hear perfectly well, enough to know Emma was in danger, that Gridley had her, that she'd bargained herself down to the rudest denominator to save him.

Mud squished between his hands as he inched forward. They were paying no attention to him. Devore and Gridley were far too intent on degrading Emma. He just needed a few more feet and enough strength to launch himself at Gridley. What happened after that hardly mattered as long as he pulled Gridley off her in time.

Emma was sobbing. He tried to hurry. She must be terrified, it was her nightmare come to life, the fear that Gridley would destroy her. Every inch he crawled was agony, his head splintering with the movement. What a terrible job he'd done protecting her.

Devore and Gridley were making crass jokes. Devore's hands were clamped around hers, keeping her still. Ren's vision cleared. He saw Gridley handle himself, his other hand between Emma's legs.

That was when Ren leapt. With a roar, he used the momentum of his body to knock Gridley to the side. He got an arm around Gridley's neck but Gridley wasn't ready to go easily. He wrestled, trying to break the chokehold. Mud covered them both, making any grasp slippery.

Gridley got away once, scrambling through the mud on all fours, but Ren reached out blindly for his ankle and pulled him back down. Gridley yelled for Devore to do something. Ren yelled for Emma to run. He was fuelled by anger, powered by vengeance for Emma, for Merrimore, for Sugarland. He would kill Gridley if he had the chance and damn the consequences.

But Emma wouldn't run. He heard Emma's voice. 'Get away from them!' It took a moment to register her meaning. Out of the corner of his eye, he saw Emma level the pistol at Devore. Ren felt his strength begin to fail, adrenaline notwithstanding. He had to end this soon or Gridley would end him.

A shot rang out and Devore crumpled, grabbing his leg, swearing. The noise was enough for Gridley to disengage, half crawling, half running to Devore's side. Ren staggered to his feet, stumbling to Emma.

Gridley roared, 'You bitch, you've shot him!' He lunged at Emma, but a voice brought him up short.

'Emma didn't shoot him. *I did.* It's about time, too.'

Ren looked beyond Gridley. Kitt Sherard strode forward, water streaming from his hair as he pushed Gridley out of the way with a hard, careless shove. 'I've got another pistol, Ren. Anything you want to shoot?' Kitt handed the butt end of a pistol to him. 'I heard Gridleys are in season.'

'Miss Ward, if I may?' Kitt took the shaking pistol Emma held and trained it on Gridley and Devore, not that Devore was much threat, Ren noted, following suit with the other gun. Kitt's shot had incapacitated him. 'Shall we shoot them now, Ren, and put them out of their misery or should we make them wait for justice?'

'You can't prove anything,' Gridley snarled. 'Your word is nothing, Sherard, not against mine. You're nothing but a pirate fancied up on money.'

'Then perhaps we'll just shoot you,' Ren put in, gesturing with the pistol. He wouldn't mind doing it if it meant he could lie down with Emma and assure himself she was all right.

'You never know what kind of proof might turn up. There was talk in town,' Kitt said slowly. 'If I were you, I'd get on my horse, ride home and consider how lucky I feel: lucky enough to stay and stand trial, or lucky enough to find a boat out of here.'

That did it. Ren watched grimly as Gridley got Devore up on a horse and the two men left, shouting threats and obscenities at Sherard, who just laughed and fired a warning shot over the top of the retreating horses to speed them on their way. After they were gone, Kitt laid down his gun and looked around. 'What a mess. Fire, mud, rain—an absolute tropical disaster.'

Ren was more worried about Emma than the aftermath of the fire and rain. 'Kitt, all this can wait, get us home.' Beside him, Emma swayed on her feet. Ren moved to catch her, sweeping her up in his arms, but unsteady on his own feet. He would have fallen if Kitt hadn't caught his elbow.

Kitt shot him a grim look. 'There's no guarantee there's any home there.'

'Better to find out now.' Ren gave a grunt and hoisted Emma up on to the seat of the gig. He would drive and Kitt would ride beside them. He was not looking forward to the effects the road would have on his head. But he was looking forward even less to extending that journey five miles back into Bridgetown if the house was gone.

'I did bring help,' Kitt told him as they set out. 'I

ran into some of the workers on the road and organised them. If the house is still there, there will be assistance.

'Did you really hear rumours in town? How did you know to come?' Talking took Ren's mind off his own pain.

'I went to the hotel, hoping to catch you before you left. I had some papers for you to sign with the quartermaster. The clerk at the desk told me you'd gone. That was when someone in the lobby mentioned in not such nice tones that there was a bit of surprise waiting for you. I set out immediately. By then, the smoke was clearly visible. I knew you were in trouble.'

'I don't know what we would have done without you.' Ren paused. 'I never saw Devore, never heard him. One moment I was surveying the fire, the next moment I was out.' Beside him, Emma's head flopped on to his shoulder. She felt warm. Ren reached a hand out to her forehead. 'Kitt, she's hot.' Anxiety laced his voice. His mind filled with the horrid images. The mud, the rain, that bastard Gridley forcing her down into the mire until she'd been soaked with it. He could do nothing but tuck a blanket more firmly around and get her home, if there was one.

It hadn't seemed that far to the still from the house, but now the drive back seemed interminable. They turned the last corner and Ren held his breath. They needed a miracle right about now. Kitt cantered up ahead. 'Can you see it?' Ren called out.

Kitt turned in the saddle, a smile on his face. 'It's still there. The wind changed in time.'

At the house, Ren insisted on carrying Emma upstairs while Kitt called out orders for two baths. Hattie, Emma's maid, was back as were a handful of the footmen and the cook. Everyone was eager to have something to do in the face of the disaster, especially when there was so much that couldn't be done. One quick glance out windows confirmed just how close the fire had come. Another five hundred yards would have cost them the house.

He laid Emma down on the bed, mud and all. 'Ren,' she murmured. She tried to sit up. 'Ren, the house?'

'We're there now. The house will be all right.' He pushed a hank of wet hair out of her face. 'Lie back and let us take care of you. Hattie's here, I'm here, there's a bath coming.'

'Ren, I'm hot.'

'I'll take care of that, too. A bath will work wonders.' He placed a soft kiss on her forehead as her eyes closed again.

Hattie bustled into the room with towels and disapproval, shooing him out. 'I'll take care of her from here. It's not right you seeing her without her clothes on and you need a bath, too. Mr Kitt has it all ready for you in your rooms.'

'I'm going to marry her,' Ren protested. He didn't want to leave her, didn't want to make the long trek back to his rooms. The *garçonnière* seemed farther away than ever.

Hattie smiled patiently at him. 'Of course you are. But not today, so off with you. You can see her once you're both cleaned up.'

Ren took one last look at Emma, so pale, so limp on

the bed, so unlike her usual self. 'I'll be back. Soon.' He'd have his bath and then he'd move his things into the room across the hall. He was done living in the *garçonnière*.

'Everything will be fine.' Hattie assured him.

When Ren returned, much later than he would have preferred, everything was *not* fine. Emma was asleep, cheeks flushed, skin hot to the touch. There was no doubt of a fever now. Hattie and another maid were bent over her, working busily with cool rags and urging her to sip tea.

'It's willowbark tea. It'll bring the fever down,' Hattie said over her shoulder, barely sparing him a look.

Ren nodded, feeling helpless. 'What can I do?'

'You can keep yourself well,' Hattie said tersely. 'There's going to be plenty that needs doing and Miss Emma can't do it. I don't want her worrying about this place when she needs to be worrying about herself and getting through this.'

As if on cue, Kitt quietly appeared in the doorway. He, too, had cleaned up and was dressed in a spare shirt and trousers of Ren's. 'She's right, Ren. Come with me. There's nothing you can do in here. But there are plenty of ways you can be useful to Emma out here.'

Ren reluctantly had to admit Kitt was right. The best way he could help Emma was to help Sugarland. They used the rest of the daylight to survey the damage. The fields were charred. The home farm would need to be entirely rebuilt, the vegetable gardens lost. Ren pushed a hand through his hair at the end of their tour. The house was intact, the still was safe, but Sugarland was no longer self-sufficient. All their food supplies would have to be brought in from Bridgetown at great expense. There'd be plenty of work, but that meant wages and that meant feeding mouths, more expenses. 'The totals are a bit staggering, a bit alarming.' Ren shook his head, but there was no question of not rebuilding. He'd simply have to find a way.

Kitt nodded. 'I can advance you funds if you need it. I have a nice bit set aside.'

'All right. We might need that.' Ren smiled gratefully at his friend.

'We?' Kitt elbowed him.

'She's going to marry me. I asked her this morning.' The morning seemed ages ago, full of sunshine and promise. Now the estate was in ruins and Emma lay sick upstairs. 'I promised her she'd be safe with me. That promise didn't last very long.'

'What happened today wasn't your fault, but I think you could finish Gridley for good if you wanted to.'

Ren nodded absently. 'I was thinking the same thing. This island isn't big enough for the both of us. Emma and I can't stay if he's here. Emma would never be safe and I don't think Gridley is in his right mind.' He cocked his head at Kitt. 'I'd like to put him on trial for arson.'

Kitt grinned. 'I think we could do that and more. I asked around like you wanted. The magistrate is definitely not in Gridley's pocket. They had a run-in a few years back. We can get a fair trial. I can find the man from the hotel. If you can find anything in Merrimore's papers about Gridley, that would help prove there's motivation.'

'I already have.' Ren told him about the journal. 'There's likely to be more.'

Kitt rocked back on his heels, considering. 'I know you'd like to do this legally, Ren, and we could see it done, but it wouldn't hurt to push Gridley a bit, scare him. I think he'd flee if he feared your righteous anger. Devore might even go with him. The others will not be a problem, those two are the ringleaders.'

There was merit to that. Gridley would not tolerate being ruined and Ren had no qualms about putting the choice, as it were, to Gridley. He would build his case, present it to Gridley and Gridley could decide how he wanted to deal with it. Goodness knew he'd have plenty of time on his hands while he sat beside Emma because he wasn't leaving her tonight. He was going to put her world back together. He'd promised, come hell or high water.

Chapter Twenty-Four

Hell came first. The fever would not abate. It was supposed to be a quick case of getting warm after a chill, but by the next day the fever had grown worse, not better. Willowbark tea and cold rags had little effect. Ren sat with her when she was awake, feeding her spoonful after spoonful of tea and broth, talking about the estate, offering every reassurance that all would be well. But she was listless and said very little.

'You should think about the wedding.' Ren tried a last attempt to engage her. 'What kind of dress do you want? What sort of flowers? We can marry as soon as you're up and about. This time next month, we could be husband and wife.' He wanted that more than anything, more than he wanted to see Sugarland reclaimed from ash, more than he wanted Arthur Gridley to pay for what he'd done. He wanted it with an intensity that surprised even him, which only magnified his frustration over his inability to control the fever.

Emma rolled her head on her pillow, 'No, Ren. You can't marry me, not now.' Her voice was hoarse and tired, but it was the most response he'd had from her in a day, just not the response he was hoping for. 'Gridley will never leave us alone.' The words came out one by one, her throat struggling to work. 'I will not risk you. He will come for you again until he succeeds.'

Ren gripped her hand, so hot, in his own. 'I will take care of Gridley and Devore and the rest if need be. They will no longer define the scope of your happiness.' He was sick of them, sick of what they'd done to her long before he'd arrived.

'Ren, I won't allow it. I release you from your promises.' Her voice was soft now as her energy faded. Her eyes closed and she slipped her hand from his. Her eyes fought their way open one more time. 'Ren.' Her voice was so quiet he barely heard.

He bent close with a smile that betrayed none of his concern. It was almost as if she was vanishing before his eyes. 'What is it, Em?'

'I love you.'

'I love you, too.' He kissed her forehead, unsure if she'd heard him. It occurred to him he had not said the words before, not to her, not to any woman, and he'd not uttered them reflexively in response to her own. Suddenly it mattered very much that she had heard him, that she knew she was the first and only woman who'd claimed that calibre of affection from him. He meant those words to the core of his being.

'Emma?' He shook her by the shoulders gently in an attempt to rouse her. No answer, no response, not even a physical resistance of her body against being shaken. 'Em? Answer me.' *I release you from your promises,*

I can't allow it, I can't risk you, I love you. Her words echoed in his mind. She couldn't force him to accept those dictates, couldn't control him. But she could... No. A cold wave of fear swept him, the reality of what she meant to do becoming clear. She meant to set him free by slipping away, simply letting go and letting the fever take her.

'Em, no! You stay with me, do you hear?' Ren was vaguely aware he was yelling. Hattie was in the room, Kitt on her heels. 'We're losing her. We need more rags, more tea, more everything!' Ren roared. His gaze landed on Kitt. 'Get the guns. We're going to Gridley's. This ends today.' It would all end today one way or another. Emma wouldn't last, wouldn't let herself last unless she had a reason, unless she knew Gridley couldn't hurt them any more.

Ren cast a last glance at Emma. 'We'll be back in a few hours, Hattie. Don't, um, let her go anywhere.'

It took only minutes to be underway, horses thundering down the drive to the main road, he and Kitt armed with a brace of pistols each. To his credit, Kitt didn't ask any questions. Ren wasn't sure he had answers, only that he *knew* Emma's fate lay tied up with Gridley's. He was not going to let her die while Gridley lived. *This* was what Cousin Merrimore had called him here for, to free Emma from Gridley's cycle of evil by whatever methods possible.

They reached Gridley's in record time, pistols out as they took the front steps, their horses left at the ready.

Servants fell back at the sight of their weapons out. 'Where's Gridley?' Ren barked, stepping towards a servant he remembered from the dinner party.

The man hesitated. Ren cocked the pistol. 'He's in his office, second door on the left,' the man stammered.

'Nothing buys loyalty like a loaded pistol,' Kitt muttered under his breath.

'Whatever it takes,' Ren responded.

'Remind me never to get on your bad side.'

'Sirs! Sirs!' the man called out to them from behind. 'He's not alone. The others are with him. They're having a meeting.'

Ren shot Kitt a wry glance. 'How's that for gunpoint diplomacy?'

'I'd say Gridley's employees don't like him very much.' Kitt chuckled. 'How do you want to take them?'

'By surprise,' Ren said grimly. Surprise would be their great equaliser. Devore would fight if he could. Devore would be incapacitated from Kitt's wound. He might not even be there. Gridley would fight. The others he wasn't sure about. 'There'll be five, no more than that.' He remembered what Emma had told him. 'They'll be selfish bastards, every last one of them. Perhaps they'll turn on each other in order to save their own hides.'

Kitt nodded. 'I'll get the door and you fly right on in.' With that, Kitt raised one long leg and gave the door a thunderous kick. The door fell in, coming off its hinges with a crash. Ren ran through, his pistol training on Elias Blakely.

Elias was the weakest link, the one most likely to cower before a show of force, especially if that threat was aimed at his personal health. 'Was it you who set the fire?' He knew good and well it wasn't, but if Elias thought he was implicated in any way, he'd go on the defensive.

'No, of course not.' Blakely's body was against the back of his chair as far as he could squeeze it, his palms up as if he could ward off Ren's pistol. 'It was the others, not me. I didn't want anything to do with it.'

'Then you knew of it?' Ren growled, not giving Blakely any quarter. He saw fear register in Blakely's eyes. The man recognised too late his mistake. In an attempt to defend himself, he'd panicked and had implicated himself as an accomplice.

Ren's gun swivelled about the room. 'How about you, Cunningham? Did you set the fire? Blakely says you did, he said "the others". Is "others" you or would you like to rat out your friends as well?'

'That is quite enough!' Gridley roared in outrage. He reached beneath his desk, Ren pivoted, but Kitt was already there, his pistol sighting Gridley.

'Quite enough what?' Ren said coolly. 'Quite enough tattling from your so-called friends? Are you afraid they'll confess it was strictly you and Devore who set the fire, you and Devore who attempted to rape Emma Ward while her plantation burned. You and Devore who planned to kill me if Emma didn't comply with your unholy wishes.' The very words fired his blood, his anger surging. If it had been his pistol on Gridley, the man would have been dead by now.

Cunningham looked repulsed. 'You said no more murders, Arthur. I told you it was too risky.'

Ren moved his gun to Cunningham. 'No more murders? Explain. You have thirty seconds.' He knew what was coming, but a public confession would make Kitt a bona fide witness now, a third party outside of himself and Emma.

Cunningham shot a look at Gridley and looked back at Ren. 'Merrimore. The man was on his way out anyway. He only had a couple of days at most. Gridley thought the will had been changed to grant him ownership of Sugarland. He didn't want to risk the old man changing it back before he passed.'

'You will never be safe here again, Cunningham.' Gridley was positively livid, half rising out of his seat before he remembered Kitt's pistol levelled at his chest.

'Neither will you,' Ren reminded him. 'Emma is ill, ill unto death because of you. If I do one thing for her, it will be to rid this island of you and the others like you. Murder, arson, assault, attempted murder—the list grows long, Gridley, and we have witnesses, too. I am sure the court will deal favourably with those who assist the case.' Ren eyed the other three in the room.

Gridley paled, slowly realising his defences were being eroded. But he wasn't done fighting yet. 'Elias prefers men, the younger the better, don't you, Elias? I don't think you'll like that coming out in a court of law. It would certainly discredit your testimony. And you, Miles.' Miles had yet to say anything, but Gridley was determined to bring them all down. 'You've been wanting to sell your plantation for over a year. I'd say this was a conflict of interest. Perhaps Dryden has offered to buy your place in exchange for a little perjury on the stand.'

'That's not true!' Miles spluttered.

Gridley shrugged. 'Who decides what true is? Even a shadow of doubt would complicate things enough to condemn your testimony. As for you, Cunningham, I'll tell them all you were an accomplice, that you knew everything and you condoned it for the sake of forming the sugar cartel. You'll say anything to save your own hide.'

'Do you want to risk it?' Ren put in, trying hard to keep his senses focused, trying hard not to give in to the anger raging through him. He couldn't afford to let his mind wander, couldn't afford to think about Emma slipping away in a misguided effort to protect him.

'I sure as hell won't sit here and let you shoot me over that little whore of Merrimore's,' Gridley ground out, his eyes lit with a mad light.

'Then leave,' Kitt said. 'I have a boat at your disposal, *all* of your disposals. You have twelve hours to be on it. It will take you anywhere you want to go on the condition you don't come back here. There will be no charges pressed if you go quietly.'

'I wouldn't recommend England, however.' Ren looked each of them in the eyes, seeing them weigh their options. 'I have sent letters to influential friends and family about the nature of your characters. You will not be received.'

'You've ruined us!' Cunningham yelled. Ren couldn't tell if the comment was directed at himself or at Gridley.

'You've ruined yourselves by targeting an innocent

woman and bullying her into compliance. If she dies, I will come after you, wherever you are, and I will not offer second chances then.'

'Shall I start shooting, Ren?' Kitt asked. 'They seem a little hesitant to make their choice. I've already taken out Devore's knee. Perhaps this time I'll shoot for a shoulder. Would you like that, Miles? Or perhaps someone is tired of their testicles.'

Miles cringed. 'I'll go. I was going anyway. But what about the plantation? You can't expect me to give it up, it's all the wealth I have.'

'I do expect it. You were party to evil for personal gain,' Ren said simply. 'Walk out with what you can carry and consider yourself lucky. I won't let the plantation go to waste. I seem to recall being told there wasn't enough land in Barbados for the free peoples to start their own farming. Perhaps now there will be, at least enough to make a beginning.'

'You would not turn this land over to those slaves!' Gridley exclaimed.

'I would. They're free, Gridley, and they have been for two years now, not that anyone in your employ would recognise that. Your treatment is abominable.'

Gridley had been pushed too far. With a mighty lunge, he threw over the desk, sending paperweights and inkwells flying. He leapt for Ren, a knife flashing in his hand. Ren darted to the side, barely missing the slice of the secreted blade. The bastard must have had it up his sleeve. Gridley came at him again. In close quarters, it was hard to get his gun aimed. Ren would have to take the shot anyway. It was Gridley or him and Gridley was a fighting with a fiend's madness.

Gridley ran at him, Ren levelled his gun, a shot firing before he could get one off. Gridley crumpled with a cry, his eyes sightless before he hit the ground. Had he fired anyway? Ren gave his gun a quick check for powder marks, for smoke, but there was nothing. He glanced at Kitt, following Kitt's gaze to Amherst Cunningham.

'I always carry my special friend,' Amherst said calmly, putting the small gun, the type a gambler expecting trouble would carry, back in his coat pocket as if this was an everyday occurrence. 'I'll take the offer of a boat, Sherard. I trust all debts are paid? I'll be at the docks at midnight.'

Ren gave the man a curt nod as he exited the room with a *sangfroid* that sent a chill down Ren's spine, the other two following sullenly. Dash it, Emma had been more right than she'd known when she'd said these men checked in their morals at the dock.

Ren nudged Gridley's still form with the toe of his boot. 'I've asked you for so much already, Kitt. Can you look after things here? I want to get back to Emma, I want her to know it's over.'

It was over. There was only peace, only calm in this place. Emma was floating. It felt good and cool. There was no worrying, no fighting, nothing to fight against. There was nothing at all. It was empty.

That bothered her. Something should be here, surely? A sense of wrongness pricked at the perfection, at the calm. *Ren.* Ren should be here. No, she was giving him up. Why? Her mind was fuzzy. The emptiness became more menacing than peaceful, dragging on her memories, dulling them before she could retrieve them. She was forgetting something very important, something she didn't want to forget.

She struggled to retrieve that memory. That was it... Ren loved her. Ren was going to marry her, but she couldn't...why? Because Gridley would kill him, because Gridley would not rest until she was his. Because she loved Ren too much to have him die for her...so she was going to die for him. Was that what she was doing here in this peaceful place? Was this part of dying?

There was only one flaw to her plan. There would be no Ren, if she died. She'd miss so much: his arms, his touch, the way he kissed her neck, nibbled at her ears, the way he enticed her to wickedness like swimming naked in their underground lake. She'd miss his gentler side, too, the side that walked in the surf and spoke of his father and his family with unmistakable love. She would miss his sense of right. A passionate man, a *good* man, loved her. Not many women could say that. It would be something to take with her to the other side, that and the knowledge that she'd freed him.

'Emma.' Her name. Someone was calling her name. Not just someone, *him*. Ren. 'Emma.' The call came again. She hadn't imagined it. How nice to hear his voice one more time. Strong fingers closed around her hand. She would have his touch once more. It was more than she could have hoped for. She was indeed blessed to have him here at the end.

'Emma!' His voice was more insistent now, less

pleasant. His words tore through the quiet peace. 'Emma, Gridley's gone. Dead. Cunningham shot him. He can't hurt you again, can't hurt me again. We are safe. I know what you mean to do, Emma. You don't have to die for me. Come back, my love, it's over.'

Emma curled her fingers around his and began the journey back towards the sound of his voice, back towards the litany of his dreams as he spelled them out for her: a home, children, a family. Things she'd given up on long ago. There might not be something to fight against, but now there was something to fight for and that was so much better.

When her eyes opened, it was to see Ren lying beside her, stretched out on his side, his fingers intertwined with hers. She had known they would be. Her body, her mind, had been aware of his presence long before she could acknowledge it. He was smiling that devastating smile, the one that showed off his dimple, the very one that had nearly undone her the first day they'd met.

'Hello, sleepyhead,' Ren drawled.

'Are you ready?' She smiled drowsily at him.

'Ready for what?' Ren's eyes danced.

'To start our life together.' Now that her decision was made, she didn't want to wait a moment longer to start her happy-ever-after. She understood what Ren had meant the night he'd told her he wanted to cherish her.

'As soon as you can get out of bed.' Ren kissed her gently. She felt tears start behind her eyes. She'd almost given this up, almost given him up.

Emma laughed. 'Out of bed? I thought the best part of forever happened *in* bed?'

'Minx.' Ren laughed with her. His smiled faded. 'Em, don't leave me again, promise? I don't want to be that scared ever.'

She looked down at their hands, locked together, her voice starting to shake with emotion. There was so much she should tell him about how she felt, about how much he meant, but all that came out was, 'Thank you, Ren.' He would know all that was encompassed in those simple words because he knew her body and soul. And he loved her anyway. What more could a girl ask for?

Epilogue

What more could a man ask for? Ren Dryden could think of nothing as he waited for his bride at the altar of St Michael's of All Angels. Kitt Sherard stood beside him, hair pulled back and dressed in a respectable jacket and trousers, not so respectably flirting with the pretty girl in the front row.

The church was full, although there were few people Ren knew personally sitting in the pews. But there were many who knew him at least by reputation. They'd come to his wedding to pay tribute to his efforts and Emma's. Thanks to their efforts, the abandoned plantations had been broken into smaller farms and given to the freedmen who had worked them for the former owners. People who had given up hope of farming their own land had a chance again and those people, black and white, had come to witness his celebration.

The doors at the back of the church opened and Ren's eyes were riveted on the sight of Emma coming down the aisle. The sunlight behind her shone on the filmy gauze of her veil and caught the seed pearls trimming her dress. She'd opted to wear white, an extravagant colour choice and hardly practical, but she'd insisted. White symbolised a new beginning, a slate wiped clean and no one knew the importance of that more than she.

Ren didn't care. She'd look beautiful in any colour. As it was, the effect was striking against the foil of her dark hair. Every step she took brought his future closer to him, a future he'd only dared to dream about. When she was close enough, Ren reached out a hand for her, drawing her close and lifting her veil. He mouthed the words, 'I love you', and watched her eyes sparkle with tears.

The ceremony started. There were prayers and hymns, vows and rings, official and meaningful in their own way, a public pledge that mirrored the private one he and Emma had made earlier in front of the witness that mattered most. They'd come early and walked in the churchyard, taking time to visit Cousin Merrimore's grave and leave a flower offering, feeling the old man's presence wash over them in blessing as they stood before his headstone, hands entwined in silence as they were now.

The bishop was nearly done. Only one last instruction remained. 'Ah,' Ren whispered as he bent to carry out the bridal kiss. 'The Caribbean, land of risk, rum and most unexpectedly, romance.'

Emma smiled up at him, her eyes sparkling. 'Especially the romance.'

* * * * *

BREAKING THE
RAKE'S RULES

For Nic, Flo, my awesome editor, who really massaged this book into excellence and took time to make it a meaningful story with a strong life lesson: you can't outrun your past, so you might as well embrace it. Thanks to Flo, Kitt Sherard does it in style.

And thanks to my agent, Scott Eagan, at Greyhaus Literary Agency who also had to put up with all my re-writes. There were lots of fits and starts and you were kind enough, patient enough to argue with me about all of them. It is much appreciated.

Chapter One

The Caribbean—June 1836

'**P**rotect the rum!' Kitt Sherard raced forward on the beach to throw himself between the oncoming attackers and the newly unloaded cargo of precious barrels. 'It's a trap!' A pistol flashed in one hand, his knife in the other as the words left his mouth, the cry carrying down the line to be taken up by his men. 'Protect the rum! Protect the rum!' He felt his men surge behind him, his first mate, Will Passemore, at his right, digging his bare feet into the sand, ready to take on the thick of the fighting.

Anger fuelled Kitt, pumping through his body over the betrayal. This was supposed to have been a standard trade done in the light of broad day; rum for farming supplies. The afternoon sun beating down on them was proof enough of that, but somewhere, something had gone wrong. There was no time to sort through it at present.

Cries echoed throughout the deserted cove as the first of the attackers emerged from the pack. Kitt took aim at the man's shoulder and fired, hoping the draw of first blood would cause the bandits to retreat. He meant business when rum was on the line, especially when that rum belonged to a friend, but he never liked to take a life.

The man clutched his arm and fell back, only to be overrun by his fellow outlaws. So much for deterrence. 'Get ready, this means war,' Kitt muttered under his breath. 'These bastards won't go easily.'

'We'll manage them, Captain.' Beside him, Passemore's jaw was set with grim determination.

The horde was on them, then. With one roar, Kitt's men met the mêlée. Kitt threw aside his pistol. This was knife work now. He stabbed wherever he could, quick, sharp jabs to shoulders, thighs, an occasional belly when there was no choice. Sweat ran in his face and he fought the urge to wipe it away with a hand. The bandits were tenacious, Kitt would give them that. At last they began to fall back—the sight of their fallen comrades was persuasion enough that whatever they were being paid wasn't worth it. 'Come on, boys, we've got them on the run!' Kitt yelled over the fighting, leading the charge to drive the bandits from the cove.

They fled with relative speed, dragging their wounded with them. Will was ahead of him, firing a pistol into the fleeing rabble. A man went down and Will leapt on him, blade drawn. 'No!' Kitt swerved to Will's side. 'We need him alive. Get him back to the ship and get him patched up. I want to know who is behind this.'

'Aye, aye!' Will said with a relish that made Kitt grin. The younger man reminded him of himself six or so years ago when he'd begun this adventure. Will hefted the man over a shoulder with a grunt. 'C'mon, you stupid bastard.'

With Will headed back to the bumboats with the wounded man and the bandits scrambling the island hills to protection, Kitt organised the beach. 'Let's get the barrels back on board, men! Look lively—we don't want them thinking about organising a counter-attack.' Kitt doubted they would. His men had given them quite a drubbing, but he knew from experience one did not take chances in this business.

Even though he'd not expected trouble this afternoon, he'd come armed, just in case. Kitt helped roll a barrel towards the bumboats, his thoughts chasing each other around in his mind. There'd been reports these last four months of bandit crews operating in the area, stealing rum and sugar from small merchant trading ships that sailed between the islands.

For the most part, Kitt hadn't taken those reports seriously. Small merchant ships, many of them more like boats and not in the best of shape, were often unarmed and undermanned when it came to fighting. They made easy targets, unlike his ship, *Queen of the Main.* Small-time bandits would prefer small-time targets. Only today, they hadn't.

Kitt ran a hand through his hair, surveying the beach. All the barrels were loaded and the men were ready to go. Kitt gave the signal to shove off and leapt into the bow of the nearest boat. It had been the worst of luck the bandits had chosen today, when he'd been hauling his friend Ren Dryden's rum. Ren would be disappointed.

Kitt had protected the rum, which was no small thing in this part of the world where rum and sugar were still the currency of the land. But on the downside, Ren had been counting on this trade to purchase much-needed farming supplies. Now, Ren was without a sale and without the goods he and his wife needed for the upcoming harvest. He didn't relish telling Ren he'd failed.

Ahead in the water, Kitt could see the first boat bump up against the side of the *Queen*. He could make out Will hauling their prisoner up to the deck in a rope sling. Kitt hoped the prisoner would provide some answers.

Aboard ship, Will had bad news. 'I don't think we can save him, Captain. He took the ball in the back. It's lodged in his spine. You'd better come quick. It's beyond O'Reilly's skill.' Not surprising news given that O'Reilly's 'skill' was relegated to stitching knife wounds.

The man was laid out on the deck, unable to be moved any further. The pain of his injury was evident in the pallor of his skin. Fear was evident, too, Kitt thought as he knelt beside him. The man knew death was coming. Kitt saw it in his eyes. 'Aye, man, it won't be long now,' Kitt said softly, motioning for his crew to give them room.

Kitt lay a hand on the man's forehead. 'Is there anything you want to tell me? Anyone you want me to notify?'

The man—or was he a boy?—shook his head. Up close, beneath the dirt and sweat, he didn't look as old as Passemore. Or perhaps they all looked like boys when they died, all pretence of bravery stripped away when it came right down to it. His brother had looked very much the same way in the last hour they'd spent together, the enormity of what was about to transpire etched in every ashen line of his face.

'All right then,' Kitt soothed him. 'May I ask who sent you? Who paid you?'

The man struggled to speak as the pain took him. There was urgency in his gaze. His words were halting. 'They. Are. Waiting. For. You. If. We. Failed. Don't. Go. Back.' His features relaxed, his breathing rattled. 'Am. I. Forgiven?' The question of every dying man.

Kitt pressed a kiss to the man's forehead and gave him the only absolution he could. 'Your debt is paid. Rest in peace.' The man breathed once more and was gone. Kitt rose. His crew was solemn around him. Kitt clapped a hand on O'Reilly's shoulder, his tone sombre. 'You know what to do, take it from here. Make sure I have anything of note that he carried.' In case there was a message to convey after all, or a clue as to who 'they' were, or even the man's name.

Shadows were falling by the time they put into port at Carlisle Bay and rowed ashore. Bridgetown was quiet for the evening, all the shops closed, people at home with their families. Out at Sugarland, Ren and Emma would be preparing to sit down to an evening meal. Kitt smiled, thinking of his friend and Ren's newfound happiness as a husband, a landowner, a man in charge of shaping his own destiny. It was what Ren wanted out of life. It was what Kitt had once assumed would have been his, too, by right, a future he'd been raised to expect without question up until the hour it was snatched away, no longer an option. Six years in and he was still grasping just how long for ever was.

Don't think on it, remembering can't change anything. The dying man had made him maudlin. Tonight, such ruminations were best set aside in light of the dead man's warning. He couldn't afford the distraction no matter what sentiments the man had conjured.

Normally, this was a time of day Kitt enjoyed, for a while anyway. Dusk was a break between the hustle of his days and the activity of his nights. Staying busy was critical in keeping his mind focused on the present. Too much solitude, too much quiet, and he knew from experience his mind would drift to less pleasant considerations best left in the past. This evening, though, the usual peace of dusk was absent. Menace stalked the stillness.

Maybe he was paranoid. Did he believe the dying man's warning? Or was it one last lie? If so, it was certainly a powerful one. Kitt could hardly afford to ignore it. He dipped his hand into the top of his boot and drew his knife. If there was an attack, there'd be no time to draw it later. He had rooms in a boarding house just off Bay Street past the governor's mansion for nights when it was too late to go home or when business detained him in town, as it did this evening. He was due at the Crenshaws' for dinner. The distance wasn't far, although tonight it seemed like miles.

At the end of Bay Street, the shadows moved. In one stealthy motion, they were upon him, three against one. One of them leapt on his back, trying to push him down, but Kitt was ready. He smashed the body into the wall of a nearby building, stunning the first attacker. His back to the wall, Kitt whirled, knife in hand, to face the other two. They were big, swarthy men. Kitt assessed the situation instantly. They would want to make the first move, would want to crowd him against the wall so that he had no room to move. They were operating under the assumption that he would fight. Kitt grinned. He would seize the advantage and take them by surprise. Knife at the ready, head lowered like a bull, he rushed them, pushing one aside with enough of a shove to keep the man off balance, and then he kept going.

But the men were fast and willing to give chase. They were closing on him. Kitt spied a house with lights on. That would do. He tore through the little gate separating the house from the street and streaked through the garden. He needed to get up and in. Ah, a trellis! A balcony! Perfect.

Kitt planted his foot on the bottom rung of the trellis and climbed upward, feeling the trellis bend under the pressure of his weight at every step. He grabbed the railing of the balcony and hauled himself up, his foot kicking the trellis to the ground as a precaution just in case the men were fool enough to try. Kitt threw himself over the railing and drew a breath of relief. He lay on his back, looking up at the sky and exhaled. It had been one hell of a day. Maybe he *was* getting too old for this.

He'd just got to his feet, feeling assured the would-be assassins had given up and ready to think about what to do next, when the balcony door opened. 'Who's there?' A woman in a white-satin dressing gown stepped outside, her mouth falling open at the sight of him.

Only quick thinking and quicker reflexes prevented a scream from erupting. Kitt grabbed the woman and pulled her to him, his mouth covering hers, swallowing her scream. He'd only meant to silence her, but God, those soft, full breasts of hers felt good against him. She was naked beneath the dressing robe, a fact every curve and plane of her pressed against him made evident.

Maybe it was the adrenaline of the day, but all he wanted to do was fall into her. His intrepid lady didn't seem to mind. She'd not shut her mouth against his invasion, her body had not tried to pull away. It was all the invitation he needed. His lips started to move, his tongue caressing the inside of her mouth, running over her teeth. Ah, his lady had a sweet tooth! She tasted of peppermints and smelled of her bath, all lemon and lavender where he breathed in her skin. She was all womanly heat against him, her tongue answering him with an exploration of its own.

Kitt nipped at her lower lip, eliciting a surprised gasp. His hand moved to cup her breast, kneading it through the slippery satin, the belt of her robe coming loose. He slipped a hand inside, making contact with warm, lemon-and-lavender-scented skin, his arousal starting to peak. He had no doubt she could feel it against her thighs where their bodies met.

An ill-timed knock on her door interrupted the pleasant interlude, followed by worried masculine tones. 'Is everything all right in there?' Kitt knew a moment's panic. There were only so many explanations for a voice like that. A father? A brother? A fiancé? Or worst of all, a husband?

His lady jumped away, her grey eyes wide as she mouthed the words, *My father*! But she was cool under pressure. Panic was already receding as she stared at him, assessing her choices and their advantages. Would she give him away? Kitt gave her a wicked smile to indicate there were definite benefits to keeping his secret. She smiled back. Apparently the decision was made.

She called into the room, loud enough to be heard through the door. 'Everything's fine, I heard a crash. It's nothing, just the trellis again.' And then, perhaps realising someone might come in anyway to be sure she was safe, she added hastily, 'I'm, um, getting dressed. I'll be down in a moment.'

Satisfied she would be left alone, she turned towards Kitt, hands on hips. 'Now, for the question of the night, who are you and what are you doing in my bedroom?'

Kitt grinned, letting his eyes appreciably roam the length of her. His rescuer was strikingly attractive. Long chestnut hair hung down her back in a heavy, shiny curtain, the sharp planes of her cheek bones and cool grey eyes creating the impression of intelligence. This was no unseasoned Miss. Maybe things were starting to look up. His cock certainly thought so. He leaned back against the railing, arms crossed over his chest, making no attempt to hide his arousal. 'My name is Kitt and what I'm doing in your bedroom is entirely up to you.'

Chapter Two

If there was a more blatant invitation to sin, Bryn Rutherford had yet to hear it. Or see it, for that matter. The
blond, tanned, mass of male muscle leaning on the rail
of her balcony was temptation personified. Even sweaty
and wearing the dirt of the day—and from the looks
of it, his day, whatever it had been, had been pretty
dirty—she could tell he was delicious. He'd tasted delicious, too, like an adventure—all wind and salt as if
he'd spent a day at sea.

She probably should have slapped him for his unorthodox silencing, but that would assume she hadn't liked
it, or that she hadn't willingly participated in it. She was
honest enough to admit that she had. And why not? It
wasn't every day a handsome man climbed into a girl's
bedroom. The question now was what was she going to
do about it? She ought to throw him back down the trellis, but her curiosity simply wouldn't allow it, nor would
the fact that he'd apparently knocked the trellis over.

Bryn returned his stare with a frank appraisal of
her own, running her gaze down the length of him in
return. Two could play this game. 'There isn't time for

what you propose, sir. I have a dinner to attend. My father is expecting me downstairs momentarily.' As if *not* having a dinner engagement would have changed her decision. One look at him had told her he would not appreciate a reticent Miss who shirked from stolen kisses. He wanted the woman she'd been in his arms, all courage and fire.

'Another time perhaps?' Bryn dared, enjoying this moment of boldness, of not worrying about the rules. Men who climbed trellises were beyond the rules to start with. She needn't worry about him telling anyone what they'd done. Such a confession would force him to the altar and that was the last thing he wanted. This man was not husband material, he was fantasy material, but she needed him to depart. Her maid would be up any minute to help her finish dressing. He would be rather hard to explain. 'As lovely as the interlude has been, I do need to ask you to leave.'

He made a show of looking around, past her into the bedroom, down at the garden below and up at the sky for good measure. 'Exactly how do you propose I do that?'

'It would have been easier if you hadn't kicked over the trellis.' Easier, but far less exciting. It was rather arousing to imagine those arms of his flexing as he pulled himself over the balcony without the help of any support. Whatever he did all day, it was no doubt 'exerting'. He fairly oozed good health from the pores of that tanned skin. Probably what he did all night was exerting, too. He wasn't the kind to sleep alone.

Bryn looked over the railing at the ground. 'Easier, but not impossible without it. If you lowered yourself over the balcony and extended to your full length, you could safely make the drop without any harm, I think.'

'Or I could hide under your bed until you've left,' he suggested with another sexy smile that sent a decadent trill down her spine. This was the most fun she'd had in ages: no chaperon, very nearly no clothes and this wicked man all to herself. She'd forgotten how much fun flirting was.

She trailed her hand down the open vee at the neck of her dressing gown, watching his eyes follow the motion. 'What a most erotic suggestion, letting you watch me undress. I must decline out of fear you will rob us blind after I leave. I can't let a stranger have unsupervised access to the house.' She flicked her eyes towards the door in warning, a reminder that discovery was imminent if he continued to delay. 'I really must ask that you go or this time I will scream.'

He laughed and made her a little bow before throwing a leg over the railing. She held her breath. She didn't want him to be hurt, but she had to get rid of him and she was fairly sure the drop wouldn't be injurious. He gave her a wink as he levered himself into position. 'Don't worry, I'm sure your estimations are correct.' Then he disappeared. A moment later, she heard a quiet thud. She risked a look over the edge and saw him rise up, brush off the dirt and trot out the garden gate into the night. In the falling darkness, her conscience might have imagined the limp.

Bryn wished he'd trot out of her thoughts just as easily. He might have if the dinner had been more entertaining. Although to be fair, it would had to have been extremely diverting in order to compete with the episode on her balcony. As it was, the most exciting thing about dinner was the empty chair across from her. It most certainly wasn't the man on her left, a Mr Orville, a successful importer, who simply wasn't up to it with his paunchy belly and habit of excessively using the term 'my dear' to start most of his sentences. The man on her right was not much better, only younger. But she understood the importance of making a decent first impression, of stroking the feathers of a man's ego. The nuances of being a lady had been drilled into her quite thoroughly by her mother, a testament to her upbringing, since she'd turned fourteen. She knew how to be a lady and how to use it to her advantage. That didn't mean she liked it.

Quite frankly, being a lady was boring, a discovery she'd made her first Season out. She preferred to think she was far more adventurous than dancing twice with the same man at a ball. She also preferred to think she was more like the woman she'd been on the balcony. However, she was smart enough to know that woman, full of fire and passion, had no place at a dining table full of her father's potential business partners. As much as it chafed, tonight she had to play the lady.

She and her father had only been ashore for three days and everyone was eager to make their acquaintance given her father's mission. The men gathered at the Crenshaws' this evening were the influential cream of Bridgetown society, the men with connections and knowledge that would be critical in carrying out the crown's charter.

These were the men she needed to impress, not sweaty, blond rogues caught in the likely act of housebreaking. The man today was nothing more than a common criminal and she'd carried on like a common hussy with him. No matter how exciting he might have been, such behaviour was not what her father needed from her. He would be scandalised if he knew what had transpired. She supposed she should be disappointed in herself. She'd set aside the teachings of girlhood at the merest temptation. But when that temptation kissed like her balcony god, it was hard to be penitent.

Bryn sipped from her wine glass and smiled at the man on her right, a Mr Selby, very aware that he was trying to sneak a glimpse of her bosom while he talked about the island's sights. Heaven forbid he actually talk about banking with a woman. She had the impression her unexpected visitor wouldn't make such a distinction. He'd talk about whatever he liked, with whomever he liked. Kitt-with-no-last-name wouldn't 'sneak' a peek at her bosom, he'd make no secret of appreciating it with a rather frank and forthright blue-gazed assessment.

'What do you think, Miss Rutherford?' Mr Selby asked, catching her unawares.

'I'm sorry, about what?' Bryn apologised, trying to look penitent, an emotion she was apparently having difficulty conjuring with any sincerity tonight.

He smiled patiently, too much of a gentleman to protest her inattention, but not too much of a gentleman to look down her dress. 'About a picnic. I thought you might enjoy a tour of the parish.'

Coward. The man from the balcony would have made her accountable for her distraction. The thought of how he might do that sent a pleasant shiver down her spine. Then again, if it had been him, her attention wouldn't have lapsed in the first place.

'I would, although perhaps it could wait until Father

and I are settled. There's quite a lot to do at the moment with unpacking.' She smiled and turned back to Orville, signalling the discussion was closed.

It became the pattern of the evening. Bryn listened intently, and responded appropriately, playing the dinner game adequately if not adroitly. By the time the cheese course arrived, signalling the end of dinner, she'd come to the disappointing conclusion evenings here weren't unlike the evenings in London. She'd hoped they would be different. She'd hoped the men would be different, too.

A little smile tugged at her lips. In that regard, at least one of them was. She wondered if she'd see him again or *how* she *could* see him again. Perhaps he ran a business in town? Perhaps it was possible to arrange a chance meeting? She almost laughed aloud at that. Her logic was failing her. He'd given her no last name, very likely on purpose. Men like him didn't want to be found. Her balcony Romeo was no businessman. Just a few minutes ago she was thinking him a criminal. Besides, businessmen looked like Mr Orville on her left, they simply didn't look like *Kitt*: part-beach god, part-pirate.

Be careful where your thoughts are leading you, her conscience warned. *This is a new start for your father. Your father needs you. You can't run around risking a scandal. This is too important for him. Besides, you promised.*

But it's a new start for me, too, her heart argued in return. She could have stayed in London with relatives where life was safe and predictable. She'd had enough of that. If she was discreet, perhaps there would be a way to have both. After all, was it wrong to want a little adventure? She'd been good for so very long. Years, in fact. Surely she was due some reward.

Eleanor Crenshaw, their hostess, rose, indicating the ladies should follow her into the drawing room. Bryn gathered her skirts and cast a last glance up the table where her father was nodding and answering questions. She hoped it was going well. She still didn't know quite how her father had managed the royal appointment. She suspected well-meaning relatives had had a hand in it. Her father's older brother was the Earl of Creighton and well-connected politically.

It wasn't that she doubted her father's abilities. Even as a younger son, he'd had his own ambitions, albeit they'd always been more of a local bent. Still, she wasn't sure it was fair to equate his experience as a country financier on the same level as the banking interests of an empire. She adored her father. She didn't want to see him set up to fail, but this had not been a consideration when the mighty Rutherfords had lobbied for the lucrative post to Bridgetown. They'd seen only the advantages.

Her father's success would see the Rutherfords strategically placed to take advantage of the crown's banking monopoly in the Caribbean. It served the grand Rutherford design to send her father overseas to expand the family interests, but Bryn hoped for more than that from this appointment. She hoped the change would give him a chance to rebuild his life after the death of his wife. For over a year her father had moped about, showing interest in nothing since her mother's death. It was time for him to move on. He was too vibrant, too intelligent of a man to simply give up on life when there was still much he could do for his family and for others.

The ladies' conversation in the drawing room politely danced around that very issue with feminine delicacy. What could her father do for their husbands? How much authority did her father have to act on his own? Was her father going to run some of his own investments? Bryn hoped not, if for no other reason than she wanted him to start slow, follow the crown's directive to the letter and complete his mission with success. It was simple enough if he stuck to the plan. But she also knew his brother had encouraged him to make some private investments as well.

Bryn was about to turn the conversation a different direction and ask about the empty chair at the dinner table when a footman entered. The man whispered something to her hostess, bringing a smile to the woman's face. 'By all means, Bradley, show him in.' She beamed at the women seated around her. It was the smug smile of a woman who has just pulled off a social coup. Bridgetown or London, apparently the look was universal. 'Our dear captain has arrived.'

Everyone burst into smiles and there were even a few titters behind painted fans. Good Lord, this Captain Whoever-he-was had the women acting positively swoony, even the married ones who ought to know better. To Bryn's left, the daughter of one of the women—a Miss Caroline Bryant—blushed and looked down at her hands in an attempt at modesty. Bryn thought it only a moderate effort at subtly calling attention to herself and whatever she wished the gesture to imply about her and the captain. In London, a girl Miss Bryant's age would have been out for a few Seasons and far better schooled in the art of dissembling.

'Ladies,' the footman intoned, coming back into the room, 'Captain Christopher Sherard.'

Bryn's gaze went to the door out of curiosity over the hubbub, her mind wrapping around the name. Captain Sherard was one of the investors on her father's list of potential hopefuls and one of the men they had not met yet. He'd been highly recommended by the Earl of Dartmoor through a friend back in London. Her father was pinning a lot of his hopes on this particular investor who had yet to materialise.

At first glance, the man who stepped into the room was striking. At second glance, he was horrifying familiar. *Kitt. Christopher.* No, it couldn't be. Her heart began to hammer as her mind connected the names with this golden god and then connected the implications. The man from the balcony was her father's prime investor!

Unexpected didn't begin to cover it. Bryn looked a third time, desperate to be sure, or was it to be 'not sure'? She wasn't certain if her heart pounded from fear of impending disaster or from the excitement of seeing him again. The way it was racing at present it might be both. Maybe she should simply wipe her sweaty palms on her skirts, ascribe it to the fact that he looked extraordinary and leave it at that.

Surely it couldn't be the same man? Long golden hair was slicked back into a thick tail tied with black ribbon. His sweat-streaked shirt had been exchanged for immaculate linen. A subtle diamond winked in his cravat as a statement of wealth and good taste. His evening clothes were well fitted enough to have done any Bond

Street tailor proud, their tight fit showing off broad shoulders, lean hips and long legs.

The physique certainly suggested he was the same man. It was the clothes that differed. They were expensive and tasteful, two traits she didn't associate with her balcony visitor. She knew a moment's disappointment. Perhaps it wasn't him after all, just a strong similarity simply because she'd been thinking of him. It would be an easy enough trick for her mind to play on her. Her pulse settled back into its usual rhythm. It was for the best. Business and pleasure never mixed, at least not well, and what sort of investor climbed balconies and kissed strange women? Not one her father could trust and not one she should trust either.

But wait… She studied his face, the strong line of his jaw, the razor straightness of his nose, features she'd seen up close today. It was the eyes that gave him away. Her heart bucked in her chest. It *was* him! The very same man who'd climbed up to her balcony, kicked over her trellis and kissed her senseless without even knowing her name.

All the fine tailoring in the world couldn't disguise the wildness in his blue eyes as they roamed the room, taking in the occupants one by one until they rested on her. Recognition fired in their cobalt depths ever so briefly, his mouth twitching with a secret smile.

Her breath caught as she suffered his silent scrutiny. Would he expose their little secret? She'd not worried about the man on the balcony exposing anything, it didn't suit that man to be caught in a compromising position. She understood him. But this one in fine evening clothes who acted like a gentleman and was supposed to be a banker? *This* was going to be tricky. He had destroyed all her assumptions and that left her feeling far too vulnerable at the moment.

A scandal was the last thing she needed. She knew very well her behaviour reflected on her father. Rutherfords were taught from birth the actions of the individual reflected on the family. Men would be reluctant to do business with a man who couldn't control his daughter. Besides, she'd made a promise and Bryn Rutherford *never* went back on her word.

His gaze left her and he moved towards Eleanor Crenshaw, making their hostess the focus of all his blue-eyed attention. Gone was the sweaty, dirty pirate prince. This new version came complete with requisite manners. He would dazzle in any ballroom, let alone Mrs Crenshaw's provincial parlour. He took their hostess's hand. 'Please forgive me for being late. I hope the numbers at the table weren't terribly upset.'

Bryn fought the urge to gape, her thoughts catching up to the implication of his statement. He was the empty chair. This grew more curious by the minute. Questions spun off into more questions. If he was supposed to have been here, why had he been scaling balconies? It was hardly standard banker behaviour.

Mrs Crenshaw was murmuring some inanity about forgiving him anything as long as he was here now to entertain them. 'Perhaps you and Miss Caroline would play another duet for us. You are both so excellently talented at the piano.' Her balcony intruder played the piano? The oh-so-modest Miss Caroline blushed again as Kitt acquiesced and escorted her to the piano, which stood suspiciously ready for such an occasion, further proof that his presence tonight was no accident. He'd been expected and in fact was expected regularly. This was no random occurrence. Well, Miss Caroline and her blushes were welcome to him, Bryn told herself. She hardly knew the man well enough to be jealous. A few stolen kisses hardly constituted a relationship. She really ought to feel sorry for Miss Caroline, who was clearly labouring under the assumption Kitt Sherard was somehow a respectable gentleman.

Bryn should count herself lucky. She'd seen his true colours this afternoon. She knew what he'd been doing and why he was late.

However, by the time the tea cart arrived and the men joined them, she liked Miss Caroline a little less than she had the hour before.

'When you said another time, I didn't think it would be so soon.' The smooth voice at her ear made her jump. She salvaged her tea cup just barely without spilling.

'I didn't imagine this party to be your sort of venue— no trellises to climb,' Bryn replied smoothly, keeping her gaze fixed forward on the other guests, but her body was aware of his closeness, the clean vanilla scent of his cologne and the sandalwood of his bath soap. He'd bathed after he'd left her, a thought that brought a flood of prurient images to mind. Hardly the sort of thing one should think about over evening tea.

'Pity, I would have pegged you for having a rather good imagination earlier this evening.' Laughter bubbled under the low rumble of his voice as if he had somehow followed her train of thought straight to his bath and knew exactly what she was thinking. 'There's plenty to climb here, just trellises of a different sort.' She ought to be put out by his innuendo, but instead all she could do was fight back a smile. If she did smile, people would be bound to notice and wonder.

His breath feathered her ear in a seductive tickle. 'Your failing imagination aside, I fear you have me at a disadvantage.'

She smiled down into her tea cup, unable to suppress it any longer. 'Oh, I doubt that very much, Mr Sherard. I don't think you ever find yourself at a disadvantage where women are concerned.'

He grinned in agreement, his teeth white against the tan of his face. 'In this case I most definitely am. Might you do me the honour of your name? You know mine, but I don't know yours.'

He would know soon enough. Island communities were small. 'It's Bryn, Bryn Rutherford.' She felt him stiffen slightly, the pattern of his breathing hitching infinitesimally in recognition, signs that he knew her already, or perhaps knew *of* her. She turned to catch sight of his reaction, wanting to confirm she'd guessed right. She nearly missed it.

He hid the reaction well. Had he not been standing so close, she wouldn't have noticed it, but she'd not been wrong in its attribution. He recognised the name. How odd that a simple fact like a name could provoke surprise between strangers. Or perhaps it wasn't so surprising. Bridgetown was a small society and news must travel fast. Every merchant, every businessman in town would know by now her father was coming, and why. It was intriguing to count Kitt Sherard among their number since she had so quickly dismissed him on those grounds earlier that evening. Did she proceed with the fiction that she hadn't noticed his surprise or did she confront him?

She opted for a bit of both. 'Does the earl know what you do in your spare time?' She was having difficulty reconciling this rogue of a man with a gentleman who'd have the ear of an earl. She was starting to think Dartmoor must have owed him an extraordinary favour to make this recommendation. Although, dressed as he was tonight, Captain Sherard might be mistaken for a lord, too.

He was studying her, hot blue eyes raking the length of her evening gown. He crooked his arm. 'Miss Rutherford, perhaps you would accompany me out to the veranda for some fresh air?' There was going to be a price. Bryn saw the subtle negotiation immediately. He wasn't going to talk in here where they could be overheard, but he would be pleased to trade information for the privacy of the veranda and whatever might evolve out there.

Say yes, the adventurer in her coaxed without hesitation. If his impromptu kisses were that good on a balcony, what might they be like on a veranda with moonlight and a little premeditation behind them? The lady in her knew better and tonight the lady held sway. *But only for tonight,* her naughty side prompted. She wouldn't always have to be the lady. She'd promised herself that, too, among other things.

Bryn decided to challenge him. 'Why? So I can risk a dagger in the back from the lovely Caroline Bryant for stealing your attentions or so that you can manoeuvre your way into my father's good graces through me? It'll take more than a kiss and a trellis to wring a recommendation from me, Captain.'

The women had been trying to lobby her all night. As much as a starlit veranda stroll with Kitt Sherard appealed to the adventurer in her, she wasn't naive enough to think romance was the captain's sole motivation. Rutherford girls were taught early to detect an opportunist at fifty paces. With dowries like theirs, it was a necessity for surviving London ballrooms crawling with genteel fortune hunters.

Bryn let her eyes lock with his over her tea cup as she raised it to her lips. 'I never mix business with pleasure. It would be best if we said goodnight, Captain, before one of us makes any faulty assumptions about the other.' Goodness knew what he must think of her after the balcony. If it was anything akin to what she thought of him, there'd been plenty of assumptions made already. Hardly the first impression either of them would have chosen to make.

His eyes glittered with humour, giving her the impression that while she had got the last word, he still had the upper hand. He gave her a small bow like the one he'd given her on the balcony, elegant and exaggerated in a subtly mocking manner. 'I have a meeting with your father in the afternoon. Afterwards, we could walk in the garden. You can decide then if it's business or pleasure.'

A meeting with her father? She knew what he thought. It would be a meeting where she was relegated to some far part of the house while men did business. Who was she to correct his assumptions? Bryn smiled, hoping the wideness of her grin didn't give her away. 'Until tomorrow, then, Captain Sherard.' The arrogant man might think he had the upper hand and the last word, but she had a few surprises of her own.

Chapter Three

Damn and double damn! Of all the balconies in Bridgetown, he'd climbed up Bryn Rutherford's, the daughter of the man who'd come to induct the crown's currency into the Caribbean and the man on whom Kitt's future business interests depended. Kitt couldn't believe his luck. What he couldn't decide was if that luck was good or bad. He was still debating the issue the next afternoon when he set out for his meeting with her father.

A certain male part of him had concluded it was very good luck indeed. Bryn Rutherford was a spitfire of a goddess. She had the lips to prove it, and the tongue, and the body, and everything else, including an insightful amount of intelligence. She'd immediately seen the ramifications of going out on the veranda with him.

Her refusal made her something of a cynic, too. For all the spirit she'd shown on the balcony, she was wary of consequences or maybe it was the other way around: consequences had made her wary. Perhaps it simply made her a lady, a woman of discernment and responsible caution. Not everyone had a past chequered with regrets just because he did. Then again, this was the Caribbean, a far-flung, remote outpost of the British empire. In his experience, which was extensive, *ladies* didn't sail halfway around the world without good reason. Did Bryn Rutherford have something to hide, after all?

It was an intriguing thought, one that had Kitt thinking past the interview with her father and to the walk in the garden that would follow. How did a girl with a well-bred, and very likely a sheltered, upbringing end up with the ability to kiss like seduction itself?

No, not a girl, a *woman*. There was no girlishness about Bryn Rutherford. She was past the first blush of debutante innocence. The green silk she'd worn last night communicated that message with clarity, even if he hadn't already seen her in that sinfully clingy satin dressing robe, felt her uncorseted curves, or tasted her unabridged tongue in his mouth giving as good as it got. Thoughts like that had him thinking he was a very lucky man. Thoughts like that also had kept him up half the night.

The other half of the night belonged to another set of less pleasant thoughts—who wanted him dead this time? The candidates for that dubious honour were usually different, but the motives were always the same. Was this latest attacker simply one of his less savoury business associates who felt cheated or was it more complicated than that? Had someone from his past found him at last and bothered to cross the Atlantic for revenge? He'd been so careful in that regard. Discovery risked not only him, but his family. He'd cast aside all he owned including his name to keep them safe. Of course, discovery was always possible, although not probable. But he was alive today because he planned for the former. It wasn't enough to just play the odds. Not when the people he loved and who loved him were on the line.

His mind had been a veritable hive of activity last night. He supposed he should feel fortunate he'd got any sleep, all things considered. There'd been critical business thoughts claiming his attention, too: would Bryn Rutherford hold the balcony interlude against him? If she did, how would that skew the business opportunities a bank in Barbados would provide? Those questions were still plaguing him when he knocked on the Rutherfords' front door.

He was taken down a long hall by a stately butler who must have come with them from England. The butler, Sneed, fit the surroundings perfectly with his air of formality. In the short time they'd been in residence, the Rutherfords had already left their aristocratic mark on the house. They'd come loaded with luxuries; carpets and paintings adorned the floors and walls in testimony to the Rutherfords' prestige to say nothing of the butler.

Kitt always made it a habit to study his surroundings. How a man lived offered all nature of insight. This house, the décor and its accessories were all designed to communicate one message: power and authority. Kitt approved of the intent. It was precisely the message a man charged with the crown's banking interests in the new world should convey. But, did the message match the man? That remained to be seen.

The door to the study was open, revealing the same luxury and wealth that dominated the hall. The butler announced him to the room in general and Kitt was surprised to see that Rutherford was not alone. James Selby, an aspiring local importer, was already present. The weasel. He must have come early. Well, Selby's limitations would speak for themselves sooner or later. Hopefully sooner.

The surprise didn't end there. Selby wasn't the only other person present. By a set of open French doors that let in the light and the breeze, her head demurely bent over an embroidery hoop, sat Bryn Rutherford. She looked up for the briefest of moments, long enough to let a coy smile slip over her lips when she met his gaze, her eyes communicating silent victory.

The minx! She'd known all along she was sitting in on the meeting. *Until tomorrow, then.* He could still see the wide smile on her face, the cat's-got-the-cream look in those grey eyes. He hadn't quite understood at the time. He understood now. She'd been laughing at him, getting a little of her own back.

'You look well settled for a man who has just arrived,' Kitt said affably, shaking hands with The Honourable Bailey Rutherford. Today, he would finally have a chance to take the man's measure more closely than he'd been able to do last night during their quick introduction at the Crenshaws'. The man was in his early fifties, with faded chestnut hair starting to thin, although once it must have been the rich colour of his daughter's. His face betrayed weariness in its lines and there was a trace of sadness in his eyes. He exuded none of his daughter's confidence.

Bailey Rutherford waved a dismissive hand in the air, the gesture showing off a heavy gold ring on one finger, another subtle sign of wealth and power. 'I can't take credit for any of this. I wouldn't know where to begin when it comes to setting up a house. My wife always handled these things. Now my daughter does.' He smiled in Bryn's direction. 'Did you meet her last night? Of course you must have.' There was pride in those last words and sorrow in the first. The sentence told Kitt volumes about Bailey Rutherford.

He was playing catch-up in that regard. Kitt would have liked to have talked to Rutherford prior to this meeting, would have preferred getting to know the man so he could assess Rutherford's character more thoroughly. Missing dinner had been unfortunate, but there'd been nothing for it. After leaving Bryn on her balcony, he'd taken a circuitous route home to avoid another encounter with the would-be assassins and then he'd absolutely had to bathe. By the time he was presentable, it had been too late for dinner.

'You already know Mr Selby?' Rutherford enquired, indicating that Kitt should take the empty chair. 'We were just talking about the geography of the islands.' They proceeded to continue that discussion, Kitt adding a bit of advice here and there, but Selby was in full glory, espousing his latest hobby; cataloguing the island's butterflies for a book. It would be a rather difficult book to write, Kitt thought. Barbados wasn't known for its butterflies. Beyond Rutherford's shoulder, Bryn rolled her eyes. Good. She found Selby as ridiculous as he did.

Thanks to Selby's windbag tendencies, there was plenty of time to let his gaze and his thoughts drift towards Bryn, who was trying hard to look demure in her quiet day dress of baby-blue muslin and white lace, her hair done up in a braided coronet, her graceful neck arched over her hoop. She wasn't fooling him for a minute.

Her very presence at such a meeting was provoking. Certainly, she'd planned to be here from the start, but in what capacity? She was no mere innocent attendee sitting here for her health, no matter that she'd dressed for the part. Most men wouldn't look beyond the dress and the sewing. They'd see her embroidery hoop for what it was—a woman's occupation.

Kitt saw it as much more—a ploy, a distraction even. He knew better. He had kissed her and a woman kissed her truth, *always*. Kitt had kissed enough women to know. He knew, too, that Bryn Rutherford's truth was passion. One day it would slip its leash—passion usually did. Kitt shifted subtly in his seat, his body finding the prospect of a lady unleashed surprisingly arousing.

Rutherford finally turned the conversation towards banking and Kitt had to marshal his attentions away from the point beyond his host's shoulder. 'I've been meeting with people all day. Now that the royal charter for a bank has been granted, everything is happening quickly. By this time next year, we'll have a bank established in Barbados and branches opening up on the other islands.' He smiled. His eyes, grey like his daughter's but not as lively, were faraway. 'That seems to be the way of life. We wait and wait for years, thinking we have all the time in the world and when the end comes, it comes so fast. So much time and then not nearly enough.'

Kitt leaned forward, wanting to focus on the bank before time for the interview ran out and all they'd discussed were butterflies. 'It's an exciting prospect, though. A bank will change the face of business and trade here,' he offered, hoping the opening would give Rutherford a chance to elaborate on the possibilities. At present, sugar and rum were as equally valid as the Dutch and Spanish currencies used as tender because the crown had not permitted the export of British money to its Caribbean colonies. As a result, actual money was in scarce supply. Plenty of people settled their debts in barter. Currency would make payment more portable. Casks of rum were heavy.

When all Rutherford did was nod, Kitt went on. 'The presence of an English bank would allow British pounds in Barbados. It would create alternatives for how we pay for goods and how we can settle bills, but it will also affect who will control access to those funds.' Kitt was not naive enough to think the crown had established the charter out of the goodness of its royal heart. The crown and those associated with it stood to make a great deal of money as a result of this decision. Kitt wanted to be associated. The charter would give the crown a monopoly not just on banking, but over the profits of the island.

'Exactly so,' Rutherford agreed, his eyes focused on a faceted paperweight.

It was Kitt's understanding Mr Rutherford's job was to make sure the charter was settled and the right players were in place. Rutherford would decide who those players would be. Although right now, Rutherford hardly seemed capable of making such weighty decisions. Then again, it might also be the effects of travel and late nights. Rutherford was not the youngest of men. Yet another interesting factor in having chosen him. Still, the bottom line was this: the interview was not going well.

It occurred to Kitt that Rutherford's disinterest might

have something to do with him personally. Maybe the man had already decided not to include him in the first tier of investors. Perhaps his daughter had told him certain things about balconies and kisses after all.

Kitt decided to be blunt. He had worked too hard for this invitation. He knew very well he'd only got his name on the list of potential investors because of his connections to Ren Dryden, Earl of Dartmoor. It had been Ren who'd put his name forward. 'What kind of bank will it be?' Kitt asked. He had his ideas, but clarification was important. There were savings banks and joint stock banks—quite a wide variety, really, since the banking reforms a few years ago—and when it came to money, not all banks were equal.

Rutherford showed a spark of life. 'Joint stock, of course. There are backers in London already assembled, waiting for counterpart investors to be assembled here. It will be like the provincial bank I was on the board for in England.'

Kitt nodded his understanding. This was good. The man had some experience. He would need it. These sorts of arrangements weren't without risk. Joint stock meant two things. First, it meant that the investors would share in the profits and in the losses. What the bank chose to invest in would be important, so would the level of risk. The less risk the better, but the less risk the fewer the profits, too. Second, it meant that shares could be traded on the exchange. They'd operate essentially like a business. This was not just a mere savings bank, it was a venture capital bank.

'Would we be loaning money to plantations?' Kitt asked, thinking of how that would change the current loan system. Right now, private merchants were primarily responsible for advancing the planters loans against the upcoming harvest so planters could buy supplies. It was what he'd done for Ren, or had tried to do for Ren before the bandits had upended the rum sale yesterday. A bank would reduce the opportunity for single merchants to finance planters. For those not on the board it would eliminate an avenue of income. No wonder there was competition for these spots.

Out of the corner of his eye, he caught Bryn reaching for something under her skeins of threads. No, not reaching. *Writing.* She was writing on a notebook. She'd been taking notes the entire time. Like Selby, he'd got so caught up in the discussion, in assessing Rutherford's assets, he'd not taken time to notice. Her part in all this was growing more interesting by the moment.

'It would depend,' Rutherford explained, 'on their collateral. Property cannot be taken as security.'

Kitt was thoughtful for a moment. Rutherford knew his banking vocabulary. That was reassuring. 'What do we mean by property, exactly?' Property, was a pretty wide term.

'It means the obvious, of course; homes and farms cannot be used as security.' Rutherford paused for a long moment and Bryn looked up, neatly inserting herself into the conversation.

'But it also means the less obvious, too, doesn't it, Father? That merchandise like rum or sugar can't be used as security either?' Kitt recognised immediately it wasn't a question as much as a prompt.

'It's not really a question of collateral then, is it?' Kitt surmised, flashing Bryn an inquisitive glance. 'We're to invest and hope there's profit. If there isn't, we're unlucky. There's no recouping of funds.' There would be no collateral. The charter had just couched it in different terms.

'Yes. Certainly, we can invest in the plantations, we just can't expect anything in return beyond a piece of the profits,' Rutherford said, regaining his confidence. 'Still, there's money to be made here.'

Kitt raised his eyebrows, encouraging the man to say more about what that money might be. Rum certainly, sugar and even tobacco in places were good cash crops. Then there was the merchandising end of things if a man acted quickly enough and knew when to get out. There was a boom going on currently, riding the wave of emancipation. Freed slaves meant more wage-earning consumers and that meant more demand for goods. Kitt knew that boom would not last, but for now it was spawning a retail layer that had originally been focused only on wholesale to large plantations.

'There's land, for starters,' Rutherford offered, looking pleased with himself.

'There's some,' Kitt said evenly, but he found the choice odd. It wouldn't have been his first option. But a non-native Englishman would. A newcomer wouldn't understand. 'Most of the land in Barbados is already under cultivation.' He'd been here for six years and knew first-hand there wasn't much left to claim unless it was bought from a previous owner. It was something the freedmen were struggling with. They wanted to be their own farmers, but there wasn't any land. This was an area where only time could teach a newcomer the realities of property ownership on an island where land was definitely a finite commodity.

Sneed entered to announce the next appointment was waiting. Rutherford nodded and turned to Kitt. 'I will be assembling the board of directors over the next few weeks. I hope we'll have a chance to talk further. I hear you're a successful businessman in these parts. You come recommended. Your expertise of the area would be useful in determining the right investments for us.'

'Quite possibly.' Kitt rose and shook the man's hand. The veiled invitation was progress enough for today. It confirmed he had not been ruled out. He also appreciated he wasn't being asked to commit today. The bank was going to happen. It was already a *fait accompli*. That was assured. What wasn't assured was the bank's success. If the bank was going to do well, it would need someone knowledgeable and strong at its helm. A weaker man might easily be led astray and subsequently Rutherford, too.

Selby rose as well. 'I was hoping I might have a private word with you before I go?' he said to Rutherford, shooting a pointed look in Kitt's direction. In general, Selby didn't like him. He was too reckless for the young man's more conservative tastes. A plainer plea for privacy could not have been made. Kitt might have been offended over the dismissal if it hadn't suited his purposes.

Kitt glanced over at Bryn. 'Perhaps you could show me the gardens? You mentioned them last night and I'm eager to see them.' He turned towards Rutherford. 'If it's all right with you, of course?'

Rutherford beamed and nodded. 'Absolutely. Bryn dear, show our guest the gardens. I didn't know you were a botanist, Captain?'

Kitt gave a short nod of his head. 'I'm a man of diverse interests, Mr Rutherford.' He offered Bryn his arm, feeling a smug sense of satisfaction at the disapproving frown on Selby's face. It served him right for coming early and then asking for a private audience on top of that. 'Shall we, Miss Rutherford? I want to see the trellis you've told me so much about. It's a climbing trellis, if I remember correctly?'

Chapter Four

'You're a wicked man to bring up the incident in such company,' Bryn scolded him as soon as they stepped outside. She wasn't truly upset with him, at least not about the potential for exposure anyway. She'd reasoned away those concerns last night. He had nothing to gain but an unwanted wife from telling.

Kitt merely grinned. 'Harmless fun only, I assure you. It means nothing to anyone but us.' Drat him, he was enjoying teasing her and that grin of his said he wasn't done yet. 'But you, miss, are another story entirely. *You* knew you would be at the meeting. I feel quite taken advantage of.' He feigned hurt, then added with a wink, 'I can't let you have all the surprises.'

Bryn gave him a coy smile to indicate she understood his game. He no more liked losing the upper hand than she did. There was safety in having control. Control meant protection against the unexpected. 'Ah, it's to be retribution then?' She couldn't resist teasing him in return. His humour was infectious, even if she needed to remember it was deceiving. It would be too easy to forget that his good-natured response veiled something more, as did her own clever answers. They were both after the same thing—to take the other's measure. What was fact and what was fiction when it came to the faces they showed society?

Bryn slanted him a sideways look as they walked. If she asked, would he give her the answer she wanted? What had he been doing in this same garden yesterday under significantly different circumstances? Twenty-four hours ago, he'd been an uninvited intruder. Today, he was received as a highly sought guest, a man whose favour her father would do well to curry. 'It hardly seems fair for you to hold me accountable for such a small thing when you were the one who invaded my balcony. If we're keeping a tally of surprises, you seem well ahead of me in that regard.'

Kitt stopped and turned towards her, his free hand covering hers where it rested on his sleeve. The simple gesture, something countless gentlemen had done on countless walks before, made her keenly sensitive to the intimacy of bare skin on bare skin. It was his eyes that made it different, how they followed his gesture, forcing her gaze to do the same until they rested on the point where his hand met hers. 'Surprises or secrets, Bryn?'

His voice was a low rumble, his eyes lifting briefly to hers as he said her name. 'I find the difference between the two to be slim indeed.' This was how sin started, with a sharp stab of awareness igniting between them over the intimate caress of a name. Oh, he did not play fair! She'd meant to be interrogating *him* and here he was flirting with her, although flirting was not nearly a strong enough word for what he was doing.

'Secrets?' Bryn feigned ignorance of his intent.

'Don't play coy with me, I much prefer your bold

mouth.' Kitt's gaze lingered on her lips. He was a master indeed at conjuring seduction out of thin air if he could turn the slightest of gestures into something more.

'What were you doing in that meeting?' It was said with the quality of a caress, but no less lethal for its intimacy. All seductions had their price.

'What were you doing on my balcony?' Bryn challenged in a breathy whisper. Now that they'd come to the crux of the conversation, the one subject they'd been dancing around, it was hard to concentrate. Most of her mind was focused on the fact they were only inches apart, inches from another kiss, from tasting the boldness of their mouths as he so bluntly put it. Her body knew it, hungered for it after only one taste.

Anticipation hummed through her, but Bryn steeled her resolve. Had he no sense of caution? Had *she*? Sneed *could* be coming out with lemonade this very minute. Maybe. The lady in her wouldn't risk it, but the adventurer would. Sneed would be terribly busy this afternoon. The odds of getting away with a stolen kiss beneath the palms were probably in her favour…

Stop it! She had to quit thinking like this, although Kitt Sherard clearly thought like this on a very regular basis if the episode yesterday was anything to go on. Bryn took mental hold of herself: *Make him accountable. Answers before kisses. Your father's business depends on it.* 'What I was doing by the window is simple. The light is best by the window—' Bryn began.

'For writing? You were taking notes,' he interrupted, his accusation implied in his tone. Kitt stopped his tracing, his hand closing over her wrist in a harsh grip. His blue eyes were harder now, their seductiveness gone.

'You can fool Selby, but not me. I know what I saw. You were there for a purpose.'

'It hardly matters,' Bryn answered sharply. She did not have to stand here and validate her presence at that meeting to this man she barely knew just because he could turn her insides to mush and ruin any hopes of logical thought. All things considered, she was holding her ground well.

Kitt shrugged, his grip relaxing on her wrist. He gave her a slow smile. It was not a pleasant smile, it was a warning. Somewhere, she'd made a mistake and he was about to capitalise on it. 'Perhaps you're right and it hardly matters. What happened on the balcony stays on the balcony, after all.'

Bryn saw the trap too late. She'd walked right into it for all her careful play up until now. He was casting her as the hypocrite. How else could she argue the balcony mattered, but her presence at the meeting did not? There was nothing for it but to answer. She met his gaze, giving no sign of having contradicted herself. 'My father needs reliable men in this venture.'

'Men like James Selby?' Kitt put in with an arch of his blond brow. 'Selby wouldn't know an opportunity if it jumped up and bit him in the arse.'

'And you would?' Bryn countered sharply, only to receive one of his disarming grins.

'Nothing bites me in the arse, princess, opportunity or otherwise.'

His candour made her blush. Her mind had run right down that rather provocative path created by his words, just as it had last night at the the thought of his bath, as he'd likely intended. 'I'm not worried about the balcony,' Bryn said staunchly, keeping an eye on the bright coral hibiscus across the yard to maintain her composure. It was far less distracting than the man beside her. 'I want to know because you will be doing business with my father. That worries me more than a few stolen kisses. If he is to trust you, he needs to *know* you.' And what about her? Could she trust him?

The question was merely one of many which had plagued her last night long after she'd returned from the Crenshaws'. What sort of man climbed balconies in sweat-streaked shirts and then turned up in expensive evening clothes a few hours later at an exclusive soirée, only to sit down at the piano and entertain the ladies as if he had manners.

'Ah, perhaps this is more about *you* than it is about your father,' Kitt said shrewdly. 'You needn't worry, I won't blackmail you with the balcony.'

'Of course not,' Bryn retorted. 'You'd be doing nothing more than compromising yourself into a marriage if my father found out and that can hardly be what a man like you wants.'

His eyes narrowed, the air about them crackling with tension. 'A man like me?' He became positively lethal in those moments. She'd trodden on dangerous ground with her hot words. 'What do you know about men like me?'

She held her ground. 'Enough to know you're not the marrying kind.' This had become a perilous verbal *pas de deux*. What had started as a probe into the nature of his business character had rapidly become personal.

'I assume you mean one without a moral code, who takes what he wants without thought for the consequences, someone who serves only himself?' He was riveting like this, a sleek, predatory animal, stalking her with his eyes. No gentleman had ever behaved thusly with her. They were all too busy pandering to her, to her fortune.

His hand reached up to cup her jaw, the pad of his thumb stroking the fullness of her lower lip with a hint of roughness to match his words. 'Your logic fails you, if you believe there's nothing to fear from a "man like me".'

'You don't frighten me.' Far from it. He excited her. Bryn swallowed hard, more aroused than insulted at being called into account for her words.

'Maybe I should.' His voice was a low rumble, part-seduction, part-intimidation. She couldn't decide which. 'I would think my sort would be *extraordinarily* interested in a woman like you: beautiful, wealthy, well positioned socially, kisses like the naughtiest of angels.' He bent close, close enough to put his mouth to her ear, for his lips to brush the shell of it. 'Princess, I am the epitome of everything you've been warned about.'

All she had to do was make the smallest of movements to fall into him and whatever he was offering. She leaned towards him, into him, but too late.

Kitt stepped back, releasing her. 'Now that's settled, if you'll excuse me? I have another appointment.'

A more cautious woman would retreat the field and admit defeat, but not Bryn. She was determined to not let him get away without an answer. A man who wouldn't give one was definitely hiding something. 'You're really not going to tell me?' She gave him a last chance to confess. 'About the balcony?'

He swept her a bow, eyes full of mischief. 'You have my permission to let your imagination run free.'

She would not let him get away with boyish charm

after the rather adult heat of the previous moments. Bryn fixed him with a hard stare. 'I can imagine quite a lot of reasons, none of them good.' Perhaps if he thought she would imagine the worst, he'd rush to amend that image. Having a poor impression of him could hardly be what he wanted when a position on the bank board was on the line. She was not naive. She knew what sort of men came to the Caribbean: adventurers, men who were down on their luck, men who wanted to make new lives. Certainly there were a few like James Selby who was here for decent opportunities as a merchant, but he was not the norm.

Kitt gave her a sly smile. 'Then I leave you with this: you're a smart woman. You already know men who scale balconies are up to no good. You don't need me to tell you that.'

The garden was quiet after he left and somehow less vibrant, as if he'd taken some of the bright, tropical colour with him. Bryn took a seat on a stone bench near the hibiscus, not wanting to go in, not wanting to encounter any of her father's business partners. She wanted time to think first.

Kitt was right. She *had* known. She'd just hoped for better. Or perhaps, more accurately, she'd hoped it wouldn't matter and it hadn't until he'd walked into the Crenshaws'. Now, she had a dilemma. Should she stay silent and let her father discover Kitt Sherard for himself or should she warn her father off before real harm could be done? Could she even do that without exposing what had happened on the balcony?

Bryn plucked at a bright orange blossom. Current evidence suggested the latter was not possible at this point without risking the consequences. Current evidence also suggested Kitt was hiding something. Her hand stalled on the blossom. No, he wasn't hiding anything, he was all but admitting to it, whatever 'it' was—further proof she needed more evidence. She was working off supposition and kisses only. She needed more than that. Too much hung in the balance. A man who compromised her, compromised her father. Likewise, if she voiced her concerns, she could ruin Kitt's investment chances.

It all boiled down to one essential question: could Kitt Sherard be trusted? There was only one way to find out. She would have to get to know him—a prospect that was both dangerous and delicious since he'd made it abundantly clear he was not above mixing business with pleasure.

Chapter Five

'I don't have pleasant news.' Kitt kept his voice low as he and Ren Dryden, the Earl of Dartmoor, his mentor in this latest banking venture, but more importantly, his friend, enjoyed an after-dinner brandy in Ren's study at Sugarland. Night had fallen and Ren's French doors were open to the evening breeze. The dinner with Ren and Emma had been delicious, their company delightful, both well worth the five-mile ride out to the plantation from Bridgetown. Kitt hated returning their hospitality with bad news.

'Tell me, there's no use holding back. I'm not the pregnant one.' Ren pitched his voice low, too, aware of how sound carried in the dark Caribbean night. With Emma expecting, Kitt knew Ren was eager nothing upset her, yet another reason Kitt was reluctant to be the bearer of such news. Ren shared everything with his wife. Kitt didn't think he'd be able to keep this from her.

'It was a trap.' Kitt still couldn't believe it, couldn't *understand* it, no matter how many times he replayed the ambush in his mind. 'They waited until we'd unloaded the barrels and then they charged, right there,

on the beach in daylight.' Not that it made much difference if it was night or day on a deserted beach. There
was no one to see either way. Things like this happened
to others who were less meticulous, less prepared, less
cynical. But he had a certain reputation, which made
him all the more suspicious about the motives behind
the attack. What had he missed? It was a simple run,
the kind he made all the time. What had he missed? The
words had become a restless, uncontainable mantra in
his mind that obliterated other thought.

Kitt rose and began to pace the length of Ren's
French doors, some small part of him registering Ren's
eyes on him. But most of his mind was focused inter-
nally, replaying the ambush, running through potential
scenarios, potential suspects responsible for the attack.
*What had he missed? This had been the first deal with
a new client he'd contracted with a couple weeks ago.
Someone, it appeared, who might not have been who
he claimed to be.*

Kitt stopped pacing and leaned his arm against the
frame of the doors. He felt dirty, as if he'd unknowingly
picked up a disease and then unwittingly spread it to a
friend. *Who? Who? Who?* pounded relentlessly in his
head, his mind was determined to solve this mystery.
Kitt closed his eyes, thoughts coming hard and fast. It
wouldn't be the first time someone had given a false
name to their agent. *Follow that line of thought, Sherard*, his mind urged. He was aware of Ren talking as
if from a distance. He couldn't concentrate on Ren's
words just now, but four managed to break through.

'They took the rum?' Ren asked quietly, neutrally.

Kitt's eyes flew open in disbelief. The day second-
rate bandits took a cargo from him was the day he'd quit

the business. 'Of course not! We fought like berserkers to protect your rum. You should have seen young Passemore with his knife, stabbing away like he fought the fiends of hell for his very soul.'

'Stop!' Ren's interruption was terse, his eyes hard as he grasped the implications. 'You *fought* to protect the rum? Are you *insane*?'

'They were bandits, Ren, they had weapons,' Kitt answered one-part exasperated, one-part incredulous. Did Ren not know him at all? Did Ren think he'd give up his friend's cargo without a fight when he knew how much Ren and Emma were counting on it? *On him?* Kitt pushed a hand through his hair. He owed Ren a debt of friendship he could never truly repay.

'We had to do *something*, Ren.'

'You should have let them have it, that's what you should have done. It's only rum, after all,' Ren scolded.

Only rum? Kitt almost laughed, but Ren would not have appreciated the humour. Ren had only been here a year. Island nuances, or the lack of them, were still relatively new to him. Rum was Caribbean gold. Taking a man's rum in Barbados was like robbing the Bank of England in London. People did indeed die for it, although Kitt didn't plan on being one of them.

Kitt looked out into the night, his mind working hard. Behind him, he heard the shift of his friend rising from his chair and crossing the room to him, determination in Ren's footfalls. 'Dear God, Kitt, you could have been killed and for what? *For rum?*' Indignation rolled off Ren. Kitt didn't have to see him to feel it.

'What would you have me do? Do you think so little of me that I would give up your cargo when I know how much you and Emma were counting on it? Counting on *me*? I couldn't just let them take it.'

The bandits had known that. Kitt's mind lit on those last words. Or at least whoever had hired them had known, had guessed that he would fight. It had been what they'd wanted. He recalled now how, after he'd shot the man leading the charge, the bandits had not been deterred. He remembered muttering to Passemore, 'This means war.' Those bandits had been spoiling for a fight, looking for one even. He remembered being surprised by their fierceness, their determination to go up against Kitt Sherard and his men—something most were unwilling to do. The rum had been a cover to get to him, or had it?

Beside him, Ren was still bristling. 'I'd never forgive myself if you died over one of my cargoes, neither would Emma. Promise me you won't take such a chance again. I don't want you dead.'

But someone did. That was the part that niggled at him. He'd had five deliveries this week. If whoever had hired the bandits had wanted him, they could have taken him any time that week and had better opportunities to do it. *All right, where does that lead you? If that's true, what does it mean?* His brain prompted him to make the next connection. It meant the rum was *not* a cover or a coincidence. Kitt tried out his hypothesis on Ren. 'They weren't trying to kill me over just any rum. They were after me and *your* rum.' And when that had failed, they'd been happy to settle for just him in a back alley of Bridgetown.

Ren blew out a breath and withdrew to the decanter. 'I'm going to need more brandy for this. What aren't you telling me?' Kitt could hear the chink of the heavy crystal stopper being removed, the familiar splash of brandy in a glass, but he didn't turn, didn't move his gaze from the opaque darkness of the night, not wanting any sensory distractions to interrupt his thoughts. He was close now, so close, if he could just hold on to the ideas whirling through his head and form them into a cohesive whole.

'There were two men waiting for me back in port,' Kitt said.

Ren moaned and gave the decanter a slosh to judge the remainder. 'I don't think I have enough. Is that why you were late to the Crenshaws'? And here you had me believing it was because you were out carousing.'

Well, that and a certain woman on a certain balcony— not that Ren needed to know that part. The carousing part wasn't entirely untrue. The fewer people who knew about Bryn's balcony the better, especially Ren, who had done so much to get him on the list of potential bank investors. Ren had enough bad news tonight without hearing he'd been kissing Mr Rutherford's daughter, no matter how accidental.

'Would it be fair to conclude those men are still out there?' Ren returned to him and handed him the glass. Kitt nodded and waited for the other conclusion to hit. It did. 'And you travelled out here *alone*? They could have had you any time on the road. Dammit, Kitt, have you any sense?'

The thought had occurred to Kitt, too. Traffic on the road between Sugarland and Bridgetown was light, especially during the heat of the late afternoon. There were places where an attack would draw no attention even if anyone chanced along. 'I was prepared for them.' Kitt shrugged, thinking of the knife in his boot and the pistols he'd slung over his saddle. Part of him had been hoping they'd try again, hoping he could wring some answers from the bastards when they did.

They were standing close together now, Ren's gaze on his face searching for answers he didn't have yet. 'Who would do such a thing? Do you have any idea who wants you dead?' There was real concern in Ren's tone and it touched him. Until last year, he'd been alone, cut off from all he knew, all social ties gone except the ones he'd created in this new life of his, but they would never be close, would never be allowed to replace the ones he'd given up. It was too dangerous. Closeness created curiosity and that was a commodity he could not afford. Then Ren had shown up and it was like coming back to life. Here was one of the two people left who knew *him* and it was gift beyond measure. 'Who, Kitt?' Ren asked again.

Kitt shook his head. 'That's not the question to be asking.' That list was rather long, definitely distinguished and would result in a needle-in-the-haystack sort of search. 'The real question is who would want revenge against *both* of us?' *That* list was considerably shorter. Ren was well liked and an earl besides. There were few who would dare to be his enemy. But there was one…

Suddenly Kitt knew with the starkest of clarity who it was and *why* it was. It was the scenario that made the most sense, and frankly, it was the scenario he preferred to the other possibilities. The other scenarios were far worse to contemplate, like the one where his past came to the island and destroyed everything he'd built, everything he'd become. If that happened, he wasn't sure he could protect himself.

He felt better now, back in control. There was relief in the knowing, in having a concrete enemy, although he doubted Ren would share that relief. It was all fairly simple now that all the pieces had come together. He faced Ren. 'I know who it is. It's Hugh Devore.'

'No, it couldn't be,' Ren answered in almost vehement denial, but his face was pale. 'Devore is gone, he promised to leave the island, to leave us alone.'

'A man will promise any number of things when his life is on the line,' Kitt said. 'He's had a year to rethink that promise and it probably didn't mean much to him anyway.' Last year, he and Ren had forcibly exiled three planters from the island after Arthur Gridley had assaulted Emma and attempted to burn down Sugarland. Gridley was dead now, shot by one of his own, but the others were at large, a deal he and Ren had struck with them to avoid exposing Emma to the rigours of testifying at a public trial.

'Do you know where?' Ren asked quietly.

Kitt shook his head. He had been the one to sail them to another island and leave them to their exile. The island had been rather remote, barely populated. They'd been free, of course, to leave that island, as long as they didn't return to Barbados.

'Cunningham went back to England,' Kitt said. It wasn't Cunningham he was worried about. Cunningham had been the one to shoot Gridley, the ringleader. He was done with the group. It was the other two, Elias Blakely, the accountant, and Gridley's right hand, Hugh Devore, whom Kitt was worried about. 'I have no idea where the others might have gone.' Devore would be dangerous. Exile had cost him everything: his fortune, his home and even his wife. Devore's wife had refused to go with him. She'd taken Cunningham's cue and gone back to her family in England.

Ren's face was etched with worry, as well it should be. Devore was vindictive and cruel and Ren had a family now; a wife and a new baby on the way, beautiful things to be sure, but liabilities, too. Devore would not hesitate to use those treasures against him and Ren knew it.

Kitt clapped a hand on Ren's shoulder in comfort. 'I'll find them.' He could handle trouble of this nature. He would protect Ren with every breath in his body. It had been Ren who had hidden him that long last night in the dark hours before the tide, Ren who had stood against the watch when they'd come. Kitt would never forget.

'You don't need to protect me,' Ren said with quiet steel. 'This is not England, Kitt, and I'm not your addle-pated brother. You do not need to sacrifice yourself for me.'

Kitt dropped his hand, his gaze holding Ren's. Ren was one of the few who could make that comment, in part because it took a certain boldness to remind Kitt of his family, and in part because there were only two people outside of that family who knew the truth. Ren was one, Benedict Debreed was the other. Kitt blinked once and looked away, the only concession to emotion he would make. 'Perhaps not sacrifice, but you'll need me to watch your back and Emma's.'

Ren grinned. '*That* offer I will take.'

The emotion eased between them and Kitt smiled back. The crisis, the bad news, had passed for now. 'In the meanwhile, I'll set up another deal for your rum and you can tell Emma everything will be fine.'

Ren's eyes drifted to the clock on the desk at the mention of his wife. Kitt laughed. Even after a year of marriage, Ren was thinking about bed, about Emma. 'You don't have to stay up with me,' Kitt assured him with a wolfish grin. 'I can finish my brandy all by myself.'

Ren hesitated. 'I can wait a few more minutes—you haven't told me about the new banker in Bridgetown yet.'

'No, you can't wait. It's written all over your face how much you want to be with her.' Kitt chuckled. 'Go, the rest of my news can keep until morning. We'll have another good talk before I leave tomorrow.' He shooed Ren off with a gesture of his hand.

'Well, if you're sure?' Ren set down his glass, already halfway to the door.

'I'm sure. Goodnight,' Kitt called after him with a laugh.

Kitt took a swallow, listening to the tick of the clock. The room was quiet without Ren and he let all the dangerous thoughts come, the ones he'd struggled to suppress these last few days, the surge of envy at all Ren had and that he could never have. It wasn't that he coveted Emma or the baby or the plantation. It was that he could never have such a family himself. Nor could he ever claim the family he'd once had.

In the last year both Ren and Benedict had married happily and against no small odds. That wasn't the strange part. Men like them, men with titles and obligations, got married all the time. They were expected to. They were expected—required even—to stand at stud for the benefit of their great families and procure the next generation in exchange for dowries that would sustain the financial burden of expanding the family line. The strange part was, despite those expectations, Ren and Benedict had managed to marry for love, to marry beyond their obligations.

In doing so, they'd turned marriage into something otherworldly, something Kitt had not thought possible when he'd made his sacrifice. But now, seeing that it *was* possible, well, that changed everything. Only it was six years too late to change anything for him. He was Kitt Sherard, adventurer extraordinaire, lover nonpareil, a man who lived on the edge of decency in his occupation as a rum runner among other things. He didn't pretend all his cargoes were legal, just some of them, *enough* of them, to massage Bridgetown society into tolerating him among their midst. He had only what he'd created for himself: a home, a ship, even his name. He was a self-fashioned man who came from nowhere, belonged to no one, was claimed by no one. This identity as a man from 'nowhere' suited him, even if it made him socially questionable. It wasn't the sort of background mamas wanted their daughters to marry into. Nor would he allow them to. That meant he should leave Bryn Rutherford alone. There was no need, no point, in tempting them both into foolishness.

She had been right today. More right than she knew. He wasn't the marrying kind. She'd only been talking about his flirtatious behaviour. The life he lived was dangerous and unpredictable, enemies lurking in the shadows, as illustrated by the latest turn of events. But he didn't have a choice, not a real choice anyway. It had to be this way. He was destined to be alone. Alone kept him safe, kept others safe.

His life kept him busy, made him rich enough to buy any pleasure he wanted, any distraction he needed to keep his mind off the past, because it wasn't just the past he remembered, it wasn't just the sacrifice he remembered, but also the guilt—he'd run to save himself when perhaps he should have stayed and saved others first.

Kitt poured a third glass, trying hard to push away the memories. He could not imagine bringing a wife and a family into the mire of his past or the peril of his present. Indeed, they would only be liabilities and they would always be at risk. He'd not be able to concentrate on his work if he was always worried about them. What was the point of having a wife, a family, if he *didn't* care enough to worry about them? He knew himself well enough to know he'd *want* to worry. It had been concern over another that had brought him to this state of life in the first place. His thoughts went to the man Passemore had shot. Was there a wife and children waiting for the dead man even now? Were people wondering and worrying when he didn't come home?

He saw his own family in the sad picture such an image painted; his once-brilliant, sparkling family. Had they learned to laugh again without him? He hoped so. He didn't want to imagine them grey and wilted—the way they'd looked the last time he'd seen them. The scandal had broken them. Did they still wait expectantly for some small piece of news about him from Benedict the same way he coveted the mail packet?

Benedict's letters were the only connection he allowed himself, the only risk he allowed himself where his family was concerned. He cherished each scrap of news. His brother, his *twin*, was courting Viscount Enderly's daughter. An engagement was in the offing.

Kitt had rejoiced over that in the last letter. It proved his choice had been worth it. The scandal had been survived, by them at least. But there was pain, too. He wouldn't be there for the wedding, wouldn't be there to stand beside his brother as a witness, wouldn't be there to act as uncle to the children that would follow. Only in the dark, fortified with brandy, did Kitt ever permit himself to admit how much he missed his brother. But to see him, to contact him, would be to condemn him and Kitt loved him far too much to risk it even if it had killed him to sever that tie. To those who suspected he still lived, he was a pariah. To those in London who believed him dead, his death was considered a good riddance and a just one.

Kitt couldn't imagine a woman who would be willing to risk stepping into his life once she truly understood it. His bed, on a temporary basis, was one thing. A woman needn't know too much about him to enjoy his bed. He had a woman in every port and in some places, he had two. But permanently? Therein lay the risk.

A hazy, brandy-induced thought came to him. What would Bryn Rutherford do if she knew how he'd amassed his fortune? Would she run screaming to her father or would she throw caution to the wind like she had yesterday? One had to wonder if Bryn Rutherford was in the habit of living recklessly when no one was looking or if it was merely a momentary lapse in judgement? Kitt hoped for the latter.

It had been rather heady business today in the garden, sparring with her, the lightness of their banter cleverly interspersed with a more serious hunt for information. She'd been a rather tenacious opponent, shrewd enough to know he was not all he seemed. He'd actually found arguing with her a bit arousing, watching those grey eyes flash, knowing her mind was working as they stood close enough to do something other than argue. He'd thought about it—about silencing her with a kiss—she'd thought about it, too. He'd seen it in her eyes. She'd been aware of his intentions when his eyes had dropped to those full, kissable lips of hers.

Here in the dim room, the darkness encroaching, the memory had the power to pleasantly rouse him. But Kitt decided against it. Kissing her would have been the easy answer and a belittling one for such a fine opponent. If he couldn't have her trust, he'd at least have her respect. It was a starting point at least. Ren had used his title, his English influence via Benedict back in London, to get his name on the list of potential investors. Kitt would not let the opportunity go languishing for the sake of a few kisses.

Kitt shifted in his chair to a more comfortable position, letting his mind drift. Bryn Rutherford was something of a conundrum. She'd been fire in his arms, eager to meet him on equal ground. Yet the woman he'd encountered at the dinner party had been concerned with propriety, which posed a most certain dichotomy to passion. Under usual circumstances, such juxtaposition would be worth exploring, intriguing even. But circumstances were not 'usual', not even for him. He had a cargo of rum to trade, new investments to consider and an assassin on his heels.

As tempting as an *affaire* was, it was too distracting for him and too dangerous for her. His safety and hers demanded he keep her at arm's length. If ever there was a time to pursue a new flirtation, this was definitely not it. He needed all his wits about him.

Chapter Six

One certainly needed their wits about them to keep up with the Selbys, or even just to be *up* with them. Bryn had awakened to the surprise—and not the good sort of surprise either—of finding James and his mother at the breakfast table. Breakfast had become a time of day reserved just for she and her father, a time to talk plans. Having the Selbys present felt like an intrusion into intimate territory.

But there they were, with plates filled full of eggs and sausage and more than enough talk to go around. James and his mother leapt from topic to topic with lightning speed in an attempt, no doubt, to show off their conversational acuity. But it was bloody difficult to follow, with an unladylike emphasis on the 'bloody'. It was a dizzying array of subjects, really, ranging from butterflies to weather to books and back again to butterflies. The book had been about butterflies so perhaps they'd never truly left the topic.

'Butterflies are a rarity in Barbados, which makes studying them a challenge. It has something to do with our position in the Atlantic that I don't pretend to understand.' James waved a fork in the air to punctuate his point. 'But it does make their presence here special. The Mimic is one of my favourites. It looks like a Monarch, but it's the story behind it that makes it so extraordinary. Scholars believe it came from Africa and was brought over on the slave ships or perhaps it was blown here on the currents of a storm.'

Not unlike many of the people who'd sought the sanctuary of the island, Bryn thought. Certainly there was the literal application of the idea. The recent abolition of slavery meant that many of the freedmen had come here as slaves. There was a figurative application, too. People like she and her father, people looking for a fresh chance, blown here metaphorically on the winds of their personal storms. Men, perhaps, like Kitt Sherard.

'I've just recently been able to add an Orion to my collection,' James told the table at large. 'An Orion is grey and blends in terrifically with things like old leaves, which makes catching one difficult.'

For an instant, the image of a butterfly garden filled Bryn's mind. It was the first interesting thing James Selby had said. She was rather surprised he had such a garden. She wouldn't have guessed it of him. A butterfly garden would be so bright and colourful, a perfect tropical accessory. She could imagine all the little butterflies gaily fluttering around.

Selby's next words shattered the image. 'I finally caught one up near Mont Michael a few weeks ago. I took it home and pinned it in the centre of my display case, I'm that proud of it.'

Pinned. Trapped. Dead. Bryn discreetly lowered her fork of eggs and opted for a sip of tea instead. Her vision had been a moment's fancy. She silently chastised herself. James Selby didn't have a butterfly garden, it had been silly to think so. Lepidopterists pinned things. It was what they did. It was what men like Selby did. He wasn't a cruel man, merely young and shallow. He'd probably not even thought to consider what his actions would mean to the butterfly even though they'd impact the butterfly considerably more than they'd ever impact Selby.

She'd met men like Selby before. They were thick on the ground in London's ballrooms. Selby would waltz through life never considering the impact he would have on others. He was an earl's grandson. He didn't have to. No one would expect it of him, not even his wife, who would only be a butterfly of a different sort to Selby; something to pin to his arm, to display in his home, another decoration along the same lines as his fine taste in carpets.

She must have had a distasteful look on her face. When she looked down the length of the table, her father gave her an inquisitive arch of his eyebrow. She immediately pasted on a smile and received one from him in return. In fact, his was positively beaming. Uh-oh. She didn't like that smile. She scaled back hers to something more aloof and polite.

She had to be careful here. She didn't want to foster false hopes and she knew exactly what was afoot: a match and one, that on paper, would be regarded as perfect in every way. Selby was young, in his mid-twenties, not unattractive in a well-kept sort of way, someone who with the right guidance could be moulded into a successful gentleman. She'd seen his file before they'd left England. She'd seen *all* of the investors' files. She'd spent the voyage studying each of the recommended investors and there'd been countless letters and communications between them and her father even before that. When she'd met Selby it wasn't as if she was meeting a stranger. In many ways she'd known him months before the actual meeting.

He was the grandson of an earl with a small inheritance of his own from his father. He was in the Caribbean managing the family's sugar interests, cutting his teeth before taking over properties in England that would come to him upon his thirtieth birthday. His prospects were not much different than those of a second son and entirely respectable. His situation and expectations were very much akin to hers.

Oh, yes, she knew precisely where this was going and why. She wasn't the only one who'd made promises to her mother. Her father had made them, too. But she'd also made a vow to herself, one that would inevitably collide with her father's plans. She only hoped when it did that her father would concede. He'd always been the permissive parent, growing up. He'd been the one who allowed her to ride astride, to swim in the swimming hole, to spend the afternoons hunting with Robin Downing, the squire's son, although he probably shouldn't have.

Selby kept talking. It was easy to smile when she thought of those afternoons with Robin. They'd both been reckless sorts—it was what had made them such good friends. As they'd grown up, though, that recklessness had transformed from dares over climbing trees to something wilder, more dangerous. More than one kiss had been stolen on those adolescent hunting trips. Perhaps there had even been a time when she'd fancied marrying Robin, but a squire's son wasn't an adequate match for the Earl of Creighton's niece and her mother knew it. Young Robin turned twenty-one and found himself off on a Grand Tour. Then her mother had taken ill and her little family was off on a tour of their own, albeit less grand, from spa to spa searching for a cure that didn't exist.

Now she and her father were here. This was to be a new beginning for them both. Bryn was honest enough to admit she didn't know what she wanted from that new start, but she did know what she *didn't* want and that was a copy of London only with different scenery. She could not be James Selby's latest butterfly, no matter what promises had been made.

'I think Selby's plantation opportunity sounds like the perfect investment.' Her father's words drew her back into the conversation with an alarming jolt, the words 'Selby' and 'opportunity' reminding her rather poignantly of Kitt Sherard's comment in the garden. *Selby wouldn't know an opportunity if it jumped up and bit him in the arse.* Now here were those same two words again in a different, even contradictory context. They couldn't both be right. What had she missed while she was busy letting her thoughts wander behind a pseudo-smile?

Selby took her silence for ignorance and leapt into the breach with an explanation couched in slightly patronising terms as if she couldn't be expected to fully understand. 'Plantation stocks are a popular method for making money. One doesn't have to do more than write the cheque. We invest, someone else manages and we pick up the profits at the end of the season. There are countless smaller islands that might support a single large plantation if one can stand the isolation.' Selby gave her an indulgent smile. 'The best part is, we might never have to set foot on the island. All the work is done by someone else.'

'If it works out—' her father picked up the conversation, his face more animated than it had been in a year '—we could have the board look into a larger investment once it's assembled. This will be a trial run.'

We. She didn't think for a moment her father meant her in that pronoun. By 'we' he meant Selby. He'd certainly taken to Selby quickly enough. She supposed it was natural. He'd exchanged letters with many of the investors months before leaving England, Selby included. Only Sherard had not written directly. All of his correspondence had come through the Earl of Dartmoor's brother-in-law, Benedict DeBreed. Like her, her father felt that he knew many of the men before actually meeting with them in person. The two of them had spent countless hours on board ship discussing each one until the faceless investors had taken on a certain familiarity.

She might have been jealous of all the attention her father lavished on James Selby if it wasn't for the fact that she knew her father needed her. They were partners in this venture—silent partners: the men were not the kind to tolerate the presence of a woman in finance. But she had a job to do that only she could do. She was to vet the ladies and determine what sort of wives and lives these potential investors had.

Investors had to be more than the sum of their chequebooks. Money might get one in the door, but one needed ethics and a particular quality about oneself to stay, especially when they would be putting other men's money on the line. That's where the mystery of Kitt Sherard came in. He had money and connections. Did he have the ethics, too? Those were the questions she'd be attempting to answer today on her shopping trip with Martha Selby, Alba Harrison and Eleanor Crenshaw.

Sneed entered the breakfast room to announce the arrival of her shopping guests and her pulse speeded up. Time to go to work and, if she was lucky, time to play a little, too. Her outing today wasn't just about vetting the women. At the very least, she hoped to draw the women out about him and where he fit in all of this. If she had her way—and she almost always got her way—she'd 'accidentally' meet up with the captain. Bryn rose and smoothed the folds of her white-sprigged skirts. This was one of her favourite gowns with its tiny apple-green flowers and wide matching green sash that set off her waist. She had a certain effect on men when she wore it. She was confident Kitt Sherard would be no different. She was very good at getting what she wanted and today she wanted answers.

She needed to be careful what she wished for. Three hours into shopping, Bryn had all the answers she wanted and more. Alas, none of them were about the more interesting subject of Captain Sherard. However, she had all the impressions she needed of Eleanor Crenshaw, Alba Harrison and Martha Selby, which also meant she had got more than an earful of the merits associated with her son. She'd not quite believed someone could be bored to death, but she was a believer now.

Selby's mother had spent a good portion of the day chattering about James's attributes, a sure sign that whoever married him would have to answer to Martha. It was also clear that Martha was more than happy to turn the financial aspects of life over to her son. She'd

mentioned more than once what a relief it was to have
James manage everything for her. 'A proper woman
should never have to worry over things like money,' she
said with a flutter of her fan. Bryn could almost hear
the unspoken words that followed the statement: *and I
am a most proper woman, thanks to James.*

To that, Alba Harrison had given a soft smile and
agreed. 'Edward handles everything except my household budget.' There was pride behind that smile, as if
ignorance was anything to be proud of. Bryn's temper
started to rise. It might have been fuelled by her disbelief that wives of investors could be so blasé about their
own financial ignorance or it might simply have been
that she was in a peevish mood, brought on by Martha
Selby's incessant prattle.

Couldn't they see such ignorance wasn't in their best
interest? The lessons of her childhood surged to the
fore. Her mother had schooled her early in life on the
subject and importance of a woman's financial independence. That was one lesson that had taken. When
men lost fortunes they could rebuild them or put a gun
to their heads in a discreet room at a gambling hell, but
it was the women who paid, the women who lost their
homes, their security. A woman risked far more by relying on a man's good sense. For that reason alone, a
woman should be an informed and active participant
in a family's financial dealings.

Bryn knew her attitude wasn't popular, but her temper had the better of her. Before she could rethink the
wisdom of her comment, the temptation to goad their
thoughts was tumbling out of her mouth. 'Don't you
ever want to know where your money comes from and
where it goes? How much it makes? Isn't it a little bit

dangerous to be so blind?' In her opinion, it was *more* than a little bit dangerous. Both her parents had instilled in her the belief that a strong financial acumen showed no preference in gender. Her father had been proud of how quickly she'd grasped the concepts of investment banking.

The ladies stared at her with identical looks of confusion. 'No, it's a relief really, my dear. It's one less thing to worry about,' Mrs Harrison said softly, her tone somewhere between polite correction and gentle instruction. Mrs Selby seemed to be making a mental note, probably something to the extent of her being an unsuitable bride for James. That stung.

Bryn squared her shoulders, stood a little taller and told herself it was for the best. She had no intentions of being a suitable bride for James. But it still hurt. She was a Rutherford. As such, she was used to being found eminently suitable. That James Selby's mother, a woman who had only a few of the barest claims to true society, would find her lacking was a bit of a blow to the ego.

They stepped into a shop on Swan Street that handled imported European furniture. The interior was dim after the brightness outdoors and it took a moment for Bryn's eyes to adjust. Even with her wide-brimmed hat on for protection today, the sun had played havoc with her vision, something she had yet to get used to after the perpetual grey skies of London.

She was still blinking when the man at the counter finished his discussion with the proprietor and turned towards them. 'Ladies, good day.' He gave them a little bow she'd recognise anywhere for its slightly sardonic nature, even in the interior of a dim little furniture shop. Then he turned the full force of his attentions in her direction, so urbane, so polite, it was hard to reconcile him with the ruthless seducer-interrogator he'd been in her garden, challenging her with his words, his body. 'Miss Rutherford, how are you besides sun-blinded?'

Kitt Sherard! Her first thought was that the fates had decided to smile on her after all. She was beginning to think they'd deserted her entirely after enduring three hours of tedious discussion *and* Martha Selby's indirect disapproval. Her second thought was that she must look like an owl. Bryn tried to stop blinking, it was hardly going to impress him. 'I'm fine, thank you. These kind ladies have been showing me the shops. And yourself?' Mrs Selby stiffened beside her. The latest of her *faux pas* coming too soon after the first. Apparently such a question from a young lady was too bold. Yet another strike against her. Perhaps she'd make a game of it and see how thoroughly she could antagonise Martha Selby. But, no, she'd promised her father better.

'I am picking up a chair Mr Friberg has repaired for me,' Kitt answered her, his smile defrosting the ladies. 'If I could offer some advice, Miss Rutherford, you need a pair of *lunettes de soleil*. They'll make your sojourn in the sun more comfortable.' He reached into an inside pocket and unfolded a pair of spectacles with green-glass lenses. 'Here, take mine until you can find a pair that suits you better.'

'I couldn't deprive you,' Bryn refused politely, aware that Mrs Selby was watching the two of them with interest. A few strikes against her were a positive deterrent. Too many, though, and she'd be a social pariah, which was not what her father needed.

'Yes, you could. I insist. I have other pairs at home, drawers full of them, in fact.' He said 'drawers' as if he meant an entirely different sort of drawers. She felt her cheeks heat. Dear lord, what was wrong with her that she saw innuendo in everything he said? 'I make them myself, it's a very useful hobby in this part of the world. It would be an honour if you accepted them as a welcome gift to the island.' Kitt would brook no refusal and surely the ladies could see that she'd resisted as much as she could without being downright rude.

But then, when she might have escaped the situation with minimal scathing, Kitt pushed his advantage too far. He didn't just hand them over, he put them on himself.

Kitt stepped forward and reached beneath the brim of her hat to fit the arms of the glasses over her ears and to adjust the lenses on the bridge of her nose with his thumbs; an act that hardly involved impassioned touch any more than tying someone's shoe or the casual adjusting of a piece of clothing, yet the act seemed alarmingly intimate for such a public spot. She knew without looking in the woman's direction that Mrs Selby found it positively lurid. She was going to kill him for this. Secret balcony kisses were one thing, as were hot looks in the garden where no one could see. Discretion, discretion, discretion. Even the wild child in her knew that much.

Maybe it was because there were onlookers and Mrs Selby had puckered her mouth up into a sour frown or maybe it was simply the intimacy of the act that made her entirely self-conscious. She noticed everything acutely in those brief moments of contact: Kitt's face close to hers, blue eyes laughing as if he knew Mrs Selby's mouth currently resembled a prune, Kitt's fingers sweeping down the curve of her jaw as he stepped back. 'There, that will do for now.' The smile on his face suggested he was up to mischief with this latest endeavour and she was not in on the entire joke.

To be sure, she was in on part of it. He'd enjoyed getting a self-righteous rise out of Mrs Selby and he divined correctly that she wouldn't mind a little fun at Mrs Selby's expense. But there was more to it than that, Bryn would bet on it. She'd bet, too, that Kitt wouldn't be around when the other proverbial shoe fell. But it would fall, she could feel it. Mrs Selby was fairly bristling beside her as Kitt took his leave and conversation was forced as the ladies finished their errands. The shoe would fall soon and she would bear the brunt of it all on her own even though she hadn't asked for his attentions.

It fell over tea in the lobby of the hotel. 'I am sorry for the distasteful instance with Captain Sherard,' Mrs Selby said, trying to sound casual and sympathetic as she passed Bryn a teacup when in reality she was neither. 'He's quite the ladies' man in these parts.' She smiled, trying to appear friendly. 'It's not your fault, my dear. You're new, you couldn't possibly know what sort of man he is.'

'What sort of man is that, Mrs Selby?' Bryn asked bluntly.

That had her nonplussed, Bryn was gratified to note. Mrs Selby hesitated, weighing her options before answering with a hedge. 'Of course, the men like him a great deal as does a certain sort of lady, but a young woman like yourself needs to take care. He has a way of turning heads without really meaning to. I wouldn't want you to read too much into his gesture this morning.'

Or his kisses on my balcony. You know he's had his hand on more than my face, Mrs Selby. Bryn smiled politely. 'Surely he's not as bad as all that. He appeared quite the gentleman a couple of nights ago at the Crenshaws'.' She smiled at Eleanor Crenshaw, hoping to engage an ally. Eleanor had invited him, after all. 'Where does he fit in? Is he a gentleman or a rebel?' Bryn asked point blank.

All three of them were stymied, exchanging awkward looks. It was Eleanor Crenshaw who answered, 'We tolerate him, of course, because he's rich and there's so little society in the islands, but he has no people. No one really knows where he's from.' She said the last in a little whisper as if it were the gravest of sins.

Bryn decided to bedevil the subject a bit further. 'Miss Caroline Bryant didn't seem to mind.' She might disagree with Mrs Selby's assessment of Kitt Sherard, but Bryn wasn't about to let this conversational opening go unused. It was the perfect chance to learn more about one of her father's investors.

Alba Harrison pitched her voice low. 'Caroline is the quartermaster's daughter.' She arched dark brows as if emphasising Miss Bryant's connection to the quartermaster explained everything. 'Captain Sherard strings her along because it's good for his business,' Alba Harrison added when it was clear the emphasis was lost on Bryn. Alba Harrison leaned forward, her words coming fast, her brown eyes intense. 'He'll do the same to you as well if you're not careful. He wants in on the joint stock bank and he'll use your influence with your father to ensure his place. It's the truth, I don't mean to be cruel.'

Yes, you do. Bryn met Alba Harrison's gaze evenly. This was nothing different than the catty politics between women in London ballrooms: the endless battle between those who held a man's attention and those who wanted it. How much of this was jealousy and how much was truth? 'I see. Thank you.' She did see, far more than Alba Harrison realised. Alba's rather vociferous condemnation of Kitt Sherard was not in character with the woman who earlier this morning had softly advised leaving all sense of finance and business to the men.

That was when Bryn realised two things: One, Alba Harrison had lied. She *was* into the family finances as deep as her husband, no matter what she professed publicly. She understood perfectly well what was riding on this opportunity with the bank. There was no doubt in Bryn's mind, Alba had come shopping with one goal in mind—secure a place on the board of investors. Second, Kitt had used her. He'd known his actions would provoke this sort of conversation. The question was, had he done it to expose Alba Harrison's true nature or to expose his? Now Bryn understood why he'd smiled. She just didn't understand the reason behind it. But she was going to.

If Alba had thought to gain favour with her warning about Kitt, she'd be surprised to note it had just the opposite effect. Bryn made up her mind on the spot. When tea was done, she would find Sherard and confront him. He would soon learn she did not care for the role of unwitting accomplice. He'd set her up and he would have to pay.

Chapter Seven

The rum at his hand was cold and the stones on his back were hot. Life was perfect. For the moment. Perfection never lasted and he knew better than most that life could change without notice or warning. He'd learned to take the moments where he could find them. Today there were no bandits, no knife fights on beaches, no assassins in the shadows.

Kitt shifted beneath the thin white sheet draped over his buttocks, the only part of him that was covered as he lay in his open-air pavilion on a raised bed that looked out over the white carpet of sand and turquoise expanse of ocean. *This* was Paradise on earth, maybe even Paradise period. And it was all his: a private home, a pristine beach, bought and paid for with rum money and danger. *C'est la vie*—such is life, the French would say. Everything, Paradise included, had a price.

'How does that feel, Mr Kitt?' The Bajan beauty working him over placed the last of the small heated stones on his back, her accented English a gentle lilt at his ear, quite a different earful than the sharp tongue of Miss Rutherford who'd likely want to skewer him the next time she saw him.

'Like heaven, love.' Kitt gave a groan of appreciation as the masseuse kneaded away the tension that
had taken up residence between his shoulder blades.
A gentle breeze passed through the open-air pavilion,
mixing deliciously with the heat of the stones against
his bare skin. After the last two days, he deserved this.
When he'd finished in town, he'd come here straight
away with strict instructions to Passemore that he not be
disturbed. This was his own private hideaway, a place
where he could relax, plan or think as the mood suited.

Right now, a little of all three suited that mood. With
Devore on the loose, he couldn't allow himself to relax
entirely no matter how tempting it was. Even in the
safety of his home, his body tensed at the thought of Devore. The man was evil incarnate, a man who calculated
his cruelty to exact every possible ounce of suffering
from his victims. He would never be completely able
to rid his mind of images of what Devore and Gridley
had done to Emma. He probably should have put a bullet in Devore when he'd had the chance.

He took comfort in knowing there was little Devore
could do to him. Outside of Ren and Emma, he had no
other interpersonal attachments and Ren would protect
Emma. It was one of the benefits of having reinvented
himself. No one relied on him. He had no one to worry
over. Still, if Devore was on the move, he'd be watching, looking for some weakness, some sort of leverage
to use against him. Devore would not hesitate to strike
at any chink in his armour, perceived or otherwise, further proof this was not the time to pursue anything that
remotely resembled familiarity with Bryn Rutherford.
Kitt would not tolerate an innocent bystander caught
in the crossfire of revenge.

His behaviour in town had been all about convincing Bryn to keep her distance without ruining his business chances with her father. His behaviour had been outrageous, but not out of character and it should have served as a final reminder of the sort of man he was; completely unsuitable for a princess like her. He'd warned her earlier with words, now he'd warned her with actions.

Right about now, the shrewd Miss Rutherford should be heading home, ready to mull over all the news the ladies of Bridgetown had imparted about him. He felt a smile of satisfaction creep across his mouth. She would be coming to her senses while he was basking in Paradise, enjoying the quiet and…*the sound of footsteps?* What the bloody hell?

Kitt reared up, dislodging the hot stones, his hand sweeping under the pillow for his knife as he leapt off the bed, his body immediately alert to danger. There was relaxation and then there was stupidity, after all. He preferred not to face an attacker in his altogether, but it was too late to do anything about the latter now.

'Passemore!' Kitt lowered his knife, the adrenaline induced tension ebbing from his body as he recognised his first mate. 'Dammit, I told you I wasn't to be disturbed. Cleo will have to start all over now. This had better be good.'

A snatch of green and a flicker of white skirts garnered Kitt's attention on the path over Passemore's shoulder. Good God! Passemore had not come alone. Kitt waved the knife in her direction with a growl at Passemore. 'What is *she* doing here?' But he knew. She'd got one over on Passemore. He almost felt sorry for William. Almost.

'I couldn't stop her,' Passemore stammered, unusually unsure of himself. 'She insisted she ride along with me when I brought the supplies out.' Kitt had left his first mate in town to load up the wagon, never guessing Bryn would want to track him down so quickly, if at all. The magpies were supposed to have sent her running the other direction with their gossip, not draw her here.

'You need to get laid, William,' Kitt muttered under his breath. He wasn't surprised his first mate hadn't been match enough for Bryn Rutherford, but he was surprised she was here. So much for keeping her at arm's length.

'Mr Sherard, I need a word with you,' Bryn began before she even came to a full stop. 'If you think you can set me up like that…' She paused mid-sentence, her eyes dropping down his length as the scene hit her full force. 'You're naked.'

'And you're staring.' Kitt grinned, enjoying taking the edge off what was likely a well-planned tirade she'd rehearsed all the way out. He'd stood naked before plenty of women and he had nothing to be ashamed of. As for Miss Rutherford, he was probably her first. His grin widened. 'See anything you like, princess?'

Of course she was staring, how could she not? He was as gorgeous as he was arrogant and Kitt Sherard was arrogant in the extreme. Not without reason. That tan, sleek body of his rivalled the gods of Olympus. Arms bulged with muscle, his torso an atlas of ridges and planes as it tapered to narrow, defined hips and a rather robust phallus announcing its presence. It was hard to look away. A girl didn't have such a fine specimen of manhood displayed for her every day. But she would not let him thwart her efforts at conversation with this rather bawdy display of man flesh. First, however, she had to find her voice. Bryn cleared her throat with what she hoped was the sound of authority and not nerves.

'Is this how you greet guests? Armed and naked?' With nearly superhuman effort, she managed to flick a cool glance at the knife in his hand. She was trying so very hard not to look, to pretend that she conversed with naked men all the time. Heaven knew what she'd interrupted. The cocoa-skinned woman had discreetly withdrawn, but not before Bryn had been aware of her presence. There were only so many conclusions one could draw about a woman and a naked man without being completely obtuse.

'Perhaps you and I disagree on what constitutes a guest, Miss Rutherford. Where I come from, guests are *invited*.' He held his arms out to his sides, giving her eyes free rein. '*This* is how I greet people who take me by surprise in the middle of a massage. Technically, that makes you a trespasser.' He gave a wicked grin that sent a tremor of excitement through her. 'There's a forfeit for trespassing.'

Yes, please, I'll pay it, the rather heated part of her imagination all but yelled in her mind. Part of her knew she shouldn't have come here. Decently bred ladies didn't seek out gentlemen and they certainly didn't go barging into a gentleman's private quarters. She was getting her just deserts for intruding. The other part of her thought those deserts not only just, but delicious. But she had to play this coolly, had to be aloof, had to appear unfazed by this blatant display of nudity. 'It hardly seems fair that you can climb my balcony, but I can't walk on your beach.'

'You want to "walk on my beach"?' He had a way of making even a simple statement sound erotic. 'There's a forfeit for that, too, princess. This is turning into a pretty expensive visit. Make sure you can afford it.'

It was her turn to laugh. If he meant to frighten her off, he was doing a poor job of it. 'You don't scare me, Sherard.' Just the opposite. He was exactly the sort of gentleman who would indulge her wild fantasies, who would be her lover without exacting marriage, but their situation was anything but ideal. She could not mix his brand of pleasure with her father's business. She needed absolute objectivity in order to help her father select the right men.

He arched a blond brow. 'If we're to go, ah, "walking", as you like to call it, we should dispense with the formalities. It sounds like a bad romance novel: *Miss Rutherford and the Captain*. I prefer Kitt.'

Kitt, reached for the sheet and wound it about his middle with a pointed glance at her feet. 'You might want to take off your shoes. And your stockings.' He paused, considering her hem. 'You might want to tuck up your skirts, too, if you want to stay dry.'

It was Bryn's turn to raise a brow. 'Anything else you'd like me to take off?'

'Not at the moment, no.' Kitt laughed. 'But I reserve the right to amend my suggestions.'

It was definitely the most decadent walk of her life, strolling barefoot on the beach alongside a man wrapped only in a sheet. But it was worth it to feel warm sand between her toes and the occasional wave the temperature of her bath gently lap against her ankles.

'This beach is really yours?' Bryn asked. The calm waves had taken some of the fire out of the intent of her visit. She felt less like fighting with him than simply wanting to talk with him, to learn about this enigmatic man who owned this peaceful Paradise while being anything but peaceful himself. Perhaps that's why he consented to let her walk along the shore instead of ushering her to the door. Refusing to see her would only have served to stoke her anger. This was distraction at its finest. Kitt had proven he was a shrewd tactician. She must remain alert. But what harm could there be in a walk when she *knew* what he was playing at?

Kitt stretched his arms wide, pride evident in his voice. 'All this is mine, the house and the beach as far as the eye can see. Since the house isn't on farmable land, the owner had no use for it. It was just a decoration and that was fine with me. I wanted a decoration. Somewhere I could be alone.' The last was intended as a pointed commentary on her intrusion.

'Your home is lovely.' She meant it, choosing to overlook his slur. The house resembled a Mediterranean villa with its white stucco and arches. A quick glimpse of the interior as she'd passed through with Passemore had revealed the place was well furnished. The gardens in the back leading down to the shore were immaculately groomed and full of colour. There was even a fountain that trickled enticingly into a tiled basin on a patio.

'Thank you, but that's not what you came to discuss.' They'd come to a cove with a wide, flat-topped rock formation set fifty or so yards from shore. Kitt tugged at her hand with a nod towards the rock. 'Are you game? We can sit on the top.'

There were so many reasons to decline the invitation. Well-bred ladies didn't climb rocks with men in sheets, they didn't walk beach shores with them either. It certainly wasn't part of the promise she'd made her mother. But the line of propriety had been crossed long before this latest breach. She'd crossed it the moment she'd sought out his company alone in his home. Maybe even before that, when she'd allowed him indecent liberties on her balcony instead of screaming for help.

And yet, her wild side argued as she scaled the rock with Kitt, hadn't she come to Barbados especially for this? How could she refuse the offer? Look where her choices had led so far: To a beautiful beach, to scrambling up a rock and sitting beside a half-naked man, letting the breeze off the water cool her skin while she took in the stunning view of the ocean and the coastline, half a globe away from the world she knew, the world that would condemn taking advantage of a moment like this. What did that world know anyway?

In a declarative act of defiance, Bryn took off her hat when they reached the top. She arched her neck, letting the sun and the breeze bathe her face. 'I never dreamed there was a place like this on earth.' Her legs dangled over the side of the rock alongside Kitt's. Below them, waves hit the rock, the spray tickling her legs. Her skirts would be damp no matter how far she tucked them up, but right now she didn't care.

Bryn gave herself a few minutes to enjoy the scene before returning to the subject at hand. 'This doesn't mean I'm not still upset with you about this morning. You can't bribe me.'

Kitt shrugged and played innocent. 'What did I do this morning?'

He was going to make her spell it out for him. 'You know what you did with your little *lunettes de soleil*. You made me look bad in front of Martha Selby and Alba Harrison, two women whose favour I need for my father. Martha Selby couldn't make notes fast enough regarding my unsuitability as a bride for her son.' She gave Kitt a sideways glance, watching for his reaction.

'You are. Unsuitable, that is.' Kitt tried to look penitent, something he obviously wasn't familiar with. 'I'm sorry, did you want to marry James Selby?'

'No.'

He grinned. 'Consider it a favour then. I don't know why you're upset.'

'It's the principle of the matter. You used me.'

'To your benefit.' Kitt threw a pebble into the water. 'Did you see Mrs Harrison's true colours?'

'Yes,' Bryn said slowly, trying to divine where this was headed. She didn't like the idea of owing Kitt any favours.

'Did you learn something more about me? Am I well maligned by the upstanding moral arbiters of Bridgetown society?'

'Yes, most definitely that.' Bryn narrowed her eyes. Alba Harrison's comment about Caroline Bryant notwithstanding, Kitt didn't strike her as the sort of man who did something entirely out of altruism. She cocked her head and studied him. 'What do you get out of all of this?'

Kitt laughed. 'My, my, we're quite the cynic. Perhaps I did it purely for your own benefit. Do I have to get anything out of it? '

'In my experience, yes,' Bryn answered honestly. 'I don't trust you.'

She expected him to be offended. The likes of James Selby certainly would have been. A gentleman's manners were supposed to inspire a lady's trust and confidence. Instead Kitt nodded, absorbing the revelation.

'That is as it should be, don't you think? You hardly know me well enough to trust me. For the record, I don't trust you for the same reasons.'

Now she was the one offended. 'Not trust *me*? What is there not to trust?' Bryn argued. She knew a moment's panic. 'You *are* going to invest in the bank, aren't you?' If Kitt pulled out, would he influence the others to do the same? Where would that leave her father?

Kitt seemed unconcerned. 'Maybe. I have to do my research.' He turned his blue eyes her way. 'Villas and private beaches don't come cheap. The question your father should be considering is not *if* I have money to invest, but *how* I made that money. I don't gamble, princess. I only bet on sure things.'

That did give her pause. Bryn saw the fallacy in her own reasoning. She'd been so intent wanting to learn about the potential investors that she hadn't thought about what those investors would want to learn about them.

'You see, it's not just about investing with your father and the royal charter. It's about investing *with* the other six men. Can I trust them with my money? Can I trust their investment choices?'

The tenor of their conversation had taken on a very personal cast. Bryn couldn't recall anyone ever speaking with her like this before. This was certainly not the kind of conversation one held at balls and her usual social venues where talk was interspersed between dance sets or limited to short bursts of time as people passed one another in crowded ballrooms. Even teas and at-homes kept 'decent' conversations between the sexes to fifteen-minute calls, hardly enough time to delve deeply into any subject, hardly enough time to do more than exchange pleasantries.

It seemed something of an irony to be having an honest conversation with this man, who made no pretence to being a gentleman beyond dressing like one when the part suited him. Did that mean the opposite was true as well? That she'd spent her adult life to date having dishonest conversations with gentlemen? If so, perhaps it was further proof ballrooms were a waste of time.

If people talked, really talked, they might learn something about each other. What was 'indecent' about that? There might be happier marriages. Then again, there might be a lot more pre-marital seductions, too, if people felt they knew each other. That was what she was feeling now—that she was starting to know Kitt, to see the man beyond the sharp wit and outrageous behaviour. That man was an analyst, a thinker with a stunningly shrewd command of human nature. He understood people and what drove them. *And* it was just as exciting as his kisses.

'Why don't you trust Selby?' she asked, deciding to test her hypothesis about his analytical skills.

'It's not him I don't trust, it's his judgement,' Kitt clarified. He spoke quietly, his voice nearly at her ear, although there was no one to hear. His body was close to hers on the warm rock slab, their legs occasionally brushing against each other as they dangled over the edge. 'He's ignorant of the world around him. Because of that, he makes less educated choices. He's young, he's eager to please and quite desperate to be seen as a man, as a leader, when that isn't where his skills lie at present. He hasn't the experience to be those things, only the money. Do you know the old proverb, "a fool and his money are soon separated"? That's James Selby in a nutshell.'

'Surely not all of his decisions are bad? He's invest-

ing in a plantation.' Kitt had her worrying about Selby.
If her father insisted on taking Selby on to the board,
would he bring the bank down or would he sit quietly
and let the more experienced men lead the way while
he learned for the future?

Kitt raised an eyebrow at this. 'Is he? I hadn't heard.
I was unaware there were any shares available.'

'I think it's on another island.' Selby hadn't said precisely where the plantation was.

'I hope it works out for him. Sugar prices are a bit
low right now, but sugar and rum are always decent
money in the long run,' Kitt offered vaguely.

'You sound sceptical,' Bryn pressed, picking up on
his hesitation. He wasn't the only one sitting on this
rock who knew a little something about reading people.

'I don't know enough to be otherwise.' Kitt tapped
his forehead with his index finger. 'Research, remember?' A further reminder, if she needed another one,
that Kitt Sherard was as people-savvy as they came.
He understood what people thought, *how* they thought
and that included her, as unnerving as the prospect was.
Her London beaux had never guessed at half the things
going on in her head. But Kitt seemed to guess them
all, even the ones she wished he didn't, like how much
she wanted him to kiss her again.

His eyes held hers for a long moment. 'I only bet on
sure things and you should, too.' A slow smile spread
across his face and Bryn had the distinct impression
they weren't talking about banking any more. 'Now,
about those forfeits.'

Chapter Eight

His hand cupped her jaw, tilting her mouth to his. Her body started to fire at his touch. She ought to fight this. But when his mouth moved over hers, it claimed all desire to resist. All the warnings she could muster, all the promises she had made, held no power here.

He kissed her deeply, slowly, and she wanted to drink him in as she had not drunk of him earlier. Those balcony kisses had been rough and rushed, the result of their rather spontaneous situation. He'd kissed her then to silence her surprise. These kisses were prelude to a game of a different sort. He smelled of sun and salt and prime male. Her hands anchored in his hair, tangling in its thick blond lengths as he pressed her back against the warm surface of the rock. His mouth moved down the column of her throat, kissing, nipping, his hand cupping a breast, lifting it to be caressed by his mouth through the thin muslin of her gown. She'd never thought of clothes as being erotic until now, until Kitt had his mouth on her, creating a delicious friction with the fabric and his teeth as her nipple hardened, laved into a decadent, straining peak by his tongue.

Her body arched against him, intuitively seeking his confirmation that he, too, was swept away by this. It was there in the erection that lay bold and strong against her where their bodies met, tactile evidence of what she'd seen with her eyes. The feel of him was enough to ignite other heady curiosities. What would it be like to touch him, to feel that part of him jump in her hand?

Bryn didn't think. She simply reacted out of primal instinct and reached for him. He was hot in her hand even through the negligible barrier of the sheet. She revelled in the power of him. He was long and hard beneath the linen where her hand shaped him through the cloth. Kitt gave a hungry groan, his mouth devouring hers, their bodies pressing into one another with an intensity that went far beyond any of her adolescent forays. This was pleasure at its finest and it was madness, too. Only disaster could come of this.

Bryn broke the kiss, levering on her elbows to sit up and dislodge Kitt from where he laid against her. Spray from a wave hit her ankles, reminding her there were other reasons this had to end, too. Tides came in. Even now the shore looked slightly further away.

Kitt looked past her shoulder out to sea, distracted for a moment, and then followed the direction of her gaze back to shore. 'We'd best head back in before we have to swim for it.' He seemed unbothered by the impending tide, but he didn't have skirts to worry about. She'd be a mess by the time she got home—not that she wasn't already a mess. Her hair had come down and the pristine, white dress she'd left the house in that morning was wrinkled from climbing and from kissing—lots of kissing. Wading back to shore could hardly make her look worse, but it could make her look wetter and that would be problematic.

In the end, Kitt carried her back to shore. It would have been humorous and quite a well-deserved fate for having enticed her out to the rock in the first place if the sheer, bare physicality of him hadn't served as a potent reminder of how many lines she'd crossed, how many rules and promises she'd broken by coming here today. Her mother would not be pleased.

Kitt set her down and gave her a once-over, assessing the damage, as it were. He shook his head, arriving at the same conclusion. 'You will not do. You'll have to come in while we set you to rights.' He gave her one of his wicked grins. 'Unless you don't mind everyone knowing what you've been up to? Then our task gets considerably easier.'

Another rule gone. A lady didn't enter a gentleman's house unchaperoned. But after this afternoon, what was one more rule? She'd broken so many already. It was quite the day for overturning the teachings of childhood. She should feel guilty. But she didn't. She felt intrigued instead. Truly, she couldn't say rules had done much for her in the past except create absolute tedium. Maybe it didn't count if a rule was broken and there was no one to see, sort of like the fallen tree in the woods. Broken rules only mattered if one was caught and Kitt had made it clear already he wasn't going to kiss and tell. For being alone with a rogue, she felt quite safe.

The inside of Kitt's house was as spectacular as the outside. For a man of questionable repute, the understated elegance of his home was unexpected. The hall he led her down was appropriately lined with consoles adorned with vases full of island flowers set at just the right intervals, the occasional painting hung over a console here and there. The drawing room was done in a dark blue and cream, striking a masculine tone while not being oppressive. A gorgeous piano sat in one corner, its lid up, its sleek body gleaming with polish and care.

Bryn ran an idle hand over a porcelain figurine of a dog decorating a side table. 'You have good taste.'

Kitt laughed and pulled the bell rope. 'You sound surprised. Is "good taste" a woman's domain? Are men not allowed to have any?'

Bryn sat on a damask-covered sofa done in dark blue to match the curtains. She was acutely aware of the sand on her skirts and the fineness of the upholstery. 'In my experience, men can have good taste, but many fail to exercise it.'

Kitt slouched into the chair opposite her, sheet and all, reminding her the house and its trappings of luxury were part of the illusion, just as his evening clothes had been at the Crenshaws'. Without those accessories, he was a rogue at heart. 'Or is it that a man of my dubious reputation isn't entitled to good taste?' Kitt persisted in calling her out, persisted in reminding her of the façade.

Bryn gave him a sharp look. 'I didn't say that. Don't put words into my mouth.'

'You were thinking it.' Kitt challenged her with his eyes, holding her gaze for a long moment before the butler entered. 'Ah, Stephens, there you are. We are going to need a hairbrush, a mirror and some hairpins. I need you to send someone to the pavilion as well. Miss Rutherford has left her shoes and stockings.'

Stephens nodded with a 'very good, sir' and departed without so much as batting an eye at her dishevelled state or questioning the attire of his employer. Perhaps there was no need to look astonished, perhaps Kitt entertained in a sheet regularly. Perhaps women left various items of clothes around his house regularly, too. Given what she knew of him, it wouldn't be surprising. Still, all told, his butler was extraordinarily well trained, on par with Sneed, who was a paragon.

She would not have thought a man like Kitt Sherard would have such a staff. Then again, she was starting to think she didn't know what sort of man Kitt Sherard was after all. Flirt? Seducer? Businessman? Rake? It was starting to sound like the children's nursery rhyme little girls played with their buttons: rich man, poor man, beggar man, thief… Kitt was a rich man most definitely. Exquisitely appointed houses didn't come cheap.

'It's all right to think it, Bryn.' Kitt returned to the topic of his taste, much to her mortification. He read her mind far too easily. 'It's what all the ladies think. I'm sure they've filled your head with a resounding catalogue of my sins.'

Bryn swallowed, feeling guilty. He was right, of course. She'd not left tea without being duly warned of his shortcomings. 'Does it bother you?'

He arched a sandy brow. 'My good taste? Does my good taste bother me? No, not really.' He was being obtuse on purpose. She could see the merriment lurking in his eyes. He wanted her to say it.

'I meant the ladies. Does what they think bother you?' It was a daring question no matter how delicately she asked it.

Kitt leaned back in his chair, looking wild and masculine, his hair falling about his shoulders. He was a god, someone untouchable. It was a ridiculous question to ask. Of course it didn't bother him. He was impervious to the slights of silly women. One had only to look at him to know that.

His eyes were laughing at her again. 'Oh, you mean do I mind that I am deemed "socially tolerable" at best? I have no choice really. I live my life, they live theirs. On occasion, like the bank charter, our lives intersect. On those occasions, I become momentarily acceptable. Money helps.' He paused, sobering. 'I won't be something I'm not for the likes of them.' His gaze rested on her with a look that made her mouth go dry. 'How about you, Bryn, will you?'

That, of course, was the very question she'd done battle with for the last year. Who would she be? Who would she *allow* herself to be?

By the time Stephens had returned with the hair things and she'd put on her stockings and shoes, then tidied her dress as best she could, Bryn knew what she had to do. She had to keep Kitt Sherard at a distance. He was a dangerous man with his mind-reading and kisses. He had her thinking and questioning all sorts of assumptions about him, about her, about the point of life in general. These were not assumptions she could challenge until she'd fulfilled one last promise to her mother. Kitt and his philosophies would have to wait.

She could justify this one lapse in the name of business. She'd come here to learn about him and learn she had. Now that was over. His behaviour today confirmed the incident on the balcony was not an isolated one. He was audacious in the extreme regardless of his excellent intuition. She needed to make her position clear before she left so there would be no more incidents like the one in town, so there would be no more need to confront him in visits like this.

'Alba Harrison believes you flirt with Caroline Bryant because she's the quartermaster's daughter and it's good for business.' Bryn finished with her laces and rose. 'She believes you will flirt with me for the same reason. I assure you, such behaviour will not be tolerated by me or by my father.' There would be no more stolen kisses. But she wasn't sure if she needed clarity on that point for him or for herself.

Kitt refused to be scolded. More than that, he refused to apologise. 'I think what happened on the rock went beyond flirting, don't you?'

She felt her face colour. Bryn busied herself with putting on her hat. 'I was trying to be polite.'

Kitt stood, finally. He hadn't risen with her, making no attempt at playing a gentleman. When one was dressed in a sheet, what was the point anyway? He stepped towards her, his body close and intimate and big as it invaded her space. 'I don't think lying is particularly polite and that's what you were trying to do. I am happy to admit I was quite aroused out there and I think you were, too.'

That was a mortal hit. Bryn's hands tangled in the ribbon on her hat, barely able to tie a bow. How dare he stand there, looking so smug over her discomfort, and the dratted man wasn't done yet.

'You're wrong, you know, Bryn. Yesterday in the garden you said you didn't trust me. But you do.' He took the ribbons from her and tied a more-than-adequate bow. He was far too competent with women's clothing.

She fixed him with a piercing stare and opted for the high road, hoping he didn't see her pulse leap in her neck where his hands had skimmed her skin. He got to her in so many ways no other man in her experience had. If she did anything today, it would be to best him in at least one argument. 'How, exactly, do you reason that?'

'You never would have gone out on the rock if you didn't.' He gave a smug grin.

'You seemed pretty certain I would.' A suspicion was starting to take root.

'Yes, I was.' Kitt's response was simple and succinct, his blue eyes watching her with a riveting intensity she doubted she'd ever get used to. He had a way of making her feel like the only woman worthy of his intentions when logic suggested otherwise. The truth rolled over her like the waves against the shore. *I only bet on sure things.* He'd managed to manipulate her one more time. A cold pit formed in her stomach, but his hand was warm at her back, his voice at her ear as he ushered her towards the door. 'While you study me, I study you.'

At the door, Bryn schooled her features into a mask of neutrality. On the drive, Passemore waited with the wagon to drive her back to town. She had a last chance to prove to Kitt he wasn't the only who was good at games. 'I suppose there's only one question to answer then. Are *you* a sure thing?' She looked straight ahead and walked down the steps to the waiting wagon. Sometimes the best way to get the last word was to leave.

Even then, it wasn't a guarantee. Kitt's laughter rang

in the air. 'What are you more upset about, Bryn, that I got under your skin or under your skirt?' His response burned in her ears the whole drive back. Not because it was insulting, but because it was true. He might have used her, but she'd let him.

Kitt soaked in his bath, eyes shut, his mind replaying, regretting, revelling in his parting words. He hated to leave it at that, with Bryn angry and feeling used. But she'd appreciate it in the long run, perhaps she'd even come to understand the reasons for it. He'd not expected her today. His strategy to keep her at a distance by letting the ladies do the alienating for him had wrought the opposite effect.

Instead of driving her away, it had driven her out here to invade his private abode. That had been the last thing he wanted. He was currently a target, Devore's target. Until that was resolved, anyone who was connected to him was potentially in danger, too. If that someone was the daughter of a wealthy banker, so much the worse. Devore would not hesitate to use her against him.

The timing was unfortunate. Under other circumstances, he would have found Bryn Rutherford interesting. What had happened on the rock was proof of that. Now, she could be nothing more than a liability, all kissing aside. In truth, he wasn't sure he'd planned to kiss her. He certainly hadn't planned to let things go as far as they did with hot caresses and her hand on his cock.

He wanted to justify those kisses as part of his scare strategy to convince her to stay away. But that wouldn't be entirely true. It had simply happened. She had looked so lovely, sitting on his rock in the sun. Then she'd raised her arms to take off her hat, her breasts rising high and firm with the effort as they pressed against the thin muslin of her gown and he'd swallowed hard, his groin tightening. He was human and male after all. At that point all bets had been off.

When she'd touched him, his body had sung with the thrill of it. This beautiful English rose had her hand on him. In all of his amorous pursuits, he'd not had a truly cultivated lady. She'd hesitated just enough to prove his speculation correct: bold and wild, but a lady still the same; a lady who did care about proprieties at the end of the day. London must have been hell on her. Society did not reward a woman for curiosity or intelligence and Bryn Rutherford had both. London was for hot-house roses, not wild ones, and Kitt suspected she was as wild as they came when she allowed it.

Kitt smiled to himself. Perhaps that explained what she was doing here in Barbados. How interesting. He wasn't the only one with secrets. She was welcome to keep them. The less he knew about her the better. The less she knew about him…even more so. He definitely needed to push her away for his sanity. He could not bed a lady and avoid trouble, not even in the Caribbean. Not only for his sanity, but for her safety, which he hoped it was not too late to protect.

He owned the beach, but he didn't own the waters. Today out on the rock, he'd thought he'd caught sight of a ship passing slowly. Ships passed all the time. He probably wouldn't have paid it any attention, if he hadn't caught a glimpse of sun reflecting off what was most likely glass. Whoever was on the ship was looking for something or someone. Given the other events surrounding the occurrence, Kitt couldn't afford to ignore the coincidence. Scepticism had kept him alive this long for good reason and now it would have to do for two. Whatever Bryn Rutherford was or wasn't, could or couldn't be, for him, she would not die for him.

Chapter Nine

'How is it that Sherard is still alive?' Hugh Devore's tone was deceptively calm as he surveyed the two men standing before his desk. But one had only to look in his eyes or note the tension in the beefy hands he splayed on the desk's polished surface to know better. He was angry and the two men on the other side of that desk—the inferior side—knew it. Devore had only to look in *their* eyes or watch *their* hands to know it.

The two men, big brutish men, twisted their caps. Good. He liked exercising his authority, liked watching them squirm. They had a lot to be accountable for. He'd paid them a decent sum of money to see Sherard dead and they had yet to deliver. They'd had three days, three opportunities to see their job completed.

'He ran into someone's backyard,' the taller of the two men answered. 'We couldn't follow for fear of being recognised.'

Devore steepled his hands and leaned back in his chair. These men had something more to fear than recognition if they failed in their task. 'Yes, I know. You told me that two days ago. What has happened since? Sherard has driven out to the countryside, he has shopped in town. The man has made himself an accessible target and yet the two of you have made no other move to bring him down. Is the amount of pay holding you back?'

It was a question that could only be answered in one way if they wanted to walk out of his office alive. They were lucky they hadn't lost a finger or two this morning as a reminder he meant business. He was in a relatively good mood for having received bad news and that was saying something. He had what might be considered a volatile temper.

'No, of course not, boss,' the other man answered smartly, quickly, his sense of self-preservation kicking in. Of course it wasn't the money. They'd been well paid and it was no easy thing to come up with the funds. Once, he could have paid them any amount and not felt the pinch. Now, thanks to Sherard and Dryden, he felt every pound that left his reduced coffers.

'Then what is it? The weapons?' Devore prompted although he knew very well it wasn't.

'He's just hard to catch, sir.'

Devore gave a hard laugh. 'He's one man. There are two of you and you come highly recommended. Surely you have some skill to manage him? What about yesterday? You sailed past his private beach, it would have been the perfect shot.'

'Yesterday, he was with a lady.' The two men exchanged nervous looks with one another. He had them on edge. Now he just had to push them to see the job done in short order. Desperate men worked more diligently than comfortable men and Devore wanted this done now. Actually, he'd wanted it done three days ago.

It had been disappointing in the extreme that the rum

ambush had failed so completely. Best-case scenario: he'd acquire Ren Dryden's rum, deal Dryden a financial setback and see Sherard dead in the mêlée of an ambush where no one was sure who had killed whom. Rum runners like Sherard embraced a certain level of danger with their career choice. His death would surprise no one.

But that had not happened. Sherard had foiled it all from beginning to end and now he was reduced to tracking Sherard with these two assassins. Devore stroked the dark bristles of his beard in thought. This was the first interesting piece he'd heard from these two. His mind was already contemplating the possibilities. Here was someone at last who could be levered against Sherard, the man from nowhere, the man with no attachment to anyone. Sherard had women, of course. The man was hardly a monk, according to Devore's sources. But one-night stands weren't worth dying for. Sherard's women to date weren't exactly the sort to inspire chivalry. Devore suspected Sherard kept it that way on purpose. 'A lady?'

The men nodded vigorously, no doubt thinking they'd found a point of empathy with him or maybe they hoped it would be a distraction from the real issue of their failure to kill Sherard. 'She was definitely a lady. She had fine clothes and a big hat.'

Devore gave them an icy smile. They would find no empathy here. Silly men, didn't they know by now he had nothing but enmity when it came to Sherard and Dryden or anything those two bastards touched? They'd taken his home, his wealth, even his wife when it came down to it. She hadn't been interested in staying once the home and the money were gone. To top it off, they'd exiled him to an island to make what he could of himself. Very soon they'd see exactly what that was and very soon they were going to pay. He would do it himself if these two got squeamish. 'Is the lady a problem? You can't kill in front of her?' he asked.

The two men exchanged horrified looks and he had his answer. He let displeasure rule his features. 'I didn't think you two came with scruples.' He paused, fixing each one with his stare in turn. 'This is a disappointing development at such a late stage of the game.'

One of them swallowed, his Adam's apple bobbing. 'We were thinking about witnesses. We thought you'd prefer not to have any. She was out on the rock with him when we sailed by.'

'Ah, that's the first sensible thing you've said. The issue of witnesses is easily solved. Kill them both.' If he'd read their faces aright, that should shock their apparent code of ethics. It almost qualified as entertainment to watch them react.

'But, sir,' one of them made the effort to protest, 'they were otherwise engaged. You wouldn't have us shoot a man in the middle of taking his pleasure.'

Couldn't they see how perfect it would have been? Two deaths were better than one. There would be no witnesses and less suspicion about a third party. Devore shrugged. 'Shooting them both—we could have made it appear to be a lovers' quarrel and no one would think to come looking for you. With Sherard's reputation that wouldn't be a hard fiction to sell.' Good lord, did he have to do all the thinking in this operation? Then again, he quite purposely didn't pay these men to think, only to act, only to take the fall should they be discovered.

His temper was starting to rise with his exasperation.

'Find out who she is, I want to know immediately.' He dismissed them and blew out a breath. Maybe that was the sacrifice he needed to make for success. He hated being out of society, but Sherard had threatened to kill him if he was caught in Bridgetown, so exile it was. But it meant he didn't know whom associated with whom. It weakened his ability to negotiate through leverage. If this woman was important to Sherard, by extension she was important to him. Devore wanted to know.

It wouldn't be long now before Sherard was dead, Dryden was beggared and his own riches returned, balance restored to his world. He just had to be patient a little longer.

Patience was a virtue, Bryn decided, for the simple reason it was bloody impossible to cultivate. If it was easy, everyone would do it. Her patience was definitely being exercised this afternoon at Mrs Selby's Barbadian-themed luncheon, complete with every Caribbean food imaginable from fried plantains to pig in souse. She was tired of the posturing, of everyone jockeying for position with her father. The game was nearly done, though. Her father would announce board within the next few days.

Bryn wasn't the only one who sensed it all coming to a head. Mrs Selby recognised it, too. This luncheon was one final attempt to ensure her son's place on that board. Everyone who coveted a spot was here with one notable exception. Kitt was not. Bryn was certain he'd been invited. Mrs Selby wouldn't risk jeopardising her father's favour by slighting Kitt, not when her father had made it plain he would receive Kitt even if she did not.

It had been a week since her rather precipitous visit

to his house. He'd not been to her father's house for a meeting, nor to any of the functions hosted by potential investors. She would have believed he'd withdrawn from the endeavour entirely if it hadn't been for the notes he'd sent to her father. But *she* had not seen him since their afternoon on his rock, which led her to this conclusion: he'd not withdrawn from the bank, but from her. *Which was for the best*, her conscience was fond of reminding her. Out of sight, meant out of mind. It was easier to keep promises when the temptation to break them was removed.

Her mind didn't want to leave it at that. Her mind wanted to know why? Did he not *like* her? Had she offended him? The former seemed unlikely after his reaction on the rock. He liked her plenty. The last seemed laughable. Kitt was not a man easily offended. He was honest about himself, about society and the world. He knew how the world worked. The truth would not offend him.

Still, it galled her that he'd disappeared without any word to her personally. *He was supposed to send you a note? Who appointed you his mother?* That was her practical side. Her less-practical side had developed the habit of getting distracted at this point in the argument: he had a mother? What sort of mother had this sort of son? Which led to other curiosities—did he have a family? Where were they? But when those considerations were done, her practical side was still there, mocking her. *He owes you nothing.* Men were like that. They could kiss a girl and have it mean nothing. Her London swains had seen her fortune, but not her, never her. They would have been appalled to know she'd swum naked in a swimming hole with her best friend, who happened to be male and he'd been naked, too. And that was only the beginning of her adventures. Kitt would merely laugh and say 'Is that the best you can do?' His blue eyes would spark as he teased her: 'I once climbed a trellis into a woman's room whom I didn't know.'

Why do you care so much? came the inevitable question. Bryn plucked at a blossom on one of Mrs Selby's flowering bushes. Because he represented everything she wanted. He was the gateway, the escape. Represents or *is*? Was he merely a symbol of something she craved or did she crave *him*? Of course she didn't *crave* him. That was too intense for a man she'd just met. He wasn't an addiction. Now she was being hopelessly romantic. She'd barely met him and they'd had only a few encounters, one of those a banking meeting. *But he rouses you, he makes you forget you're a Rutherford and makes you remember who you are...who you were before the rules, before the sickness took your mother and three years of your life, before you lost Robin. He makes you remember your true self.* If that was the case, it was no wonder she was desperate for him. Without meaning to, he was coaxing her back to life.

'Would you like some cake?' Selby materialised at her elbow, a real flesh-and-blood contrast to all Kitt represented: neat brown hair to Kitt's dishevelled blondness, composed manners to Kitt's insincere, mocking bows, placid security to Kitt's wildness. He offered her the plate in his hand. 'It's a chocolate rum cake, but there's coconut sugar cakes at the dessert table if you'd prefer.'

Bryn took the plate. Chocolate sounded perfect. Rum sounded better, even though she knew the spirit baked out. Martha Selby would never serve a tipsy dessert.

'Thank you.' She hoped James would politely retreat. Instead he sat down on an empty chair and motioned for her to join him and the practical lady in her head went to work.

You could have this one. A few smiles, a few light touches on the arm and he'd come up to scratch. Kitt Sherard offers no guarantees. You don't even know where he is. This one offers guarantees aplenty: marriage, security, a family, prestige, social standing that matches your own—all the things your mother wanted for you.

'Did you enjoy yourself today?' James asked. It was her first visit to his home. She understood the point of the luncheon had been for the Selbys to impress her father with their quality of living and no doubt they had. The Selbys lived just outside of town in a big home with wide verandas and shady gardens. Martha Selby had made good use of those gardens today, setting up tables and chairs under the cool palms.

'Your home is beautifully appointed,' Bryn offered neutrally, fearing where this was leading. As the only unmarried man among the coterie of her father's select investors, it had been natural to pair James with her when the group met with their wives. As a result, she'd spent a considerable amount of time with him in the interim. It hadn't necessarily improved him. *But what is there to improve? On paper, he's perfect.*

James leaned forward. 'I would like to ask you something rather personal, if I may.'

As long as it's not a proposal. It wouldn't be though, would it? It was far too soon to be making decisions of that nature. 'Of course, Mr Selby.' In truth, she didn't want to hear his 'personal' question, but a lady had no other answer. It was hardly a question at all.

'Has Captain Sherard been troubling you?' She wondered if Kitt's extended absence had emboldened him now that there was no chance of Kitt hearing him.

'He's hardly here to do any troubling.' Bryn smiled to allay his concern, but also to make the subtle point she didn't approve of asking after a man who wasn't there to defend himself. 'I hardly know him well enough to find him troubling or otherwise.' Perhaps he'd extend that message to himself as well.

James didn't smile back. He lowered his voice further. 'He will be back, though. He's out on one of his infamous runs through the islands.' There was a hint of derision in his tone. 'My mother indicated he'd been overly forward when the four of you met up with him while shopping.'

Bryn wanted to laugh. James was so very serious. She tried to answer with an appropriate amount of reserve. 'It was nothing. Your mother was just looking out for my best interest.'

'She was right to do so. Captain Sherard is in no lady's best interest,' James said with a touch of manly protection.

Probably true. James would be appalled if he knew even half of what had transpired between her and Kitt. She decided to steer the conversation in another direction. 'Where does he go on his runs?' This was something she had not heard.

'He runs cargoes between the islands. He has a fast ship, the *Queen of the Main*. Most of his cargo is rum, so you can imagine the people he deals with.' Oh, she could imagine. James would be stunned by the vivid images that conjured up: Kitt at the helm of a boat, wind his hair, his shirt open at the neck.

'It's all very unsavoury.' James's distaste was written in the scowl on his face.

Very dangerous, too. That explained the knife. The image of Kitt naked and wielding a knife was engraved on her mind for obvious reasons. It had not occurred to her until she'd got past the 'obvious' part of that image how odd it was he'd had a knife handy while getting a massage. Who kept a knife with them when they were relaxing?

Now she knew and the answer wasn't nearly as satisfying as she'd hoped. It merely spawned other questions and more curiosity. She'd been able to justify her interest in Kitt as purely business at first. But this new flare of interest was far more personal. Who was he? She knew so little about him. *And you should keep it that way. What could knowing more about him do but cause trouble?*

She was still debating this when her father walked over, smiling broadly to claim her. It was time to make their farewells to their hostess. Her father was still smiling as they left the Selbys.

'What has you so happy? Did your discussion go well?' Bryn asked, opening a parasol as the open barouche headed back towards town.

'Yes, I think the group is forming well. We should be able to send a preliminary report back to England on the next mail packet in a week or so. But I'm smiling because of you. I saw you with James. Do you like him? He's a solid young man with great potential.'

Bryn hated to spoil her father's good mood, but there was no sense in prolonging a lie or creating false hopes.

'He's nice enough, a perfect gentleman, but he's not for me. I don't think anyone is right now. It will take me some time.'

Her father nodded and leaned over to pat her knee encouragingly, misunderstanding her remark. 'There will be someone.'

'Maybe, some day.' She smiled to assure him. Until that time, there was Kitt Sherard and his audacious kisses. It occurred to her that perhaps the reason she'd behaved so badly with Kitt was that she knew nothing could come of it. In that regard, he was safe. There would be no professions of love. Just physical pleasure, just coming alive. And that was enough, more than enough. In short, there would be nothing to break: no engagements, no hearts, nothing. Just life. Just living. He offered a far simpler arrangement, which was, unfortunately, quite appealing to a woman who felt chained by complicated promises.

'You're smiling, Daughter, and that's a start.' Her father's voice held a laugh, something she hadn't heard from him in a while. 'Whatever has put that smile on your face, I'm glad for it. We are coming alive again, you and I both.'

Now if only the reason for that smile would come back, Bryn thought. Where was her pirate prince?

Chapter Ten

Kitt took the helm of the *Queen*, feeling alive at sea in a way he never quite achieved on land. The ship moved beneath him, gently bucking over the waves, like a woman finding her pleasure. He never tired of either image, the woman or the ship, although these days the image of the woman had taken the very definite shape of Bryn Rutherford as she'd been on the rock, as she'd been on the balcony: hot, curious and willing in his arms.

There were other images, too: her storming down the path full of righteous indignation only to find him nude; her untying the ribbon of her hat and lifting it from her head, her hand on him. For a woman he was trying to avoid, the list of images he carried in his mind was rather long and colourful. In short, arousing.

Of course, that might also have something to do with the fact that he'd been without one for far longer than he was used to. This trip had not allowed enough time to avail himself of his usual port-to-port favourites. There'd been business to handle, which had been hectic due to the impending cane harvests. There'd been extra business, too, like arranging another trade for Ren's rum barrels. And, as always, there'd been information to gather, which involved a lot of listening, head nodding and a judiciously placed question here and there on his part, sometimes accompanied by judiciously placed coins. The good information was never free.

Kitt turned the wheel to put the ship's nose to the wind, the sails full against the blue sky as he headed for Bridgetown and home. That was a dangerous word. Home made a man weak just as friends made a man vulnerable. It was a sign he'd been here too long. He was starting to feel comfortable. He was starting to feel hopeful. There were signs of that hope sprinkled throughout his life. He had his villa, his ship, he had Ren and soon Bridgetown would have a bank. Civilisation was coming to him and Bridgetown both. There was no escaping it and it was not the time to start feeling 'comfortable'. He should be feeling increasingly vigilant. With civilisation came more opportunity for his past to be exposed.

Perhaps he should consider leaving. The western Caribbean was still fairly untouched by the English, still fairly lawless. It would be hard to find him there. It would keep him from entertaining fantasies about Bryn Rutherford. She'd definitely be out of reach then. He was going to have to see her again. He couldn't communicate with her father by letter for ever if he wanted to be part of the investment group.

The ship entered the bay and his blood hummed. He told himself it was because he was eager to talk to Ren. Something was definitely afoot. The islands were brimming with activity. There'd been reports of new plantations trying new crops. It sounded very industrious, very interesting, even very lucrative. Plantations were the backbone of the Caribbean economy. Since the sixteen hundreds, people had been cultivating a variety of new crops, some with success, some not. These islands were seedbeds of innovation for those willing to risk it.

Kitt also knew these islands were seedbeds for other more notorious activities. When innovation was of a less-honest nature, it was called swindling. That was what had him worried. He wanted word of James Selby's plantation. When he'd been approached by an acquaintance of a regular connection on one of the smaller islands, Kitt had listened intently. The Sunwood project, he'd called it, a chance to experiment with new strains of cotton and cane. Perhaps this was the one Selby had spoken of. It would be something to start from.

Why do you care so much about what Selby invests in? his mind prodded. Selby was welcome to his own mistakes, but this time those mistakes involved Kitt's money. If he was going to invest in a bank, it had better be a good one. He wasn't going to throw money after poor investments. That was the easy answer, the one that didn't require any further thought.

The harder answer was that Bryn's father was involved, at the very least by association. Selby's foolishness would reflect poorly on the bank. If her father was involved, then she was involved, too, and that was intolerable to Kitt. He'd seen too many innocent bystanders brought down by the foolishness of others. He hadn't been able to save them. But he'd be damned if he stood by and watched it happen again if he could help it.

That was all. He put a firm lid on that analysis. It had everything to do with the past and nothing to do with Bryn personally. With that, his thoughts came full circle, back to the woman who'd started them. It was nearly impossible for him to think about the pending bank without thinking of Bryn. Had she missed him? Had she noticed he was gone? Stupid questions both, and hardly worthy of a man who'd refined the art of physical pleasure without emotional attachment.

Is that what he meant by 'Had she missed him?'? Miss as in she was sorry he was gone? Did he want her to miss him? Why? He liked her well enough. She was out of the ordinary, a challenge. But to what end? To see if he could have a woman like that without the trappings of his old life to recommend him? To see if Kitt Sherard, rum runner, could win a cultivated woman of high birth—the sort of woman who, by rights, should never look twice at such a man, a woman who was reserved for a lord? Or was she more than a game he played with himself? Neither proposition was answered easily or comfortably for a man who prided himself on remaining unattached and emotionally aloof.

Had she spent her time wondering such things, wondering about him? Or had she spent the week deciding James Selby was a better choice by far? She would have had ample opportunity to make the comparison. There would have been parties and meetings—had she sat in on any more of those? He couldn't imagine Selby finding her attendance at meetings a womanly behaviour.

In England, he wouldn't have even viewed Selby as competition. But that life was over. Here, Selby had the advantage. For all her protests to the contrary, perhaps Bryn would see that. Again came the question—why did he care? There were plenty of women who were glad to warm his bed and make no demands, yet she was the one who made his blood heat with anticipation when he thought about this evening, the reason he was back in Barbados so soon. The banking board would be announced tonight at the gala. He would be there for that, as would Ren. And Bryn. He'd see her tonight, perhaps tonight he'd test his many hypotheses about the attraction she held for him and sort this out once and for all.

It had been a difficult decision to sail with so much going on, but he had a business to continue and he wasn't worried about being left off the board. His money spoke for itself, as did his business sense. The good women of Bridgetown might look down their noses at his unorthodox methods, but their husbands were all too happy to make money with him.

Kitt called for the anchor to be lowered. As eager as he was to be home, the trip had been incomplete in some ways. There'd been no news about anyone who might be stalking him and that was decidedly unnerving for two reasons. First, he usually had a good idea of who his enemies were and why. Second, because of the first reason, it affirmed the suspicions he'd voiced to Ren. Ghosts of the past had come back to haunt them. But not for long. When he got things settled on land, he'd go do a little hunting of his own by sea. It was necessary and it might even give himself a chance to purge this growing obsession with Bryn Rutherford.

It occurred to Bryn that she might be developing an obsession for Kitt Sherard. Bryn's eyes hunted the lantern lit gardens for him, searching the crowd with her gaze from the darker perimeter. He should be here. Tonight was the bank's celebration gala and his ship had been sighted in the bay that afternoon. Not that it did her any credit to admit she was looking for him, it was just something to pass the time, a reason to disengage from the crowd for a moment.

She'd done her duty as her father's hostess and greeted all the guests. Now, she wanted a moment to step back and see the results of her planning. Although invitations had only gone out a week ago, this party had been conceived of months before. The supplies for it, including the cases of champagne, had crossed the Atlantic with them in anticipation of this precise outcome; the assembling of the bank's charter members.

Across the garden, she could see him deep in conversation with Selby and Harrison, his face animated as he spoke. Bryn couldn't help but smile. Her father had done it. Tonight was his triumph—a triumph that went beyond banking, although she was the only one present who knew it.

A server passed by, bearing icy glasses of champagne on a silver tray, the bubbly liquid sparkling like gold diamonds in the lights. She reached for one, but someone behind her was faster, whisking two glasses off the tray.

'Silver and gold, perfect colours for tonight's party, don't you think?' Kitt materialised out of the darkness beside her. He handed her a glass, bemused by her gasp of surprise.

'You do have a way of taking a girl unawares.' Bryn took a sip of the sharp, fizzy champagne, trying not to give away the excitement his presence raised in her or the fact that he'd succeeded in catching her off guard. She'd expected to see him first.

'You were looking for me. Miss me, did you?' Kitt chuckled, taking a swallow.

'Were you gone?' Bryn answered coolly, annoyed

that he'd been spying on her. He'd been here longer than she'd thought and he'd been watching her. She'd wanted to have all the control.

'Minx.' Kitt smiled and it went straight to her knees. He was even more handsome than she remembered. A week aboard ship had served to deepen his tan and bleach his hair to a sleek white-gold. He fairly vibrated with potent good health, his presence more intoxicating than the champagne. She was definitely developing an obsession.

'I must confess, I was worried,' Bryn said casually. 'You were the first asked and the last to sign.' Worried, because she'd feared somehow her secret indiscretions had affected Kitt's decision and her father's success would pay for her indiscretions, although they were hardly her fault, at least not the first one. She hadn't asked Kitt to climb her balcony and she hadn't known who he was at the time.

'I had business,' Kitt offered vaguely.

'Rum?' Bryn guessed. 'I suppose we're lucky you came back at all. The way Selby tells it, rum is a most dangerous business.'

Kitt laughed outright at that. 'It used to be—it's far tamer these days in most cases.' But he would say nothing further about what he'd spent the last week doing, and Bryn sensed there was far more to it than simply trading barrels of rum for farming supplies. Kitt Sherard was not a simple man, why would he lead a simple life?

Kitt nodded in her father's direction. 'He's done well. This is an important night for him and for England. History will mark this occasion.'

She had not thought of that. It was just the sort of

comment Kitt would make when she was convinced he was nothing more than a habitual flirt. Was he the only one who saw it? Did the others see it, too, or had they also lost the forest for the trees? Everyone had been so intent on the immediate gains of banding together for investment and personal profit. Bryn cocked her head to one side, giving Kitt a considering glance. 'Is that why you're here? Posterity?' Goodness knew he didn't need the group to make money.

Kitt raised a broad, nonchalant shoulder. 'Maybe it's my way of thumbing my nose at all of it, a little bit of irony. In the end I was good enough.'

A very telling comment and a surprisingly revealing one, too. For all his airs to the contrary, Kitt Sherard wanted to prove himself. It was there in his magnificent house and his private beach and it was here tonight in his decision to join a most respectable group of gentlemen. She did wonder why. Something else she could add to her growing list of questions about the stranger who'd climbed her balcony. She knew shockingly little about the man with whom she'd shared some rather liberal intimacies.

Across the garden her father motioned for her to join him. It was time for the official announcement. Selby was already with him, standing on at his right shoulder. 'I have to go.' It was dratted timing. She'd just got Kitt to herself. She wanted to say something, to arrange to meet afterwards, but that seemed forward. It seemed desperate, too, an admission that she had indeed missed him.

Kitt's eyes hardened, looking over to her father and Selby. 'Who do you go to? Him or Selby?'

She kept her gaze neutral, her smile mysterious. 'Who

do you think?' If he really understood her the way he intimated he did, he knew the answer. In the meanwhile, it was a novelty to know that she could summon at least the faintest stirrings of jealousy or covetousness. The idea that Kitt Sherard coveted her just a bit sent a feminine thrill down her back and maybe, just maybe, she walked away with a little more swing in her hips in case she was right.

'Is she or isn't she?' Kitt muttered, watching her go. Bryn Rutherford would give the devil a run for his money when it came to temptation.

'Is she or isn't she what?' Ren sauntered up, a glass of champagne in hand for the anticipated toast.

'You weren't supposed to hear that.' Kitt took a swallow of his champagne. At this rate, he'd need another glass.

'Then don't talk out loud.' Ren laughed. 'I presume the she in question is the lovely Miss Rutherford? May I also presume the question is: is she a temptress with experience or merely a temptress who has no idea of her skills?' Ren paused. 'I am being delicate with my terms, of course.'

'Dammit, yes, that's exactly what I'm considering. Is she or isn't she a virgin?' Kitt blew out a breath. The crowd had obscured Bryn from view and he couldn't watch those hips sway across the garden.

'Does it matter?' Ren asked, both of them watching Bryn reappear as she kissed her father on the cheek and smiled broadly at the group assembled around him.

'Only in the sense that it dictates how far I can take things and the price that might be paid for it.' It struck Kitt that it didn't really matter to him personally. Vir-

ginity had never been something he'd thought much
about, but in this case it mattered.

Ren laughed and slapped him on the back. 'Oh, that
I've lived to see the day Kitt Sherard is infatuated.'

'I am not infatuated,' Kitt argued in firm undertones.
'I am merely planning my next conquest.' Even as he
said it, he knew it was a lie. He *was* infatuated. Ren
had hit it on the head. But nothing more. Infatuation
was tolerable on occasion. It wasn't as base as lust, nor
as noble as love, but somewhere in between. Perhaps
Bryn was even savvy enough to understand that. Maybe
she was infatuated, too, and knew the difference. He
might have been watching her from the shadows, taking in every delectable inch of her in that tight-fighting
aquamarine silk, but she'd been looking for him, too.
He didn't imagine the way her pulse had jumped when
he'd joined her. How interesting, they were both *infatuated* with each other.

Her father chimed a fork against a goblet, calling for
attention. A small dais had been set up for the occasion and Rutherford stood on it now with Bryn on one
side and Selby on the other. The lantern light loved her,
bouncing off the discreet *brillants* in her hair and the
tasteful diamond choker about her neck. Virgin or not,
she was indisputably a lady of quality.

Kitt's eyes drifted to Selby and something twisted in
his gut. Selby looked well in his evening clothes, every
inch an earl's grandson. He was just the sort of man for
Bryn: young, attractive, respectable. He would never put
her in danger—then again, he'd never excite her either.

On the dais, Rutherford raised his glass and began
his speech. Kitt forced himself to listen, dragging his
thoughts away from Selby and Bryn. 'Thank you, ev-

eryone, for coming tonight. This is the beginning of an historic turning point in the history of the island and in the history of the British empire. It also marks the beginning of our partnership, long may it prove prosperous.' There was applause and everyone drank.

'You should be up there with them,' Ren growled at his side. The other investors were clumped together in the front row, congratulating one another.

Kitt shrugged his nonchalance. 'I'm in, that's all that matters.'

'You don't have to keep yourself apart.' Ren's response was fierce. 'You've been safe for years. No one even remotely connects Kitt Sherard with Michael Melford. Surely, there's no harm in—'

Kitt shot him a hard, silencing look. Ren had crossed an invisible line. 'I cannot take that chance. I can never be sure and the risk is too great.' He could not be discovered. His family was counting on it, and now his brother's future bride, whether she knew it or not, was counting on it, too. She and her unborn children. Oh, yes, the risk had grown exponentially.

Ren didn't know when to stop. 'I don't think Miss Rutherford minds. I think she'd be very interested in whatever you had to offer, the way her hips were swinging.'

'She might, but I cannot ask her to risk it.' Although God knew he wanted to. Each time he saw her it was becoming harder to resist acting on the attraction. Who was he fooling? Every time he saw her, he *did* act on the attraction and so did she. Each time things went a little further, became a little more explosive. There would come a time when neither would be able to pull back. Kitt relished it and rued it.

Ren was not cowed by his stare. 'Seems like there might be more than a little infatuation going on.'

'Sod off, you…' The last of his unsavoury comment was lost in the tapping of another goblet. Rutherford wasn't done with his announcements.

'What's this?' Ren asked *sotto voce*, but Kitt shook his head, he didn't know.

'If you would all humour me one more time, I would like to offer a second, more personal toast,' Rutherford announced.

Kitt listened, but his eyes went to Bryn. There'd been a moment's surprise on her face. She had not expected this either.

'Tonight also marks the beginning of my partnership with James Selby as we embark on a new venture at the Sunwood Plantation. May this, too, be the start of new innovations and scientific research into the agriculture of the island.'

Kitt felt Ren stiffen beside him, both of them exchanging quick looks. This was the plantation project he'd heard about on his rounds. He wished he knew more, wished he wasn't so sceptical of Selby. On the dais, Bryn looked out into the crowd, searching for him. He met her gaze, holding it. He would never reach her. People were moving around them, making their way to the long dinner tables laid out under the white canopies.

He could see she was stunned by the news. Something protective inside him wanted to go to her. She hadn't known, which meant one thing: Rutherford hadn't researched it. He had merely taken Selby's word and Selby was a man easily misled. Kitt's gut knotted with suspicion. He needed to know the location of Sunwood Plantation.

'What are you thinking? It's on one of the smaller islands. I can send you the co-ordinates. It's about a day's sail away.' Ren intruded on his thoughts.

Kitt's response was grim. 'I'm thinking it's all happening again.'

Chapter Eleven

It had all happened without her! The thought ran through her head in a repetitive loop. Her father, who was in the habit of telling her everything, hadn't told her this. That was the part that hurt. When had he decided this? Why hadn't he told her? She feared it was because he wasn't sure. Why else would he keep the secret except out of concern that she would argue with him?

In her disappointment, she'd instinctively sought out Kitt in the crowd. He'd been as stunned as she, perhaps even more so. His expression had been grim, as if he knew something she didn't. She was desperate to talk to him, but that would have to wait. Dinner was at round tables of eight and she'd spread the investors across all the tables in the hopes of building interest from others in the bank. She was seated with Selby at her father's request. There'd be no chance to talk to Kitt until much later, if at all.

'He's a poor sport, that one, an absolute loner,' Selby said, his head nodding towards Kitt's table where everyone was laughing. The handsome Earl of Dartmoor was seated, too, and champagne was flowing freely. They looked as though they were having fun.

'I don't know why you would think that,' Bryn replied in Kitt's defence. This habit of Selby's to malign Kitt was most unbecoming.

'He can't stand the idea that anyone else can make money. I'd wager he's envious over the plantation. He'll probably try to sabotage it at some point. If I were your father, I'd be on the watch for something sly.' Selby shook his head. 'I vow, he'll be difficult to work with. If his pockets weren't so deep, he wouldn't have been asked to join.'

None of you would have been asked to join, Bryn thought rather uncharitably. Did Selby really believe all this nonsense about friendships? This was business, pure and simple. It was about who had money. Even now, the tables reflected that. There were the prime investors her father had gathered, a secondary group, and then there were the connections, all the people who hoped to persuade the investors to invest in them.

'Just think about it—any time an idea comes up, Sherard seems to take issue with it,' James persisted with a huff.

'You are quick to condemn him,' Bryn pointed out a tad more sharply than she meant to.

Selby shot her a hard look. 'You are quick to defend him. There are better gentlemen present who hold you in great regard. I would aim higher if I were you, Miss Rutherford. You've done an admirable job of setting up house for your father. This party is a splendid example of that. The other women like you, too. I would warn you not to throw away all the good you've done by championing a bounder who is best left to the company of men.'

This was a new side, a harder side, of James Selby. Bryn reached for her wine glass. 'I shall certainly consider that.' She smiled to suggest he was forgiven and trailed a hand along his sleeve. 'Enough about Sherard. Tell me about the island—where is it exactly? Perhaps I could get you to write those co-ordinates down?' Bryn shifted in her seat to better show off the tight bodice of her dress. James's eyes followed.

She'd been surprised by his outburst. The man did possess some spine after all. Too bad it was supported by bile. There was no love lost between Selby and Kitt. It could create some difficulty on the board if the two insisted on competing. She could easily see her father in a bit of a tug of war. Her father liked Kitt, but it was Selby who'd availed himself of her father's time and ingratiated himself. Kitt had been aloof and absent, not the best of recommendations if her father had to choose between them.

You should apply that same standard for yourself. Who should you believe? Selby, who tries so very hard to be all a gentleman should be, who has supported your father at every turn, or Captain Sherard who takes liberties with you, sails away without notice and shows up late for dinners, making it clear his priorities do not lie here, all of which points to the fact that he is hiding something.

Bryn was still considering these competing ideas when the guests departed shortly after midnight. Kitt had departed much earlier—at least, she guessed he had, to her disappointment. He'd not said goodbye to her. For all she knew, he'd slipped out the garden gate. Selby and his mother were the last to leave.

Selby clasped her father's hand warmly, congratulating him on a wonderful evening. Not for the first time she wished she could like him more. Selby was safe, comfortable. He would be a doting husband, all a girl should wish for, and yet he stirred her not one iota, except to irritate her. But she'd stirred his gentleman's blood enough to get the co-ordinates.

'We'll leave for the other parishes, day after tomorrow, early in the morning, before it gets too hot,' James was saying. That got her attention.

'Are we going somewhere?' she enquired politely.

'I hadn't had time to tell you, we've just decided.' Her father smiled broadly. 'Some of the other investors thought it would be a good idea to make a survey of the island and see what's out there to invest in. We'll only be gone a week. James has lined up some people for us to meet with.' Her father was leaving on a trip? One more thing he hadn't told her.

A sense of panic began to well. How had everything got so far out of control without her knowing? It wasn't that her father needed her consent. It was just that she was used to being consulted. The closeness of the last two years was slipping away.

The Selbys left, the door shut behind them, the house quiet after being filled with the noise of guests all evening. She smiled at her father. 'I could make us some tea and we could talk it all over,' she offered. 'It was a grand evening.'

Her father shook his head and started up the stairs. 'I will pass, my dear. I am too tired and I have busy days ahead. James is coming by tomorrow to go over some things about the Sunwood project. They're going to need a little more start-up capital than originally thought to get the new crops in—'

'Yes, about that,' Bryn interrupted. 'Did you research

it? I was surprised by the announcement. I had no idea you were considering it. What do we know of it?'

'James knows of it. He would not lead me astray. It would hardly enhance his reputation to have an investment go foul at this juncture. He knows what he's doing. I have every confidence in him.'

But Kitt had thought otherwise. *It's not that I don't trust Selby, it's that I don't trust his judgement.* Who was she to trust? The gentleman or the rogue? Perhaps Selby was right. She was unduly influenced by Kitt's good looks and flirtatious ways.

With her father gone to bed, there was no sense in staying up. Bryn picked up a lamp and made her way to her own rooms. She didn't expect to sleep, she had too much on her mind: her father's new investment, Selby's comments about Kitt, all the little revelations of the evening. All of which led back to the very point she'd been considering since the day Kitt had taken her out to the rock: did she trust him?

Perhaps she did. She'd certainly been quick enough to seek his opinion tonight and even quicker to question Selby's choices instead of questioning Kitt's. The bigger question was why she trusted him. Was it true? *Did* she defend Kitt because she was drawn to him? Was infatuation influencing her decisions? There was admittedly a lot of him to be infatuated with.

She wasn't naive enough to believe she was the only girl who'd ever been swayed by good looks, or even swayed by *Kitt's* good looks to be specific. But for a woman who'd promised herself freedom, it was hardly something to be proud of. Bryn stepped inside her room and set the lamp on her dressing table, and began to absently pull the pins from her hair, her thoughts trying to sort themselves out. What was she playing at with Kitt? How far could she let it go without compromising her dreams? Her promises?

'Very lovely.' A voice spoke out of the darkness beyond the scope of the lamp and she grabbed up her hairbrush out of reflex, prepared to wield it like a club, although she recognised the voice all too well. Perhaps all the more reason to have a club.

'Speak of the devil!' She gasped. 'What are you doing in here?' Kitt's long form emerged from the shadowy folds of her canopy bed. 'Although I should hardly be surprised. You have a knack for showing up in odd places.'

'I couldn't leave without saying goodbye to the hostess.' He gave an impish grin and walked towards her. He'd taken off his evening jacket. She could see it now, folded at the end of her bed. Without it, his shoulders looked even broader, his waist even narrower, his maleness more prominent. He took the brush from her hand. 'What were you thinking to do with this? I don't recommend it as a weapon of choice.'

'A girl has to use what she has at hand.'

Kitt put the brush down. 'Did you learn anything else about the plantation?'

'Are you planning on investing after all?' She was trying to view this interaction with a level of objective detachment that had nothing to do with the fact a handsome male was in her bedroom after midnight, walking slow, seductive circles around her like a stalking tiger. Instead, she tried to focus on Selby's warning. 'Selby thinks you like to discourage others on purpose.'

'What do you think, Bryn?' His eyes never left hers as he circled.

'I don't know what to think,' she admitted honestly, her voice a little hoarse.

'As it should be. I don't know what to think either. I don't know enough about this to think anything, which is both worrisome and relaxing. Maybe there's nothing to worry about. Maybe there is and that should be a concern to your father. If he's being taken advantage of, the whole bank board will look foolish.'

'The Rutherford coffers can handle a loss,' Bryn said, trying to convince herself Kitt's words didn't raise some alarm.

'It's not about money. It's about reputation. This would be a loss of credibility at the fledgling stages of the bank's formation. It could be devastating.' Kitt's voice was velvet in the darkness, seductive even delivering bad news. *Potentially* bad news, nothing was certain yet. She couldn't jump to rash conclusions.

'What are you going to do?' She was certain he was going to do *something*.

She could almost feel his grin as he came up behind her, hands at her shoulders, his breath at her neck, feathering her ear. 'I am going to find that island.'

'And if you don't?' She was sure he could see the race of her pulse, her body firing so easily at his touch. It was as shameful as it was delicious.

'Either way, we'll know if we have anything to worry about, princess.'

'Do you know where to look?'

'No, but I have some ideas.'

Bryn licked her lips in a slow motion, an idea coming to her. She held up the paper she'd carried in her pocket just out of reach. 'I have the co-ordinates.' She watched Kitt's eyes light up. 'But, I'll want a forfeit for them.' He was leaving, again. Everyone was going somewhere, except her. Maybe she could go, too. Bryn turned in his arms, pressing her hips lightly against his in suggestion. 'When are you going?' She gave him a coy smile, her gaze dropping to his mouth.

'Oh, no, minx, you are not coming along.' Kitt's voice was husky, though. He was not unaffected by her little flirtation.

She flicked her tongue over her lips, her hips moving more strongly against his. 'I didn't say anything about that, did I? Maybe I just want a proper goodbye kiss.'

This time it was her tongue that initiated, her tongue running over the even line of his teeth and the smooth planes of his mouth as it explored. It was her mouth that moved over his, drinking and tasting the full flavour of him, her hands that anchored in his hair, drawing him to her, against her, until she could feel the unmistakable press of his erection.

'What are you doing, princess?' Kitt's voice was no more than a groan.

'Giving you a reason to come back.' She gave his lower lip a final tug with her teeth and stepped away, knowing full well her own breathing was as ragged as his.

It was his cue to depart. There was only so much she was willing to risk with her father just a few doors down and her own thoughts so unsettled. 'You can find your own way out?'

Kitt gave a snort. 'I hear the trellis works pretty well.'

Bryn waited until he'd swung a leg over the balcony railing and disappeared over the edge before she followed him outside, her eyes marking his progress as he jogged through the now-deserted garden and out the gate. The only way to trust him would be to test him. Bryn knew what she had to do. She had a day to get on that boat. Round one might have gone to him, but round two had gone to her, he just didn't know it yet.

Chapter Twelve

She was giving him a reason to come back, all right. That kiss was still on his mind two days later as he sat in his cabin, the *Queen of the Main* heading out to sea once more on the evening tide. He was supposedly charting a course for Selby's island, something his mind was only half-engaged in. The other half kept getting sidetracked by memories of Bryn's warm body pressed up against him, very deliberately. It was the deliberate part he kept going back to.

As enjoyable as the kiss was, he couldn't shake the feeling that she'd done it for a reason. If the reason wasn't to tag along, what was it? He'd replayed the scene over in his mind numerous times, much to his body's chagrin. But nothing stood out. That particular mystery would have to wait until he returned. Perhaps the kiss was nothing more than what she'd suggested—a reason to come back.

But that carried its own set of complications. Beyond their clandestine, rather spontaneous meetings, what more could there be for them? A woman of her quality was meant for a gentleman. *If you were in England, you'd have rank and be more than acceptable.* The thought was shocking in its rarity, although it wasn't shocking in its occurrence, poised as it was on the aftermath of recognising Selby as competition.

The idea was not one he trotted out often. It wasn't something he'd even allowed himself to think of in the years he'd been here. This was a land of self-made men and he'd successfully fit that mould, setting aside his former life. Never once had he regretted that decision, never once had he looked back and missed what he'd left behind.

Not even now, his conscience reprimanded forcefully. *She changes nothing.* Bryn Rutherford was a passing fancy. From a logical standpoint, he knew all the reasons she appealed. He could tick them off on one hand. He'd been celibate too long, his libido was on edge; she was new and different; she was beautiful and fine, intelligent and daring, and, to top it off, they'd been thrown together by business interests, forced to encounter one another. Fancies passed, storms passed. Like a storm, he simply had to ride her out.

Kitt shifted in his chair, trying to subdue a growing sense of arousal. Perhaps riding *her* out was not the best comparison at the moment. He went back to the map, refocusing his thoughts on a less exciting topic. After five more minutes of working he sat back and rubbed his temples. He must be entirely distracted. Usually he was a very good mapper. He picked up Bryn's paper and studied the co-ordinates again. Perhaps Selby had got them wrong? Perhaps Bryn had written them down wrong? Those thoughts did nothing to dislodge the sense of unease that had ridden him since the gala dinner. It couldn't be happening again, but early signs suggested it was. He had to find that island and it had, *absolutely had*, to have a thriving plantation on it.

Kitt was about to give it another go when a loud thump drew his attention to the wardrobe. Nothing. He scanned the room, looking for evidence something had fallen off a shelf. Perhaps it had come from outside. The thump came again and Kitt swore in frustration. Great, now he was hearing things. If this kept up, he'd never get anything done. To assuage his curiosity, he strode over to the wardrobe and flung open the door, only to be proven wrong.

Out tumbled Bryn Rutherford with an 'oomph' and a most unladylike oath on her lips.

Kitt stepped back in time to avoid being trampled. He crossed his arms over his chest. 'Well, at least you can swear like a sailor.'

'Stuff it.' Bryn glared and struggled to her feet. 'Do you have any idea how long I've been in there?'

Long enough to be deliciously rumpled. 'You weren't supposed to be in there at all.' She'd probably have a bruise or two tomorrow on that sweet *derrière* of hers, but it served her right for all the trouble she was going to cause him. He strode to the door, already making calculations for what this delay would cost him.

'Where do you think you're going?' Bryn tried to stagger after him. She hadn't any sea legs to speak of at the moment. Kitt reached out to steady her.

'Out on deck to tell Passemore to turn this ship around. I'm taking you back to Bridgetown, as much as the delay grieves me.' The tide and the breeze would be wasted now, but he was *not* taking her with him.

Bryn chose that moment to throw herself in front of the cabin door, effectively blocking his exit. 'I'm going with you to find that island.' She meant it, too. Her grey eyes stormed with stubbornness and Kitt knew he'd make no headway arguing with her. He'd let her have her moment. He leaned against the wall, arms crossed, and watched her. She was fascinating to watch, all those emotions rolling across her face at once. A lady without her ladylike mask of blandness on. Not for the first time, he thought what a trial London must have been for her and what a trial she must have been for London. Society wouldn't have known what to do with her. Lucifer's balls, *he* barely knew what to do with her. He'd have to try another tactic since reasoning was out of the question.

'You do understand, Bryn, that I am bigger and stronger than you, even when you're in a temper. I can simply throw you over my shoulder, remove you from the door and go about my business.'

'The hell you will.' Her eyes shot bolts of lightning and her hair hung forward over her shoulders. She looked like an avenging Fury. If she had a weapon, she'd be positively dangerous, lethal even.

'What a lovely mouth you've acquired,' Kitt drawled with a touch of indolence. It wouldn't do to show any ounce of weakness. 'Do you talk like that at home? Because I have to tell you that will not impress the likes of James Selby.' She managed to blush, but she didn't move from the door.

'I want to go with you,' Bryn repeated staunchly, ignoring his comment. 'This concerns my father. I deserve the right to go and see his investment.'

Kitt ran a hand through his hair. 'Damn right this concerns your father. What do you think he'll say—better yet, what do you think he'll do if he discovers you've hidden away on my ship?' Did she understand the implications of stowing away?

'He won't know. He's out with Selby visiting the other parishes. He'll be gone all week,' Bryn answered with a tilt to her chin that said, *Ha, take that*.

He sauntered towards her, crowding her a little with the bulk of his body. It was time to remind her that she'd stowed away on *his* boat and the two of them were explosive together. He would ensure she made good on that promise of a kiss she'd given him. 'It's not only that. Have you thought about us and the fact that we'll be alone with no one to stop us?'

She had no ready answer for that except for a blush that crept up her cheeks. He pressed his advantage. 'Or is that the real reason you came aboard? Maybe you want an excuse to exercise those passions of yours.'

Her cheeks flamed. Kitt smiled wickedly. So, she had thought of that, too. His hands rested at her waist, his thumbs pressing lightly on the low bones of her hips intimately, suggestively. 'Make no mistake, princess, if you came here for a taste of me, I am up for it.' More than up for it, actually. He wanted her the way a thirsty man wanted water. He hoped a sip or two would quench that thirst and he could move on.

'All that within the span of a day?' Bryn challenged, holding her own against the onslaught of his rather aggressive flirtation. Well, good for her. He'd see what she'd do with round two.

'A day?' he questioned.

'Selby says the island is only a day away. We'll be there and back before my father returns.'

'That might be a problem, princess. According to Selby's co-ordinates, there's nothing there. But when I

reverse them, there's an island three days away. Either
Selby wrote them down wrong, or he's been had, and,
by extension, so has your father.'

'No, that can't be.' Bryn had paled. She moved away
from the door to the table with rapid steps. Her finger
drew lines on the map, retracing his trail. 'The plantation managers have written. There was an actual letter.
They needed more money for the new crops.'

An absolutely classic move in a classic scheme. This
was looking more like land fraud with each revelation.

'That's why you have to go back, Bryn. I don't know
what we're going to find out there. It may be dangerous and it may not be a quick a trip.' If the island was
a fraud, he would want to hunt down the men behind
it and there was still Devore to find. He could be gone
indefinitely.

'It's every reason why I need to be there,' Bryn protested. 'Do you think James will believe you if you
come back and tell him his island isn't there? He'll see
it as another competitive ploy to outwit him. He'll believe me, my father will believe me.' She swayed suddenly on her feet.

Kitt moved swiftly to steady her. This was more than
not having sea legs. 'How long has it been since you've
eaten?' He helped her to the edge of the bed.

'This morning, but I'm fine.' She insisted although
the pallor of her face told a different story. Kitt, tell me
what's really going on?' The earnestness in her eyes
settled it. He would probably regret this but how could
he ask her to stay at home and wait? If it was him, he
knew he'd never tolerate such a decision. Why should
she? Kitt drew a resigned breath.

'I'm going to get you some food and when I come

back I'm going to tell you the tale of a Scotsman named MacGregor.'

She smiled at him, coy and alluring even in distress 'I'll be right here.'

Yes, she would be, Kitt thought grimly, exiting the cabin. It wasn't until he was in the galley gathering up food that it hit him. The minx had won. She was going to stay and it hadn't even required his consent, it had just happened. One minute he'd been spelling out the concern for her virtue and the next she'd been bent over his map, tracing routes with her finger.

For better or worse, she'd be in his cabin for the next six days. What had he been thinking? That was the problem. He knew what he'd been thinking and what he'd been thinking *with*. The organ of record wasn't the brain in his head.

He was going to let her stay! Elation surged. Bryn had not been sure her stowaway ploy would actually work. There'd been a moment when she'd thought he actually would toss her over his shoulder and personally row her ashore if that was what it took. He'd looked quite formidable standing there, legs apart, arms crossed and quite appealing, too, with his shirt open at the neck, sleeves rolled up, breeches tight, hair loose. Lord, he had glorious hair, glorious *everything*. And he'd wanted her. In spite of his anger, he'd wanted her. That had definitely worked to her advantage.

Yes, you won, you get to stay for six days. Six days alone with the pirate captain himself. It's what you wanted—an adventure. What will you do with it? What would she do with it indeed? Would she act on it or would she play the lady and resist? The reality of what she'd agreed to put a damper on the mental festivities. She'd not bargained on six days, just the one.

One day would be tolerable, surely they could keep their…what…their lust…their desires…in check for that long? But six days? Kitt's parting words rang strong in her head, the memory of his hands on her hips burned like a brand. He'd made it clear he was willing. The risk had doubled exponentially. But so had the reason for taking it: the island wasn't there! She hoped it was just a case of Selby mixing up the co-ordinates. Foolishly, she'd let him write them down. But if Kitt was right? It didn't bear thinking about. It would be a debacle before the bank even got under way, something her father's reputation couldn't afford.

Her father's reputation wasn't the only one to consider. This voyage could ruin hers entirely. She could only hope they'd beat her father back and that Kitt's crew could be sworn to secrecy. But, if the island truly didn't exist and it was discovered she'd gone out with Kitt Sherard for nearly a week unchaperoned, there would be no more attentions from gentlemen like James Selby, even if nothing had happened in truth. Which, ironically, made the case for adventure all the stronger. If she wasn't found out, then no one would know what had transpired. If she was found out, everyone would assume the worst regardless of the truth. If she was dammed either way, she might as well indulge.

Would Kitt follow through or had he been bluffing in an attempt to scare her into returning? What were the odds of *that*? Even if that had been his intention, something *would* happen in truth. He was right about their rather explosive history. The smallness of the cabin would make the conclusion inescapable. The size of the quarters would demand a level of daily intimacy she'd not factored in, but she did now and a shiver of anticipation ran down her spine. This was the adventure she sought.

The door to the cabin opened and her heart pounded at the sight of him. There was something undeniably sexy about a man with food. Kitt moved his maps to the side. He laid out the bread and cheese on the table. He gave her a wicked half-smile, catching her watching him as he poured red wine into a stoneware goblet. Her heart flipped a little when he said, 'Come and eat, your table is laid.'

Just like that, the decision was made. *When* he asked, she'd be his. It wasn't a question of 'if' any longer, but a question of when and how, and where. All very titillating considerations.

Kitt took the seat across from her and helped himself to some cheese. 'Have you ever heard of a place called Poyais?' When she shook her head, he went on. 'Not surprising. The reason you've never heard of it is because it doesn't exist.' He nodded towards his bookshelf. 'I have a book about it. though. That's how far someone went to convince others Poyais existed. I bought the book because it seemed interesting, a cautionary tale about what people will believe.'

'Authors invent places all the time, it's part of fiction,' Bryn said, not quite following.

'This wasn't an author. This was a self-fashioned adventurer, Gregor MacGregor, and this is no tale out of the past. He's still alive, apparently. He called himself the cacique of Poyais, telling people he was the head of a new nation somewhere near Belize. He recruited people to go and settle.'

'But no one did, surely,' Bryn said, disbelieving. 'No one sets off across an ocean to a place they've never seen. They had no proof it was even there.'

Kitt raised an eyebrow, forcing her to consider her words. 'How is Poyais any different than what Selby and your father have done?'

'They have letters from the overseer,' Bryn argued. 'They have scientific reports about the crops Sunwood intends to grow and market projections for profit.'

Kitt rose and strode to his bookshelf, taking down a slim volume. He tossed it on the table. 'Those settlers had a book. Flip through it. They could read about the size of the country. It's slightly larger than Wales, by the way. They could read about its climate, the natives. Anything you could want to know is right there.'

Bryn reluctantly thumbed through pages full of maps and drawings, paragraphs of descriptions about fauna and wildlife, all of it very specific, very detailed. Most unfortunately, she saw Kitt's point. Technically, there was no difference between this book and the reports that had been sent to Selby and her father. 'It doesn't mean the letters to my father are not real, just because Poyais wasn't.' The Poyais book had worked because it successfully mimicked reality after all.

Kitt leaned across the table, his gaze serious. 'You're right. This might be a false alarm on my part. It might be nothing more than Selby's incompetence with the co-ordinates. *But*, keep in mind it wouldn't be the first time someone tried to pass off the imaginary as real. New lands are full of opportunities, just not always the right kind.'

Selby wouldn't know opportunity if it bit him in the arse. It would be too much to hope he'd be able to separate the good ones from the bad. Now, he'd potentially dragged her father down with him.

She eyed Kitt with speculation, a horrible thought occurring to her. 'How is it that you know so much about land swindles?'

The gaze he gave her was equally serious. 'Because I've been involved in one.'

'I see,' she said quietly while her stomach churned over the bread and cheese. It was as bad as she thought. Kitt might be right about the island, but Selby was right, too. Kitt Sherard was not to be trusted. What fools they'd all been. What a fool she had been. She hated that realization the most. She'd been willing to trust him with more than money. She'd been willing to give him her body and quite possibly her heart.

Chapter Thirteen

Bryn tried to muster a sophisticated tone that betrayed none of the hurt she felt. 'You're concerned now because you're on the other end. Is that it? It's your money being swindled instead of the other way around.' Perhaps he'd used the Poyais book to run a swindle of his own.

Kitt's eyes darkened and he drew back as if she'd struck him with a physical blow. He pushed back from the table and rose, striding to the window. 'No, it isn't that way at all. Quite the opposite, in fact.'

'Really?' she prompted, her voice doubtful. But nothing more was forthcoming.

'Really.' Kitt's tone carried a finality with it. 'That's all you need to know, Bryn. You'll have to trust me on this one.'

She wanted to be disgusted with him, but the look on his face when she'd accused him had made *her* feel guilty instead. Maybe it was unfair to hold his past against him. Doing so made her no better than Martha Selby. Who was she to deny him a new start? Wasn't that what she was after herself? Perhaps she had no business condemning him. Her tongue had run ahead of her thoughts.

Now they were back in limbo, in the same place they'd been in the garden. Could she trust him? It all returned to that. In truth, he'd given her no reason not to even though he managed to always leave her with more questions than answers.

Kitt turned from the window and held out a hand. 'Come out on deck, I want to show you something.' It was a peace offering. He was sorry for snapping, for being mysterious, and she was forgiven for her accusation.

Bryn glanced outside the window. There wasn't much to see. 'In the dark?'

Kitt gave an exaggerated nod. 'Most definitely in the dark.'

She followed him out on deck, but once they got there, he stepped behind her, covering her eyes with his hands. 'You cannot look until I tell you. Do you trust me?' He'd understood her dilemma in the cabin, his words echoed it. This was to be a trial of sorts. If there was to be anything between them, there had to first be this. Her pride left her no choice in the matter. It was quite the experience walking the short distance to the railing with Kitt behind her, her body entirely dependent on him. It was erotic, too, her other senses heightened by her blindness. She could smell him, could smell the salt of the sea, could feel the breeze against her face.

He turned her around so that her back was against the rail and, she was facing the centre of the ship. At least she supposed that was the direction. His mouth was at her ear, low and pleasing. 'All right, now…look!' He took his hands away and she gasped.

Above the centre of the ship was the largest, fullest, gold moon Bryn had ever seen, hanging so close to the boat it looked as if the mainsail could pierce its rim.

'It's beautiful.' Her voice was no more than a whisper of awe. Kitt's hands had moved to her waist, wrapping about her. It was hard to remember the quarrel and her disappointment in the wake of his touch. All she could remember were the reasons to like him, to want him. She could feel the beat of his heart, slow and steady against her back, life surging through him, through her. The night had become profound as she stared at the moon.

Perhaps this was what she'd travelled across the world to see, to feel, these unbridled moments when nothing mattered but this oneness with herself, this primal thrill. There were no rules, no expectations, no past, only the present, only this moon, only this man and the knowledge that in this moment, nothing could hurt her except hesitation.

'I can hardly believe this is the same one we see in London,' Bryn breathed. She'd seen harvest moons, of course, and perhaps they rivalled this giant glowing orb in some way, but this was a moon nonpareil. 'I want to touch it.' She wanted to do more than touch it. She wanted to dance, wanted to shout her thrill to the skies, wanted to set aside her doubts. This was living life at its finest.

She turned in Kitt's arms, her own arms twining about his neck. 'Thank you for not sending me back. Thank you for this.' His hips were hard against hers where their bodies met, his need for her evident against her stomach.

'Don't ask me to play the gentleman, Bryn,' Kitt growled, his voice husky as he wet his lips, his gaze a sapphire smoulder when it locked with hers in silent communication. If he kissed her tonight, there would be nothing to stop them. And afterwards, there would be nothing permanent, there would be no promises.

'Understood,' she whispered. Absolutely, and completely, understood. After all, it was really the only way she could have him and her promises, too.

Her mouth lifted to his, opening eagerly to him, the fire beginning to ignite in her veins once more. She let it come, slow and steady like a flame running along a fuse. These long kisses were a well-worn trail now. She knew the taste of him, the feel of him, but passion's edge was no less keen for the familiarity. Tonight, they would get to the other side of those kisses, they would take the trail further than they'd ever been, perhaps even depart from it altogether.

Her body was primed for the adventure; heat gathered low in her belly, the place between her legs pleasantly damp in anticipation. Kitt danced her backwards to a large crate, lifting her to its lid. His hand ran warm and firm up her leg, pushing her skirts up until he palmed her mons. 'No pantalettes, again? Tsk-tsk, my naughty girl,' Kitt murmured between kisses, kneading her mound with a stroke that matched the motions of his mouth.

This was a new fire he stirred in her, a slow burn that grew until she ached with it. His hand pressed downward, finding a sensitive spot and she moaned at the sharp, sweet stab of unexpected pleasure. 'Do that again,' came her breathless request.

'Like that, do you?' Kitt's teeth pulled at the soft flesh of her lip, his hand pressing once more.

'Ohhh!' This time the cry was one of anguished pleasure. She was sure now once more was clearly not going to be enough. Bryn arched against him, her body clamouring for more, for surely, instinct told her, there must be more. This new pleasure was merely a prelude to grander things as his kisses had been a prelude to this.

'If it's more you're wanting, you'll have to brace yourself.' Kitt's eyes smouldered, two coals mirroring the fire raging in her. She wanted more and he wanted to give it to her. He lifted her arms and she watched him loop them through a skein of rope hanging above her head. Kitt gave a satisfied tug. 'Do you know what I mean to do?'

Bryn shook her head, the ache in her obliterating all ability to speak. She didn't much care what it was only that it filled her, only that it satisfied the throbbing pulse at her core. He knelt between her legs, his hot eyes locked on hers from his crouch. 'I mean to give you pleasure, Bryn.'

She felt his fingers on her as they parted the lips of her private flesh, then came the press of his mouth, the decadent flick of his tongue over the place where the pleasure had started and she was lost. Bryn sagged against her rope bonds, letting them take her weight, her eyes closed as she let the ecstasy of his wicked caress wash over her. She lost herself in the sensations, each one building upon the other until the pleasure could not be separated from the ache, until her body vibrated with it, warning her the end was near, and it was, falling upon her swiftly in an intense, shattering wave as she arched hard into Kitt's mouth.

She was boneless afterwards. She let Kitt untie the rope, let Kitt rub her wrists where the rough hemp had chafed, let Kitt wrap an arm about her and draw her close as they sat on the crate. 'So that was pleasure, *real* pleasure?' Bryn mused drowsily, her head lolling against Kitt's shoulder.

'Aye, it's a form of it, an uncompromising form of it anyway.'

Bryn wanted to protest. There'd been nothing un-compromising about it, nothing held back, everything physically, emotionally exposed, for her at least. But she knew what he meant. The act left her untouched in the ways that mattered to the Church and to society. A chivalrous pleasure indeed. She smiled against his shoulder. 'You said you wouldn't play the gentleman.'

'Do you know a lot of gentlemen who do *that*?' Kitt's voice contained a trace of humour. He was playing with her again in that bold way of his.

'No,' she said quietly. She knew intuitively there would never be a comparison for the roguish Kitt Sherard, who did not hesitate to pleasure a woman beneath a full moon, yet took care not to let the plea-sure leave her spoiled. It made for an odd juxtaposi-tion. What did that say about him? Rake or gentleman? Heaven knew what it said about her. Ladies did not enjoy being tied up by rough ropes and pleasured even more roughly.

Kitt rose suddenly, dislodging her from his very comfortable shoulder. When she was slow to rise, he bent down and scooped her up in his arms. 'Off to bed with you. We have an island to find in the morning.'

'What about you?' The fog of pleasure had lifted and she was starting to think more clearly. It occurred to her belatedly that he had not had his own release, or rather that she had not provided him any satisfaction in return. Robin had taught her that much at least in theory, if not in practice.

'It's a hammock for me. I'll bunk with the crew.' Kitt gave the door to his cabin a gentle kick and pivoted inside, careful not to bang her legs against the frame. He dumped her on the bed quite unceremoniously, making it clear there would not be another romantic overture.

Bryn raised up on her elbows. 'That's not what I meant.' She let her eyes rest meaningfully on his trousers where they pulled at his hips, a certain sign the evening had not been complete for one of them. She remembered the feel of him, the hard length of him the day she'd held him on the rock.

Kitt's eyes narrowed. 'I'll take care of it. I think you've had enough pleasure for one night.'

But just for one night, she thought as Kitt shut the door behind him. She sank back against her pillow with a sigh. Satisfaction now would lead to craving later. How could she *not* want more? Kitt had shown her pleasure existed. It had been so entirely different than what she'd experienced with any of her London bucks and their chaste kisses.

Bryn blushed guiltily in the dark. Should she even compare? Did a lady do such a thing as measure lovers against one another's performance? Love was supposed to transcend such crass consideration. But they hadn't loved her. They'd wanted her name, her fortune, the prestige of being connected to the Rutherfords. Kitt wanted nothing more than the moment. Could she settle for that? Would the pleasures of the moment be enough?

Bryn stared at the ceiling in the dark, letting the rhythm of the boat rock her towards sleep, rock her towards dreams of Kitt Sherard with his blue eyes, his flirtatious ways, his dares, his bold conversation, his unique way of looking at the world. A cynic's way, to be sure, but there was independence and strength, too. He was his own man, he answered to his own code. It was an intoxicating way to live.

He was daring her even now to follow him down that path. For her own sake, not his. This was not because he wanted a partner on that journey. She had no illusions there. Kitt Sherard was too wild. The woman who attempted to tame him would lose him. She could run wild alongside him for a while, but that was all. He'd made it clear tonight he would not share his past. There was a limit to what he was willing to give, a sure sign he had something unpleasant to hide. Perhaps even something criminal. Such a supposition made sense. Why else would he try too hard to be the impossible; a man from nowhere, unless there was something terrible to hide?

This was not new to her. She had known this all along. Men who climbed trellises and all that. This was where her promises collided with her father's. Enjoying Kitt for the moment was not the new start her father had envisioned. He'd envisaged remaking London for her, finding her a nice gentleman like Selby, setting up a house and starting a family of her own just as she would have in England, only now it would be somewhere warmer where they could escape memories of death and fading life.

What happened when fathers and daughters disagreed on their destinies? It wasn't as if this was a choice between Kitt and her father. For one, Kitt wasn't offering. For another, it was bigger than that. This was a choice between living the life she wanted for herself and the life her father wanted for her. It was a lot to think about, especially when she wasn't entirely sure what sort of life she wanted for herself, only that it wasn't raising James Selby's children under his mother's watchful eye.

Kitt, on the other hand, would have beautiful, wild children and no mother-in-law. The thought came out of nowhere and it made her laugh at the sheer ridiculousness of it. Being with Kitt wasn't about the future and it certainly wasn't about a pattern-card future. It was rather ironic that she was envisioning a traditional future with a non-traditional man. Still, one could not dispute the fact that it was a pleasant image to fall to sleep by even if it was a most improbable one.

Kitt had more than one image to fall asleep by as he lay in his hammock among the snores of his crew. Bryn continued to surprise him with the depths of her tenacity, her devotion. He'd known tenacious women before. Women were usually tenacious when they wanted something. It was a selfish tenacity at best, something that bordered on being spoiled. But Bryn's tenacity was of a purer sort. She was tenacious on behalf of others. This current task was proof enough. She was driven by devotion to her father, even though it placed her at considerable risk.

That kind of devotion was unique. Everyone had families, but not all chose to dedicate themselves to those families. Growing up, he'd been surprised to learn his family was the anomaly. His parents were the unusual ones who had not shuffled their twin boys off to the nursery without a second thought until they were old enough to be shuffled off to boarding school.

True devotion, because of its rarity, stood out. The Drydens had it. It was what had appealed to him most about Ren. Bryn had it, too. He'd seen it in her eyes at the gala dinner. She'd been proud of her father. For all her cool demeanour and clever words, she had a soft side. She would love deeply, intensely when she decided to. The recipient of that love would be a lucky man. But she would not give it idly. There was a reserve about her that he recognised and understood all too well, in part because he possessed it himself. It was one thing to play at physical pleasure, it was another to attach any deep emotion to it for the sole reason that while devotion was rare, it was also quite expensive. He knew what devotion had cost him. What had it or what *would* it cost Bryn?

Tonight had pushed things to that most dangerous edge, the edge he was always so careful to avoid. They skated close to the two things he avoided: his past and emotionally driven pleasure.

Even now, with time and space between himself and the pleasure he'd given her, his body demanded its own release, insisted upon it, the image of Bryn claiming hers fresh in his memory.

Kitt's hand slid along the hard length of his cock. She'd been magnificent; a wild creature come to life, sprung from her cage. He'd nearly come undone when she'd whispered those three heady words against his mouth, 'Do that again.' He'd gone one better and done more, knowing exactly what she wanted, what she needed. She'd leaned into the ropes, eyes shut, letting the fantasy take her and in doing so, becoming a fantasy herself, bucking against his hand, crying out her pleasure, pleasure he provided.

His hand began to pump in harder, shorter jerks. There was a manly intoxication in being able to bring a woman to completion so thoroughly. That Bryn Rutherford trusted him to provide her that completion created a whole other level of intoxication. It created complications, too, because, damn it, it wasn't going to be enough. They were physically explosive together. He knew they wouldn't stop with the pleasure tonight. She'd already offered more, offered to be a partner in that pleasure. The male in him would take that offer. He couldn't resist her.

His rhythm surged a final time, his body reliving the feel of her coming against him, his own release following at last. Now he could sleep. There would be time to think about complications tomorrow.

Passemore woke him all too soon. 'Captain, we've reached the co-ordinates! You'll want to be on deck. Come and see.'

Kitt rolled out of the hammock, pulling on his shirt and forgoing boots. This was it, the moment of truth. Sleep faded in the wake of urgency as he followed Passemore up the ladder to the deck. Someone handed him his spyglass. He surveyed the blue expanse, hoping against hope he was wrong, that James Selby had for once done something right. After a minute he collapsed his spyglass and let out a sigh. 'Passemore, can you wake Miss Rutherford and have her come up?'

He was going to have to tell her the news. The island wasn't there.

Chapter Fourteen

'What do you want to do?' Kitt leaned on the rail beside her, the morning breeze in his hair as he looked out over the water. There was a grimness to his features she'd not seen before, yet one more side of this multifaceted man. It was a deeper side, too, than the mischievous charmer he so readily displayed to the public. The ladies who vacillated between being charmed by his manners and dismayed by his boldness would hardly recognise the man beside her on the rail.

'You can't turn back now,' Bryn answered slowly. She'd been weighing her options ever since he'd called her up on deck to show her the blue expanse where the island should have been. He would turn back though, for her sake. She'd not bargained on six days away from home and all it entailed. They both knew it.

Kitt shrugged. 'We can. We can tell your father the island isn't there.'

Bryn shook her head. She would not fail her father. 'All that proves is Selby gave me the wrong co-ordinates. It doesn't mean the island isn't out there. You said so yourself. You think the co-ordinates direct us to a different island further out.'

'I think there are other considerations besides Selby's intelligence,' Kitt said sternly. He would protect her from herself if nothing else. 'Last night should have proven to you there is more at work than simply hunting down an island.'

Bryn turned so that her back was against the rail. She could look him directly in the face from this position. Her suspicions were growing. 'You're trying very hard to get rid of me. You want me off this ship so badly you're willing to sacrifice a day's worth of travel.' She paused, studying his features. 'What did last night prove to *you*?'

'To be honest? It proved to me I can't protect you, not from me, not from what might be out there.' Kitt gave a sweep of his hand to indicate the ocean. 'Who knows what we might find at the island?'

And who knew how far they'd go the next time passion swept them away? But they did know. The next time there would be no holding back. He'd already warned her and she'd already decided what she wanted. 'I can take care of myself, Kitt. Nothing will happen that I don't want to happen.'

His eyes told a different story. She had to remember he liked being in control, too. It wasn't only up to her. But that wasn't entirely it. The passion wasn't the whole story. He wasn't solely concerned about what lay between them. 'You don't think Selby mixed up the co-ordinates, do you?' she supposed quietly, having to shield her face from the sun with her hand as she looked up at him.

'No. I think there's someone out there running their version of the Poyais swindle.' Because he'd been there in some form or other. He was reliving his past through this. She could see that more clearly this morning than she'd seen it last night.

If Kitt was right, her father was caught in the middle of it. Bryn's heart sank. 'We won't know for sure until we reach the island.' But the island was two long days away and patience had never been her strong suit. If she didn't keep herself busy, she'd go mad in the interim with worry. She caught sight of Will Passemore climbing the ropes. 'Do you think your first mate might have a spare pair of breeches and a shirt?'

'Oh, no, you are *not* climbing around on anything,' Kitt said quickly. 'I don't want to have to drag you out of the ocean.'

'I don't have to climb, but I have to do something. I can't just sit in your cabin for two days waiting.' When Kitt seemed reluctant, she pushed past him. 'Fine, I'll ask Mr Passemore myself.'

'I'll do it.' Kitt caught up to her. 'Just no climbing, agreed?'

'Agreed.' She grinned.

It wasn't enough to keep her off the ropes. He should have asked for more, Kitt realised at some point in the afternoon, after he'd had a few hours to let the reality sink in. Will's borrowed clothes fit her far too well. She was curvier than Will and that made all the difference when it came to those culottes she was sporting. They showed off a nicely turned ankle, because of course she opted to go barefoot, and they pulled a mite tight across her *derrière*, reminding him acutely of the body beneath. Probably not just him either. He wasn't the only man on board who would notice. He didn't want that to become a problem.

'Will!' Kitt called his first mate to him at the wheel. 'Do you see that?' He jerked his head to where Bryn was swabbing the deck with admirable effort. To her credit, she had made herself useful.

'Yes, Captain.'

'What do you see, Passemore?'

'I see Miss Rutherford washing the deck, sir.'

'Who else do you see?' Kitt prompted.

'I see O'Reilly, sir.' Passemore cleared his throat.

'I see O'Reilly, too, and he seems a little, shall we say, distracted? I don't want any of my men distracted. Do you understand?' Over the past twenty minutes, O'Reilly had been giving Bryn's deck-cleaning skills far more attention than the sails he was supposed to be mending. If O'Reilly put his eyes on her *derrière* one more time, he was going to flatten him.

Passemore gave a curt nod. 'I understand, Captain. I'll make sure the crew is apprised of your attitude on the subject.'

Kitt chuckled. 'Apprised of my attitude, is it? And what exactly is that?' Order on board was important and it was his job to ensure it occurred, but he could still poke some fun even at himself.

Passemore's mouth twitched. 'As you are so fond of telling me, "you need to get laid". Miss Rutherford has you surly as bear after winter, as prickly as a hedgehog in winter, as—'

Kitt laughed and cut him off. 'Despite your rather tired clichés, I get your meaning. I prefer a stag in rut, they're more majestic creatures. A hedgehog , really? That seems like it would be awkward business.'

He felt like a hedgehog, too, with all its quills extended, all prickly and aroused as he went through the motions of doing his job.

By late afternoon, Kitt had had enough. He needed to expend some energy and his crew did, too. 'Passemore! Set a course for that island over there and see if we can sail the ship into the bay on the east side.'

A general whoop went up from the crew as the news carried down the line. Everyone knew what that meant: Free time on a pristine beach. Within the half-hour, the ship was anchored, the dories loaded with his twenty-member crew and Bryn, rowing towards the island.

Kitt had chosen the island well. There was plenty of beach and jungle for his men to explore and a pretty, sheltered cove past the headland for privacy. He gave Passemore instructions and took off with Bryn in tow for the cove.

'I'm sorry,' Bryn said, catching up to his long stride. 'Maybe the breeches weren't such a good idea.'

At least she wasn't oblivious, he'd give her that. It wasn't her fault she was built like a goddess with the kind of beauty that dared a man to claim it, possess it if he could. Goodness knew Kitt wanted to be that man.

'Oh, but maybe it was worth making you angry just to see this place!' Bryn stopped, taking in the white beach and the water. She tossed him a teasing smile. 'This beach might be nicer than yours.'

Kitt felt something in him begin to relent. He'd over-reacted. She'd only been trying to keep busy, she was worried about her father, she was in an entirely new part of the world with no friends to speak of. Except him. He wondered if she realised that, too? She was rather dependent on him at the moment whether she wished it or not. Probably the latter. She was definitely an independent sort. So was he. He wasn't used to people being dependent on him. Oh, there was his crew and there was Ren, but that was different. Or maybe *this* was different.

It struck him that he could make this adventure good for her if he wanted and he did want to. There was so much he could show her. He wasn't a heartless bastard, just a horny one.

'What was that!' Bryn pointed to something in the ocean. 'There it is again.'

Kitt shielded his eyes with his hand and followed her finger. He grinned. In terms of showing her things, he could start with that. 'Dolphins. Do you swim?' A swim was just what he needed to take his mind off things.

She smiled at that. 'Probably better than you do.'

Kitt already had his shirt over his head before the import of what she'd implicitly agreed to sank in. She could not swim in her clothes, or rather Will's clothes. She'd swum naked with Robin, but this was different. Robin had been her friend. Kitt was rather more. Sensuality rolled off of him as naturally as most people breathed.

Kitt tossed a look over his shoulder. 'Well, come on. What are you waiting for?' he prompted. 'We'll be in the water. I'll hardly see anything. Besides, it's not every day you get to swim with dolphins. They're usually not so far in. Unless, of course, you're bluffing me about those swimming skills?'

That did it. He was daring her and she'd be a fool not to go. He'd been far more intimate with her body last night and she had not hesitated. When would she ever have such a chance again? She'd already come this far.

Bryn stripped out of her clothes, leaving on only her chemise. She folded the garments neatly and left them on a warm rock with their towels while Kitt laughed, gloriously flaunting his nakedness. His clothes had been thrown haphazardly on the beach.

He was right, though, it hardly mattered in the water. As soon as she began swimming, Bryn quickly forgot about clothing or the lack of it. There were too many other things to focus on: the warmth of the water, the gentleness of the waves in this protected area away from the open ocean, the powerful feel of her body exerting herself.

Beside her, Kitt was a sleek athlete, cutting through the water with strong, confident strokes. When they reached the dolphins, Kitt motioned that they should dive under the water and swim alongside them.

She could not believe she was doing this! Unmitigated joy bubbled inside her as they dived. This was incredible, almost indescribable. Beneath the surface, they mimicked the dolphins' undulating movements, rising every so often for a breath. After a while, the dolphins seemed to understand they were playing with them. The dolphins starting leaping, showing off their acrobatic skills, much to Bryn's delight. She and Kitt trod water, content to watch the graceful creatures and be among them as welcomed guests.

'We should probably swim back in,' Kitt suggested. The dolphins had settled back down, their leaping done for the afternoon. 'There's more I want to show you.'

Bryn couldn't imagine what more there could be that would rival this, but there was. On the way back, Kitt showed her a small reef full of coral and colourful fish. They swam past the rocks where the sea turtles gathered to sun themselves, their large brown shells gleaming. By the time they regained the beach, Bryn was pleasantly exhausted.

Kitt retrieved their blankets and spread them on the sand. 'This is heaven, everything is so different here.' Bryn stretched out on a blanket, not caring if her chemise was plastered to her skin, not caring what it revealed. She felt full of life at the moment—nothing so trivial as nudity mattered. She was starting to understand Kitt's comfort with it.

Kitt stretched alongside her as they lay face-to-face. He lifted a hand to push a wet strand of hair behind her ear. 'Then you fit in perfectly. You're different, too. I don't know any women like you.' His voice was husky, perhaps evidence that he was caught up in the moment, of the profoundness of what they'd experienced; nature at its finest. Or perhaps, she thought, her heart giving a little leap, it was evidence of what the admission cost him, that the words were more than mere flattery. She knew he found her attractive, his body had told her that in many ways, but to hear the words and to hear them spoken by this sea god, this Poseidon on the beach, went beyond an appreciative look.

He moved into her then, drawing her body along his, his mouth taking hers in a long, slow kiss that asked the question for him. No man, not even Robin, had made her feel this way. No man had ever asked for what he was asking. Her body answered without hesitation: 'Yes, yes, I will be yours in this moment out of time.' There was nothing beyond this. There was no tomorrow, no future, only the present, only this beach, only this man, only now.

Kitt peeled the wet chemise over her head and tossed

it aside. He drew his hand down her breastbone, his touch possessive as his eyes drank in her nakedness like a fine wine; something to be savoured and lingered over, then he bent his head to her breast and sucked, his tongue licking small circles around her peak, slowly, venerating until her back arched, thrusting upward to meet his mouth, clamouring to be part of this reverent experience. This was not a heated, carnal claiming driven by lust. This was *worship*. Instinctively, her hands went to his head, tangling in the wetness of his hair, wanting to touch him, wanting to be part of this intimate communion.

He moved lower, kissing her navel, his hands framing her hips as he held her, taking a more intimate kiss between her legs. Her body pulsed for him, for what she knew could come. But he did not take her with his mouth as he had the night before. Instead, he levered himself up and positioned his whole body between her legs, letting the length of him lay against her mound, announcing, previewing what he intended next.

'Oh, God, yes, Kitt,' she moaned, as if he needed further urging, further confirmation that she wanted this. She was far beyond wanting—at some point it had become a need she would not be complete without. He moved into her then, a slow thrust that filled her, her lips moving in a thousand silent hallelujahs as Kitt claimed her, over and over, invoking the primal rhythm of the ocean in the push and ebb of his thrusts, his phallus stroking a place deep inside her with each pass until the intense friction of his efforts had her moaning incoherent words, her body bucking, her legs wrapped about his hips in an attempt to draw him even closer.

She was not alone in this. Kitt's eyes were riveted on

her, his blue gaze nearly the shade of midnight with desire. The muscles of his arms bulged with the effort of lovemaking, his body taut as climax loomed. They met it together; a final thrust, a final cry, and they were falling, blue sky above them, white sand below them and a universe of pleasure in between. She'd been wrong earlier. *This* was heaven and this man beside her, within her, was angel, saint and sinner all in one.

She floated back to earth slowly, confronted by the realisation that Kitt Sherard was more than the proverbial sum of his parts, manly or otherwise. He'd shown himself to be both a man who could have sex—that had been last night, a physical game between two willing players—but here on the beach, he'd shown himself to be a man who could make love and *that* man knew the difference.

'I can see why you love the Caribbean so much,' Bryn murmured sleepily, her finger tracing idle designs on his chest. 'Do you ever think of going back to England?' She was already regretting the time when she and her father would return to cold, dreary England, their mission accomplished.

'No, I don't think of England as home, not any more,' Kitt answered. She was almost sorry she'd asked. His tone had lost some of its usual ease. His body and his gaze moved away from her. He tucked one arm behind his head and looked up into the sky. 'My life is here, with my ship, my men, my business.'

'And your villa?' Bryn interjected.

'Yes, my villa.' Kitt chuckled. 'I'm starting to think you covet my villa. It seems to come up in your thoughts on a regular basis.'

'It is rather magnificent,' she teased, knowing he

would hear the innuendo. She wanted to return to their earlier intimacy, wanted him to trust her with part of himself no matter how small. She wanted to know him.

'Now I'm starting to think we're not necessarily talking about my "villa".' They were back to the sexy banter that was second nature to him, the casual nonchalance he wore so easily. Conversation with Kitt carried an edge. It was always a battle of wits. Was it armour, too? She wondered what depths lay beneath all that cleverness. What did he work so hard to hide?

Bryn was loath to let the profundity of their recent moments go. She shot an upward glance at his face, watching him study the clouds, his eyes thoughtful. Those moments were worth fighting for. She would risk it. 'Kitt, tell me something about yourself. What was your life like back in England?'

'You assume I had a life in England,' he challenged, but the question had made him vulnerable. It was there in the way he sat up—a sudden movement that dislodged her from his shoulder and sent her scrambling to sit up as well. They faced one another, eyes duelling.

'You want to know something about your lover, is that it?'

Kitt's tone was dangerously silky. She should take his tone as a warning, but Bryn would not retreat. She met his gaze with the tenacity she'd met his other challenges. He'd not succeeded in scaring her off yet. 'Yes.' She smiled, a tigress to match this lion of a man.

'Very well.' Kitt gave a grin. She wondered if it was meant to distract her. He did that sometimes. Doing it now was a sign of how deeply disturbed he was over her question. 'If I tell you something, you have to answer my question, whatever it is.' He laughed at her hesitation. 'Ah, it's a little different when the shoe's on the other foot, isn't it?'

Her chin went up a fraction and she squared her naked shoulders. 'Fine. One answer of mine for one tale of yours. I have nothing to hide.' Kitt, on the other hand, could make no such claim and they both knew it.

Chapter Fifteen

Kudos to Bryn. She had him cornered. Her request
should not have surprised him. A man could not make
love to a woman and not expect her to ask questions.
It was a woman's nature to seek that attachment. Yet,
he'd bolted upright and tried to dare his way out of it.
Perhaps not his best reaction. It would only confirm
for Bryn what she already suspected—he had a past he
would not willingly trot out for just anyone.

He should have known by now Bryn didn't scare. A
dare only caused her to entrench further and now here
they were, ready to exchange battle stories as it were.
It was some consolation to note that while she'd taken
the dare it hadn't been without hesitation.

'My life in England was…predictable,' Kitt said. He
settled back on his blanket and pulled her to him. Her
warm skin felt reassuring against his as he picked his
words, trying to weave a suitable truth from the fabric
of his tragedy without giving away too much. Perhaps,
too, he could use this intimacy for other purposes that
would demand more of her attention than this exchange
of stories.

'I doubt it.' Bryn's head had found its way again to the notch between his shoulder and his chest where it fit perfectly.

'Well, you can believe what you like. It was predictable.' Inside that predictability he'd had all the security of being raised the son of a peer and all the luxury, too. He had not fully appreciated what that meant until he'd been without the privileges it had provided. He understood now in retrospect it was what had driven him to purchase the villa—a chance to recreate some of that security. He had proven he could recreate the material security, but not the other, the security of knowing people loved you.

'Predictability has its benefits, but I could see the whole of my life laid out before me, the next thirty or forty years unless I died of ennui before that.' That was almost true. He *could* see his whole life laid out; what his parents wanted for him; what life had to offer a second son who was loved or not by his family. The options were minimal. The prospect had not especially bored him, but it had frightened him. Even then he could see the potential for his life to amount to nothing but one entertainment after another. As much as his family cared for him, he wanted more. It had been equally frightening to not know what more might be.

'An opportunity arose to leave and I took it.' He'd been restless in the months leading up to that 'opportunity'. He often wondered if his 'sacrifice' had been selfishly motivated after all. If he hadn't been restless, would he have been so eager to take his brother's place? But that was part of the story he couldn't tell Bryn.

'And you left, just like that?' Bryn snapped her fingers. Kitt thought he heard admiration in her tone. She'd taken the story to the intended conclusion—he'd left because he sought a new challenge. He was doing fairly well with his story. He'd managed to leave out places and people, or any reference that tied him to the aristocracy.

He could answer this latest question without any artifice. 'Yes, I did. Once I decided to leave I went. I took two trunks and whatever money I could lay my hands on.' He didn't want Bryn making him out to be any sort of hero. What had followed had been anything but the stuff of legends. He'd left within the hour of making the decision. It might have been the quickest exit in history. He could still see that last scene with his father, the two of them in the front parlour, his father's drawn face as he gripped his hand and pressed a thick wad of pound notes into it. *'Be gone, don't come back. You can never come back, promise me?'* Words whispered in love, not hatred, a father's desire to protect his son. Kitt knew all about promises. To break that promise meant to die, to be killed, to resurrect a scandal his mother's social expertise would have taxed itself to put to bed. Kitt had given his word and he'd become the prodigal son who could never return.

Bryn snuggled into him. 'I don't believe you. There has to be more to it. What compels a man to give up all he knows and sail into the unknown?'

'Why don't you tell me? I suspect our stories aren't terribly different at their core.' That was probably an outright lie. She wasn't protecting a twin from an unthinkable scandal, but it was time to turn the tables. He couldn't sustain this pseudo-truth telling much longer. 'What compels a lady of your background to leave the comforts of England and throw her virginity away on a pirate rogue she knows little about?' She tensed at that and he chuckled. 'Did you think I wouldn't notice? Tell me, were you bored, too, Bryn?'

He'd not said it meanly, but his words were a direct hit all the same, challenging her on so many levels. Her eyes narrowed, her body stiffened as she pulled away from him.

'I expect nothing from you, Kitt.' She levered herself up on her elbow, her hair hanging in a chestnut sheet over one shoulder. She looked as tempting as Eve in the garden. His body was thinking of things other than questions. It was thinking how he wanted her again, this time on top of him, her hair falling over her breasts, not Eve, but Godiva riding her steed.

Kitt mustered some self-discipline. He wasn't fooled. Virgin or not, she knew how to use her assets to advantage. He'd shifted the conversation to her and she was uncomfortable with it. She was trying to retake the offensive, but the truth was he had her on the run. So be it. She wasn't the only one who wanted something. He wanted answers, too. He felt compromised over the fact she'd not told him she was a virgin, never mind that he'd suspected it. Part of him argued that she should have said something, should have warned him. *Why? Would it have made a difference?* He knew it wouldn't have, not at the critical moment.

'Well, I do expect something. I expect a story. That was our bargain. What are you doing here, Bryn? What are you doing with *me*?' He'd turned on his side, propped on his elbow to match her. 'Who's the man who drove you to the Caribbean?'

Her eyes dropped and he knew he'd hit a target. 'Why does it have to be a man?' She was avoiding a direct answer. It heightened his curiosity. How could it *not* be? 'Because you're beautiful, you're intelligent, you're wealthy, all the things a London gentleman is raised to admire.' He could almost see it written on her face: Of all the questions in the world, he'd had to ask that one.

Bryn shook her head. 'It's complicated. I don't know where to start, really.'

'Take your time.' Kitt gave her a lazy smile, but he did not mock her hesitation. 'I've got all afternoon.' He wanted to know, wanted answers to the puzzle of her. Since he'd met her, there'd been pieces that didn't fit.

When she spoke, her words came slowly. 'My mother wanted me to be a lady, the very finest lady, the sort that was beautiful and polished, who knew all the rules, who could command a room with the nod of her head. It was what I was trained for since I turned fourteen. Eventually, I persuaded myself I could do it, that it would be enough.'

'Why did you need to persuade yourself?' Kitt watched her, waiting patiently. It struck him that she was putting this together in words for the first time although the thoughts were clearly not new to her. He felt a twinge of guilt. She was being entirely forthcoming with him and he had told her a piecemeal truth.

'Time was running out.' She furrowed her brow and ran a finger through the little river of sand separating their blankets while she gathered her thoughts. 'I'd had my debut at eighteen. It was quite the success. I was supposed to follow it up by making a stunning match the following year—after all, I'd been the toast of the Season. Rutherford girls are never out more than two Seasons. But my mother took ill with consumption. We didn't go back to London. Instead, we went to the country, we went to the seaside. We went wherever we thought she'd get well. My father and I devoted the next three years to her, to chasing hopes. '

Bryn looked up, her grey eyes misty. Kitt swallowed, tempted to make her stop. 'London and fashionable marriages lost their appeal in the wake of our family tragedy. My father loved her quite intensely. He would have gone to the moon to save her.'

'And you loved her, too. You wanted to marry for her sake?' Kitt divined in soft tones. If she'd been willing to give up three prime years of her life, it was not surprising Bryn had been willing to risk her reputation by sailing off with him to preserve her father's standing. 'You wanted her to know you were settled and taken care of?'

'I wanted her dream to come true. She'd invested a good part of her life in me. I thought it was only fitting she be rewarded.' He saw Bryn's throat work, trying to fight tears. 'She was running out of time. My young adult life had been devoted to my parents, naturally. It was just the three of us, it had always been just the three of us. We were close.'

He could understand just what those three words meant and the loss they implied. He'd lost that, too, not just with his family, but with his twin. It was something Ren would never understand. Ren might be half a world away from his family, but they were still there, he was still part of them in a way Kitt would never be a part of his family again, the way Bryn's family would never be whole again. It was a blow and a comfort all at once to know someone else understood exactly how that felt and he could never tell her.

She looked again, studying him. He must have looked

bewildered in his private discovery. 'Am I making any sense?'

Kitt reached for her hand. 'Yes, absolutely.' He could see where the story was headed, how very difficult those last years must have been for a girl of Bryn's vibrancy, to be limited to accompanying an invalid from post to post when her heart yearned to be out dancing and *living* and yet her heart was devoted to her family. She would give anything for them.

The truth of his own situation wasn't much different, but he could not tell her what he'd sacrificed for his family without the risk of making that sacrifice useless. 'But her dream came at the expense of your own?' Kitt understood that side of the coin, too. Saving his family had come at a high personal price: guilt and anonymity.

She looked at him, surprised perhaps at the insight. 'Yes. I was far more wild than she knew and far wilder than I truly understood at the time.' Bryn smiled. 'I had a friend, Robin. He and I were wild together. We grew up best friends and we stayed that way. But my mother saw trouble on that particular horizon. She was probably right. I would have married Robin, but she aimed higher for me and our mothers conspired to politely separate us. They understood our relationship was no longer proper. He was a squire's son, you see, not quite on the same level except in wildness.'

Kitt nodded. 'Your mother wouldn't approve of me.' He had some answers, but he wanted more. What was she doing with him?

Bryn shook her head. 'I think in her younger days she might have. In my heart, I believe she was wild once, too, although I have no proof for it. That's the part I never understood. What I remember of her was that she was so perfect, so proper, yet that didn't match the stories in the village. My parents were something of a local legend. He was the reserved youngest son of the earl who had won the heart of the beautiful Esme Hatfield, a woman who was as high flying as she was lovely. The villagers said she could have had any man, even my father's sophisticated cousin who was in line for a marquisate. But in the end, true love triumphed. I could never reconcile my mother with that vision of unbridled *joie de vivre* and it makes me wonder if "true love" exists or if it's an illusion.'

Kitt threaded his fingers through hers in the sand. 'Are you a romantic or a cynic, Bryn Rutherford?' It was hard to tell.

She looked down at where their hands joined. 'I've come to believe that there are no happy-ever-afters for ever, Kitt, just happy-ever-after moments. We should do our best to collect them and enjoy them for what they are and not worry about what happens next. That's what I'm doing with you. I think you understand that.'

'I'm not sure if that is a beautifully expressed sentiment or extraordinary cynicism,' Kitt replied. Whichever, though, it explained much about her, about the source of her passion, her willingness to give it free rein. 'Would today qualify as one of those moments?' Kitt asked softly, aware that the sun was starting to go down on the horizon. They, too, were running out of time. There was an hour at most before they had to return to the boat.

'Yes.' Her reply was breathless, her desire shifting her focus from the conversation to other things.

'Then let's send it out in style.' Kitt kissed her hard and dragged her up over his body, ready to do battle with the ghosts of her past. 'Come ride me, Bryn, I want you.' This would not be a languorous coupling, there would be no reverence. It would be rough and exciting, an exorcism of the past. He knew what she was doing with him. It was time for her dreams now. She wanted to fly…*with him*. He could set her free. He only hoped when she came back to earth the landing wouldn't be too hard.

He wanted her. The knowledge made her blood fire, made her adventurous as she straddled him, her body poised just above his straining phallus so that its tip could touch her private furrow with the lightest of caresses, creating an exquisite torture for them both as she moved across his tender tip. Her hands splayed on his chest, her thumbs teasing his flat nipples into erectness as he'd teased hers. But Kitt wouldn't let her play alone for long. His hands slid beneath the long coils of hair hanging over her shoulders to cup the breasts hidden beneath the chestnut curtain.

'You fit in my hands like you were made for them.' Kitt groaned, his eyes dilated with the potency of intimate touch. 'Slide down on me and show this man some mercy, my Godiva.'

She sheathed herself on him, feeling her body stretch, welcoming the strength of his erection. This was glorious and new, to have him deep inside her at her request. This time, she'd taken him and there was power in knowing the journey to pleasure was up to her.

Bryn began to move, slowly at first, exploring the possibilities of this new position. Her muscles contracted and released around him as she slid up and down his length, shuddering each time his phallus passed

178 Breaking the Rake's Rules

over the secret place it had found before. Once, twice, three times—the more it passed, the more she wanted it.

She moved on him faster, increasing their pleasure. She was gasping her delight now, Kitt's head thrown back, his body tight in ecstatic agony as he arched into her, his hands digging into her hips as they surged towards release. When it came, it was explosive and consuming, leaving no doubt this was indeed a moment she would not forget, a thousand sensations to live on for a lifetime.

Chapter Sixteen

Eventually there would be hell to pay for this heaven. She was no fool. But not yet.

She knew what happened to virgins who gave away their virtue. *If they were caught.* The size of Bryn's world had shrunk to this ship, this man, this journey. Nothing outside of that mattered. She had everything she needed right here in this cabin, in this bed.

Kitt laughed when she told him, his chest rumbling beneath her ear where she lay against him. 'The Caribbean does that to a person. It reminds you what matters, what's truly important. It's not big houses, or piles of money.'

'You have both,' Bryn argued, but not too heatedly. She was content, lulled into drowsiness by the rocking of the boat and the heat of Kitt's body beside her in the captain's bed. It was easier to think of here and now than it was to think beyond that. She didn't want to think of the missing island and what it might mean or what it might mean if she were caught with Kitt. Even if she wasn't caught, what would happen between the two of them once they returned home? There were to be no expectations, it was what they'd both agreed upon and yet she wouldn't mind if there were.

'Yes, I have both, but with the understanding that nature could take both away at any moment. The Caribbean is beautiful and deadly, kind of like a woman,' Kitt teased. 'One hurricane, one tidal wave, one disaster and it's all gone. Talk to any of the natives and they'll tell you the only way to survive is to live for the present. The future offers no guarantees.'

Was this a carefully veiled warning not to question him about the future? 'And yet the British have come and planned for a future,' Bryn said thoughtfully, wondering if she dared risk the question his comment provoked. 'It's hard to say who has the right of it.'

It was on the tip of her tongue to want to ask him if he planned for the future or if he counted himself among the natives in that philosophy. It was hard to tell with Kitt. He had forsaken any acknowledgement of the past. Had he done that with the future as well? On the surface, he retained some of the trappings of a future-minded British man—the villa, the investments, the ship, the business—but then he'd make comments indicating he lived his life in a more present-focused fashion. Where did a relationship fit? Did he even have 'relationships' the way she and the rest of the world understood them?

'You've gone quiet,' Kitt prompted. 'What are you thinking?'

'You don't want to know.' She could hear the drowsiness creeping into his voice. This was not a subject to fall asleep by. Talking about relationships would likely queer the pitch prematurely. The last thing Bryn wanted was for Kitt to become aloof and he most surely would if he thought she had any of those expectations she said didn't matter.

She let him drift off, content to be in his arms, content to be with her thoughts, to sift through the dazzling events of the day. She'd swum with dolphins and made love to a man on a beach. The next few days promised to be filled with more of the same. But then came the reality. They would go home to Bridgetown and it would be over.

Kitt had made it plain since the beginning he would not play the gentleman. He would not 'do the right thing' by her at the end of the voyage, brought up to scratch by feelings of guilt. If he thought she entertained such notions, he'd withdraw entirely and go back to his hammock in the crew quarters. That would be intolerable. There *would* be an end, but she'd think about that later, much later, and heaven forbid she do anything in the interim to hasten that end. She wanted to hold on to Kitt, to this newly discovered magic, as long as she could.

They'd come back to the boat and eaten a dinner of shellfish and bread in his cabin by the light of a lantern. They'd strolled the deck hand in hand, the crew making themselves absent to give them privacy. Back in the cabin, Kitt had made love to her in his bed, for the third time that day, his stamina for passion meeting the demands of their bodies. He'd warned her she'd be stiff tomorrow and he'd given her a chance to beg off, but she would not hear of it. If there was no guarantee how long this would last, she didn't want to waste a minute.

She'd not guessed it could be like this. She'd thought passion, once satisfied, would diminish. But with Kitt, she was hungry for more. For the next few days, she could have all she wanted. But what then? That was a dangerous path to travel down. She'd take her moments and leave it at that. She would not think about it. This was a chance to live the philosophy she'd so bravely spouted to Kitt on the beach, to reach for the blithe promises she'd made herself. She would seek moments and not create expectations beyond them. Kitt was the perfect man with whom to explore the efficacy of that new criterion. He had told her bluntly expectations would be useless.

That was fine with her, she'd had enough of gentlemen.

The experience he offered was ideal—meaningful lovemaking without creating those expectations he was so keen to avoid. Bryn looked at the man sleeping beside her, a thought coming to her. He'd got the better part of the deal today. She'd told him more than he'd told her. How much of his desire to avoid expectations rose from his desire to avoid the past? One could hardly build a future without it. The present was different. It didn't require a past or anything else. The present could sustain the unsustainable: perfection. The very reason for perfection's success lay in its temporary condition. But it provoked the question: how did one make a dream last? It was a heady question to fall asleep by. She couldn't help but feel if she knew the answer to that, she'd know the answer to everything.

Bryn slept late the next morning, awaking to find the bed empty and her body sore. Not unpleasantly so, it had been well used on sand and sea. She dressed in one of the plain skirts she'd packed, regretfully eschewing the borrowed breeches after the turmoil she'd caused yesterday. She'd miss the freedom of those clothes but she didn't want to make things difficult for Kitt, even by accident. She borrowed Kitt's brush and plaited her hair into a thick braid before going out on deck to greet the day and whatever it brought.

That sentiment turned out to be quite optimistic. A man she didn't know by name was at the helm, Kitt was at the rail with his spyglass, Will Passemore beside him. The snatch of conversation she overheard didn't sound promising.

'They picked us up again last night, Captain,' Passemore was saying. 'I don't know if they're following us or if they're just sailing in this general direction. The ocean's free country. It doesn't have to mean anything.'

'Given our circumstances, I wouldn't back that bet.' Kitt sounded surly.

'Who's following us?' Bryn said brightly, causing both men to turn and face her. Kitt slammed the articulated spyglass closed, not amused by her intrusion, a sure sign he was hiding something.

'Maybe no one,' Kitt said, shooting Passemore a look that clearly indicated he was not to tell her anything.

Bryn pretended not to notice. She came at the question from another angle. 'Why would anyone be following us at all?'

Kitt smiled. 'Exactly. It seems unlikely, we're just being cautious.' He put an arm about her shoulders to steer her away from the rail. 'Have you had breakfast? Let's get you some food.'

Something was definitely wrong. She'd give him five minutes to confess before she demanded an answer.

'Are you going to tell me?' Bryn asked between bites of sweet breakfast ham and toast. The five minutes had come and gone. Kitt had said nothing, trying to reroute her curiosity with food. Kitt's cook was more than competent and his larder was far better stocked, she suspected, than the standard ship's, but it would not be enough to distract her from the business at hand.

'It's not your concern.' Kitt's voice contained a quiet force that heavily suggested the conversation was to go no further. There was something he wasn't telling her, yet another sign the trouble was beyond trifling. She worried more when people didn't tell than when they did. Her parents had kept her mother's illness from her until it simply couldn't be denied. While she'd understood their reasoning, she didn't agree with it any more than she agreed with Kitt's choice now.

'Ignorance does not protect.' Bryn pushed her plate away and met him with a hard gaze over the wooden table. 'If there is danger posed to a ship I'm on, it is definitely my concern. Peril to my person is always my concern.'

Lucifer's balls! She wasn't going to let it go. 'It could be nothing.' Kitt blew out an exasperated breath. How was he to tell her that he hadn't come out here just to look for an island? How did he tell her he had men out to kill him quite possibly in retribution for an altercation last year? Keeping such company hardly recommended him. He'd asked her to trust him and yet there was so much he needed to hide from her.

It most certainly was a stain on his credibility, too, when it came to her father. He needed the board to believe his opinions, to be swayed by his advice rather than Selby's at this juncture. It was bad enough that she suspected him of some involvement in a previous land swindle, even if she didn't understand what that involvement had been.

That rationale sounded a bit thin even to him. *Perhaps that's not all*, a little voice inside him spoke up. *Perhaps it's not the bank you're worried about so much as her. What would she think to see your roguish life up close? It's one thing to know about it, another to see it in action.*

He wanted her safe, that was all, just as he would want any passenger on his ship safe. This had *nothing* to do with the fact that his body craved her, that he knew when she was in a room, that she permeated far too many of his thoughts these days.

'Kitt? I demand an answer. If our positions were reversed, you would, too. The only difference is that *I* would give you one. Yesterday was proof enough of it. I told you more than you told me. You owe me.' Her tone was sharp, her gaze challenging. She believed her words for now because it suited her purpose. Kitt doubted she'd feel that way if the shoe was truly on the other foot, if she risked his good opinion. *And yet, she's risked her virtue, something far more valuable. What more does a woman have to risk when it comes to her reputation?*

'We don't know it's anything at all, just another boat out sailing.' Kitt tried his last line of defence, but it was weak and she laid siege to it with devastating ferocity.

'Yes, I heard that part on deck. I also heard your response to it. You don't believe it's nothing, ergo, you believe it is something *and* you have an idea of what it is.'

Kitt rose from the table. 'Come walk with me. I don't want to discuss it here.' He wanted to be back on deck to check the ship's progress and to gain a measure of privacy. The next shift would be getting ready to go on and men would be drifting down for food.

Outside, the intruding ship had made no move to sail closer, keeping its distance and giving every appearance it was going about its own business. Bryn leaned against the rail, her face showing the glorious effects of a hatless day in the sun. A small trail of freckles brushed the arch of her nose. She looked fresh and vibrant, except for the shrewd look in her eyes, a reminder to Kitt that he was up against a most enticing equal.

'Are you concerned the ship might be some of your enemies?' Bryn asked, cutting right to the heart of the matter. 'I know your business is sometimes dangerous, although if it's simply the matter of trading I don't pretend to understand why.' There was a scold in there for him, that he'd somehow not been forthcoming when he should have been.

'Rum is not my only cargo,' Kitt answered. 'Last year I ferried four men into exile after they tried to burn down a plantation and force a cartel in order to leverage sugar prices. Two of them took the situation poorly. I would not put it past them to have revenge on their minds and designs on my person.' Although he wished they'd picked a better time to come after him than when he had Mr Bailey Rutherford's daughter on board. But perhaps they knew and had done it for just that reason. Bryn would certainly limit his options for dealing with them if they made a move.

He watched Bryn cock her head to one side, a habit she had when she was thinking. He could nearly see her mind fitting all the pieces together. It was only a matter of time now. 'Is that why you climbed my balcony? You never did tell me.'

Kitt nodded. 'They were waiting for me when I stepped ashore.' Perhaps knowing would be for the better, a very real reminder that the life he lived was unsuitable for her, just in case she was entertaining ideas to the contrary. Now she knew. He must always be vigilant in his line of work; vigilant for opportunity, vigilant against danger.

'Now you are paying for having done your civic duty and rid the parish of rotten scoundrels,' Bryn surmised with an arch of her dark brow. 'Assuming you're right about the nature of that ship, of course. It was quite selfless of you, knowing you'd be the one to draw their fire eventually.'

That set off alarm bells. 'Oh, no, you don't, Bryn. Do not make me into a hero.' That was the last thing he wanted. What he *needed* was for her to understand the danger in associating with him. 'It can't change anything.'

Bryn's voice was dangerously quiet. 'I don't want to change anything, I just want to understand it.'

'For your father's sake?' Kitt asked sharply, feeling as if he was about to be in over his head. The moment she acknowledged this inquest had stopped being about her father's banking and had become more personal, he would be.

'No, for mine.' Bryn speared him with her stormy eyes, her gaze pinning him to the rail with their intensity. 'Is it so wrong to want to *know* you, Kitt Sherard?' There it was, the admission that proved it.

He did not hesitate to answer. Better to say it now than to say it later. 'Yes, it is if it leads you to think differently about our situation. When we get back to Bridgetown, this will be over.'

'If that's what you want.' Bryn looked out over the water, her jaw tight in the wake of his harsh words. She refused to meet his gaze, perhaps realising she'd gone too far, maybe even further than she'd meant to go. Goodness knew he had. He had not meant to be so blunt.

'It's what I want. It's what has to be.' He wanted to add that she'd agree if she really knew him, but that would give her an opening he couldn't afford. He could not let her know him.

She had no response for that. In the distance they watched the worrisome ship veer off, sailing away from them. 'Too bad it didn't sheer off a few minutes earlier. You could have saved yourself a lot of trouble,' Bryn said drily. 'I guess there was nothing to worry about after all.'

'Bryn, you knew when we started this—' Kitt began, only to be interrupted by a cry of 'land ho' coming down from the crow's nest, a reminder that their second island loomed. He didn't hold much hope for this discovery. The island was too remote. It would be too difficult to populate it, to support it. Great, the morning was just full of fraud. 'Get a towel and whatever you need, we're going ashore.' Kitt pushed off the rail and went to join Passemore at the helm.

Other than not being the home of an innovative, new plantation, the island held promise in other ways. With luck, maybe he and Bryn could get back to what they did best: sex on a beach one more time before he had to pull away from her entirely for her own good.

Chapter Seventeen

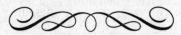

'**W**hy did we pull away? We could have taken them on that island!' Hugh Devore's fist came down on the captain's desk, rattling the inkwell and other accoutrements. 'What's the point of following them out here only to turn back?' When he'd decided to follow Sherard's ship out of the harbour, he'd not bargained on being gone so long. Three days out and he was growing impatient. He had other business that demanded his attention.

'It's called protecting my ship,' the captain, a big burly Jamaican he'd hired because the man's size and temperament matched his, growled, unfazed by his surly manner. 'Besides, it's what Sherard wanted. He was too ready for us. His crew has been watching us all morning. They'll see us coming, they'll be prepared. I won't wreck my ship for your vengeance.'

Devore had to admit to the merit of the captain's thinking and tried to shape it to his advantage. 'We know where they are and where they'll be. Let's lull them into complacency first, let them think we were nothing but another trading ship. We can take them when they leave.'

'We'll see about that,' the captain argued. 'The *Queen of the Main* is a fast ship and Sherard's a canny one.'

Devore sat down and stretched his leg. His knee was starting to ache from the exertion of being at sea. Sherard had done this to him, caused this pain. He'd shot him in the knee as a show of power. He would extract pain in return from Sherard ounce by ounce until Sherard wished he had killed him outright when he'd had the chance. 'Nonsense, it's the perfect set up,' Devore insisted, helping himself to the captain's brandy. A battle at sea would have no witnesses. He would have preferred to have stormed the beach and killed Sherard, crew and all, on land. But perhaps the captain was right and it was better to wait.

It probably didn't much matter where it happened as long as it did happen. It was perfect *and* necessary not just for his personal vendetta, but for the security of his other business ventures. He wasn't certain what Sherard was doing out here, but it seemed ominous that the man had sailed with the banker's daughter on board just days after Rutherford and Selby had invested in Sunwood Plantation.

'I told you this would happen.' Elias Blakely spoke up from his corner where he'd watched the whole exchange. Usually, he was a quiet mouse of a man, sharp with numbers, but not much else unless his profit was threatened. Then, Blakely could be as lethal as the next person.

Devore shot Elias a hard look intended to make the man squirm, but Elias didn't back down. 'We should have let the plantation scheme go when Rutherford showed up. The situation was too hot. But you had to go and overreach yourself, taking money from men who were bound to ask questions.'

'Selby didn't ask questions,' Devore ground out defensively. They'd decided last year it was much more lucrative to run imaginary plantations than to run real ones. But the money was real enough. Men were eager enough to invest for a quick profit. They paid them, too, a nice sum within the first month to inspire trust and to foster future investment, which of course would be much more than the initial outlay. Men like James Selby were happy to donate to 'the cause', never guessing the only thing they made back was money they'd already given. But men like Kitt Sherard were dangerous. They and their questions were avoided at all costs.

'You think he was looking for the island,' Elias continued. 'We're sunk if he tells anyone. He'll come after us.'

'Yes, you nodcock!' Devore snapped. 'That's why we have to take him before he gets back to Bridgetown.' There were other reasons, too. He and Blakely weren't exactly welcome in Bridgetown after the debacle last year. Dryden and Sherard had made sure their presence would not be tolerated. Once Sherard reached Bridgetown, Devore could only rely on hired men to get to Sherard.

'What about the girl?' Elias asked.

'Sherard owes me a woman, by my count.' After he'd lost everything at Sherard's hand, his wife had sailed for England and her family, refusing to follow him into exile and poverty. 'She'll have to die, too,' Devore replied grimly. He'd kill the girl first and make Sherard watch on the off chance the girl mattered to him. She was the banker's daughter—it was entirely possible Sherard was simply using her to lever his way into respectability. Although, what he'd seen through the spyglass on deck a few nights ago hadn't looked like play-acting. Perhaps he'd have that chestnut vixen spread for him—a nice consolation prize for all the upset Sherard had caused. Maybe he'd make Sherard watch. That was a better idea yet.

Who would have guessed one of the plantation investors would actually have known Kitt Sherard, who was in turn carrying on with another investor's daughter? Fate and coincidence had conspired quite cruelly against him just when he was back on his feet and making money. Devore squeezed the stem of the brandy snifter with such force it snapped in his hand. Having Sherard's woman would be small consolation for all the upset the man had caused. Damn it! Devore pulled out a handkerchief and wrapped his bleeding hand where the glass shards had bit into his palm. It wasn't supposed to be this way.

It wasn't supposed to be this way! Kitt's primal instincts were barely leashed as he thrust hard into Bryn's welcoming wet core, the waterfall sluicing over them both, Bryn's cries swallowed up by the pounding cascade. He wasn't supposed to want her, to keep her. She was supposed to be merely another lover, one of many and one of more to come.

Her legs were wrapped tight around him, her body balanced between him and the water-smoothed surface of rock wall under the falls. Her neck arched back, her body bucked. Perhaps she, too, felt the wrong rightness of this, perhaps she knew as he did that this had to be the last time. Practical realities demanded it.

He buried his mouth against Bryn's neck, his climax fierce and powerful as he pumped into her one final time. Kitt let the climax claim them both, giving himself over to these last minutes of peace. He knew full well in the clarity that accompanied the intensity of release, his mind would be swamped with all that needed doing in the aftermath of this journey.

There would be a new voyage to plan, one full of danger and without Bryn. He would find the bastards who had set up the land scheme and bring them to justice before they could ruin any more bank accounts and reputations. He'd seen first-hand how families suffered from schemes such as this. It was clear now that the plantation was a swindle. There was nothing on this island except jungle and falls. It was beautiful and lush, like the woman in his arms, but it was not home to an investment property. The best they could do now was set a fast course for Bridgetown before her father returned and be there to prevent him from investing any more money.

Against his skin, he could hear the pounding of Bryn's heart starting to slow into its usual rhythm. These last moments of intimacy would have to do, would have to last. Even if he hadn't proven it to her, this trip had proven to him what he'd already guessed in theory: there was no place in his life for a woman like Bryn—a woman he could easily become attached to, a forever woman. His life was far too unpredictable, too dangerous. *And he liked it that way*, Kitt reminded himself. He'd made this choice long ago. He wasn't going to give it up, risk it all for a woman. He'd have to give up the woman, this beautiful, vibrant woman.

Separating himself from Bryn would be tricky. There would be her father and the bank, a partnership that would potentially put him in contact with her from time to time. Much of that business could be conducted by letter. Eventually the bank would set up formal offices on Bay Street and there would no longer be a reason to call at Rutherford's house, a situation Kitt thought he could help along when he returned. He had a currently vacant property that would do well for the office, something he'd acquired in a card game a few months back.

'Come back to me,' Bryn whispered at his ear, her hands combing back his tangled hair. 'You're a million miles away.' She held his face between her hands, her eyes meeting his. 'Don't worry. We'll find the people responsible and make things right. For a man who says he cares about nothing, you take too much on yourself.'

'It does me no good to see the bank's reputation tarnished before it even opens.' Kitt stepped out of the falls and reached for a towel. Perhaps waiting to put distance between them was a bad idea, perhaps he needed to start that process now. It would be easy enough. A swift journey home would demand his attention on deck. He'd not have time to worry about the chestnut beauty lying in his bed. He wasn't comfortable with this version of Bryn Rutherford who saw too much. It was simpler when he was just a rogue on a balcony with no history. That was the problem with relationships. You got to know someone, façades were stripped away until all you were left with were truths.

Bryn would not like those truths when she came to

them. Right now she saw a hero, but soon she'd see a man who had broken with his family, a man who was loyal to a few rare friends, but mostly loyal just to himself. In short, she'd see in him all that she wasn't and she'd abhor him for it. All he would be able to say for himself was that he'd been honest about it, he'd warned her.

Kitt watched her wrap the towel around her hair and reach for her clothes. He watched her glorious nakedness disappear beneath the fabric, memorising each curve, each line. He was going to miss this. He slipped on a pair of loose culottes and held out his hand to her. Best to get it over with. 'Are you ready? It's time to go.'

Time to go *home*. Bryn reluctantly took Kitt's hand and let him help her over the rocks. The idea did not appeal at all. Time to go home meant the end of this adventure, it meant confronting her father about Selby's mistake. Most of all, it meant the end of this interlude with Kitt. Everything would change when they reached Bridgetown. It was changing already. She wasn't entirely convinced Kitt's thoughts had only been about the land swindle, but about them, about *her*. He was already leaving, trying to distance himself from her.

It was probably for the best. How would they keep this affair up in Bridgetown? He certainly couldn't keep sneaking into her bedroom and one too many trips out to a garden would eventually be noticed. But those were just practical reasons for ending it. If they kept this up, it was bound to reach a point where it meant something, at least to her. In fact, that point might have already been reached, promises to the contrary notwithstanding.

It had become readily apparent to her over the last

few days that she could make all the vows she wanted about not falling for a man, about not leaving herself vulnerable to the emotions that came with physical contact, but those vows could only serve as warnings, they could not actually force her to take their advice, nor could they stop it from happening.

On board the *Queen*, the crew was a unified mass of moving energy, everyone busy with their tasks. Kitt's orders had been plain: make Bridgetown with all speed possible. This would be no leisurely sail home. There would be no side sojourns to swim with dolphins, no waterfalls to bathe under, no languorous afternoons spent on sunny beaches. In short, no time for her.

Bryn took up an unobtrusive post at the rail where she could watch Kitt and stay out of the way, of which the latter was clearly what he wanted. The sting of separation hurt, there was no doubt about it. Even now, with the feel of his body still imprinted on hers, her hand still warm from his grip, she felt bereft—something she had no right to feel, she reminded herself sternly. She had no right to feel abandoned, no right to wallow in self-pity like a jilted miss, no right to feel anything. They'd implicitly agreed it would be this way.

Apparently she wanted to rub salt in her emotional wounds. She couldn't stop staring at him. Her eyes followed him around the deck, watching him work. He remained shirtless, putting his muscles on display as he heaved ropes and raised the sails, his culottes riding scandalously low on his hips, reminding her she knew precisely what lay beneath them.

Overhead, the sky started to cloud, the wind rising.

'It'll make for good speed!' Kitt called to Passemore, who questioned the weather.

'Are you sure we shouldn't stay in the cove and shelter until it passes?' the first mate called back.

Kitt shook his head, shouting to be heard. 'We cannot delay in reaching Bridgetown. With a wind like this, we'll make excellent time, perhaps even outrun the worst of the squall.'

Bryn turned her gaze skyward. Grey clouds gathered, blocking out the setting sun. The peaceful blue-skied day was gone, replaced by an ominous dusky light. The island was still visible behind them. She much preferred Passemore's suggestion to Kitt's idea of a fair race between them and nature. Overhead, a fork of lightning lit the sky in the distance, at once both terrible and beautiful in its power. Passemore gave Kitt a final challenging look, but the rest of the crew seemed oblivious.

'We've sailed through far worse.' She heard Kitt laugh and clap Passemore on the shoulder. 'You take the helm and I'll finish with the sails.' He disappeared to the far end of the ship.

Bryn turned her gaze outward to sea. They were definitely picking up speed. The serene blue waters had turned the colour charcoal, no longer a flat, peaceful sheet of ocean, but an erratic collection of choppy, white-topped peaks as the *Queen* cut through them. She could feel the ship roll beneath her feet. She hoped Kitt was right and they would outrun the weather. Otherwise, it might be a very long night. It was going to be a long night anyway in an empty bed.

The first raindrop caught her on the nose, a fat, wet

splat. She blinked, wiped it away and blinked again, her eyes catching a shape on the horizon that had not been there before. There was a ship under full sail and it gave every appearance of closing fast.

Chapter Eighteen

Hell and damnation! Kitt swung down from the rigging, calling for his spyglass. Passemore had it waiting before his feet hit the deck. 'Is it the same one?' Kitt asked, putting the scope to his eye. This was disastrous. He needed clear sailing to Bridgetown, but fate and nature seemed determined to conspire against him, first with the storm and now with this mystery ship reappearing out of nowhere.

'I think it is, Captain,' Passemore affirmed. 'But the ship is unmarked so it's hard to tell.'

Kitt gave a grim nod and handed the glass back to Passemore. It was his belief, too, that it was the same ship. 'Run up the quarantine flag and let's see what she does.' A ship meaning no harm would respect the warning and leave them in peace with their sick. Only a ship bent on menace would ignore the quarantine, or even suspect the quarantine was a lie.

Another fear began to surface. If it was the same ship, it had picked them up fairly quickly after they'd left the island, suggesting to Kitt it had deliberately lain in wait for them. He looked up at the white sails filling with the full force of the wind. The *Queen* was fast. This would not be the first time he'd outrun storms and villains. Now that the *Queen* was under full sail, the other ship would be hard pressed to keep closing. He made a decision. 'Passemore, let her run. If these bastards want us, they'll have to catch us.'

Passemore grinned with far more enthusiasm than Kitt felt. 'Aye, aye, Captain.'

Kitt risked a glance to where Bryn stood at the rail looking out over the sea, soaking in the rain. The silly woman, she should be off the deck. Didn't she know she was in danger up here? Of course she didn't. He hadn't told her, not explicitly. He grabbed up an oilskin from the storage trunk they kept on deck and strode towards her. His tone was gruff and sharp when he spoke, anger disguising his concern. 'You should have gone to the cabin the moment it began to rain. I don't need you sick with a chill.'

'We had a squall or two on the crossing, I can manage bad weather,' Bryn said confidently, but she didn't shrug him off when he draped the oilskin about her.

Kitt had every intention of ushering her to the cabin, but she twisted out of his grip, refusing to be mandhandled. 'Will they catch us?' Bryn asked, her gaze riveted on the dark shape of the ship trailing behind them.

'They may not want to. I've run up the quarantine flag. We'll know soon enough if they mean business. Now, let's get you somewhere warm and dry.' This time, she let him lead her away from the rail and he knew relief as they gained the shelter of the cabin, not just because it afforded her protection from the elements, but also because it afforded her safety.

If this boat behind them meant menace, Kitt would

prefer it not know a woman was on board. He wanted a fair fight if it came to that. He'd match his men man for man and the *Queen*, too, against any roguish frigate's crew in the Caribbean. But he absolutely didn't want a fight where Bryn was used as leverage against him. There would be nothing fair about that.

Bryn was no fool and his gruff tones hadn't masked his concern. She reached for him as he turned to go, a firm hand on his arm. 'I have two pistols in my valise and I know how to use them.'

Kitt gave her a curt nod, understanding her implicit message. *If the worst happens, I'll be fine. You needn't be distracted by worry for me.* It was a gesture entirely her, selfless Bryn thinking of others before herself even in a potential crisis and it was the undoing of him. His mind screamed a desperate warning: *Not now, not now!*

'The *Queen* is fast,' he assured her, trying hard to betray none of the emotions rocketing through him as he stared into those eyes of hers, so hard and determined. His insides were chaos. He'd not imagined it would happen this way. He'd always thought if, on the remote chance, it ever *did* happen to him, it would happen in bed, a beautiful woman staring up at him with soft, dreamy eyes. It most definitely wouldn't happen in the midst of a crisis with a woman telling him she was priming her pistols. That was when he knew. Love had found him and at the worst of all possible times. It was a hell of a time to realise he'd fallen for Bryn Rutherford. But it didn't matter. It couldn't change anything, it could only hurt more. He would get over it. He'd hurt before and he'd survived.

'You won't need them,' Kitt repeated with a final grim nod before stepping out into the rain, shutting the door firmly behind him and wishing he could leave his emotions behind as easily.

She won't need them, he silently vowed, pulling his arms through an oilskin slicker and joining Passemore at the helm. The rain had picked up substantially, but that was expected. The storm was bound to get worse before it got better. Beyond the rail the dark ship was keeping its distance.

That was expected, too, either because the storm and the *Queen*'s speed had not allowed any further gains or because the quarantine flag had done its job. The distance was reassuring, but Kitt suspected it was for the former reasons and not the latter. If the flag had worked, the ship would have probably charted a different course. Even small-time pirates would not have made the effort to go after a quarantined ship. Still, it would be difficult to overtake them. Byrn could put her pistols away.

If it wasn't for Bryn, Kitt would have opted to turn and fight, the only sure way to end this guessing game once and for all: who was indeed behind these attacks on his person. Outrunning the ship simply delayed that particular resolution for another day. It was clear to him that he was the target of this chase. At least that gave him something to bargain with if it came to protecting his ship and protecting Bryn: himself. But he would not go easy. He would put his faith in the *Queen*'s speed.

'I thought you said this ship was fast!' Devore fumed, water dripping in his face in a cold, steady stream. The rain was miserable and they were making no headway in catching Sherard's ship. The storm was working to Sherard's favour, but not theirs. Every time Devore looked up, it seemed they were falling further behind.

'The *Queen*'s a fast ship, I'm doing all I can!' the captain yelled over the wind, as surly as Devore. Devore swore and turned away, kicking a foot at a coil of rope in frustration. Dammit all! This was supposed to have been easy. They'd lain in wait, sails at the ready to take the *Queen* swiftly before Sherard could get it under full sail.

Even then, they'd been outplayed by the rising wind, but not before Devore had caught sight of something of interest in the spyglass; Sherard had gone to the woman at the rail, his hands lingering at her shoulders as he'd wrapped an oilskin jacket around her. It was definitely not a neutral act. He could have sent someone else with the jacket, he could have simply handed one to her. Sherard's gesture spoke of a caring that went beyond politeness. It confirmed what he'd seen through the telescope earlier. Sherard had developed feelings for Miss Rutherford. Devore almost rubbed his cold hands together in glee. Before, he'd counted on deep-seated honour to make Sherard accountable. He didn't think Sherard was callous enough to stand by and watch any woman under his protection suffer regardless of his attachment to her. But now, this was different, this was better. A woman Sherard *cared* about would be exquisite leverage indeed. It guaranteed Sherard's capitulation if they could just capture the ship.

'We need more drastic measures.' Devore returned to the captain at the helm. 'We've got to slow him down, make him turn and fight. You have cannons. It's time to use them. Shoot to disable the ship only. I don't want to sink it.' Not yet anyway. He wanted to do that when

Sherard could watch. Oh, this was perfect. With the limited visibility of the rain, Kitt Sherard would never see it coming, not until it was too late.

The first shot shook the cabin, sounding like a clap of thunder had occurred directly overhead. Bryn screamed in abject shock, the force of the sudden explosion sending her reeling on to the bed. Outside the cabin door, footsteps pounded across the deck, the air filled with the abrupt shouts of men racing to do a task. Bryn picked herself up off the bed, a terrible thought occurring. It hadn't been thunder, but something worse.

Bryn scrambled for her valise tucked away at the bottom of the wardrobe. Now seemed like a good time to retrieve those pistols she'd boasted of to Kitt. Her heart was racing and she took a few breaths. A shaky hand didn't do anyone any good, nor did a shaky mind. She needed to be calm, she needed to think with cool detachment.

Her hands closed around the smooth butt of one pistol, then the other. The feel of the familiar grip offered some measure of comfort. She'd bought them before she'd left England and had taught herself to shoot. She was by no means an extraordinary marksman, but she'd find her target in close quarters. She hoped she wouldn't have to prove it.

Bryn checked to make sure the safety was on and returned to the bed just in time. The ship made a sudden lurch. They were turning back! There was a low rumble and the clank of chains from under the deck somewhere. It sounded as if cannons were being rolled out. That meant engagement. Someone had fired on them. Worse, it likely meant Kitt couldn't outrun them.

Oh, the curiosity was killing her! Bryn fought the urge to go out on deck and demand information. She wanted to see the damage first-hand, wanted to know what was going on. Most of all, she wanted to see with her own eyes that Kitt was unharmed. But she was practical, too. She understood on deck she was a liability: a distraction to Kitt and a danger to the crew. If she were taken, their lives could be forfeit to save hers. Kitt would be forced to bargain, to choose whose lives mattered. It would be an intolerable situation. So she did the right thing, the hard thing. She sat on the bed with guns primed and aimed at the door in case the worst happened, occasionally risking a glance out the window, but since it was in the bow and they were turned sideways to face the oncoming ship, the window could tell her little of the action.

The volley of cannon fire rattled the cabin, this time from the *Queen*'s own. It was returned. Outside, men yelled, items shattered and crashed. She thought she heard Kitt's voice calling to reload the cannons. It was comforting to know he would fight to the end, but what would that end look like? Would Kitt and the *Queen* prevail? Bryn thought not. A ship would not fire and demand a battle if it didn't think it could win.

The *Queen* was a merchant ship, and its prime weapon was speed. Its cannons were primarily for protection, not for deliberately provoking other ships into a fight. It was quite likely only a matter of time. Kitt could not hold them off indefinitely. That decided it. She would not meet her fate quietly sitting in a cabin waiting for it. Bryn cocked her pistols and stepped out the door.

The deck was a ghastly scene straight from a pirate novel, exacerbated no doubt by the dark weather.

Wind whipped at her hair, the slanting rain pelted her newly dried skirts. Debris lay strewn about. She could see where the first shot had severed part of a mast and ripped through a sail. The jagged mast piece lay on the ground, looking much larger at her feet than it had up in the air.

It was all she had time to see. A body barrelled out of nowhere with a yell, taking her to the wet deck with a bone-jarring thud just as something whizzed overhead, ripping the air. 'You are supposed to be in the cabin.'

Kitt! She pushed at his heavy form, trying to regain her breath after the sudden impact. But Kitt would not let her up. His voice came low and fast at her ear. 'How can I protect you if I don't know where you are? If you don't follow instructions? Cannon balls are indiscriminate things, Bryn. They don't care who or what they hit.'

'They're coming, Captain!' Passemore scrambled across the deck towards them. Kitt rose. 'They just launched the longboats. Shall we fire again?'

'Fire as long as you can,' Kitt barked out for everyone to hear. 'Cannons are our best chance. We want to keep them at a distance. Do not let them board this ship!' His voice was full of authority. Men ran to obey, but Bryn saw the futility of it in his eyes. She grabbed his arm, forcing him to look at her.

'It's not going to work, is it?' She willed him not to lie to her. She was too smart. She knew the numbers. Kitt had a crew of thirty. It appeared the numbers were against them, three to one.

'Don't worry, they won't sink the ship, Bryn. They don't want the *Queen*, not right away at least.'

She searched the grim lines of his face. 'What do they want?'

'They want me.' His eyes moved beyond her, looking at a point past her shoulder, his mind already calculating options and discarding choices of which she knew there weren't many. The question now was not if they'd surrender, but when and how.

'No, Kitt. You can't.' Bryn's grip tightened on his arm as if she could hold him there with her strength.

'If anything happens to me, Passemore will see you to safety. Get to your father. Tell him what we found.' He shook his head, his tone softening for a moment, his eyes caressing her face with their gaze. 'I am sorry, Bryn, for dragging you into this.' He kissed her on the forehead, a quick hurried gesture. 'Stay in the cabin. Hide, defend yourself. I'll have men posted outside the door, good men, it will be hard for anyone to get through. You will not be alone.'

But not with him. Bryn understood that message and worry ripped through her. What was he going to do? He simply couldn't turn himself over. Of course he couldn't be with her. It would be tantamount to suicide for them both to be caught together. Strategically, she understood that. Emotionally, though, it was all she wanted. If she could see him, she would know he was safe, she would have a chance perhaps to protect him. Out of sight, she could control nothing.

'No, that option is unacceptable,' Bryn said, her challenge taking Kitt by surprise. She was *not* going back there to sit and wait. It was the very thing she'd come out here to avoid. If she went back and sat on the bed with her pistols, fate would just outwait her. The end to this adventure would be inevitable and obvious. 'There has to be another way.'

Kitt stepped close, frustration evident in his eyes.

She involuntarily backed up a step. She'd crossed a line with her latest bit of defiance, but she'd not give in. In her gut, Bryn knew she had to win this argument for both their sakes. Kitt was worried for her and that had limited his perception of the options. 'Bryn, I need you to follow directions. How can I keep you safe?' he ground out the old argument.

'No.' She shook her head, an idea forming. She spoke quickly, the words coming rapidly, racing against time. 'You're only saying this, only acting like this, because I'm a woman. What if I wasn't?'

Kitt gave a wide grin, some of the grimness receding from his eyes, his voice full of mischief the way it usually was. 'Now that would be *very* disappointing.'

Chapter Nineteen

If Bryn didn't have to be a woman, he didn't have to be the captain. Of course, in his case, success was less assured. Depending who was on that ship, someone might recognise him regardless of disguise. If it was Devore, as he suspected, Devore would know him. *But* if it was someone else entirely, or if Devore didn't board the ship, he stood a chance of escaping detection. Not that it mattered as much for him as it did for Bryn. Bryn's disguise took away leverage that could be used against him. It ensured her safety. His disguise simply enhanced the element of surprise.

Kitt rummaged through O'Reilly's things in the crew quarters, looking for a knit cap. His own soaked and worn culottes would certainly pass muster as crew attire, but he'd been bareheaded and a cap would go far in hiding his hair. Any distraction would help. He had no illusion that pretending not to be himself would resolve this ambush favourably. But it would be a start. There was still the issue of keeping his ship and crew intact and being able to sail away when this was over. For that, he'd need a knife, a nice long sharp one.

Back up on deck, he gave Passemore a wink and instructions to wave the white flag. 'We want to be able to sail away when this is done.' He'd not lied to Bryn. He wasn't worried about being sunk. But he did worry another volley might render the *Queen* too incapacitated to sail away in a timely manner and it would be better to get this ruse under way sooner than later.

His men assembled, waiting in an orderly but dangerous line, for the longboat of invaders to reach them. They knew without being told this was no textbook surrender. They were to be vigilant and wait for their moment. He almost missed Bryn entirely, his eyes picking her out at the last moment. His optimism rose. This just might work.

A beefy Jamaican was the first on board, a mean, wicked-looking man. The captain no doubt. Kitt narrowed his eyes, keeping his attention on the man who would be his opponent. The Jamaican walked down the line, his voice deep and barking, carrying over the wind. 'Where is Captain Sherard?'

Come on, come a little closer. Kitt's hand closed around the handle of his hidden knife. He wanted to be the one to answer that question, but only when the brute was close enough to seize. Kitt didn't want the gambit working the other way. He didn't want one of his men pulled out of line and forced at knifepoint to reveal his identity. He wanted to do all the revealing, all the knife work. Nobody took what was his. This audacious bastard needed a lesson in that.

When no one answered, the captain stopped by Bryn five men down the line from him. Kitt swallowed. *Move away from her.* He wondered if he could reach her in time. There would be a mêlée. The captain had not come alone. Kitt counted twenty men in the longboat with him and another twenty were probably on the way. He wasn't looking for a fight. He was looking for leverage.

'Will no one tell me?' the captain yelled again, starting to move forward once more. 'Shall I select one of you to tell me?' He halted by Passemore standing beside Kitt. The captain turned to call back down the line. 'I shall start slitting throats, beginning with this one.' That was his fatal mistake.

Kitt knew he wouldn't get a better chance. He grabbed the man from behind, knife at the man's neck. Anger and rage pulsed through him as Kitt hauled the brute to the rail, his men leaping into instant action, weapons drawn from secret locations on their persons to minimise any heroics on the part of the Jamaican's crew.

'One move and he dies!' Kitt bellowed, making sure the other ship could see him. He was betting whoever was left over there wasn't fool enough to fire on the *Queen* with so many of their own men on board. He was relieved to see the oncoming longboat turn back. There'd be no reinforcements. Cowards and mercenaries, then. Kitt thought. Not a crew like his who had been together, who could rely on one another. He raised a bead of blood to make sure the other ship knew he meant business. He could not afford to bluff, not with Bryn, his crew and his ship depending on him. Truth was, this captain was dead regardless. To let him go gave him a second chance to blow them out of the water.

'You surrendered!' the captain ground out, starting to sweat. He'd probably just come to the same realisation. 'You are not respecting the rules of the game!' It was a desperate plea, one captain to another.

'*I* ran up a quarantine flag and *you* did not respect

that,' Kitt growled, pressing his knife tip. 'The rules had been broken long before now.' Whatever he did, he'd have to do it soon. It was a dangerous guessing game now. If his men released the crew and allowed them to return to their ship, would they fire on the *Queen*, sacrificing their captain, or would the captain's presence be enough to prevent it? Maybe it didn't matter if the captain lived or died. It was hard to know in what capacity the captain was most valuable.

'Passemore!' Kitt made his decision. 'Round up the men who don't wish to be shot. Take them below to the hold as our prisoners! They will be dealt with in Bridgetown.' Short twenty men, the ship would be hard pressed to follow them at full speed. 'Except that one.' Kitt pointed to a smaller, younger fellow. 'Have him take a message back. If they aren't under way in ten minutes, I will execute the captain.' He hoped it wouldn't come to that. He hoped whoever was on board would understand they were beaten for the day and retreat.

It was the most important question of the day. One look at the captain's face told him the man didn't know the answer any more than he did.

He had eight minutes left to answer and the first mate—the captain's brother as it turned out—was staring him down. Devore cursed and kicked the table leg with his good foot. Damn and double damn. Sherard had him in a bind. Did he risk firing on the *Queen* and sacrificing a third of the crew for the sake of a second try? Even then, at such close range, the *Queen* would be able to fire again. The damage Sherard had already done to the boat was going to cost him. Would the remaining crew follow his orders? He wasn't the one in charge, just the one paying the bills. If he did let Sherard have his captain, where would he find another one? Captains without scruples were expensive. He'd have to start all over and that would definitely put him behind.

On the other hand, Sherard's ship was limping, too. This might be his only chance to take Sherard. It was frustrating to have the man at such close range only to let him slip away. The captain was only one man. If he let Sherard make it back to Bridgetown, the stakes rose substantially. This went from being a personal vendetta to taking on the crown's banking and legal system. He'd be wanted for fraud.

'What will it be, mon?' The first mate glared, fingering a wicked blade with feigned idleness. 'A short life or a longer one? If they do my brother over there, I will do you a minute later.'

Devore unconsciously fingered his throat. That made the decision a bit easier. 'We'll pull away, of course.' He smiled. 'A fine captain like your brother would be too hard to replace. Tell the crew to make ready to depart.'

The first mate gave a cold smile. 'A very good decision, mon.'

Maybe not a good decision, but the only decision. Devore helped himself to a hefty serving of the captain's rum. After all, fraud was fairly difficult to prosecute and they'd have to catch him first. Sherard would understand today hadn't been a victory, it had been a draw. Sherard would have to live with the knowledge that he was still out there, still coming for him and that kind of knowledge made it hard for a man to sleep at night. Oh, no, this was definitely not a victory for Kitt Sherard, but perhaps it was a tiny victory for *him*.

* * *

Kitt's crew gave a victory cry as the dark ship moved off into the rain. The movement was slow—the *Queen*'s cannons had done some damage, giving as good as it had got. They were safe now. They could look to mending their own hurts. It would be wet, messy business in the rain. The weather was not pleasant, but thankfully it hadn't worsened. By morning, the sun would be out, but Kitt didn't want to wait until then to get under way with twenty prisoners and the enemy's captain on board. Any sign of weakness could be an incentive for them to attempt a mutiny.

He put Passemore in charge of repairs and gestured for O'Reilly to join him. It was time to get some answers. He allowed himself to seek out Bryn with his eyes. She'd dedicated herself to cleaning up the deck. Her face was white, but stoic, as she worked. He wished she was in the cabin, getting warm and dry, but he understood why she wasn't: too much adrenaline. He could no more expect her to sit than he could expect it of anyone else right now. Men needed to work after a battle, needed to have purpose. He wanted to go to her, but there was no time and this was not the place. He had to be the captain first and there was still a job that needed doing, further testament Bryn could not be part of his life.

He drew a breath for fortitude. 'Come on, O'Reilly, let's go see our guests.' But O'Reilly had seen the direction of his thoughts. The big man clapped a hand on his shoulder.

'Your woman did well today.' O'Reilly's face split into a grin. 'I doubt many women could have pulled it off. She didn't flinch when the captain stopped right in front of her. Of course, I was next to her and I wouldn't have let the captain touch a hair on her head.'

'Thankfully it didn't come to that.' Kitt smiled politely. O'Reilly meant well, but that was the problem. Bryn made men feel chivalrous. Men would fight for her, die for her whether she wanted them to or not.

He could not have that, not for himself or his crew. Today had gone right by luck. There was only so much he could control. He couldn't control where the captain stopped along the line. He couldn't control who the captain picked as a first victim. If O'Reilly had been forced to protect Bryn, there would have been blood spilt and quite a lot of it. Bryn stripped away all objectivity from a situation. He couldn't have it, he simply couldn't have it.

Down in the hold, Kitt gave O'Reilly his instructions. 'I want to know who was behind this ambush today. Remember, you're the ship's doctor. You're supposed to patch people up, not rip them open,' he cautioned O'Reilly when the big man cracked his knuckles with a bit more glee than Kitt would recommend from a physician. 'We're going to play nice.'

'Of course, Captain,' O'Reilly said respectfully. 'And if that fails, we have plan B.'

Her plan had worked brilliantly—so brilliantly, in fact, that she'd never been so scared in her entire life! Bryn slipped out of the oilskin slicker, having finally allowed herself to seek the sanctuary of Kitt's cabin. She was cold, something she'd thought she'd never be in the Caribbean with its sticky, underwear-forgoing heat. Her teeth were even chattering.

Bryn carefully peeled the wet clothes from her skin.

She'd borrowed some of Kitt's since Passemore's had obviously done little to hide her more feminine assets. Kitt's clothes had been far larger, though, and she'd had to make liberal use of rope to tie up his pants. Now, all that extra cloth was haunting her. Her cold fingers fumbled on the extra fabric, her tired legs threatened to tangle in the legs of his culottes. At least, the effort kept her mind from wandering down less pleasant paths.

Finally, she was free of the wet clothes. She wrapped a blanket about her, letting warmth start to creep into her skin, but thoughts began to creep in, too, images of the day and with them came the horrible 'what ifs' she'd not dared to dwell on as the events had unfolded for fear they would steal her courage. But now, there was nothing left to restrain them, nothing left to keep them at bay and they came, in floods and in torrents.

Always Kitt was at the centre of those images. The desire to see him, to assure herself he was safe, or maybe it had been the desire to assure herself *she* was safe, had driven her on deck. Her eyes had known where to look for him. He'd been everywhere, shouting orders, lending a hand where it was needed and he'd saved her from her own careless foolishness when the cannon ball had whined overhead. He'd been vibrant and alive in those moments. But that man had also been a stranger.

She did not know the grim captain who had argued with her to seek the safety of the cabin. He was so different than the laughing, cocksure Kitt she knew, to whom everything was a game, even life itself. That had not been the case today. Today had been serious business.

She understood why. This ambush had not been a game to the captain who'd boarded them. When he'd stopped in front of her, it had taken every ounce of her bravery to see those moments through. He could hardly have stood there more than a few seconds, but it had seemed an eternity. The only thought she'd been capable of thinking in the interim was that he'd not been bluffing. He would have killed to get his answers. He was a brute. But when Kitt had drawn his knife, she'd known Kitt would have, too. She'd hardly recognised the ferocious man who'd leapt into action five men down from her.

There were people who claimed they'd kill for something, but those were just words. Worse, in her own bloodlust, in her own desire for safety, she'd wanted him to do it. She'd wanted him to kill the man and put an end to her fear. Kitt had proven better than that, though. He'd seen the long-term advantages to keeping the captain alive. He was below deck even now, interrogating the captain for information. What did that make *him*? Was Kitt a brute just with better looks? No, that was unfair and she knew better. She'd made quite a discovery today. Deep down, hidden away beneath the armour of his carefree nonchalance, Kitt was loyal to the bone.

Today, Kitt had protected his crew, his ship and her by any means possible. He'd not hesitated to draw blood to see it done. All of which pointed to the reality that this, or things like this, had happened before. She'd not missed the fact that his crew had taken each progression of the battle in stride. They'd fired cannons with efficiency, they'd been prepared to flawlessly enact the mock surrender without giving away their captain's identity. Flawlessness required practice. Proof enough, these things not only happened, but they happened with *frequent regularity*. Today, she'd had a glimpse into the real life of Kitt Sherard. This is what he spent his days doing, this was how he'd built his fortune.

It was, admittedly, quite a lot for a girl to take in. Although, why she should find it shocking escaped her. *You knew. You've known from the start. Good men don't climb balconies. Good men don't roam beaches in bed-sheets. Good men don't make love as if they won't see tomorrow.* She *had* known. She really had. But as the saying went, seeing was believing.

The door to the cabin flew open, helped by the wind. Kitt stepped inside, all dripping, soaking, six feet of him. Every inch of him a man against all, a man who had won. Bryn's pulse raced, her eyes unable to look away from the sheer attractiveness of raw, potent male on display, a man fresh come from battle.

'Bryn!' The hoarse word ripped from Kitt's throat as he crossed the room.

She rose, dropping the blanket, meeting him halfway. She was seeing, and heaven help her, she was believing.

Chapter Twenty

Heaven help him, he could not be gentle. Kitt pulled her to him in a rough embrace, his mouth ravaging hers in his need, his wet, soaking body pressed to her naked one, selfishly drinking in her heat, her life. How he'd wanted to do this for hours! How he'd wanted to wrap his body around hers, wanted to immerse himself deep inside her, to assure himself she was safe.

Bryn's hands were frantic on him, tugging at his wet clothes until they had him out of them, his body as naked as hers. 'Are you cold?' She was managing a one-sided, breathless conversation between kisses. 'Come to bed, I can warm you better there.'

Kitt bore her backwards to the blankets. 'I thought you'd never ask.' He followed her down with a laugh, feeling alive, feeling the fear that had gripped him the last hours effectively banished. Her legs were open to him, welcoming him into their cradle. His erection, already full, surged pikestaff-hard at first contact with her soft flesh. This would not take long. Three thrusts, maybe four and he'd be spent. There was no finesse as he entered her hard and fast, primal thrust after primal thrust as he buried himself inside her.

He found her ready for it. Her legs wrapped about his hips, taking him deep, her core wet and slick, ready to accommodate his rough entry, even revel in it. Beneath him, her body arched, bucking in the hasty pleasure of their coupling, her climax as feverish, as intense as his when it came. This was not about first times or last times, lucky guesses or second chances, this was about drinking the ambrosia of life.

He lay embedded inside her long afterwards, reluctant to leave the shelter of her feminine harbour. They were entwined completely, intimately. When at last he moved, it was to roll on his side and take her against him, her buttocks curled against the curve of his groin. Consummation and comfort; he craved them both. He'd had his consummation, wild and ferocious, but he still sought the comfort of holding her close, the assurance that she was there, whole and safe. 'Bryn, I nearly lost you today. I'm so sorry.' It was easier to talk without seeing her face. She was warm against him. It felt good, it felt right. *Moments of happiness are not sustainable*, he reminded himself.

'Nothing happened. I'm perfectly fine, not a scratch to show.'

But the distance between 'not a scratch to show' and being blown to smithereens, or having her throat slit, was a matter of mere inches, the matter of luck changing in a heartbeat. If he'd tackled her a second later, if the Jamaican captain had singled her out instead of Passemore, if the captain had not turned his back, if a hundred other variables had gone awry, the day could have ended very differently. Only a fool would pretend otherwise.

He said as much out loud, but Bryn merely turned in his arms, to see him face-to-face, her body pressed to his. 'I'm no fool, Kitt. I know just how close it was today.'

The quiet intensity of her voice was nearly his undoing. He enfolded her in his arms. What had he been thinking to let her come? He should have sailed straight back to Bridgetown the moment she'd tumbled out of his wardrobe. But he knew what he'd been thinking. He'd wanted her too much and he'd known he could have her, at least for a little while. He'd been selfish and in his selfishness he'd risked her.

He should tell her, say the words, but he found the only words that would come was a litany of 'I'm sorrys'. He was sorry for things he couldn't begin to tell her. He was sorry for exposing her to danger, for exposing her to his life, sorry that he couldn't change it. Most of all he was sorry that the world of Kitt Sherard had no place in it for a woman like Bryn Rutherford, a decision that was made long before he met her.

Bryn pushed back a bit to take his face between her hands. 'You saved us all today. There's nothing to be sorry for.' Then she slipped beneath the warm cocoon of their blankets and burrowed to the bottom, her hands announcing their presence on his calves. Her lips followed them up, past his knees, to his thighs, until there was only one place left for them to go. Kitt's breath caught in anticipation of what she meant to do.

Her hand came first, running the length of him, preparing him, until he felt himself come exquisitely to life beneath her fingers. Then came her mouth, her sweet delectable mouth. Her tongue stroked his tender head with quick, teasing flicks across his slit. Kitt could feel himself bead for her. He closed his eyes, letting the pleasure sweep him away, letting it drown out the impossible wanting, the guilt of his selfishness. He could have this moment, this gift. She ran her tongue the length of his under-ridge and he moaned; she mouthed him, sucking hard until he sobbed with the ecstasy of it, rocked with the ecstasy of it until the blankets had fallen away, revealing Bryn in all her beauty between his legs, each stroke sending him closer to the edge of his release.

Kitt arched, barely able to articulate a strangled caution to Bryn, but she was ready. She caught him in her hand, holding him as he spent, his phallus pulsing, throbbing with its climax. The moment was as intimate as they came. He'd never been held through it, never seen a woman watch him come with awe riveting her face. He wanted to remember her this way for all time. How had she known this was exactly what he needed? She'd given him acceptance to simply be himself.

She would try and change him. Bryn wondered— would he understand that's why she'd done it? Beside her, Kitt's breathing was slow and even. 'Happy?' She ventured the brave word in the dark. She snuggled against him, her head finding his chest as surely as his arm wrapped about her, drawing her close.

'Content.' Kitt sighed as if to emphasise his point.

'I'm…content, too,' Bryn echoed. She would rather be happy, but content was a more realistic word. Content implied she was satisfied with what she had, while understanding it was all she *could* have even if she wanted more. Kitt pressed a kiss in her hair. It made her bold or perhaps the tender gesture made her desperate. 'What happens when we get back to Bridgetown?'

Difficult words, but they had to be spoken. They'd pretended they both knew what would happen, they'd even pretended they were satisfied with that. Well, at least she had and she suspected he'd pretended to be satisfied, too. The man who'd made love to her tonight would never truly be satisfied with such an understanding any more than she. How much longer would they go on denying the truth? If they didn't address it now, it would be too late.

'You know what happens, Bryn. This is over. It has to be.'

'Is that what you want?' Bryn asked softly, trying to ignore the slow pain growing in her heart.

'It's what has to be. Today should have shown you how impossible it is for it to be otherwise. We were lucky. We won't always be lucky. And, yes, these sorts of situations will happen again and again just like the day I met you.'

'The assassins chasing you into the garden?' She forced a laugh, trying to find a way to argue against his decision. Surely he wasn't climbing balconies *every* day.

'Even before that.' Kitt sighed in the darkness. 'That day, we had a rum drop-off to complete. It was supposed to be simple, but it was a trap designed to ambush us. The man who warned me about the assassins died in my arms. Now it seems we have another layer. The captain in my hold was kind enough to inform me that Hugh Devore is the mastermind behind the Sunwood swindle. Apparently, while he's not out ambushing my rum sales, he's coaxing wealthy gentlemen into investing in a plantation that doesn't exist.'

An ambush over a typical trade, a dead man's warning, being chased by assassins and climbing a stranger's balcony. All in a day's work, quite possibly all in *every* day's work. She would never know what he would be facing when he went out. What was worse? Knowing or guessing? Today's reality had been fairly frightening. 'You're trying to scare me off,' Bryn said quietly.

'Is it working?'

'It's not that I don't understand, Kitt, it's that I want to try anyway.' She was out on the very furthest limb of her tree of confidence now. It was a thin one, it might snap at any time and send her plummeting. *Don't betray me, Kitt. It took everything to say those words.* She was not a weak woman, but she felt vulnerable just now.

'You do me a great honour, Bryn.' His answer was neither refusal nor acceptance, but something in between and it would have to be good enough.

The rain had stopped in the night, leaving behind a brisk breeze that blew them steadily and quickly towards Bridgetown. At the rail, her hat once more firmly on her head, Bryn watched the port loom ever closer in the afternoon sun with growing trepidation. Had anyone missed her? She'd told the servants she was going to stay with a new friend. It hadn't been a lie, only she'd been gone longer than she'd planned. The servants would know she'd packed to be gone a day or two. Instead, she'd been gone five, nearly six. Was that all? It felt as if a lifetime had passed. Still, all should be fine. Her father was not scheduled to be back until tomorrow.

'We'll drop anchor here.' Kitt materialised at her elbow, breaking into her thoughts. 'I'll row you in, unless you'd prefer Passemore or O'Reilly?' He was letting her decide where it ended. They'd not talked of 'it' since the prior night. She'd spent her bravery the night before. If he was going to leave it up to her, she'd hang on to him as long as she could.

'I'd prefer you if you have the time.'

'Are you nervous?' Kitt leaned beside her on the rail, his blue eyes on hers, the gesture feeling personal and sincere. How many times had they met on this spot on the rail since leaving port? She would miss this. He'd become friend and lover combined into one. It would be difficult to go back to being less.

'I'm thinking how disappointed my father will be to hear about the island.' He would be disappointed. It was a severe blow, but it was also a lie. She hadn't solely been thinking of her father's reaction although she probably should be. Back to Bridgetown meant back to business, back to being the banker's daughter. Her father needed her.

Kitt did more than row her in. He carried her valise and he walked her the distance from the docks to the house at the end of Bay Street. But he said nothing, their walk accomplished in abject silence. Bryn reasoned it was better for him to be silent than to say things he didn't mean or make half-promises he had no intention of keeping. It would hurt more if he lied to her. In truth, it was hard to imagine it hurting more than it did. She was hurting pretty badly right now, as if something was being ripped from her.

She'd thought she'd be safe this time. Kitt wouldn't betray her and he hadn't. He hadn't used her, hadn't seen her as a means for personal gain, he hadn't needed anything from her. He'd given her gifts beyond compare, experiences that exceeded her dreams. Because of all that, it wasn't supposed to hurt, there wasn't a reason for it to. *Since when did love need a reason? Admit it, you fell for him. All the promises you made yourself about adventure and happy ever afters being momentary could not protect you.*

They reached the gate separating the house grounds from the street. He swung it open for her and handed her the valise. 'I'll call on your father in a couple of days when he returns and talk with him about the island. I'll see what we can salvage. But then I'll go back out again. It's important we find Devore.'

Devore—oh, yes, the grand villain in all this. Bryn dragged her mind back to practical matters. For a moment she'd forgotten about that island, the missing one, the one they'd set out to find. Instead, her heart had leaped, thinking it saw a flicker of hope. She'd been thinking about a different island, about salvaging something else, an entirely different reason to talk to her father.

Kitt began to speak, but the front door suddenly opened with some force. Bryn froze, her mind going blank except for one thought: her father was home, James Selby with him. She'd known there was going to be hell to pay, but she'd hoped for a little time, a reprieve in which to marshal her resources, to think through her explanations. Apparently the devil was keen to collect his due.

Chapter Twenty-One

'Thank goodness you're all right!' Her father hugged her tight. His warm welcome was more than she deserved. 'When you didn't come home as expected, Sneed sent for me. We had no idea where you'd gone.'

'I'm fine.' Bryn pasted on a smile, guilt surging at the worry she'd caused. He'd cut short his business trip because of her. He had every justification to be furious. He could have shouted at her, could have berated her, could do far worse than that and yet he'd hugged her, his concern for her safety overriding all the other implications of her absence.

Her father's grip on her loosened and she could feel his attention shifting over her shoulder to Kitt. 'Thank you for seeing her home, for watching over her. Please, come join us on the veranda for a glass of falernum.'

It was masterfully done. Her father had set in motion the script by which he wanted her homecoming recorded for the public, for the servants, for James Selby. He was saving face for her, standing between her and disaster. He was saving face for Kitt, too, treating him as a trusted business acquaintance for all to see.

Beside her father, Bryn could see Selby visibly stiffen,

his eyes narrowing as they fixed on Kitt. Selby didn't believe the fiction, but he'd go along with it to curry favour with her father. There was nothing he could take issue with at the moment. 'Bryn darling, why don't you rest, have a bath brought up if you'd like.' Her father attempted to gently dismiss her. After all he'd done, she didn't want to defy his authority, but she would not leave the aftermath of this homecoming to a protective father, a jealous suitor, and a man who'd faced down pirates in a storm, not when that aftermath was about her.

She looped an arm through her father's. 'I will last a little longer.' She shot a look at Kitt. 'We have news that you both need to hear and I'd like to be there for it.'

Selby bristled and she realised too late the connotation he'd put on her words. Bryn rushed on hastily. 'It's about the Sunwood investment.' She wasn't about to blurt out the island didn't exist on the front lawn.

Hearing it over falernum wasn't much better, but at least it was private and it certainly served to distract everyone from the unanswered question of what she'd been doing with Kitt for five unchaperoned days. Of course, she'd rather have had a more pleasant distraction for them. Selby turned a startling shade of white and her father went very still as Kitt laid out the findings.

'I sailed out to the co-ordinates Selby gave Bryn.' Kitt gave Selby a sharp look. If Selby had lied, now would be the time to come clean. For her father's sake, Bryn almost hoped that would be the case, although it would certainly damage Selby's reputation. But Selby said nothing. 'I even thought I may have written them down in reverse,' Kitt added charitably, more face saving, this time for Selby. It was generous of him given that he owed Selby nothing and Selby was looking daggers at him.

'I sailed out to the other set of co-ordinates as well although they seemed too far out to be believable. But I wasn't ready to give up. The map did show a set of islands in that direction and there were islands there, just not developed islands.' Kitt paused and looked directly at her father. 'I thought you'd want to know right away.' He would not apologise for being the bearer of bad news. 'I am sure you understand this could mean trouble for the bank if it got out you and Selby had been taken advantage of.'

Her father nodded slowly, his shoulders, which had borne so much, starting to slump. Bryn's heart broke for him. They'd been so close to the fresh start he'd coveted, the bank nearly operational, the charter fulfilled, only to have it all poised on the brink of ruin.

'No one has to know,' Selby said quickly. 'We'll simply stop investing and that will be the end of it.' That was how Selby's rather facile mind worked. Everything was black and white, but Bryn saw the grey space. They couldn't simply walk away from this.

'We know who is behind this. I have the name,' Kitt said tersely, trying to avoid direct disagreement with Selby. 'We have to go after him. We are ethically obliged.'

Selby glared. 'You dare much to speak of ethical obligations after spending five days alone with a woman of good reputation.'

Bryn winced and took a hasty sip of falernum. Her father shot her a look. 'Were you with him? Is that where you went?'

'Yes.' She would not lie. She fixed Selby with a hard

stare, daring him to defy her. 'You do yourself little credit by painting with a sordid brush.' That was the difference between them. Selby was interested in self-protection, but she was interested in protecting others. She would not make Kitt pay for her bold plan.

She turned back to her father. 'Captain Sherard did not invite me. When I learned he was going out to see the island, I hid aboard the ship. I did not make my presence known until he was at sea and could not turn back.' The explanation seemed to placate him, but her father was an astute man. There would be more questions in private.

'I was glad I risked it,' Bryn continued staunchly, avoiding Kitt's eyes. 'Now you have two witnesses to the fact that the island doesn't exist, just in case there is any challenge to Captain Sherard's word.'

'I would not expose your presence needlessly,' Selby put in hastily. 'Sherard's word is enough for me.' He was quick to grovel after his misstep.

'As it should be,' her father spoke sharply. 'As the primary investors for the bank, we all rise and fall together. Dissension in our ranks cannot be tolerated. Anyone who cannot accept that is welcome to leave our association.'

'I couldn't agree more,' Selby affirmed. Bryn saw the faintest signs of a smile twitch on Kitt's lips. This was the victory she'd angled for with the announcement she'd share with all and sundry she'd been aboard the ship. She'd forced Selby to have to publicly acknowledge Kitt's word and accept his verdict. It was a secondary triumph to have removed herself from needing to make that testimony.

'So do we go after the villains?' Kitt circled the conversation back around to the point at which Selby had derailed it. 'I can have my ship ready and at your disposal the day after tomorrow.' He could have an official mandate for this next voyage.

'I think we must. I will assemble the board of directors tomorrow and explain the situation to them.' Her father blew out a breath, a man dreading but prepared to take responsibility for his errors. Her father had never shied away from his duty. He would not shirk it now.

Kitt leaned forward and spoke in earnest. 'Definitely assemble them, but do not play the martyr. Tell them you and Selby had made the investment as a trial in the hopes that if it was successful the bank could choose to be involved later. Tell them we've since learned it's a land swindle and we are setting out to bring the criminals to justice.'

Her father's face began to brighten. 'Yes, that could do the trick. There are no lies there. Your own involvement proves that. James and I truly *had* hoped to bring Sunwood to the investors' attention. We will look proactive in our response and in the immediacy of it. Thanks to you, Captain, we learned of the fraud right away before more than initial money was sunk into it.'

Bryn felt some of the knots in her stomach loosen. Kitt had managed the situation in a way that would not only save face for her father, but for the bank. Her father would look like a hero. The venture would be saved. She wanted to throw her arms about Kitt, wanted to thank him, but there was no chance. The men stood up and shook hands. Kitt barely looked at her, giving her the briefest, remotest of polite farewells. He might as well have been taking his leave of any hostess.

Selby gave every impression, however, of wanting to linger. Her father diplomatically disabused him of the notion with a firm hand on his shoulder. 'James, I am counting on you to call the meeting. Invite everyone for eleven o'clock tomorrow.' It was his *congé*. James smiled politely, his shoulders squaring with the importance of the task.

Her father had one last parting thought for him. 'James, a man is defined by the choices he makes in his hour of crisis.' In other words, James's future on the board would be contingent on his ability to embrace the phrase 'discretion is the better part of valour'. Nothing that occurred in this house was to be bandied about with anyone, not his magpie of a mother, nor with the other investors.

Her father's brave façade faded the second James Selby passed through the gate. He turned to her with worried eyes, looking every day of his fifty-five years and then some. She could do without reminders of his mortality. 'Why did you do it?' he asked quietly, sinking down into a chair in the little-used front parlour.

'Captain Sherard had indicated after the toast at dinner he was concerned about the nature of the investment. That made me worry, too, and I couldn't just sit back and wait.' But it had been more than that. The words tumbled out. 'You were leaving, going off with your new friends and partners on a trip you hadn't told me about, you were investing in plantations without a word of it to me.'

She twisted her hands in her skirts. 'You didn't need me any more and here was an opportunity to show you I was still useful.' She didn't feel twenty-three at the moment. She felt about eight, very small, very vulnerable. She'd felt vulnerable with Kitt, too, that last night. She didn't particularly like it. Exposing one's feelings was nasty, uncomfortable, risky work. No wonder Kitt was so reluctant to do it.

Her father's features softened, his eyes misty. 'You don't need to be useful to me, Bryn. You're my daughter, you're my whole world.' He waved a hand to indicate the house about them. 'We're here for you as much for me, after all.'

Complete acceptance of who she was flaws and all, the kind of acceptance she'd offered Kitt. The similarities struck her hard. Had it been as difficult for Kitt to accept as this was? Her father put a hand on each of his knees and straightened. 'This would be easier if your mother were here. She would know what to do, what to say. I'm afraid these sorts of delicate conversations elude me, they always have.' She sensed he was gathering himself. 'Do I need to bring Sherard up to scratch?'

'No, we had an agreement,' Bryn answered evenly.

Her father raised his eyebrows. 'Might I enquire as to the nature of the agreement? I may be old, Bryn, but I know what happens between men and women in close quarters. Captain Sherard has a certain reputation and you are a beautiful woman, so full of life like your mother. Do not play me for a fool.'

'Sherard is not the marrying type. I will not have him forced into anything he does not want,' Bryn said with finality. She wanted Kitt, but not like that—not bought and paid for with her father's money and influence. There were a hundred men she could have had in London under those terms. Such an arrangement would trap them both. Neither of them were looking for that sort of marriage.

Her father tapped a finger on his leg in thought. 'Sherard might not be the marrying sort, but James Selby is and he's made no secret of his esteem for you.' She started to protest. They'd had this discussion before. Her answer hadn't changed. Her father held up a hand to stall the interruption. 'Selby is a good man, a steady man, Bryn. With my guidance, he will become more astute. He is young yet, unpolished. He is bound to make mistakes like the Sunwood project in his eagerness to prove himself. But I will make him my protégé. He can be taught. If you need a husband, he would do admirably.'

What he meant was if she was pregnant, if there were consequences for her five days with Kitt. She looked down at her hands, her face colouring. Her father was offering to buy her a husband, to set that man up for life with the Rutherford connections and the banking charter all to make her and her child respectable. It was a generous offer, a loving offer that spoke again of being completely accepted flaws and all. 'Selby wouldn't be so bad,' her father argued with soft persuasion. 'Sometimes the quiet ones are just what wild souls need. They can have a calming, balancing effect.'

'Like you and Mother.' She looked up and shook her head. 'But that was true love.'

Her father looked uncomfortable for a moment, a look that was gone as soon as it came. She might have imagined it. 'Perhaps it's time for a confession. It was always love for me, but I think true love came later for her.'

Bryn wanted to argue—she had cut her teeth on stories of her parents' fairytale romance—but something in her father's gaze stopped her.

'I had no chance. I was a younger son, I was retiring.

I liked my numbers, I liked calculating odds. I had little use of society in practice. She was such a bright flame, always the centre of everyone's attention. My cousin the marquis was much the same, handsome, wild. Everything came easy for him, even Esme. When things come easy, it is hard to appreciate them. He did not appreciate Esme as a gentleman should appreciate a lady.

'There was a compromising incident, there was scandal, my cousin blamed Esme and would not do the right thing. Scandal is always more bearable for a man, especially when he has a title. Not so for a beautiful untitled woman with little claim to society beyond her looks. The Rutherfords understood my cousin's hesitation to marry so far beneath himself, but my brother was earl by then and he was eager to see the family redeemed. Suddenly, as the only unwed male close at hand, my odds started to improve. I couldn't believe my luck. Then you were born and I knew I was the luckiest man alive.'

Bryn knew she'd been born early in their marriage. A new suspicion took her as she let the story settle. 'Am I yours?'

He grinned. 'Most definitely. You were born twelve months almost exactly after the wedding.'

'And the scandal? Was there any truth to it?'

He nodded. 'Yes. She had been…well, indiscreet with my cousin, but that's not the point. Everyone makes mistakes. We don't love them the less for it.'

'You never held the past against Mother,' she said, implying that Selby would. He was all that her father said, but he was also petulant. His remark this afternoon indicated as much. He would hold Kitt Sherard over her head whenever he needed leverage for the rest of their lives. No amount of money or prestige her father threw Selby's way would change that.

Her father rose, perhaps sensing they'd reached another impasse on the subject of James Selby. 'Think on it, just in case. I'll have Cook make your favourite for dinner tonight.'

Bryn didn't want to think on it, but it was inescapable. No matter how far down in the bubbles of her bath she slid, she could not escape her thoughts. The story her father had told her threw her world off balance. It forced her to call into questions assumptions she'd taken for certain truth, assumptions about love, about marriage.

Whenever the villagers had recounted her parents' courtship, they'd conveniently left off the events leading up to it, the cousin mentioned only as a secondary character in the tale who had surfaced as competition for the charming Esme's hand, but who had been out-wooed by the quiet hero. There'd been no mention of Esme's desperate circumstances, or of the callous marquis's rejection, only of her father sweeping Esme off her feet in a whirlwind courtship.

She saw also how much her own situation paralleled her mother's. She, too, was wild. Her mother had feared her daughter would follow in her footsteps, throwing herself away on the squire's son who might also be too wild to care about the consequences. No wonder her mother had wanted her with someone stable, someone well situated like her father.

Bryn ran a cloth over her arms, washing them free of bubbles. It was no wonder her father favoured Selby. He saw himself in Selby. Perhaps she should, too. Her father was far wiser and far worldlier than she'd given him credit for. And, apparently, she was far less. True love didn't exist. Practicalities did. Perhaps the James Selbys of the world were the best a girl could hope for. Even her parents' marriage hadn't embodied the ideal, no matter what the local legend purported.

Perfection didn't exist because it *couldn't*. It wasn't a happy prospect. It was, however, a sobering one that required more answers than she had and those were answers that included the past, whether Kitt was willing to dredge it up or not.

This wasn't only about romance and love. In a larger sense it was about truth, something Kitt had been skating around. She had, too. She'd convinced herself it didn't matter in her new paradigm of living for the present, of living for herself. But it did.

If she was to go forward with Kitt, if she was to force him to admit he cared about her, that he didn't want this to end, there had to be truth. There had to be explanations about his past, which did exist whether he wanted it to or not. Everyone had one, even the man from nowhere. That his past involved an encounter of some sort with a land swindle seemed to make it even more pertinent considering their circumstances. These were answers she had to have no matter how painful they might be. Nothing more could happen without them.

Chapter Twenty-Two

'*I have a warrant for the arrest of Chase Melford on grounds of fraud.*' Kitt was dreaming of the past, of promises. They were all gathered in his father's office: himself, his mother, his father, his brother, older by two minutes and the heir. '*He is named as an active collaborator in the Forsythe scandal.*' His brother's face, Chase's face, was ashen as he listened. His brother probably was guilty and probably had been oblivious to what he had done. Finances weren't his brother's strong suit. He had other talents. Chase wasn't reckless, but he didn't often think about the long-term implications of his actions. He was heir to an earldom, he didn't have to.

Then had come the charges. If found guilty, he would face imprisonment. A title, his father's connections, wouldn't protect him now. Too many of the nobility had fallen in this scandal. In their desire for vengeance they would not protect one of their own if that one was guilty or if that one would provide a convenient scapegoat. It was said the Earl of Audley's heir had suffered a nervous breakdown over his investment in the non-existent island somewhere out in the Caribbean. Kitt had been friends with Audley's other son, Ashe Bedevere.

Kitt had thought his brother would faint at the mention of imprisonment. His brother would not survive this. The family would not survive this. But he would. He could save them and he could save himself, give himself the freedom he'd been craving. This was his chance, *their* chance.

Kitt crossed his legs and drawled indolently, 'You've got the wrong man. It's not him. It's me. He's entirely unaware. One might say I wooed in his name, to quote a little Shakespeare.'

His mother moved to protest, but a sharp look from his father silenced her. 'We are identical twins.' He explained the obvious to the inspector. 'It was no hard thing. I'm the one who convinced our friends to invest.' He quelled Chase's argument with a look only a twin would understand, a silent message: *let me save you. I love you. The family needs you to survive this intact.* Chase's eyes had met his: *Are you sure? I will trust you. I love you, too.*

The inspector had been hampered then by legalities. The warrant had the wrong name on it and could not be enforced. He'd left with a threat to return. 'I'll be back.'

I'll be gone, Kitt thought with a quiet calm—the magnitude of what he'd done hadn't fully settled, but the need for action had. His mind was already working. How much time did he have before the inspector was back? An hour?

The moment the door shut behind the man, Kitt was up the stairs, calling for a valise and all the money he could find in the house. He fired off instructions. Trunks could be sent to Ren later and Ren would get them to him. Chase was beside him, arguing all the way between orders. But not his practical father, who remained below, staring up at him from the bottom of the staircase with admiration and sadness before he moved to comfort his wife. His father understood it was the only way to save the family.

The transformation in his status amazed even him and he'd been the one to put it in motion. Only the night before, he'd been the darling of the ballroom, charming maids and matrons, his biggest concern in life being how to avoid his mother's matrimonial shenanigans. Less than twenty-four hours later, he'd become *persona non grata*, running for his life. 'My son, you can never come back—do you know what you've done?' his father had said, embracing him one last time.

He knew precisely what he'd done and he knew why he'd done it: to take all the stain upon himself, to save the family. Within an hour, he'd left it all behind, even his own name. Michael Melford could be traced. Kitt Sherard—a man from nowhere—couldn't be. So he'd become Kitt Sherard—Christopher from one of his middle names and the patron saint of travellers, Sherard for his mother's maiden name. He was a man with nothing but what he made for himself.

There was more to dream about, but the sun wouldn't let him. He had to wake and deal with what the day brought, starting with a meeting with the board of directors to sort this whole mess out. That wasn't the only sorting to be done. There was sorting to do with Bryn as well. Had things gone well for her after he'd left? Did she understand he'd meant it when he'd said 'no expectations'?

Kitt splashed water on his face and reached for a clean shirt. He'd not played fair there. He knew what she thought—that he wouldn't marry her because he refused to abide by society's dictates in that regard. The reality was quite different. He couldn't marry her because of the risk to her and to his family.

How could he tell her what he'd done? What if she knew the nightmares he dreamed? If he told her the truth, she might understand. But one more person knowing Kitt Sherard was nothing but a mask for another man put them all at risk. If England ever discovered him, he was dead. He could offer Bryn very little. They could never return to London. This was a secret that had to be kept for ever.

Kitt finished dressing and broke his fast downstairs with the other boarders. He spoke little, his mind on the upcoming interviews, on other fantasies. Would Bryn be surprised to know he would have her if he could? The realisation had stunned him the first time he'd thought it. But the more he took it out and examined it, the less shocking it became. He took it out now as he walked to the meeting.

He had fabricated domestic fantasies aplenty of a future with Bryn lending her touch to his home; Bryn wading in the surf, her skirts held above the waves, her hair flying loose about her shoulders as she laughed with him; Bryn in his bed, the big mahogany one at the villa with the down bedding. Bryn with his son, *their son*, on her hip. Ah, that was the most dangerous image of all. A child. One more person to protect. It was the most potent, too, the one with the power to lure him away from the lonely discipline he'd worked so hard to acquire.

* * *

He was not the first to arrive at Rutherford's. Harrison and Crenshaw were already there, and Selby. He shook hands and greeted everyone, his eyes distracted already as they searched the room for Bryn. He wondered if she would sit in. She had valuable information to contribute, to be an alibi for his story if nothing else. But perhaps it was best she didn't. There was no need to bring their association to anyone's attention, especially if Selby's reaction yesterday was anything to go on. Selby had immediately jumped to sordid conclusions.

Unfortunately, those conclusions were accurate, but irrelevant to the situation. They only served to muddy the waters. The first priority was to get permission to go after Devore. Technically, he didn't need permission. He'd go after Devore regardless. Permission would simply determine on what grounds. Did he have permission to make the land swindle part of his vendetta or would this remain a private affair between the two men?

The rest arrived and took their seats around Rutherford's long dining-room table. Bryn was not coming, but Rutherford left the doors open ostensibly to catch the breeze. Kitt hid a smile. Bryn was in the house and he'd wager his fortune she was listening somewhere.

Rutherford made an initial statement about the situation and turned to Kitt. 'Mr Sherard undertook a short voyage to the supposed destinations. I'll ask him to share what he found.'

Kitt nodded and began to speak. 'The Sunwood Plantation does not exist at these co-ordinates…' He unrolled a map and pinned it down with candlesticks. He pointed to different places, tracing his voyage. It seemed like he talked for ages. He shared what he had found, how he had found it and gone on to a second set of co-ordinates to be sure. There was outrage and questions. He fielded the questions patiently, explaining how the scheme was set up, how this was not the first time. It was easy enough to do out here in the uncharted ocean with thousands of islands.

When he finished, silence descended on the table. Selby had been uncharacteristically quiet, as well he might, since it was his rashness that had brought this upon them. Now, Selby leaned forward, locking eyes with him. 'How is it that you know so much about land swindles? You seem highly informed for a man of your background.'

Kitt braced himself on his arms and leaned across the table. 'What are you saying, James? Is there an accusation you wanted to make?'

'I don't know—should I be concerned about one? You have to admit your recommendations are not the best.'

Kitt raised an eyebrow at this. Those were fighting words. There was much he would tolerate for himself, but he would not hear a word against Ren. They had been friends since their school days, not that he could call on that allegiance now without giving too much away. To do so would indicate he had noble connections in England as opposed to the fiction he and Ren fabricated here—they were business partners. How else would the lofty Earl of Dartmoor know a rum runner? 'Careful, James. You question Dartmoor's reputation.'

Crenshaw broke in. 'Gentleman, an internal squabble is hardly beneficial to us at this point. We have more important concerns. Selby, I think there is no purpose in doubting Sherard's information in this instance.'

Kitt gave Crenshaw a curt nod of thanks and backed away from the table. 'You all have much to discuss and you know my opinion. Rutherford, I'll avail myself of the hospitality of your garden while you talk amongst yourselves.' He shot James a look. 'I don't want to unduly influence your decisions.'

Rutherford began to protest that he was on the board of directors, too. Kitt raised a hand to stall any further comment. 'I am and I have offered my opinion. My boat and my services are at your disposal. Perhaps you would discuss things more freely in my absence.' He wanted to go in search of Bryn and there was truly nothing more he could say. He would go after Devore no matter what their decision.

In the garden, the air was cooler, the heat of the afternoon had not yet settled. The smell of sweet hibiscus was on the breeze and it soothed his temper. He drew a deep breath, letting some of the tension go from his body. Selby deserved a thrashing for his comment. He stilled. Someone was in the garden with him, behind him. He could feel them.

'I want to know the answer to Selby's question.' Bryn's voice was quiet.

'You were eavesdropping. I thought you might be.' He could not look at her. If he did, he'd be lost. He held himself rigid, willing her not to move into his line of sight.

'Don't make this about me, Kitt. You told me you were involved in a land swindle. I did not press you then for an answer, but I am asking for one now.'

'Why should I tell you? If you're asking, you've already assumed the worst. Obviously you have doubt.'

'I have what you've allowed me to have.' There was

some steel, some heat in her voice. 'I think you want me to believe the worst. When I first met you, you led me to believe you were nothing more than a house-breaker, only for me to discover you a few hours later in the company of gentlemen.'

Kitt snorted. 'Your logic is ludicrous. Why would I want that?' But she was far too close to the truth.

'It's how you keep people at a distance, how you ensure you're alone.' Bryn didn't hesitate with her answer. She'd thought this out and that frightened him. What else had she thought out? What else had she realised despite his attempts to obfuscate it?

'I'm not in the habit of keeping beautiful women at a distance.'

'Only the ones that upset you. I disturb the balance of your universe,' Bryn argued.

'I suppose you upset a great many men then.' They were moving ever so slowly away from the intent of her conversation. Kitt was beginning to feel a little relief. Maybe he could distract her after all.

Then she ruined it. She pulled on his arm, forcing him to face her. 'Dammit, Kitt, tell me—did you swindle men out of their money or was it you who was swindled?'

She was furious. Her face was flushed, her eyes almost feverish in their intensity. He'd pushed her further than he'd realised. 'Tell me. Everything depends on it.'

Everything did. The board's belief in his information, his credibility, more than that, his future depended on it. If he told her, he could win her, he could outbid Selby. But she'd never be able to tell another. Could he trust her with that? Why did everything that happened between them in this garden come down to trust?

'I can't tell you because my life depends on it, Bryn,' he said simply. He felt tired, defeated, as if he'd fought this battle for too long.

Bryn sat down on the bench and motioned for him to sit beside her. He didn't. He didn't want to be that close to her. 'It's hard, isn't it? To trust another. You wanted me to trust you. It didn't seem so difficult when you were asking it because you knew I could trust you. But I didn't know. Now, the shoe is on the other foot. I know you can trust me, but you don't know, not for sure.' She reached for his hand, not willing to accept his resistance. 'I trusted you with my body and with my reputation. That is a woman's life. You can trust me with yours, Kitt.'

But he wasn't going to. Bryn felt defeat lurking. She was going to lose, not just this argument, but *him*. He wasn't going to tell her and she simply couldn't tolerate that. He knew it, too—this was a decision not only about sharing his secret, but a decision about them. It was his last defence in pushing her away. Then suddenly, he sat and he began to talk.

'My name hasn't always been Kitt. My brother was involved in the Forsythe scandal in England in thirty-one. Do you remember it? It was over a Caribbean island that was supposed to be colonised. Unwittingly, my brother invested and convinced several families to invest heavily as well. As a consequence, a lot of people lost a lot of money. Some lost their lives. Some had invested so deeply they committed suicide. One young man had a nervous breakdown. He never recovered. He's in an asylum today.'

She watched Kitt's profile, the firm line of his jaw working as he spoke. It took all her discipline not to prompt him. He would share in his own time. 'I could save my brother, but I couldn't save them. My brother and I are identical twins born two minutes apart. I took the blame and I fled. He and my family would be exonerated by my departure and by my assumption of the guilt. People will pity them, but people will hate me. I can never go back to England. Some of those people may even hate me enough to hunt me. I may not have to go back to England to seek death. It may find me. Do you understand? People believe I cost them their loved ones, their livelihoods.'

Bryn nodded. She understood other things, too—the depth of commitment to family it took for him to make that sacrifice. The hidden depths of nobility, real nobility, that had nothing to do with rank. His sacrifice made hers look minute in comparison. He was a bold man, a brave man, who had doomed himself to exile for the sake of his family. She was not foolish enough to argue platitudes with him, that perhaps there was another way or that maybe in time things would be different.

'Maybe I could have saved more of them if I had stayed.' Kitt's gaze was faraway. 'Perhaps I could have helped some of the families, maybe I could have done more if I'd stayed, but I couldn't bear to see my brother suffer, couldn't bear to see my family become outcasts. No matter how many people I helped, I wouldn't be able to save my family. In the end, I chose my family over others—the few instead of the many. And maybe I chose my own freedom over all of it without fully understanding the price.'

He turned to look at her. 'Now you know why I know so much about land swindles.' She knew a lot more than that.

'Thank you. Your secret is safe with me, always.' She squeezed his hand. He had told her much, but not everything. He was protecting her still. It had not escaped her attention that he'd omitted names, his real name particularly. But it was enough. He would tell her more when he was ready.

Kitt rose. 'I should go. I'll be leaving to go after Devore in a day or two no matter what they decide in there. Until then, it would be best if we kept our distance from one another, I think.'

If he came back. She heard the underlying message. Going after Devore was dangerous. She'd seen that danger first-hand. 'Do you have to go?' It was a stupid question, but it made Kitt smile.

'If Ren or Emma, or you, want to be safe, I have to go. Devore is a menace to us alive. He's a menace to your father and the bank as well.' He bent forward and placed a kiss on her cheek. 'I will see you again and we will talk when it is settled.' He swept the back of his hand along the line of her cheek. 'Don't look so glum, Bryn. You have victories enough to celebrate today.'

It was a significant victory to know he was not guilty. At the end of the day, he was a good man who cared for others no matter how he tried to muddy the waters to the contrary. Her conscience was free to love him and she would. For now, that would be her secret. She reached up for his hand where it lay against her cheek. 'Be safe.' She would tell him the rest *when* he came back.

Chapter Twenty-Three

It was safe to assume Sherard knew the island didn't exist and by now he must surely know they were behind the plantation swindle. Hugh Devore paced the floor of what passed as his office, nothing near as elegant as the one he'd had on Barbados. That was one more sin to lay at Kitt Sherard's feet: the lack of any luxury, any comfort. It had taken months to get this far. Just when they were making progress, Sherard had to interfere again.

It proved he was right. They should not have waited to go after Sherard. But Blakely had made a strong case of operating from a position of strength and Devore had agreed. At the time, it seemed sound. Now, Hugh Devore wondered otherwise. A position of strength also meant there was more to lose. They had the business to protect from exposure. The scales had tipped. No longer were they hunting Sherard, he was also hunting them. Their offence had been minimised.

'We have to act now and we have to act fast.' Devore spun on his heel to face Blakely and the first mate. Damn, but his forces were reduced. He had to act fast for other reasons, too. He'd lose the first mate once the man's brother was free. He had no illusions the pair would stay around after this last run in with Sherard. He'd temporary lose his ability to chase Sherard on water until he could find another captain.

'Beyond revenge, killing Sherard won't stop the swindle from leaking out,' Elias Blakely put in weakly. He was getting nervous and Devore worried about losing him, too. Blakely had no ethical qualms about swindling people on paper when it was just numbers in a ledger, but when lives were on the line, the man became positively squeamish.

Devore whirled on him with a hard stare, enjoying how it made the man squirm. 'Is revenge not enough? Have you forgotten what Sherard has done to us? Have you forgotten what you had? The luxury in which you used to live? Sherard took that from us, dropped us off on an island with only what we could carry. He made us no better than worms.'

'He let us live,' Blakely answered. 'We escaped a trial.'

'At a price!' Devore roared. 'It is no small thing.' This was not the time for Blakely to have cold feet. But he was right about one aspect: there were more people involved. Silencing Sherard would not prevent others from knowing. By now Sherard would have told Rutherford and Rutherford would have told Selby.

If he was lucky, it would stop there, the two investors being too embarrassed to confess it publicly to the bank board. If he was unlucky, the bank board would know, too. Devore felt a moment of stinging regret. If not for Sherard, if not for the failed sugar cartel and the debacle at Sugarland, he too might have been asked to sit on the board as one of Barbados's leading financiers.

Heaven knew he'd had the money to do so at one time. Sherard could pay for that, too.

Blakely piped up one more time, a sure sign of how nervous he truly was—nervous enough to stand up to him rather than face Sherard. 'We should take what we have and go. Barbados is dead to us, we can never go back there. In fact, the whole Caribbean is dead to us. Sherard will not rest until he finds us. We should go up to Florida or to New Orleans and start again.'

It wasn't a bad idea, but being chased off left a sour taste in Devore's mouth. He nodded, a plan starting to form. Blakely was right. Now that things had come to a head, there wouldn't be anything left here for them even if they did have their revenge. 'All right, two days, Blakely. You have two days to organise our departure.'

Blakely gave a tremulous smile, hardly daring to believe he'd won an argument. 'What will you be doing?'

Devore fingered the sharp blade of his letter opener. 'I will be picking up a passenger, a little insurance to make sure Sherard keeps his distance.' He motioned to the first mate. 'You're with me. You and I have a trip to make to the mainland. I've decided a new start requires a new bride.'

The start of 'life without Kitt' hadn't gone well. Bryn had lasted in the house all of a half-hour after yet another bankers' meeting began before she'd grabbed her market basket and stormed out to shop. Not that it counted as truly storming out. There'd been no one to see. The men had all been gathered around the big table in the dining room, deep in conversation. No one had paid her any attention or known she was gone, or for that matter even known she was in a temper. Not even Kitt, who had greeted her with stiff politeness when he'd arrived in the company of Mr Harrison and Mr Crenshaw as if they'd not shared an incredible conversation the day before, in some regards a life-changing conversation. Apparently, 'life without Bryn' was going better for him than 'life without Kitt' was going for her.

She'd not thought it would be like this. She'd imagined something more tragically romantic when she'd pictured them meeting in the interim—eyes full of soulful, secret looks of longing, of regret that there couldn't be more all in hopes that some day it might be possible. Good lord, she'd never thought of herself as the swoony type. She was supposed to be more practical than this, more like Kitt. It would get better. In a week or two this would all be over. She and Kitt could move on to exploring other possibilities.

Bryn selected some fruits from a stall and put them in her basket, realising too late one of them was rotten. She had to pay attention! She couldn't wander around absentmindedly thinking about Kitt. She'd get herself run over by a cart or...

'Miss? Could you come with me?' a big beefy man said at her elbow. Where he'd come from was anyone's guess. She'd not been aware of him when she'd started shopping, then again, she'd not been aware of much. His tone was polite, but he was not familiar to her. 'I have a message I need you to relay.'

Bryn studied his features, trying to recall if she'd seen him before, someone perhaps from the gala dinner. No, she did not know him. 'I'm not expecting any messages. Forgive me, but we have not been introduced. Perhaps you should arrange a meeting with my father directly.' It was a bit haughty of her and she smiled to soften the politely delivered blow, but her instincts cried out that such a tactic was necessary. Something about him made her uncomfortable. Perhaps it was simply that he stood too close to her, crowding her. 'If you'll excuse me? I'm meeting some friends.'

He didn't budge. His eyes narrowed, sending a chill through her in spite of the warm sun. 'Liar. You left the house alone and you're meeting no one.'

Cold fear came to her. She'd been followed and she hadn't even known. This was her fault. This was what she got for letting her thoughts daydream over Kitt. She needed to get away. She had no weapon to hand, no real weapon at least. Her hand closed over the rotten piece of fruit in her basket. It would do.

Bryn took a step back and threw the slimy missile, hitting him squarely in the face. He yowled in disgusted surprise, his hands clawing at his face to wipe away the oozing fruit, his attentions distracted momentarily. Bryn dropped the basket and ran...straight into a solid wall of unfriendly muscle who wasted no time wrestling her into a quiet alley away from the eyes of the market. There was no time to scream, barely even time to fight before she was shoved rather roughly into a dark interior, the door of the old storehouse clanging shut behind her taking the light with it. She could see nothing, but her captor was still with her. She could hear him breathing in the dark.

'What is the meaning of this?' she railed, trying to get her bearings, her mind reeling. She was certain now that this was an abduction attempt. Had anyone noticed? Was someone from the market even now on their way to her father?

'You will see, the boss has plans for you,' came the reply, thick with an island accent.

'Who is the boss?' she tried, desperate for information. Anything she could learn would help her escape and, if not escape, then help her negotiate. What did they want?

Light flooded the little chamber for a moment before it was cut off by a bulky form. 'I am the boss.' The man from the market. She recognised the voice and the shape.

He approached, walking with a pronounced limp. That limp should mean something to her. Her mind raced, trying to recall the memory. He was close, crowding her again in the dim room as he had in the market. She stood her ground, refusing to back up. In the small space there was nowhere to move, no way to evade him that wouldn't make her look foolish. To back away would appear cowardly and give proof to her fear. Better, she reasoned, to meet him with her chin up.

He chuckled at her show of defiance. 'Sherard has himself a spitfire this time.' He put his hand beneath her chin, turning her face this way and that in the dimness. 'A pretty one, too.'

Devore. The name came to her. Kitt had told her once that Devore limped as a result of a bullet he'd put in the man's knee. She understood much of this now. Thwarted at sea in an attempt to keep Kitt from reaching land, knowing Kitt would expose the swindle, Devore had decided to take her hostage. Perhaps he thought to use her as leverage for Kitt's silence. Perhaps he thought to blackmail Kitt into abdicating his claim of fraud. Perhaps she was to be the lure to draw Kitt out into the open. Perhaps he simply wanted to strike back and take something of value. He might have misjudged her worth if that was what he hoped.

'You assume too much if you think Kitt will come for me,' she said with a nonchalance she didn't feel.

He started to move about her in a predatory circle, his eyes crawling over her form with undisguised lascivious intent. 'I don't assume too much at all. I saw him on deck with you that first night out, before you knew we were there.'

Her cheeks burned, but Devore wasn't done. 'Now that I know what you like, I'll be sure to provide you with the same service.' Bryn cringed inwardly at the thought. Outwardly, she remained stoic, her eyes forward, focused on the wall. Even with a theoretical understanding of her role in Devore's private battle with Kitt, his next words were chilling.

'I've decided…' Devore came to stand in front of her. She looked past him to the space over his shoulder '…that we shall be married. That will put you beyond Sherard's reach as long as I live.'

'He will kill you!' Bryn spat, her words hastily and poorly chosen in the wake of Devore's shocking revelation. The proposition invoked no small amount of fear.

'Ha! So he does care? I thought so.' He smiled evilly, grabbing her wrists and dropping a loop of rope over them. He tugged and she felt the rope bite into skin as he jerked her forward. 'Philippe, the blindfold please, we're ready to go.'

Brave or not, Bryn did struggle then, putting up a fight as the other man bound a cloth over her eyes. She wanted to know where they were going, wanted to seize any opportunity to get away. But she was no match for his muscled brawn any more than she had been in the marketplace. But it was Devore who ended it with a stiff slap across her face that left her stunned by the show of brutality.

'There will be no resistance, my dear. If you try my patience, you will learn there are worse things than a slap in the face.' His calm tones belied the violence he'd just meted out. 'Philippe, I think a gag is in order, too. I'll wager this one's a screamer.'

The gag smelled and she involuntarily turned her face away in an attempt to avoid it. But Devore pressed it to her mouth and nose, forcing her to breathe deeply of the foul rag. Her head began to swim, her mind registering too late this was no mean gesture designed to be a show of power. She felt consciousness slipping away, the one thing she was desperate to hang on to, the only thing she had left that gave her any control. A small, panicked moan escaped her. 'No…' But that was all.

Kitt was desperate to hang on to his sanity. The bankers' meeting had gone on for what seemed an interminable amount of time. How much more was there to say? Devore was guilty of fraud, he needed to be brought in. Yet these men were determined to turn the decision into a two-hour discussion. Didn't they see they were losing valuable time? Even now, Devore might be sailing away with his profits. If he escaped them, the bank's reputation would be ruined before it even started.

But the bank's reputation wasn't Kitt's only concern. He was losing time, too—he wanted this settled so he could focus on Bryn. What could he risk offering her? It had been torture to see her that morning, to be in her house, to know she was near and not be able to reach out to her. He wanted this latest adventure to be over. He wanted to know she was safe.

He'd barely slept the previous night. His thoughts had been haunted with 'what ifs'—what if he gave up his business? He didn't *need* to run cargo. He was wealthy enough to live off investments and live more tamely. But that wasn't him. It would be like giving up his soul. And yet Bryn moved him, touched him at his core with her love for adventure, with her loyalty. To turn his back on what she offered him was no small thing. He'd felt the absence of her in his bed quite acutely for reasons that went beyond sex. By the time the sun had risen he was no closer to an answer.

Sneed entered the dining room, quietly passing an envelope to Rutherford. Kitt followed the interaction with his eyes, his mind desirous of any distraction. The conversation had long since bored him. Rutherford looked perplexed, turning the note over in his hand.

'I believe this is for you, Sherard.' Rutherford looked down the table at him as Sneed brought the unopened envelope. Kitt took it, apprehension running through him. This was no ordinary note. Passemore brought the mail to the boat or to the house. How would any note know to find him here? Or why?

Kitt slit the envelope and read. It was a wedding invitation done up on formal, heavy cream paper. His gaze stalled on the first line at the sight of Hugh Devore's name. His heart began to pound. The next line confirmed his fears. The bastard had taken Bryn. Devore had her even now and had done who knew what to her while they'd sat discussing their options. And it was his fault. He'd exposed her to Devore. Devore somehow knew Bryn mattered to him, although he'd certainly given Devore plenty of chances to learn of it. He'd been careless. This was a direct blow, not so much about the swindle, but about personal revenge. Devore blamed him for his wife's desertion. Now he sought to take a woman in place of the one Kitt had taken from him.

Stay calm. Show these gentlemen nothing, he counselled. Panic would do no one any good, certainly not Bryn. He looked up at Rutherford and the others, eyeing them in turn. 'While we have been discussing our situation *ad nauseam*, Devore has taken action.' After hours of noise and babble, silence fell on the table, awkward and heavy. Kitt tossed the invitation into the centre. 'He's taken Rutherford's daughter.'

Chapter Twenty-Four

Rutherford paled. 'We must go after him.' He'd already half-risen in his seat, prepared to rush to Bryn's aid, all foolish, noble loyalty. It twisted the knife of guilt a little more in Kitt's gut. He'd jeopardised Bryn.

'It's what he wants.' Selby spoke coolly from his place at the table, his voice drawing everyone's attention.

'Of course it's what he wants,' Rutherford said impatiently. 'He means to ransom Bryn for our silence on the matter of the island.'

'No, it's what *he* wants.' Selby jabbed a finger in Kitt's direction. Kitt bristled. What fresh conspiracy did Selby seek to convict him of now? 'Sherard would like nothing better than to marshal your legitimate resources to fight his less-than-legitimate-war with Devore. Why risk himself when he could have the bank intervene instead?'

Kitt watched Harrison's eyes narrow. 'What is this about, Sherard? Is there any truth to it? There had better not be a secret agenda.'

'Do you expect him to answer that truthfully?' Selby cut in before Kitt could respond. 'Devore wants revenge for Sherard and Dryden exiling him and the Gridley gang last summer.'

Kitt shifted uncomfortably in his seat. Selby had said too much. Couldn't the man see he'd nearly betrayed Bryn? A smart man at the table would see the missing link of logic. Crenshaw decided to be that man. 'I thought this was about the land swindle. What does abducting a banker's daughter have to do with Sherard's little vendetta? I thought Rutherford had the right of it: Devore wants to trade the daughter for our silence.'

Selby paled, recognising his mistake too late. To explain further meant publicly pairing Kitt with Bryn. Kitt tensed, waiting for Selby to back down. 'Well, Sherard was the one that discovered the island was a hoax,' he said weakly.

Kitt decided to enter the fray. These men would talk themselves to death, meanwhile Bryn was in some very real peril. 'We have to go after her. We can sort out the particulars of my motives later.'

'We don't know where he's at,' Selby said sulkily.

'Yes, we do. It's on the invitation.' Kitt pushed the card towards Selby. Tortoise Island, six o'clock. It was just past three now. Barely enough time to get his ship under way and go, but perhaps Devore was counting on that; there wouldn't be enough time to ride for Ren and rally the plantation workers. There would only be enough time to assemble Kitt's crew and whichever investors might choose to come.

Selby picked up the invitation and tossed it back down again. 'If it's so obvious where to find her, it must be a trap.'

'Of course it's a trap,' Kitt said through gritted teeth. He was going to strangle Selby in a minute. 'That doesn't mean we don't go.' That sounded very similar to something Bryn had said to him not so long ago. Then, he'd been the Selby in the room.

Kitt pushed back from the table. 'The *Queen* sails at four. If anyone feels inclined to come, be on board. The tide won't wait. If we mean to make Tortoise Island by six, we need to catch it.' They needed the wind to hold as well. He didn't want to alarm Rutherford, but it would take all the speed the *Queen* could muster to make that deadline. He was starting to suspect that had been Devore's plan all along—to have them arrive too late.

Not that the marriage would be binding. Devore would be a bigamist if he claimed marriage to Bryn. It wasn't the theoretical that worried Kitt, it was the practical. Devore wouldn't hesitate to consummate the marriage such as it was and Bryn wouldn't hesitate to fight it even though she'd be no match for Devore's brute strength.

Kitt strode down the front steps of Rutherford's town house at a near run, stuck on the image of Bryn resisting. A litany took up residence in his mind: *Don't fight, don't fight.* But he knew she would. She wouldn't give in even at risk to her personal safety. Bryn was stubborn and tenacious. Heaven help him, it was what he loved about her.

Something pulled on his arm and he turned to see Selby beside him, jogging to keep up. 'Sherard, stop and face me like a man!' Selby nearly shouted. That did it. Kitt had all he was going to take from the likes of James Selby, who had arguably brought all of this to a head with his foolish investment.

Kitt seized him by the front of his jacket and hauled

him up against a fence post, roaring his displeasure. 'Take your hands off me or I will squash you like an ant!'

Selby was not daunted. 'Are you happy now? You have everyone running to do your bidding, to rescue Miss Rutherford for you, to finish your vendetta for you. Do you care for her at all or is she just a means to more of your sordid ends?'

Ah, Kitt understood the man's rage. He should have known. Perhaps he *had* known and had conveniently chosen to ignore the facts. Selby was in love with her. Of course he was. What man wouldn't worship Bryn Rutherford from afar? Or up close if he could? Like he had. A man like Selby wouldn't dare the latter. Still, Kitt was in no mood to tolerate Selby's assumptions.

'I should call you out for that!' Kitt snarled, his face close to Selby's. Let the man see his anger. It would make his forgiveness seem all the more generous. 'Your feelings for her do you credit, but your emotions do not.' He shook Selby once and stepped back. 'Curb your temper before it makes you foolish.' He could spare no more time for Selby. He had a boat to make ready and a woman to redeem.

Beyond that, he didn't dare to think of what came after. Bryn would be despising him by now. No matter how moving their last conversation had been, no matter how many subtle promises had been made, no professions of love would override the fact that the danger he put her in was very real. It was no longer hypothetical as it had been on the ship. She was experiencing it first-hand and she would not thank him for it. She could not ignore that part of his life. If she was smart, she would understand why she couldn't be part of it. If *he* was smart, he'd give up his fantasies. He couldn't have her. He couldn't let her live this way for him.

He was regretting having been so cool towards her that morning. She might even be wondering if he would come for her. He hated that the most, that Bryn would doubt him, but he'd given her no reason to believe otherwise. How many times had he warned her he would not play the gentleman? But surely she knew someone would come? Maybe that didn't inspire much confidence if she thought those someones would be her father and Selby, hardly two knights in shining armour when it came to overcoming the likes of Devore. *I am coming, Bryn.* He cast his gaze to the sky as he hurried towards the harbour. The winds would hold. They had to. He would reach her in time. He had to. Nothing else mattered.

Kitt would reach her in time. He would come, if not out of his own volition, out of her father's. Bryn stretched and twisted on the cot, trying to find relief for her sore arms without upsetting her stomach with any sudden movements. Whatever had been on the rag had made her nauseous. When she'd come to the journey had been over. The blindfold and gag had been removed, a sure sign they were no longer necessary. But she was just as helpless. She was stuck on the cot, her hands still tied and the rope connected to a ring fixed in the side of the hut.

Were they still on Barbados? Had they sailed somewhere else? If she managed to get free, where would she go? At the moment, such considerations seemed moot.

The hut opened, admitting the hulking form of Devore. He was carrying a box. 'You're awake, just in time. Do you know what is in here?' He lifted the lid and set the box down across her lap. He parted the tissue and pulled out a gown. 'Your wedding dress, isn't it lovely? I got it in a trade a while back with a merchant ship.' He shook out the expensive confection. 'It should be close enough to your size.'

'The same way you were trading for Kitt's rum? By ambush?' Bryn managed to get out past her dry lips. 'I'd rather go naked.'

'That can be arranged, my little virago.' He set the box down and walked to the crude little table and the pitcher that sat on it. 'Thirsty?' He poured a cup of water and Bryn tried to appear uninterested while he drank it front of her, giving a wet, satisfied smack of his lips when he finished. 'It's cold. It's very good water actually. Would you like some? Perhaps we could reach an agreement? You put on the dress, and I'll give you a drink.'

Bryn was far more interested in what the deal implied. Her hands would be free! Free hands created possibilities. Her mind was whirring. Free hands could smash the water jug, free hands could pick up a pottery shard from the broken jug and wait for a moment to swipe the jagged edge across Devore's leering face. She would take the deal, but she didn't dare appear too excited by it or Devore would suspect something. With great reluctance she eyed the water jug, her posture feigning defeat as she managed one hoarse word. 'Yes.'

Devore bent over her, slicing a thin, wicked blade through the ropes, the big paunch of his stomach in her face as he cut. He laughed at her discomfort, but he held out the cup of water and watched as she drank it. The water was good. She let it slide down her throat, but her enjoyment was short lived. He yanked the empty cup away. 'You've had your drink. Now, put on the dress.' His eyes gestured to the box on the cot and he settled into the hut's one chair.

Dread settled over her. He didn't mean to leave. He laughed again, this time at her hesitation. 'Don't give me this maidenly modesty act, Miss Rutherford. You have no modesty. I saw you with Sherard, with him buried between your legs.' He played with his knife, drawing her eyes to the long blade. 'Get on with it before I decide to not be nice, although I should warn you, I like it when you fight.'

Bryn slid down the short puffed sleeves of her gown, her fingers slowly working the laces at her back. For now, what choice did she have? To undress herself was better than having someone else do it for her, a scene she rather thought Devore would enjoy a little too much. The man was repulsive. When the time came, she would have no trouble slicing, gutting, cutting, whatever it took. She had no empathy for this cretin who took so much pleasure in degrading others. That time would come. There was a rescue party on its way to her. Devore had arranged it, a final showdown between him and Kitt. The only question was how would Kitt compete against Devore's men. She was merely the bait to draw Kitt out.

'Now the chemise,' Devore growled, a hand riding his crotch. 'No sense wearing anything beneath that wedding dress when I'll be taking it off you soon enough.'

Bryn closed her eyes. *Just get it over with. Watching can't hurt you.* It was with some relief that she slipped into the dress, her skin covered once more. There was a rap on the door of the hut and she clutched the loose dress to her. One of Devore's henchmen entered.

'Best get on with it, Boss. We've got Sherard's ship in our sights, just rounded the headland.'

'The headland!' Devore roared. 'How did he get so close? We were supposed to have seen him long before this.'

The man shrugged, backing away from Devore's wrath. 'You can go see for yourself, Boss.'

Devore lurched to his feet, grabbing her by the wrist in a vicious grip. He dragged her towards the door. 'It looks like we'll have to speed things up a bit.'

'You're in an awfully big hurry to die,' Bryn snapped, tripping behind him, her feet tangling in the skirts. 'You can't possibly think you're his equal in combat. He's faster, stronger, younger, he'll wear you down.' Perhaps she could sow some doubt that would turn Devore from this course.

She shouldn't have provoked him. Devore hauled her to him, drawing his knife, the blade the only thing between them. 'This is the great equaliser. I don't need to be stronger or faster. I only need to prick him with the smallest of cuts and the poison will do the rest, a nice trick I picked up from the natives.'

'Killing Kitt won't stop people from knowing about the swindle. You can't kill all of us.' It was all bravado at this point. The knife was a frightening weapon indeed. The relief she'd felt in hearing Kitt had arrived was replaced by a paralysing fear. Kitt could die without even knowing what had wounded him, without knowing that she loved him.

'I'm not interested in stopping the news,' Devore sneered. 'I'm interested in revenge. When I've had it, I will sail away with my new bride.' He brandished the knife dangerously near her face. 'And when I've tired of her or she has displeased me one too many times, I will discard her, too. How long do you think you'll last, my dear? A few days, a week? Years?'

Bryn wanted to make a grand gesture as she stumbled ignobly behind Devore out into the sun. Perhaps a braver soul would opt to prick herself on the deadly blade right now and end it by taking away Devore's leverage, or say something grand like 'I'd rather die than contemplate years with you', but it wasn't true. She wanted to live so very much. She wanted to swim with dolphins, shower beneath waterfalls, and make love on white sandy beaches with Kitt. All of it with Kitt. If that made her a coward, then so be it. She would find a way to warn him.

Devore brought her up short at the treeline where the jungle gave way to beach. 'Don't think about warning him. I have a blade for you, too.' He motioned to a big, swarthy man with scars on his chest. 'If you cry one word of warning to him, Baden here has orders to give you a nice scratch. I wouldn't risk it, my dear. Can you imagine the guilt Sherard would carry with him knowing you died for him? That alone would kill a man. It's not a pretty death either. I've seen men afflicted by the poison. It isn't pretty nor is it fast enough. It grabs hold of your bones and it won't let go until you scream, your body contorting, twisting this way and that looking for relief. Surely marriage to me would be a far better alternative than that.' He yanked her chin up, forcing her to meet his gaze. 'You never know, you might just find you have a taste for a man like me.'

Bryn spat in his face, allowing herself one small piece of defiance. 'Never.'

He laughed. 'Well, that's for you to decide. I'm off

to greet our guests. Baden, you might want to tie this one up in case she gets any ideas about running. I want her to have a front-row seat to Kitt Sherard's demise. His luck has just about run out. He's only got this far because I allowed it.'

Bryn's eyes darted past Devore's bulk, trying to catch a glimpse of Kitt, of what Devore had planned. Devore turned, following her gaze, the tension in his form belying his confidence. For the first time, Bryn realised he was afraid. If she'd been able to look past her own concerns, she might have seen it earlier: the brutality, the bullying, the poisoned knife, the tactics of a coward. That didn't mean he wasn't dangerous. The knife especially posed a very real threat, coward or not.

She caught sight of Kitt, a band of men fanned out behind him as he gained the beach. Her breath hitched. Devore had every right to be afraid.

Chapter Twenty-Five

He looked glorious! For however long she lived, the image of Kitt would be burned on her mind. He was Poseidon rising from the sea, or Apollo come to earth. His skin gleamed in the sun, sleek and greased from liberal quantities of oil, his bare chest crossed by a bandolier of pistols, a long knife sheathed at his waist. But it wasn't the weapons that made him formidable. It was the set of his jaw and the hardness of his eyes. This was no Poseidon or Apollo. This was Ares, god of war, come to do battle. Hope surged. Poisoned knife blades diminished in the face of this avenging warrior.

'Let her go, Devore!' Kitt's voice rang out with authority across the beach. His men faced Devore's in a menacing line, each of them bristling with weapons. Kitt's message was clearly communicated: this could be a blood bath. His men were prepared to fight for her. 'It's me you want.' Kitt held his arms wide in a pointless gesture of peace. He was armed to the teeth. It didn't matter there wasn't a weapon in his hand at present. He could have one there in seconds.

When Devore said nothing, Kitt called out his offer

one more time. 'Me for her!' He slipped the bandolier from his shoulders and let it fall to the ground. Bryn's throat tightened. This was a trade Kitt had made before, for his brother. She knew in a horrifying moment of truth that Kitt loved her. He had sacrificed himself once for his brother out of love and now he intended to do the same for her. No, that wasn't what she wanted. She didn't want him to simply turn himself over, to submit to Devore. She wanted him to fight, to make Devore pay.

Apparently it wasn't what Devore wanted either. 'I don't want a trade, Sherard. I want you to suffer,' Devore called out. 'Submission is too easy. There's no pain in it. I want you to suffer as I've suffered. I lost everything that had worth to me, thanks to you, and just when I'm getting back on my feet, you come along again to kick me back down. Well, no more.'

Devore stepped back to her side, his knife flashing in his hand, the tip hovering beneath her chin. Bryn drew back, trying to make herself as small as possible, but Devore held her fast. This was not the plan! 'This blade is poisoned, Sherard. One prick and she dies. I am taking her with me aboard my ship as I sail into a new life. If you follow us, she dies. If you attempt to do me any harm, she dies. Do you understand?'

He understood Devore's repetitive litany too well. Any misstep from him and Bryn died. Kitt's hand flexed around the handle of his own knife, a throwing blade, specially balanced for accuracy and speed. He just needed an opportunity. Bryn lived as long as he let Devore go. But that required leaving Bryn in Devore's hands and that was intolerable. Bryn would not suffer for him, because of him.

It was clear Devore wasn't bluffing. Bryn's pale face was proof enough Devore's threat was real. Kitt assessed the options with lightning speed. Devore would kill her right there in front of him or kill her later, perhaps, with the slightest provocation. Letting Devore go now didn't buy Bryn more time, only more danger. He needed a clean throw, he needed Devore to step away from Bryn so there was no risk of him accidentally pricking her. And yet, if he could somehow put Bryn in charge of Devore's blade, it would give her power, a tool to defend herself with. Would she understand his message?

'You are more of a coward than I thought, Devore.' Kitt began to pace, hoping to distract Devore with his ceaseless movements. 'Taking a helpless woman, using her to blackmail me into compliance and resorting to poison, all speak of cowardice. I would have expected better from you. Perhaps you've lost your courage without Gridley around to call the shots. Perhaps he truly was the brains of the operation. Are you afraid to face me man to man? What will your men think of their boss if you refuse?'

Kitt drew a circle in the sand and stepped inside. 'I dare you to join me. Man to man, knife to knife.' He couldn't afford to look at Bryn's face. He would lose his focus, his detachment. He'd felt it slip the moment he'd seen Devore's knife slide beneath her chin. He didn't need her panic to know the risks. He was the more agile of the two, but Devore had a poisoned tip—it more than made up for the bulk and limp of him. Devore didn't need to be fast, Devore only needed him to be careless. Kitt knew he had no margin for error.

There was a rustle in the ranks of Devore's men. 'C'mon, Boss, give the bastard what he deserves,' someone called out. The sentiment was taken up with cheers along the line. Kitt grinned. Devore would not be able to back down now. Devore stepped into the circle. Despite the danger to himself, Kitt let relief ease his thoughts and focus his body. Bryn was safe for now. As long as he kept Devore in the circle, Bryn was safe.

Kitt feinted, testing Devore's tactics. Devore growled and threw a handful of sand. Kitt was ready for it and darted backwards. His men roared their disapproval of the underhanded ploy. He heard Passemore call out something derogatory. The proverbial sabres were starting to rattle. His men would fight. Passemore had instructions to launch a full attack if he fell, to get to Bryn at all costs.

Kitt and Devore circled. He watched the man's bad leg, he watched the sweat bead on the heavier man's forehead. Devore would want to have this over quickly. Devore lunged, lowering his head like a bull, his head aimed for Kitt's midsection, his free hand attempting to grab Kitt's wrist. Kitt dug his feet into the sand and took the blow, grabbing the man's shirt and wrapping his fist in the fabric to throw him. Devore tried to grab hold of Kitt, but couldn't. There was no shirt, only slippery skin that offered no traction. Devore lost his footing, momentum overbalancing him. He went down, Kitt's blade slicing into him as he fell.

It was chaos on the beach then. Devore's men rushed the circle, only to meet Kitt's crew, weapons drawn. Kitt pulled his knife free, his one thought on getting to Bryn.

All sorts of accidents happened in mêlées like this one and the fighting was far too close to her.

Kitt punched and stabbed, cutting a path towards her, his thoughts immediate: get Bryn, get to the boats, get to the ship. There were no thoughts beyond that. One brute remained between him and Bryn. Kitt drove his knife deep into the man's belly without hesitation. His next cut was through Bryn's bonds. They were free, the boats fifty yards ahead of them.

They ran, his hand tight over her wrist as he dragged her towards safety. He didn't care, he just wanted off the beach, just wanted Bryn safe. He shouted to Passemore to cover their retreat and swept Bryn into his arms, carrying her through the surf to the row boat. Others joined him to get the oars under way. Minutes later, Passemore had the rest on board and they were away, leaving the bloody beach behind them.

He had her. Bryn was safe! She was in his arms, because he wouldn't let her leave them. But victory had struck him dumb. All of his thoughts had run out. He'd not thought beyond the beach, hadn't allowed himself to think of them both leaving the beach alive. What next? He didn't know. That wasn't quite true. He *did* know what was next, the one thing he'd promised himself he'd do if he got her off the beach. He'd see her on a boat to England, back to where she belonged. After today, her father would certainly support such a decision. As long as she was here, there would be those who would try to get to him through her. He couldn't expose her to that. They'd barely lived through it once. He couldn't imagine living through it again. He loved her too much. He was going to do the only thing he could. He was going to give her up. But first, he had to walk away and that was proving hard to do. His mind was made up, but his body was not.

'Thank you,' Bryn said quietly into the silence that had grown up between them. They were at the rail of the ship, the rest of the crew had gone about their jobs, their busyness giving the two of them privacy without leaving the deck. 'You were brilliant today, so fearless, so brave.'

'I was scared,' Kitt said more sharply than he intended. He would not be made into a hero over this. It was his fault this had happened in the first place, that she'd been in danger at all.

Bryn's hand was light on his arm. 'Of course you were. I think that is what real courage is about; going forward even though you're frightened, even though the outcome is uncertain.' She paused and bit her lip. Kitt waited for her to continue. 'Which is why I want to try and be courageous now. I promised myself I would do something if I saw you again. It was all I could think of to keep myself from going crazy with fear when I was with Devore. I don't pretend it's something you want to hear, but it's something I need to say.'

Bryn turned to face him, forcing him to look at her. His stomach rolled into a tight ball. This was where she told him how much she despised the man he was, how much she regretted what had passed between them. Kitt steeled himself. He'd known from the start it would come to this. A woman like Bryn Rutherford was far too good for a man like him. Today, she'd seen him kill without hesitation. When all of this had started, it hadn't mattered. But in this awful moment, he'd never wished so much to be a different man, to have a different life.

'When Devore was making his threats, I kept thinking of all the things I wanted to do and all the things I had done. The best things were the things I'd done with you. And everything I had yet to do, I wanted to do with you. I didn't look for this to happen. I thought I'd be safe with you, but I'm not. I fell anyway, Kitt. I love you.'

I thought I'd be safe with you, but I'm not... He understood that part. He'd expected that much. It was the part after that caught him by surprise. *I fell anyway... I love you.* It took a moment for him to realise she'd not meant it literally. She meant the safety of her feelings, of her heart. She didn't despise him. Quite the opposite. She loved him. It was a stunning gift, one he couldn't accept.

'I cannot offer you anything decent, Bryn.' His resolve was wavering. He'd never get her on a ship to England at this rate. 'I can't keep you safe. There will always be the potential of another Devore. Even if I gave it all up, I can't erase my past and whatever may lurk there.' *Maybe he could, maybe there wouldn't be any more enemies, maybe no one would look for him. Maybe his identity was safe. Maybe...* The possible began to chase the impossible around his mind in a dizzying circle of reason. 'I just don't know what I'm capable of. If I did, it would be different.' Kitt fumbled with his thoughts, overwhelmed. When things seemed too good to be true, they probably were.

Bryn's grey eyes lit up. She meant to do battle. For him, Kitt realised. 'I don't want it to be different or you to be different. I don't want "decent". I've had my share of what passes for decent gentlemen. You are far more than decent with your love of family, with your loyalty.' She fixed him with a hard stare. 'I want you,

Kitt Sherard, rough edges and all. The question is do you want me?'

'Rough edges and all?' Kitt gave a faint smile, but it was no laughing matter. His insides were still roiling, but for a different reason. Did he dare take the leap? He wanted to. If he leapt or not, Bryn had his heart. Nothing would change that, not England, not a thousand miles of sea.

Suddenly, it was all too much. He needed her desperately, needed to feel her around him, needed to be inside her, to know she was his beyond words. 'Come with me.' Kitt's voice was gruff, filling with emotion. His hand closed about hers, leading her to his cabin, the door barely shut behind them before he claimed her with his mouth, her back against the wall.

'Kitt.' She moaned his name into his mouth, her hands cradling his face, her body pressing against his, wanting this as much as he did, needing it perhaps more.

'Are you sure, Bryn?' He drew a ragged breath. 'Devore, he didn't…?'

'No, he did nothing that could truly hurt me,' she murmured, Devore and his filth couldn't touch them, couldn't haunt them any more. Her hand slipped to his trousers, cupping him, stroking him. 'There are some rough edges of yours I like more than others,' she whispered at his ear, her teeth catching the tender part of his lobe. 'Undress me, Kitt. I want to be naked with you.'

He slid the gown from her. He'd burn it the first chance he had, but for now he wanted to worship with his hands, with his lips, his tongue, wanted to erase every trace of Devore's touch from her skin. She was his, and only his. Primal fire consumed him as he took her down on the bed. He'd nearly lost her today. One slip of the knife and she would have been gone, beyond any skill he had to bring her back. There are some things a man couldn't fight with pistols and blades. Those were the things that scared him the most.

He came down between her legs, revelling in how she opened for him, how her legs went about him to draw him close. *This* was one of those things. He had no illusions now that being with Bryn would grow less intense with familiarity or time. That scared him, to lose himself so completely in another. It also ignited him, fired him deep at the core of his soul. This was living at its most frightening, but loving at its finest.

Kitt thrust deeply with all the surety of a man who knew he was home. He let his body say what his words could not. She arched against him and he came hard, wringing a satisfied cry from her as she clung to him, their bodies overcome with pleasure, overcome with life. It had been a near-run thing today. He vowed silently it would never be so near again. He rolled to his side and pulled her to him as his heartbeat slowed, the enormity of what he'd committed to coming to him in post-climax clarity.

'It will be hard, Bryn. Life with me won't be easy.'

Bryn smiled up at him. 'I know. I like it hard.'

Kitt laughed. 'You're a naughty wench when it comes right down to it.' He sighed and blew out a breath. 'It's been quite a day: rescuing damsels, a fight to the death…falling in love.'

Bryn traced a circle around his nipple. 'All in a day's work for the notorious Captain Sherard from what I hear.' She paused and levered up on one arm to look at him. It was one of his favourite poses, her hair hanging over one shoulder, her eyes fixed on him. 'You haven't answered my question and Carlisle Bay looms. I want you, Kitt. Do you want me?'

'Do you doubt it?' He'd worshipped her with his body. What more was there to prove? Meaningful words were not his strong suit. He could banter all day, flirt all night with empty words. But meaningful words? He'd denied himself those for so long.

'I do not doubt it. I don't want *you* to doubt it or yourself. Say the words,' Bryn coaxed.

Kitt met her gaze solemnly, his voice quiet, intuitively understanding this would be the most reverent moment of his life. 'Yes, Bryn Rutherford. I want you, for ever, for always.'

There would be vows and public declarations later to satisfy the law and the church, but these words satisfied their hearts and meant so much more. Somewhere in the back of his mind, a little voice whispered, *it's a trap.* Yes, indeed. Love was a trap. A glorious, well-sprung trap in which he was utterly caught.

Epilogue

No one ever said loving Kitt Sherard would be easy, but it was an amazing journey as he revealed little pieces of himself to her. Bryn understood she would not get it all at once, but she had a lifetime to learn him, a lifetime to love him whoever he was—notorious Kitt Sherard or Michael Melford. She loved both the rogue and the gentleman, but most of all, she loved the man they'd combined to make. That man waited by the warm surf of the beach to claim her as his bride.

Beside her, her father gave a misty smile as he walked her down the runner of red carpet covering the sand. 'Your mother would be proud of you. You have followed your heart and that's all she would have wanted.'

Bryn smiled, too moved for words. Kitt was her heart, her future. Her father placed her hand in Kitt's and stepped back. He joined the guests gathered on the sand—all three of them and one of them asleep: Ren Dryden and his wife, Emma, who held a baby in her arms.

Kitt squeezed her hand, smiling down at her as the vicar began the ceremony. 'Dearly beloved, we are gathered here today…' Dearly beloved, yes, indeed, Bryn thought. They could have had a grand wedding at St Michael's in Bridgetown, filled with citizens wanting her father's favour, wanting to bask in Kitt's success in bringing the land swindle to justice. But Bryn had wanted something more meaningful, a private celebration of their love with people who mattered.

She hardly heard the ceremony. She was too caught up in Kitt's gaze. It held hers with a look that communicated his pledge to her better than any words. If her voice shook as she said her vows, it was to be expected. It wasn't every day a woman was loved so thoroughly or so well. It was an overwhelming prospect to know she'd wake up to this man, to this love, for the rest of her life.

Waves rolled lightly over their bare feet as the vicar pronounced them husband and wife. This was the life and it was hers to claim, hers and Kitt's. Kitt tipped her chin upwards and covered her mouth with his, sealing their vows with a kiss, sealing them together, for ever.

* * * * *